Bestselling Egyptian author **Ibrahim Ess** TV personality, and political commentator. novels and other books, and he lives in Cai

Translator of the winning novel in the Independent Foreign Fiction Prize and winner of the Saif Ghobash–Banipal Prize for Arabic Literary Translation, **Jonathan Wright** was formerly the Reuters bureau chief in Cairo. He has translated Alaa Al-Aswany, Youssef Ziedan, and Hassan Blassim. He lives in London.

The Televangelist

Ibrahim Essa

Translated by
Jonathan Wright

hoopoe
AN IMPRINT OF AUC PRESS

This paperback edition published in 2016 by
Hoopoe
113 Sharia Kasr el Aini, Cairo, Egypt
420 Fifth Avenue, New York, NY 10018
www.hoopoefiction.com

Hoopoe is an imprint of the American University in Cairo Press
www.aucpress.com

Exclusive distribution outside Egypt and North America by I.B.Tauris & Co Ltd., 6
Salem Road, London, W4 2BU

Dar el Kutub No. 25542/14
ISBN 978 977 416 718 8

Dar el Kutub Cataloging-in-Publication Data

Essa, Ibrahim
     The Televangelist: A Novel / Ibrahim Essa.—Cairo: The American
     University in Cairo Press, 2016.
         p. cm.
         ISBN 978 977 416 718 8
         1. English fiction
         823

1 2 3 4 5   20 19 18 17 16

Designed by Adam el-Sehemy
Printed in the United States of America

THE MAKE-UP ARTIST DABBED POWDER on Sheikh Hatem's forehead with the finesse of a professional.

"That's perfect, Mawlana," she said, looking to him for approval.

"God bless you, Georgette," he replied with a laugh.

Anwar Othman made the same lame remark he'd been making all year long, ever since he became the host of Hatem's program.

"All those people you lead in prayer, your disciples, the people who ask you for fatwas, how do you think they'd feel if they saw you putting on make-up before filming?"

"The Prophet used to henna his hair and put kohl on his eyes. For God's sake, enough of these silly questions of yours, Anwar," Hatem replied, firmly but cheerfully.

Sheikh Hatem had found Anwar unbearable from the first time they met, when the Dunya channel suggested him as his partner in a new program. The channel had persuaded Hatem to change the format of his program to broaden its appeal. Instead of standing among the audience or having young people sit in front of him on stands while he told stories or preached, he now had a daily program in which he took questions from viewers of all ages and social classes. In fact the channel's argument never really convinced Hatem. The people who came to hear his sermon in the Sultan Hassan mosque every Friday were ordinary people too, and they filled

1

every inch of the mosque, which could hold several thousand people, not counting the ones who sat outside. And when he went to his father's house near the Citadel on Tuesdays, hundreds of men and women came seeking baraka and blessings or asking for fatwas or for money. He deferred to the owners of the television station because the fee they offered him was tempting, but right from the start something about Anwar had reminded him of an insect.

"He's like a pesky fly that gets inside the car when you've put the air conditioning on," he once said, "and you keep opening the window to get it out but it doesn't go, and then it buzzes against the window and you think it's planning to get out, but as soon as you open the window it goes and lands on the back of your neck."

They laughed. Hatem spoke with such solemnity, recited the Quran so eloquently, and was so quick with sayings of the Prophet and stories from the Prophet's life that it came across as a contradiction when he spoke in a way that didn't conform to the usual image. It took people by surprise but, at least as far as Sheikh Hatem could see, they approved of the fact that a preacher who gave fatwas was a man like them, a man who sometimes spoke rudely, who had material demands, and who liked to say outlandish things. They seemed relieved that sheikhs were closer to them than to God. He knew that the image people had of him was shaken when he sprang a joke on them. People would no longer treat him with the respect due a sheikh or a mufti. Oddly he liked that, to see their reaction, because deep down he wanted to subvert the image people had of sheikhs, which television perpetuated.

He still remembered clearly how one day, at a time when he was finding his way out of the cocoon of adolescence and thinking hard about his aptitude for the role in life he had chosen, he had been sitting on the second floor of his father's house near the Citadel. They had turned the room into a large hall where dozens of visitors would come and sit, each

with their own objective—to get a look, to obtain a fatwa or charity, to ask Hatem to intervene with an official, or to seek a recommendation for a job. In a quiet period after a long night, when those who were left were about to go to dawn prayers, his father took him aside in a private room at the end of the hall and sat him down in front of him. They were both exhausted and his father's face had a mysterious look that he couldn't decipher. Between them stood a barrier—the painful memory of his father taking a second wife, a divorcee twenty-five years younger than Hatem's father. His father remarried when Hatem was just starting out in the media. At the time he was only a preacher in a government-run mosque but he had caught the attention of congregants through the quality of his sermons. The mosque would fill up and people recorded his sermons on cassettes. Hatem suppressed the pain of his father's second marriage and neither of them had said a word about it for all those years. They had never confronted each other on the subject, or even thought of doing so, even when his mother, humiliated and pushed aside, told him that his father's new wife was pregnant and that his four sisters had decided to boycott their father's house. None of them ever took their children there again. Hatem had said nothing. He just hugged his mother, in that intense and natural way typical of a son's relationship with his mother. But as if something was amiss in the order of the world, his father's second wife gave birth to a boy that died the moment it was born. When they told Hatem, he was in a studio recording his program.

"We have all this medicine and science," he had told the audience, which was paid to attend. "Yet there are still children who die coming out of their mother's wombs. Yes, folks, God sometimes likes to remind us that we are nothing."

His father was entering his eighties in good health but he was willingly turning his back on the world. There in that room, just before dawn prayers and after the gathering had broken up, on the occasion of this rare meeting that his father had requested, Hatem felt that destiny was knocking on the door and something new or unexpected was about to happen in their lives.

"What's wrong, Hatem?" asked his father.

"Nothing, Father."

"Why can't you believe you're a sheikh?" his father replied.

He was stunned by the remark, not because it was a surprise, not because it was correct, but because it came from someone he thought had been content just to look on for the past five years.

"But am I a sheikh, Father?"

"What else? If you're not a sheikh, then what are you? You know the Quran by heart and you know how to recite it, you lead people in prayer and give sermons, you've memorized fatwas and you give fatwas of your own, and you have a wealth of stories about the Prophet. All that certainly gives you a place among the sheikhs. In fact your success with people gives you a leading place among them."

Hatem sighed and revealed something he had never before revealed candidly or comfortably, even to himself.

"Does that make a sheikh! That's a civil servant with the rank of sheikh. You know what I am, Father? I'm a merchant of learning."

Then he wrapped his arms around his father and muttered, "Come on, Father, let's go to dawn prayers. Would you like me to recite the Yassin chapter for you during the prayers?"

"No," his father replied earnestly. "I want the dawn supplication in the second prostration, because you say it so beautifully."

Proud of his father's opinion, Hatem had laughed and said, "Very well. I should do a request program for people who are about to pray."

The lights went up and the make-up woman finished powdering Anwar's forehead and cheeks while he did up his buttons.

"Medhat," he asked the director, "is my tie straight? Could you check?"

Sheikh Hatem no longer had stage fright, those palpitations in his rib cage or the cramps in his guts before the live feed began. The director and his assistants were sitting in the control room, along with the producers who would grunt into Anwar's ear through the small earpiece attached to a wire strapped to his back, prompting him, encouraging him, or calming him down. Sheikh Hatem shouted to them through the glass:

"Hey guys, could someone put my picture on the monitor so I can check it, or else I'll lay a curse on all of you."

They burst out laughing.

The picture came up and he checked everything was in order. Then he heard the director's voice:

"Everything's ready. Anwar, Sheikh Hatem, we're going on air. Three, two, one, action."

Anwar smiled. He looked nicer than he looked in real life.

"Ladies and gentlemen, good evening," he said. "Peace be upon you and the blessings of God. Welcome to a new installment of our program. Today we have with us the preacher and Islamic scholar, his grace Sheikh Hatem el-Shenawi."

He turned to Hatem and the camera panned out, showing Hatem smiling as he bowed his head.

"And good evening to you too, Anwar. Let's hear your questions, sir, and see what traps you've set for us tonight."

They both laughed.

Whenever Hatem saw the red light that lit up on the camera, he went on alert like a performer ready to perform. The red light activates latent powers of adaptation. You change from a human being to a televised creature on display, cheerful even if you're annoyed, serious when you're feeling flippant, dignified in the midst of a farce, respectable even in the face of lewdness. Hatem had quickly adapted to this style of performing. Many people needed time to get used to the red light as the signal for adopting a persona or a voice that was not theirs and to become completely captive to the magic light, whereas Sheikh Hatem was a trained creature almost from the first moment. It was as if he had lived by the red light all his life and it was with him wherever he was—in the pulpit, giving a lecture, posting on his Facebook page or on his website, among friends, with his followers, in a restaurant, at a wedding, in his car when people noticed and greeted him, shook hands with him, praised him, asked him for baraka or blessings, or asked him a question like someone asking a famous comedian that they happened to meet on the corner to tell them the latest joke. People were so inquisitive they would even ask for his latest fatwa if they saw him in the bathroom at a fancy fish restaurant. When he got out of his car and went to the elevator, the security men and the doormen would crowd around him, savoring his presence, seeking a memento of having shared a space with him so that they could tell their families or friends about it. His whisper, his laugh, the way he knitted his brow or the way he walked—everything was monitored and followed, so he put on his own red light, somewhere between his mind and his body.

This imaginary divide, or interface, confused him and forced him to constantly obey the red light, because one never knew who might be watching. Often he even caught himself staring at the ceiling of his bedroom, waiting for the red light to flash on so that he could assume the persona he adopted when performing. His real self seemed to have gone missing or been dissolved. He had started to find his real self strange or had forgotten what it looked like, so he would resort to the self that he had trained himself to adopt and that he felt at ease with. Because of this, those close to him—the rare ones who retained old ties to him—thought he was silent and aloof. They thought it odd that a man who was usually so talkative should be silent. He was also surprised by his silence, but he saved his energy so that he would be ready when the red light came on. He needed to be in perfect health and on the alert so that when he received an order he could obey and when he was summoned he could appear. One day he discovered that in the company of his father and his sisters he was the trained red-light creature and not his real self. He had reached the point where he was no longer certain who he was. He no longer knew if he was a new version of Hatem el-Shenawi, different from the old one that was no more, or whether he had changed into something that combined the human being he used to be with the training and skill of the person who obeyed the red light. All this put the relationship between him and his wife Omayma on ice for years, during which time neither of them ever thought of taking it out of the freezer and putting it under the hot water tap to thaw out. Their feelings were preserved in ice to keep them from going bad but they were never taken out to reinvigorate their marriage. What they had in common was this sense of being adrift as they sought out their true selves. Fame and luxury had changed him, and he had changed her. On the rare evenings when he wasn't caught up with the television programs, the recordings, the soirees or the sessions with businessmen, producers, and sponsors, they would sit together. But the atmosphere would soon chill and the conversation would wither. The links frayed but never broke, and the two of them largely kept their distance.

"God damn the red light," he said.

He could hear the music of the commercial break after Anwar's dreadful introduction. No ringmaster in any circus could have done better. Hatem thought of the peddlers who used to come round with toys.

"Put it on its chest it lights up, put it on its legs it lights up, it lights up red," the peddlers cried.

"Welcome back. I can tell you that this episode will, God willing, be very important and very serious, and we'll pose many of the questions you have in mind about religion and the world. Our telephone numbers and email addresses are on the screen as usual and you can also send SMSs to the number on the screen. Sheikh Hatem el-Shenawi, I welcome you again and I'd like to ask you about the saying that wealth and children are the adornment of life in this world. How can we turn this adornment into something that serves God Almighty?"

Hatem checked that the red light had switched to him this time so that he could start. He followed the light like a sunflower follows the sun. When it came to him it was time to react to what the anchor had said. He smiled, nodded, and sighed to the camera as if Anwar had spoken pearls of wisdom, though what he had said was really quite naive and trivial. Hatem knew that Anwar had hardly read a verse of the Quran and the last book he had read was the textbook of the last subject he was tested on in university. He knew for sure that Anwar didn't pray. Anwar worshiped the red light, a true devotee. Before he came he always memorized the Quranic verses he was going to cite in the conversation and he would jump in whenever there was a gap and recite the verses as if he had been born in a minaret. As a result many people thought he had memorized the whole Quran, and not just the script for the program.

Hatem leaned his head back and held out his hands in front of him with his prayer beads. His vocal cords received orders to sound solemn and impressive. The words came out of his mouth into the microphone attached to the edge of his suit jacket.

"Look, Anwar, what does the verse say? It says 'wealth and children.' So wealth comes first, because if you have children but not wealth that means poverty and want, which you don't want. Then it says 'the adornment of this life.' What are we to understand from that?"

Mischievously, playfully, yet with true professionalism, he pressed Anwar to respond.

"Go on then, what do you think?"

Then with a smile:

"Are you only clever enough to ask questions? Come on, what's your answer, brother?"

Anwar laughed and looked into the camera lens as though the exchange was part of a script they had worked out months earlier.

"We should read it as meaning that wealth and children are the most important things in the world," Anwar finally volunteered.

Hatem broke into the end of Anwar's sentence with a laugh.

"No, my good man, it means that wealth and children are not this life. They are just an adornment, and not the essence of life. They are not life. Isn't it the All-knowing and Almighty who says in His noble book *We have adorned the lower heaven with lamps*. 'The lower heaven' is the sky that we see, rather than the rest of the seven heavens, and the lamps are the stars in the sky. The sky has a role and the stars have a role. The stars appear one day and not the next, but does the world come to a halt? Not at all. If the stars disappeared the sky would continue. Its role lies in rain, sun, the atmosphere, and the ozone layer before they make holes in what's left of it. And this exactly parallels the relationship between this life and wealth and children. They are an adornment like the lamps, and notice that we use the same word to describe the two—we say 'the lower life' and 'the lower heaven'—because we know that there's more than one heaven and more than one life. So wealth and children are an adornment, a veneer, a brooch on the lapel of your jacket, dye for gray hair, like the couple that I have." He stroked his head to get a smile from Anwar, and Anwar complied immediately. The camera moved from Hatem looking at Anwar and stroking his hair, to Anwar's smile, and when he was sure that the director had caught it, he took his hands off his temples and continued. "Money and children are all well and good but they're not the issue. They are the crème Chantilly on this lower life, a cherry on the cake but not the cake."

Theatrically, Sheikh Hatem broke off there.

"It looks like you're hungry with all this talk of cake," he added.

"Very well, now that you've made our mouths water, we'll cut for a break, Mawlana, and have a bite to eat before we come back," Anwar answered quickly.

Anwar turned to the camera, proud of how the program was going and confident he had chosen a good moment to stop.

"God willing, we'll resume the conversation with our sheikh, the great promoter of Islam, Hatem el-Shenawi, after a short break," he said. "Stay with us."

As soon as he was off camera, Hatem lost interest. Adverts appeared on the screen—dancing colors, sexy girls running around after soft drinks, with close-up shots of their lips, glossed the color of peaches, as the liquid poured suggestively into their mouths. Then a half-naked young man appeared and an irresistible woman sauntered up to him, took a deep breath, and let her hair loose as if rehearsing for when she would let it down for him. Then a bottle of perfume suddenly appeared on the screen like some new elixir that would attract women and make them fall in love.

The cameraman pulled the earpiece out of his ear and said, "My God, you were brilliant, Mawlana."

"Thanks," Hatem replied.

He turned to the director, who was sitting in the control room, and raised his voice.

"Haven't I told you to speak to the owner of the station or the general manager and tell them that Hatem el-Shenawi doesn't want indecent ads running during his program," he said. "I mean, I go on and on about morals and Islam and then some girl jumps on a guy as soon as Anwar says 'let's cut for a break.' I'm starting to feel that 'break' is a bad word."

The director's guffaws boomed into the studio through the internal loudspeakers and the cameramen laughed in turn. The cameramen often gathered around him as soon as the taping was over or during the breaks, asking him questions about religious matters, most of them trivial and vacuous. He talked himself hoarse explaining to them that they needn't trouble themselves with useless knowledge or worrying that there were things they didn't know. But, as the cameramen changed and new faces appeared asking pretty much the same questions, he realized it was pointless and he had to keep his cool as he swallowed the inane questions. He gave brief, reassuring answers that were no less inane than the questions but that at least poured cold water on their curiosity. All of them—the sound technicians who had earpieces in their ears as if they were palace guards, the workers who did the wiring, the ones who dusted the table where they sat and cleaned it with some foul-smelling substance or wiped away any footprints on the floor, or sprayed a mist to polish the glass, those who spruced up Anwar's and the sheikh's clothes—all of them fell silent and stopped scurrying about and whispering to each other as soon as the voice rang out from the control room:

"Three, two, one, action."

The red light gave the order to Anwar, who opened his mouth and smiled.

"We're back after the break and we're still with Sheikh Hatem el-Shenawi. Before the break we were talking about wealth and children as the adornment of this lower life."

Hatem broke into Anwar's sentence to liven up the discussion after Anwar's rather flat introduction.

"Look, dear brother, the verse talks about wealth and children as the adornment of this life. Then you find another verse saying, *The day when man flees from his brother, his mother, his father, his consort, and his children.* Look at the order God has put them in, to show the horror of the Day of Judgment. He says, 'You with the money and the children, come and see on the Day of Judgment what you'll do with your children.' On the list, who do you flee from first? Your brother, who's your ally, who comes from the same womb, who is of the same flesh and blood, then your mother, who's the most precious person in your life. In other words there's nothing more terrifying than forgetting and running away from your own mother. I don't think there could be anything more contemptible to show you've reached the level of complete terror. After that comes your father, then the consort, that is your wife, then your children, lovely, and of course the list might be in ascending order of proximity of relationship, starting with the brother, who could handle it if you abandoned him, then your mother, who might forgive you running away. If she saw you as a child running away, she would forgive you. You know what a mother's heart is like. Then the same for your father, then comes your wife, who might shame you in this world if you tried abandoning her. Then comes the ultimate test of the great terror—abandoning the fruit of your loins on the Day of Judgment and running away from them—and they of course are the adornment of this lower life."

Sheikh Hatem paused for a moment, thinking that the explanation might be hard for Anwar and the audience to understand. He then decided to lighten it up to pull together all the disparate strands.

"That's nice and it's new. So tell me, is that the first time you've heard that?" he said.

Anwar shook his head.

"No, but it's right on the mark, Mawlana."

Hatem responded with firm dignity in a tone that reproached anyone who might think he was joking. "But see how God finishes off the verse. He asserts His divine wisdom by saying, *And the good deeds that endure are best in the eyes of the Lord as the basis for reward, and for hope.* So not only do the good deeds that survive you bring better rewards. No, here there's an inevitable addition, that they are better as the basis for hope.

That means you should put your hope in what you do that's substantial, not in the adornments you're attached to, whether money or children or whatever."

Anwar, unable to bear these moments of earnestness and Hatem's stern gaze when he started talking like a sheikh in a turban and a caftan, hurriedly looked up and put the palm of his hand to his ear to hear the voice of the producer read him the name of someone who called in by phone.

"We have a telephone call from Samir in Cairo," he said. "Good evening, Samir."

The voice started off as a mumble, saying, "Peace be upon you and the blessings of God, Mr. Anwar and Sheikh Hatem."

"And peace be upon you, Samir," Anwar replied.

"And peace be upon you," Hatem mumbled with him.

The caller broke the moment of silence that broadcasters hate, especially Hatem, because they suggest hesitation, slow thinking, and badly prepared questions, but the substance of Samir's question was very far from welcome.

"What news of Omar, Mawlana, or have you forgotten him?" he asked.

The call was cut off and the phone line made a whistling sound.

The call hit him like a right hook knocking out a tooth, delivered by a boxer that struck and then disappeared in a flash. People who appear on live programs are used to calls that are stupid or weird, or that insult them to their faces and then mysteriously cut off, or that are set up by malicious, envious rivals. This call could have been like one of those, and he could have let it pass, but this one had such an impact on him that Anwar noticed and tried to cover for him. He avoided looking at Hatem's face or making any reference to the phone call, but instead went on with another call. Anwar definitely knew who Omar was, and Hatem knew that Anwar knew who Omar was.

*

Hatem thought back to when his wife Omayma announced that she was going along with a proposal that their son Omar should go abroad for treatment. Hatem had expected a big battle with the doctors but Omayma had disarmed him by agreeing. Her attitude surprised him and he questioned it:

"It's strange that you didn't refuse!"

"Why strange? It's logical and common sense and it's in Omar's interest. I'm sure it's in his interest," she said.

"It's in his interest to leave us, and live alone in a foreign country, and in a place like that?" he answered.

That provoked her.

"I had to agree. The boy needs very special care and therapy. And if you still cared and paid attention, you'd see I've run myself ragged looking after him. I'm ready to carry on and even die for his sake, but as long as there's hope of a solution, why shouldn't he go away?"

She waited for him to answer but he didn't, so she continued, "And besides, what does being far away mean? Can you be far away these days, what with cell phones and the Internet and Skype? Thirty years ago people used to talk about 'being far away.' And besides, I'll go and see him to keep an eye on him from time to time, and the whole thing will just take a year or a little longer."

He remembered how the doctor smiled as he pulled him over to the incubator where they had put Omar moments after he was born.

He had taken Hatem's hand and said, "Don't worry. This is just a precautionary measure, I swear the boy will be just fine."

He pulled the baby in his white wrappings from under a warm light inside a metal crib and lifted him toward Hatem.

"There you are, Hatem, the crown prince," he said.

Hatem was smitten, instantly and forever. He was overwhelmed with tenderness for this fragile bundle of human flesh. Somewhere deep inside him, perhaps in the lining of his kidney or somewhere in his heart, there was a burst of emotion and affection that grew inside him until it seemed to prevent him from being himself, because he was so worried about Omar. If Omar had a temperature Hatem was in torment, as though the boy was going to die and he was going to die with him. If Omar fell ill, Hatem was shaken. He went back to his books, searched in all the biographies of the Prophet and looked through all the bound volumes in the hope of chancing upon someone whose child had the same disease, but he found none. When he thought about the death of the Prophet's son Ibrahim and the Prophet's sadness, he fell to pieces. If, in one of his sermons or lectures, he stumbled into a story about a father losing his son, he would break down in tears.

Like all fathers he didn't think any father had ever worried about his son as much as he did. When he saw him asleep in his crib he was in agony because he loved Omar so much and was so attached to him. Omar had been born after years of desperate waiting and frantic efforts by doctors and laboratories. They had calculated peak fertility times for having sex, which made sex more like a laboratory experiment than something intimate, wild, and passionate. He was on the rise at the time and his fame was spreading but every night he was pulled down by the feeling that for some reason they didn't deserve to have children. When Omar finally arrived he tried to protect himself from his weakness toward his son through learning, piety, manliness, and fame. He was strong and self-sufficient, or so he deluded himself, and he had no problem being weak toward a single creature. His weakness toward Omar would strengthen him against the world. Omayma opposed his obsession with his son and consulted psychiatrists (this is what he gathered from her without them discussing it openly), in the hope that he would get over his obsession, but all attempts failed.

Then one day Omar fell into a swimming pool in front of Hatem's eyes on an outing to the club. Omayma screamed at the pool attendant and the people around Hatem—fans, people seeking fatwas, and a crowd of club members—all dispersed. Hatem didn't hear what Omayma said, but he understood what she meant. He was speechless, paralyzed. Every muscle in his body started to go limp, none of his senses worked properly, and a strange feeling came over him. They pulled Omar out and brought him to Hatem in the arms of his swimming instructor, with his mother behind him, stooped, terrified, anxious, bewildered, and confused. Hatem was very distant and didn't know how he managed to stand up and walk with Omar and Omayma and take the child to the hospital, where Omar lay in a coma for weeks. At night Hatem spent time alone in the dark room, shaking and banging his head on the wall, slapping his cheeks, pulling out his hair, and muffling his cries by biting his hand. Then after two hours he left the room and realized he would have been relieved if he had been told that his son had died. From that day on, his sense of guilt and of abandoning the boy guided his behavior toward his son, who did not die.

He knew that Omar's trip abroad would be a relief for Omayma and a reason for hope. Besides it was what the doctors had recommended. But it pulled a stone out of the wall that was their relationship, like that stone that Sinmar the architect inserted into the palace he built for the king. Sinmar knew how to find the stone that, if removed, would bring down the whole palace. His reward was that the king killed him for fear he might use the secret against him. Omayma was pulling the stone out of its place and finishing off the demolition of the dilapidated wall. Omar was his life.

Hatem didn't hear the question that the next caller threw at Anwar. But, with the red light on, he somehow managed to keep talking, spouting grandiose nonsense interspersed with prayers, Quranic verses, and hadith of the Prophet. It was the kind of material that would serve in response to any question—his usual recourse whenever he had to improvise. Eventually Anwar, aware that the sheikh hadn't been listening to the viewer's question, stepped in to save him by throwing him a quick clue. Hatem picked up the clue and got back on track immediately. But while this 'game of professionals' was playing out between them, Hatem was asking himself who that first caller that had floored him with the question about Omar was. Was it the father of one of Omar's friends? But the voice sounded old. Was it Omayma? But the caller was a man. Who would know that Sheikh Hatem's son was unwell, in order to be able to ask the question in the first place?

"Thank you for that thorough answer, Sheikh Hatem el-Shenawi, and now we have a call from Raouf in Alexandria. Go ahead, Raouf, we can hear you."

The voice was metallic, as if it came from wires wrapped in plastic rather than the vocal cords in the throat of a human being.

Raouf, or the man who gave his name as Raouf, said, "I'd like to ask Sheikh Hatem el-Shenawi whether it's true that the Prophet ogled his neighbor's wife."

Anwar's heart leapt because this was a question that would enliven the program. In his eyes Hatem saw the gleam of a spectator watching the bull entering the ring and heading for the matador. Anwar interrupted the caller.

"That's a serious question, and it deserves us asking what exactly you mean, brother Raouf."

From the rhythm of Raouf's speech Hatem had the impression he was reading from a piece of paper. Raouf replied:

"One of the Christians who works with us heard me say something about Islam and he got angry and shouted at me, 'Well, you should know for a start what your Prophet did. Muhammad, may God bless him and grant him peace, and I ask mercy of God, looked at the wife of his neighbor and his son, Zeid bin Haritha.'"

Hatem smiled.

"He told you it was Zeid bin Haritha?" he said.

"Yes," Raouf confirmed.

"And he didn't mention Zeinab bint Jahsh at all?" asked Hatem.

"He did in fact say a name something like that."

There were murmurs and an anxious shuffling of feet among the cameramen. Anwar found himself out of the picture so he decided to find a way back in.

"Sheikh Hatem," he said. "Clearly with some callers we're getting into a debate with other religions that we shouldn't get into because it could get acrimonious."

Hatem laughed, easing the tension in the air.

"Well, it's clear that Raouf was anxious and confused and that leads us to remind all the viewers and all those in the live audience here with us today—an assembly of learning on which blessings from heaven descend—that they have to ask religious experts so that they don't get confused or misunderstand things. This remark that the viewer cited, quoting a Christian colleague of his, and I say this with full respect for our fellow human beings and compatriots, is one of a bunch of accusations made by people who hate the Prophet of Islam and are ignorant about him, and that is the incident of the Prophet's marriage to Zeinab bint Jahsh, may God be pleased with her."

Anwar realized that this was a climactic moment but the director in the control room, whispering through his earpiece, was giving him frantic instructions.

"Break, Anwar, time for the commercials," he said.

Everyone was hot to hear Hatem's answer.

When Anwar cut to the break, Sheikh Hatem cried out, "You sons of devils, how could you do that? Now there are three or four million people watching who are dying to hear the story of this wife of his neighbor."

He heard the director's voice shouting boastfully, "See the suspense, Mawlana!"

Anwar submitted to the hands of the woman fixing his make-up.

"But Mawlana, isn't that Raouf guy a Christian?" he said.

"How would I know?" Hatem cut in. "Ask Georgette who's wiping your face and doing your make-up."

Georgette gave them a smile that revealed nothing.

"Every religion has all sorts of people, Mawlana," she said.

Anwar jumped in jokingly.

"Watch out for your livelihood, Georgette," he said.

Hatem was almost certain that the call had come from the control room and that the person who made it was from the production team and that his colleagues were impressed when he ended the call so professionally. Hatem leaned back, staring into space and turning away from Anwar and Georgette toward a new cameraman who was always wearing him out with questions such as what Lot's wife was called and how old Noah was and how the people of Sodom and Gomorrah reproduced if the men had no interest in women and in what language the ant spoke to King Solomon (on that occasion Hatem said he didn't know but it was probably dubbed into colloquial Syrian, like all the soap operas these days!). After a program they did on how just the Caliph Omar ibn al-Khattab was he asked a real stunner: "Was Omar ibn al-Khattab bald?" Hatem thought he might be about to ask another question about Maria, the Prophet's Egyptian Coptic wife, so he pre-empted him. "Is there any greater baraka than that of Maria the Copt, that Alexandrian beauty who so impressed the men of Medina?" he said.

He looked at the wooden screens behind the cameras and the plastic panels around the room, the technicians sitting on four seats behind a console that looked like an electronic organ, with round headphones on their ears, the frantic movement, and the jostling as they arranged the wires along the ground or rolled them up in enormous spools and plugged them into electrical sockets. He looked at the peeling paint, the torn wallpaper, and the dark noisy corners that were the antithesis of the corner that the camera filmed, with its cheerful colors, bright lights, and ordered glitter. He looked up and saw all the metal rails and the dozens of interlocking poles, the high ceilings, the aluminum scaffolding, the massive spotlights fixed to the ceiling, carefully distributed and attached, very high up, and that steel arm like the ladder on a fire truck with a camera on the end that moved and turned like the eye of heaven looking down at their fake, artificial patch of light—a little island of smart furniture, bright colors, tailored clothes, and a polished floor amid a world of terrifying chaos, invisible ugliness, and hidden pretense.

"We're back after the break."

The red light took everyone by surprise. Anwar repeated the question posed by Raouf, stressing the words and clearly wanting to whet the appetite of the viewers. Then he asked Sheikh Hatem to reply.

"We'd like to hear, Mawlana, your answer to these allegations propagated by the opponents of Islam, this skepticism about the integrity of the Prophet. Apparently they want to portray him as a man who lusted after women and who was driven by his desires, God forbid, whereas we of course deem him to be above all failings."

Hatem nodded and said, "First of all I'd like to affirm two truths: first, that a Muslim who is well educated and knows how to defend Islam is not afraid of questions and does not tremble in the face of accusations, and second, that Muhammad ibn Abdullah was both a prophet and a human being, in other words there is a human side to the Prophet. Now we're talking about the story of his marriage to Zeinab bint Jahsh, may God be pleased with her. But we're not going to say anything that isn't in the standard texts, and what does that mean? That means the major works of Quranic exegesis by recognized scholars. I'll keep myself out of this and tell you only what's in their books. The story has its roots in the

Quranic verse *Behold! You said to one who had received the grace of God and your favor: 'Keep your wife, and fear God.' But you hid in your heart that which God was about to make manifest: you were afraid of the people, but it is more fitting that you should fear God.*

"In Bukhari, citing Anas bin Malik, we find this verse: *You hid in your heart that which God was about to make manifest.* This verse was revealed in connection with Zeinab bint Jahsh and Zeid bin Haritha and it is said that 'God never revealed to his Prophet a verse harder on him than this verse.' See, Anwar, how seriously it intrudes on the Prophet's private affairs. So much so that Hassan and Aisha said, 'If the Prophet of God had suppressed anything that God revealed to him, he would have suppressed this verse because it is so hard on him.' And notice, Anwar, how openly that possibility is discussed—'if the Prophet of God had suppressed anything.' An impossible assumption and some people imagine that it discredits the Prophet, yet Hassan and Aisha say it and the books of exegesis carry it, so if something had been suppressed this would have been the most likely verse because it has a divine disclosure of private feelings, what the Prophet's private feelings were on this occasion, and note, these are his feelings as a human being, not as a prophet, first because he wanted Zeinab for himself, second because he hid those feelings, and third, because he was afraid of people 'and God is more worthy to be feared.'

"In other words, folks, when we find ourselves in a weak position and too embarrassed to declare an opinion or our feelings because we can't confront people with them and we're worried what people will say, then this is quite natural. Even the Prophet Muhammad felt it, and the story says that 'In the evening Zeid took to his bed. And Zeinab said, "Zeid couldn't handle me. He wouldn't do things with me, but not because they were things that God had forbidden, but because he wasn't my equal."' Now listen carefully, no one go far from the television, folks, and don't answer that phone that's ringing beside you, please, because listening to only half of what I have to say would be dangerous. Zeinab herself, who would later be the Mother of the Faithful, is narrating the most intimate details of her relationship. She's speaking, in books that will be read by millions of people until the Day of Judgment, about things that happened in the conjugal bed. She even says that her husband wasn't capable. Of course we understand here what she means when she says he wasn't 'capable' and 'he couldn't handle me.' It's clear she was surprised how bad he was in bed. Then Zeid realized. If it had been an ordinary incident, it would have passed without her noticing, and if he hadn't been able to handle her on other nights before, it wouldn't have mattered. But what happened that night suggested such obvious impotence, driven by God's will, that Zeid went to the Prophet the next morning and said, 'Zeinab is tormenting me with her tongue, and going on and on, and I want to divorce her.' And the Prophet said to him, 'Keep your wife, and fear God.' People have disagreed over how to interpret this verse. Some of the commentators, including al-Tabari and others, maintain that the Prophet made some complimentary remarks to Zeinab bint Jahsh while she was married to Zeid and then Zeid told the Prophet that he wanted to leave her and complained that she had been rude and disobedient, that she had insulted him and had boasted of her high birth.

"In other words, we have a wife finding fault with her husband on the grounds that he didn't have a noble pedigree while she was a woman of high rank and good family. This can happen even in the household of a husband and wife who are Companions of the Prophet. So we can also understand the human side of the Companions and don't think they were angels descended from Heaven, but human beings who tried hard to discipline and improve themselves. Then the Prophet said, 'Fear God'—in what you say about her, that is—'and keep your wife.' The commentator Muqatil says, 'The Prophet came looking for Zeid one day, and he saw Zeinab standing there. She was fair-skinned, beautiful, and buxom, one of the finest women of the Quraysh, and he fell for her and said, 'Praise be to God, who turns men's hearts.' Zeinab heard what he said and mentioned it to Zeid, and Zeid saw what was happening and said, 'Prophet, give me permission to divorce her. She's giving me a hard time and tormenting me with her tongue.' And the Prophet said, 'Keep your wife, and fear God.'"

Hatem leaned his head back and raised his string of amber prayer beads to his chest. He checked that the red light had not gone off and that the story had silenced the studio and that the director and the control room technicians were too enthralled to engage in their usual distractions. A phantom, maybe his old Rifai master, flitted behind the cameraman standing by the camera fixed on Hatem's face. He unexpectedly did something that someone like him just does not do while broadcasting live: he stopped talking for some seconds and stared at a point far from the focal point of the camera lens. Everyone was puzzled, but the machine at work inside Hatem took over, dragging the sounds out of his prodigious memory. The words took shape without passing through any mind or monitoring. His voice was louder when he resumed, as if he were hiding the fact that he was thinking of something completely different.

"It is said that God sent a gust of wind that lifted the curtain when Zeinab was scantily dressed at home," he said. "The Prophet saw Zeinab and she made an impression on him and, when he came asking for Zeid, Zeinab realized that she made an impression on the Prophet. When Zeid came, she told him what had happened, and it occurred to Zeid to divorce her. The Prophet was worried people would gossip if he married Zeinab after Zeid, given that Zeid was his adopted son, since adoption was permissible in Islam at that time, although it was later banned. He had even given his name to Zeid, who was known as Zeid ibn Muhammad."

Hatem came to his senses and heard his voice telling the story, and he decided to stop and break in with an explanation, because he felt that Anwar was trying to interrupt him and catch the camera's attention by reacting to his story with amazement, playing the part of a viewer watching at home.

"But there are imams," Hatem continued, "who think that the Prophet fell in love with Zeinab, Zeid's wife, and there's another text that says, and I quote, 'Perhaps it was some joker who used the word "love" because this could only come from someone who was unaware that the Prophet was incapable of such things or from someone who had little respect for him.' All these stories appear in the works of respected commentators but, if the story is offensive to the Prophet and discredits him, would it have appeared in a text that is recited from high above the seven heavens, the Quran, by which we will worship until the day when people rise from the dead and are gathered together? Even if it does contain things that Muslims are embarrassed about or consider shameful. Folks, would the commentators on the Quran have singled out this verse for all this explanation, of which I have given you only a quarter or maybe less?

"So Raouf, or whoever you are, the Prophet married Zeinab bint Jahsh to undo the ban on marrying the wife of one's adopted son, because no one could marry the wife of his adopted son unless the Prophet himself had done it, thus lifting the ban. And see what it all led to? Anas bin Malik says, 'When Zeinab's obligatory waiting period was over after the divorce, the Prophet said to Zeid, "Let me get engaged to her." And Zeid went off and found her leavening her dough. And Zeid said, 'When I saw her, the fact that the Prophet wanted to marry her was too much for me and I couldn't look at her. I turned my back on her and withdrew and I said, 'Zeinab, the Prophet has sent asking to marry you,' and she said, 'I can't do anything until God gives instructions.' Then she went off to the place where she prayed and the revelation was revealed, and the Prophet went in to her.'"

"There's nothing to embarrass us in this story. On the contrary, we can be proud that the Quran has taught us to be completely transparent about the Prophet's important private and intimate affairs. The incident of Aisha's necklace is in the Quran and is there anything more serious than the Prophet having suspicions about his wife and refusing to have anything to do with her for a month or two while everyone is talking about her honor? Could there be anything more embarrassing than the story of Zeinab and Zeid if it were to happen to one of us at home, God forbid, but when it happens in the Prophet's household it becomes part of the Quran by which we worship when we pray. A strong Muslim is a knowledgeable Muslim, and a weak Muslim, Anwar, is a Muslim who is ignorant."

The phantom had appeared and disappeared in a flash. Then it reappeared facing him and coming toward him. It walked past the cameras into the frame of the picture to appear with Hatem on the screen. Did he miss his old Rifai sheikh so much that the sheikh had come to see him? Had the sheikh come to give him his blessing, to join him or to pick a fight with him, by coming to him from his youth to remind him that he had forgotten about him? Despite his composure Hatem was stunned that Anwar hadn't noticed, and he was unsure whether it was a silly trick and nothing to be frightened about or a phantom that reflected the guilt that was feeding on his nerves. He clammed up and looked down toward his chest, until Anwar saved him by wrapping the program up.

They were heavy, the stones that had piled up on his heart over all the years—a burden of anxiety that showed no signs of easing. When he was left to himself for a while the anxiety ate away at him, like woodworm in the rafters of a house. What hurt him most was that he simply couldn't speak his mind: the white corridors with high ceilings where his fame had spread and his star had risen were now walls that imprisoned him, forcing him to conform to the image that television had created. When he entered these studios for the first time, everyone ignored him or looked away. He was just a sheikh coming to earn a few pennies, a mosque imam on a salary that wasn't enough to feed him, who wrote a column interpreting dreams in an evening newspaper and shared the fee with the sheikh in whose name it was published but who was ancient and senile. The sheikh had come to him at Friday prayers and proposed that Hatem help with the column because he was tired of doing it day after day. Then he discovered that he was expected to write it daily in exchange for half the fee—an arrangement that the old sheikh considered to be generous on his part and that Hatem saw as a gift from heaven that would help him makes ends met at a time when his income was meager and his needs expanding.

It was through this same elderly sheikh that he came to know the novice editor who was working on the team that produced a fatwa program broadcast by an Arab religious channel from Cairo. On one occasion he invited him to take part in a program ('you go on air in two hours, Mawlana'). It took him a while to grasp the meaning of 'on air,' but he soon got the idea. The sheikh who was supposed to be the guest had backed out and another sheikh was urgently needed to save the program. Maybe the producer had mixed up his telephone number with someone else's, or perhaps he felt that this young and available sheikh wouldn't feel insulted to be called in at short notice, only two hours before broadcast time. Naturally he agreed. It was the first time he had been driven in a car sent out by a studio to pick him up. When he thought back to that night, hardly any of the details escaped him. The job offered him a glamorous future, but with a dark side too. He might travel far, but his new life would also be a trap. The driver realized that the sheikh was new and didn't know the basics of the job, from the way he sat next to the driver because he was confused and too humble to sit in the back, the questions he asked about the presenter, and about where the program was watched. The driver set off, displaying his experience and knowledge, explaining to him the precise details, telling him that the program paid the sheikh a thousand pounds.

"But the producers will take advantage of you because this is your first time and so they will reduce the amount, but mind you don't accept less than five hundred because they'll share out the rest between them and it won't go back to the budget, Mawlana."

Then he added, "And all we make out of it is a tip from the guest, I swear, sheikh."

Then the driver began to talk about his decision to retire so that he could get an early pension to marry off his two daughters and how he then found work driving his car for a car service and from that he discovered the offices that specialize in dealing with Arab television stations, and by making friends, by treating people respectfully and being polite, he started working directly for the station without going through the company boss, who would skim off some of his earnings.

In spite of the depressing nature of the conversation and the fact that the driver was clearly angling for a tip, Hatem was happy to be entering this world, even through the driver. His future was still murky but through the swirling mists he could see glimmers of light that drew him into the corridors of the very same studios that he now knew by heart, preferring some to others depending on when they had last been renovated. On that first occasion he was no one compared to the people impatiently awaiting his arrival, just someone who sat on a chair in front of the presenter so that people could make a living. He discovered the rules of the job from the looks, whispers, comments, shouts, gestures, instructions, and obscenities exchanged across the studio and from the hidden room that he knew was the most important room— the control room, where the director and production team worked, along with dozens of pieces of equipment and screens. Later on, when he was confident of his authority, he asked to see the control room. He went inside and teased them, no longer intimidated and contemptuous of how routine and easy their work was.

The basic principle in this business was that it was a job. He never ran into anyone who tried to delude him, or themselves, into thinking that it was a real vocation. As soon as anyone thought it was anything more just a way to make a living, they soon lost their job. There was a magic in it, and a touch of madness, but if you felt you were working for some goal other than making a living, then it would spit you out. From being its jailer, you would become its prisoner. The conceptual difference between a virtuoso and a session musician was very much evident in the reality of this trade.

He had learned to play the lute, but was anxious not to let on to anyone. This was a secret he had kept to himself since he was a student at the middle school of the Azhar institute. He went to the institute wearing the compulsory uniform—a loose black caftan and that white turban that by the end of the day was full of dust and dirt after all the running and playing and throwing balls around in the institute courtyard with the high walls. He remembered the rustle of the caftan's hem and the stomping of his feet beneath it when he ran after his fellow sheikhs at play in break time. They forgot about the dignity of the uniform and were ignorant of the roles that awaited them—roles in which play had no part. He loved the lute so much that he went to study under a lutist called Ezzat, who lived behind their street. Hatem went there diligently, twice a week after school and before the afternoon prayer. The lutist lived with his widowed and childless sister, who had time on her hands to lament her bad luck, which had robbed her of a husband when they were both still young and of an apartment that had gone to her husband's brother because it was registered in his name. Ezzat's good nature made him resistant to depression, and by working at night and sleeping all day he was spared having to face his miserable sister. Hatem was a willing student and his favorite: he even overlooked delays in paying the fees for lessons. Ezzat told him that the pioneering Egyptian composers of the nineteenth century were given the title of sheikh, as in Sheikh Sayed Darwish, Sheikh Salama Hegazi, Sheikh Abul-Ela Mohamed, and Sheikh Zakaria Ahmed. Except for the Egyptian composers who were Jewish, all of them wore turbans and caftans.

Ezzat's sister, meanwhile, took it upon herself to complete Hatem's education. One day she found him sitting in a corner of the sitting room waiting for her brother to wake up.

She walked in on him and started making small talk, then she asked him, "Please, my little sheikh, would you cast a spell to protect me from evil."

Hatem didn't understand what she wanted.

Purring like a cat, she added, "What, don't you know how to do it?"

She decided to teach him: she suddenly came up to him and pressed herself against him, breathing heavily. With trembling fingers, she stroked his hair and his face. Hatem froze but he couldn't help but be aroused. She undressed him and within a few minutes of him discovering the mysteries of sex and crossing the bridge from childhood to adulthood his lute teacher was standing at the door in shame. The sister picked up her clothes and Hatem sat rigid with fear. Then Ezzat went off to the bathroom in silence.

The excited widow gave him a kick and said, "Out you get now, and come any time at night when he's not here."

He went out into the night alone, although some of the studio workers were milling around him, shaking his hand just to feel close to him or greeting him to express their admiration and affection. The tenacious crowd that waited every day for him to come out of the big studio door headed to his car, which was well known, a landmark that betrayed his presence or heralded his approach. There was no escaping the daily ordeal of people asking him questions. In fact, in his ability to put up with them he discovered that he retained something of his old self—his willingness to listen patiently to stupidities and to deal with people who stared at him and stretched out their hands seeking money or asking him to intercede to get them a job. He had realized long ago that he hated them as much as he sympathized with them or cared about their needs, but along a path that was so long that he thought it would never end, he had come to understand the aggressiveness, the determination to extract something from you—money, a recommendation, a business card or even a telephone number, anything—because these people were desperate and defeated, not because they deserved it or because of anything they had done or any shortcomings on their part, but because of you.

You were always responsible for the disparity that gave you your status while they were driven by poverty or by hardship to come to you seeking your friendship and flattering you so you would give them what was necessarily their due. Necessity gave them the strength of the desperate as well as the weakness of the beggar, the rudeness of the abused as well as the politeness of the mendicant. He could sense a cruel but suppressed aggression when he was physically surrounded by a group of people pressing their requests, seeking jobs or holding up medical reports and heart and chest X-rays. The jostling, the noise, and the size of the crowds showed him that, although they had trained themselves to appear weak, they might change instantly into ruthless troublemakers. They were torn between, on the one hand, a feeling that their dignity had been offended and that sycophancy and begging were beneath them and, on the other hand, such desperate need that they thought little of seeking alms and even thought of it as work. He could see it in their eyes, which pinned their hopes on him but did not look directly at him. They hardly ever looked you in the eye when they made their requests or when they put out their hands or told the repeated stories that they, and you, knew by heart, or when they came back to you for the fourth or fifth time citing some new difficulty or telling you how the person you sent them to had let them down, or that they had a new prescription for a more expensive medicine or that a new surgical operation was needed.

Anything and everything. He had seen it all, heard it all, and experienced it all since becoming famous and joining the circle of celebrities. He hadn't seen this with other sheikhs who appeared on the same programs as he did or who gave fatwas on television. The people who came with requests and those in need were experts by instinct. They could tell which sheikhs it was worth asking for charity. Some of the other sheikhs were not targets in the same way. On the contrary, they were enemies because of the way they dispensed advice to beggars, shouted at them, pushed them away, and were openly tight-fisted. But Hatem el-Shenawi ranked with those film stars, soccer players, and television presenters who were portrayed as allies of the poor and who felt deeply guilty about their fame or who begrudged themselves their wealth, because inside they feared it might be a temptation or a test, illicit or transient. They were prey to this petty harassment, the kind of siege that Hatem faced when he came out of the studio at the appointed time, known to them all. At zero hour, half an hour before the end of the program that was broadcast live, they gathered at the entrance to the studio. They managed to get past the gate of Media Production City by various means. Then they would easily find their way to the pavement opposite the studio building. There they would wait, either opening a Quran and reciting from it, to fend off anyone who tried to question them, because who would dare to interrupt someone who was engrossed in the Quran, or going

31

over their complaints with each other, exchanging sob stories and maps showing how to reach people who gave assistance. As soon as the program ended they would rush to their positions at the door and on the pavement. When they heard that Hatem would soon come out, they surged to meet him and he could hardly hear anything from all the voices shouting over one another. With patience and experience he had worked out how to escape the circle that tightened around him, despite the shouts of his driver Sirhan to keep them away, the intervention of the security personnel, and the pushing and shoving of the studio workers. He had tried everything: silence, ignoring them, being kind and sympathetic, shouting and screaming, appealing to them, running alongside the car and then jumping in when it was already moving and driving straight off. But in the end the only fitting reaction was to surrender.

On this occasion a phone call from Khaled Abu Hadid's secretary gave him added impetus to leave the studio more quickly.

"Am I monitored that closely?" he said. "I've hardly stepped out of the studio and turned my phone on."

"That's because we miss you so much, Mawlana," said the secretary. "And anyway everyone was watching the program, and Khaled Pasha decided we couldn't have dinner without you, Mawlana."

He put his cell on speaker and put his foot on the accelerator, turning his head to see how far back he could reverse, then turned hard right to avoid the car parked in front of him.

"Well, I certainly wouldn't want to keep the other sheikhs waiting for their dinner," he answered. "Some of those guys will eat you up if they don't get their dinner on time."

The secretary laughed. "I'm on my way," Hatem added. "The driver's on holiday, so I'm driving myself."

The secretary quickly feigned being upset.

"You should have told us, Mawlana. We would have come and picked you up," he said.

"What for? No one ever said I was blind, and besides, it's not far to the estate."

The secretary seemed to want him there instantly.

"Do you know the short cut to al-Manashi by the desert road?" he asked.

"Don't worry. God's with us."

He turned off the phone and concentrated on the road. He was no longer able to be alone. He avoided private meetings with himself. He wouldn't go home till late. He would be there early only if the house was full of people, as it sometimes was because of the random hours he worked, with producers, his team of assistants, or people coming to talk about new projects. He couldn't remember the last time he had sat down and buried himself in a book. He felt that he knew everything he needed to know, that he had memorized everything he required for his work, that he was set up like a device with a hard disk in which all the information had been filed away and could be accessed at any moment. Besides, he was fully aware that he wouldn't be able to read if he tried. With appalling arrogance, he felt that any new writings would just reproduce the classical sources. He didn't need any simplifications or dumbing down. The original books were a treasure trove and he had taken the gems and the diamonds. Digging for more would be torture. For many years he couldn't put a book down till he had finished it and even memorized it. Whenever anything on paper came into his hands he would drink the ink and store away the information. He was a camel fully loaded with the water of knowledge in a television desert that didn't give the people invited to appear on screen a chance to stop to read and reacquire the ability to think. Most of the people in television had memorized the texts and taught their audiences to learn by rote, but he would die if he thought he was like them or representative of them. He felt profoundly ill at ease when he had to deal with himself, face himself, have a discussion with himself, or be self-critical. He was at an age when he could no longer bear honesty. Being honest with himself was a malignant virus and if it got inside his body it would attack the whole robust system that made him resilient. Posing questions was lethal and it would be best if the inner mirrors in which he might see himself were broken. He left the studio after the program and made his way through another crowd. It took up more of his time and kept busy the brain cells he still had.

He put the CD of Sheikh Mohamed Rifaat in the player in the hope that it would warm him up inside. Sheikh Rifaat's voice sounded distant and there was some interference that created a hissing that impaired the purity, clarity, and grandeur of his voice. Yet in spite of all the damage that time had done to the remaining serviceable recordings of the great Quran reader, the vigor and warmth of the voice was overwhelming, beguiling, and soothing. It seemed to reflect both the sheikh's own mysterious history and the warm memories that came back to Hatem whenever he heard Sheikh Rifaat. For Hatem's generation, and those before him, the radio had left a deep impression. For years the sheikh's voice had monopolized the Quran readings in the month of Ramadan, a time when the radio alone commanded people's attention and was often on. Sheikh Rifaat had become, psychologically and spiritually, a symbol of the month of Ramadan. If Hatem heard him at any other time of year or in anything other than a family setting, the experience would be tinged with sadness, nostalgia for family, a sense of the passage of time, and comforting memories of an innocence that was long gone. When he heard him, he metaphorically curled up in the fetal position, his mind at peace.

When he was fuming with anger, he would go into the bedroom of his son Omar at night. It had some features that reminded Hatem of his own childhood, but he didn't feel at ease and the washing machine in his mind didn't stop turning—washing and wringing his thoughts, extracting the dirt stuck in his brain—until he saw Omar asleep with his chin on his knees and his legs folded up against the back of his thighs, his fists clenched, with one arm folded under his head and the edge of his shoulder and the other arm on top. Then he might move close to Omar and lie down in the clothes he had come home in after a work trip or a program or a seminar or some other horror, and curl up alongside his son, lying in exactly the same position without turning over or stretching out.

His wife found him like that one night and laughed. That was the day they had gone to see Dr. Shehab, the marriage counselor, who was shocked when Hatem had come to see him, which undermined Hatem's confidence in him from the first moment, because why should the doctor imagine he was above having a deep disagreement with his wife? Did the wise doctor think that sheikhs never failed or that they didn't have feelings? Omayma complained that Hatem had run away the day Omar fell ill. She told him about Hatem's absence while his son was in a coma, where he had gone and how he had left her alone to face the disaster. Hatem hadn't wanted to say where he was, neither to himself nor to her, out of fear for his reputation and his programs and his money. Then she told the doctor how Hatem had come back twenty-two days after Omar had gone into a coma. She'd found Hatem sleeping like a child in Omar's bed. Hatem put up with what she said only because the doctor realized how stupid and rude she was being. On that day she cursed and swore, insulted, broke down, wept and sobbed, slapped her head and her face. He felt more pity for her than he felt for himself, given the way she had insulted him in front of a doctor they hardly knew. She was hysterical and he tried to calm her down. He took her hand and stroked it and patted it. It was as if some demon had rented her body for an hour on the cheap. She pushed the door and went out, leaving him alone with the doctor.

There was a silence that neither made any effort to break, but after a while Hatem said:

"So now you know there really are such things as hysterical women."

They both laughed.

"Beat them and leave them alone in bed,"[1] Hatem continued. "All that stuff you hear me say on the program is indeed what God said, but he sets one condition—those who beat their wives or refuse to sleep with them have to be real men, and I'm sorry to say we're not real men."

"Remember the old saying, 'a carpenter never fixes his own front door'? Well, my door looks to be off its hinges too, doctor," he went on, continuing to joke with the doctor. "What do you say we set up an association called the Loose Door Association for Medical Consultations and Religious Fatwas?"

Hatem arrived at the entrance to the estate to the sound of Sheikh Mohamed Rifaat's voice. Devious Khaled Abu Hadid was always waiting for him in his country mansion in this spot in the remote suburbs. The estate covered dozens of acres and had high, forbidding walls. They might have a bite to eat or a banquet in the garden in the summer or in the halls when winter came. But when he wanted to show his constituents that he had divine legitimacy, he would cleverly take his guests instead to a place in the heart of the town where he had his electoral campaign headquarters. He had started in a building overlooking the main square, near the mosque of the most important local saints. After a few months he had bought the whole building and turned the apartments into offices, headquarters for his staff, reception rooms for his guests, and rooms where he met provincial and municipal officials. Then he stripped the partition walls out on the ground floor and turned it into a large meeting hall for communal banquets. Abu Hadid's main objective was achieved merely by announcing that a religious delegation was coming to visit him. As each sheikh arrived, he went down to receive him from the street entrance, where the cars were parked, and then escorted him through the crush of dozens or hundreds of local people. The sheikhs' followers pestered them with requests and tried to get as close as possible, jostling with the guards. Then, when the whole delegation went through the square to the mosque, the scene marked Abu Hadid in the consciousness of the poor people in his constituency as someone who was blessed, because some of the sheikhs' baraka and sanctity had rubbed off on him. Abu Hadid chose the sheikhs he invited like an impresario. Sheikh al-Ibyari, for example, was the most famous and most highly paid Quran reader in the whole country. When their food had settled and they had washed it down with a cup of tea or coffee, the sheikh's voice would boom out with a prayer of lamentation. People recorded his voice enthusiastically, as if it opened the gates of Heaven for them, though it's hard to imagine the gates of Heaven or even a small window in one of Heaven's side rooms opening on top of Abu Hadid's election headquarters.

Hatem knew there would be at least six preachers at Abu Hadid's reception that night, some in turbans and some in Western suits, because the man was generous. He paid them a fee for attending as soon as they arrived and they couldn't leave without a parting gift of some kind. All of them were the stars of their channels: some were fanatics and bigots, while others were easygoing and pleasant. Abu Hadid tried to satisfy all tastes; his gatherings were inclusive and he never missed an opportunity to bring people together. He bribed people with such skill that the people he bribed never felt they were demeaning themselves or being bought off. He bribed them and then begged them to do what he wanted, mouthing religious platitudes to the sheikhs and kissing some of them on the hand and always opening his arms, usually with his head bowed, when he was speaking to one of them or seeking their favor. He always sounded deferential toward them when he spoke reverentially in front of a gathering of the people he had invited to meet his sheikhs, as he called them. He had even contacted Sheikh Galal Abdel-Muhsin before the last elections and asked him to grace him with a prayer, and the sheikh told him he was going to win the elections by a margin of three.

"May God bring you good news, Mawlana," Khaled said he told the sheikh, "but three what?"

Khaled turned to the audience and said, "I swear, my knees were knocking during the conversation. That's right, three what? After all that, I'd win by three votes? Or maybe he meant three hundred or three thousand."

"And maybe thirty thousand," someone shouted out.

They laughed and Khaled Abu Hadid added quickly, "Come on, how many votes are there in the constituency in the first place for me to win by 30,000 votes? Anyway, the result came out and I found there was a three in there, it was true. I had three times as many votes as my opponent."

"Allah, Allah!" people said in awe.

Hatem leaned over toward Sheikh Sorour's ear and asked, "Do you believe that story, Sheikh Sorour?"

"Really!" Sorour replied in a rough whisper. "The man feeds us and treats us with the highest honor and you want me to say that all his elections have been rigged and the candidate he faced was from the Muslim Brotherhood so they rigged them again for double measure. Let him have his say, Sheikh Hatem."

Sheikh Said Sorour was a religious singer that Khaled Abu Hadid never forgot to invite. Sorour was blind and Hatem had dealt with many blind sheikhs, some of them very perceptive, from the time when he studied in the Azhar institutes, when he performed at funerals, gatherings, and saints' days, and when he was at university. He had seen many blind people behaving as if they could see, but Sheikh Sorour was the only blind person who behaved as though everyone around him was as blind as he was. Sorour was the most powerful religious singer in the Arab world of our time, and also the stupidest person in the Arab world. That's how Hatem had always seen him, even before Said Sorour became famous by recording a religious song with a young singer who had a contract with one of the religious stations for a Ramadan song. The singer came up with the idea of giving Sheikh Sorour a part in the song, and Sorour's voice was in fact a stunning match for the young singer's voice. The song was a success that astounded Sorour, especially when he heard his voice being used as the ringtone on the cell phones of passengers on the microbuses going up to Muqattam, where he lived. But Sorour's stupidity far outmatched his vocal talent. His lack of discipline, his addiction to hashish, and his extraordinary ability to squander his money on failed marriages and loose women all undermined his credibility. The deep bond between him and Khaled Abu Hadid survived, however, perhaps because neither of them was required to put on an act for the other, so although he was a sheikh, Sorour gave Khaled an easy and legitimate opportunity to challenge comfortably and safely the intentions and consciences of other sheikhs, enabling him to vent his repressed hostility toward sheikhs that he knew were full of hypocrisy about his own hypocrisy.

When Hatem arrived that night Sorour had already started singing, accompanied by the powerful aroma of Moroccan hashish procured especially as a gift for Sorour, so that the circle would be filled with a sound from heaven. Hatem made his way through the melee of onlookers and bodyguards. People who had already taken their seats called him by name. He fumbled to remove his shoes and several people came forward to help him take them off and carry them away. People smiled at him admiringly with languid eyes. The banquet, served by Khaled Abu Hadid's guards and constituency workers, was laid out in a spacious, circular hall spread with carpets of the kind used in funeral tents. On the walls he noticed calligraphies with verses from the Quran, all of them about patience and gratitude, and on the floor there were low seats arranged in a horseshoe pattern, where Abu Hadid's guests were seated at tables a few inches off the ground, laden with many kinds of food, especially those rich in fat. People were chomping on large pieces of turkey, and there were roast ducks placed here and there across the tables, along with plates of grilled meat, kebabs, and kofta. The kofta lay in every corner, wherever you looked and wherever your hand happened to land. There were trays of rice with nuts, bowls of mulukhia with chunks of lamb floating in them, plates of taro with veal, and stuffed cabbage, eggplant, vine leaves, and zucchini arranged on top of each other, with a rich gravy oozing out of them. The guests greeted Hatem and Khaled Abu Hadid appeared, staggering like an overweight elephant as he invited him insistently to sit next to Sheikh Fathi, barking orders at his bodyguards, who treated his order as a divine decree. Sheikh Hatem wasn't as interested in Sheikh Fathi as Sheikh Fathi was in him; in every one of his television appearances Sheikh Fathi criticized Hatem and attacked his opinions. Hatem sat down anyway, welcomed as he yielded to the arms that squeezed him in next to Sheikh Fathi. He saw Mukhtar el-Husseini, the head of a Sufi order, looking at him with a smile, and his heart rejoiced.

Where have the sheikhs gone, Hatem wondered when he saw the men barefoot around the tables. None of them were wearing caftans or turbans or the kakoula, the splendid gown worn by Azhar graduates. Time seemed to have ridden roughshod over the warm, comfortable attire in favor of this urge to modernize, stripping the clerics of their old appearance and giving them a Westernized modernity—long, bushy beards and Western, twenty-first-century suits on bodies with heads from the twelfth century. Out of them all, only Mukhtar el-Husseini was wearing his white uniform and green turban.

He had a kind, childlike, innocent face and a dignified smile, and he was shy and thoughtful, too timid to interrupt or eavesdrop. He wasn't as gluttonous as the others; in fact he would mutter a little bismillah before reaching out for a piece of food, then chew it carefully before taking another, closing his eyes and relaxing. The ruling party's members of parliament from the province that included Abu Hadid's constituency were all in attendance, squeezed in between the sheikhs, reaping the rewards of fame in the form of duck legs and pieces of kofta. In front of him, standing, sitting, jumping up, or scoffing food, there were many police officers and generals in civilian dress, some of whom he recognized because they looked the part and others he had actually met on various occasions. There were also current and former ministers and governors who came to network with other powerful people or because they were tempted by the extravagant hospitality of Abu Hadid, who bought and sold influence with such civility that the offense seemed quite innocent, indeed quite normal. The hot food and the large helpings gave Hatem a lump in the throat, only partially relieved by the sight of Mukhtar el-Husseini, who seemed to be supporting him and encouraging him to bear the unbearable. In fact Hatem felt that the only sympathetic person at the banquet was Mukhtar el-Husseini, who signaled to him that he would like to talk to him in private later.

"Of course, Sheikh Mukhtar," Hatem told him. "That would bring me a thousand blessings."

"God bless you and preserve you," Sheikh Mukhtar replied bashfully.

Hatem then realized that Sheikh Fathi at his side had lost his appetite as soon as he sat next to him. He could hear the hatred in the way Fathi was breathing as he slowly chewed the meat. In response to this hatred, Hatem decided to mobilize his secret reserves and lure Fathi's snakes from their lairs.

*

After all, that's what he had trained to do as a teenager with the Rifais, the Sufi order that specialized in handling deadly serpents. The old Rifai that was hiding inside him came to the fore. He remembered how it all began—when Sheikh Zein, the head of the order, ran into him at a funeral reception. Hatem gave the funeral oration and the sheikh then summoned him. Hatem stood in front of him, small and insignificant, looking up at a man who seemed to be standing when he was only sitting, and who seemed to be as high as the sky when he stood up. The man had an aura, a radiance, a charisma that was terrifying, especially to someone like Hatem, who felt as if he had received an unchallengeable summons from a sovereign lord.

"What's your name, son?" the sheikh asked.

"Hatem el-Shenawi."

"Fifteen, sixteen years?" he asked with a smile.

"Fourteeen and four months," Hatem answered firmly.

Sheikh Zein laughed.

"And have you had time to learn the meaning of life, so that you can explain to us the meaning of death, my boy?" he asked.

The question took Hatem by surprise. He acted dumb and replied:

"I based my oration on God's book and the commentaries on it and the practice of the Prophet, may God grant peace and honor on him and his family and all his Companions and those who came after them and do good deeds till the Day of Judgment."

The sheikh made a sign as if some secret had just been revealed to him.

"My boy, parroting is one thing and knowing is something else. Learning is one thing and divine inspiration is something else."

It was rather mysterious.

But then he added, "You're in the fourth year at an Azhar institute, aren't you?"

"That's right!" Hatem said, amazed at the man's accuracy.

"Tell your father that for the month of Ramadan, which starts in two nights, you'll be traveling with Sheikh Zein of the Rifais, celebrating Ramadan by fasting in the expectation of reward in the afterlife. And come quickly," the sheikh added.

Hatem tried to hold him back as he walked off.

"But my father won't agree, and besides I don't want to go," he said.

"You're coming, my boy," he said without even taking the trouble to look back.

He did in fact spend a month on the desert fringes of Cairo and some days with the sheikh in his mansion. He remembered the Rifai spell:

"I entreat you, you that dwell in this place—snake, scorpion, or serpent—come flying to me by order of the Merciful One. If you disobey you will die at the wishes of the Living One that never dies."

Hatem remembered the boy standing in front of Sheikh Zein in that house in the center of the terrified village that had been attacked by snakes some days earlier. The people were so frightened that they had abandoned the village and summoned the Rifais. Sheikh Zein decided to bring along three young men from the order, including Hatem, who watched in silence. When Hatem panicked the sheikh grabbed his collarbone between the thumb and the index finger of his rough hand until he calmed down despite the pain.

"This isn't magic," the sheikh had said. "These are not spells, or even baraka. This is a science, a skill. Don't rely on things you've been taught; learn from what makes sense. Don't believe what you see; see what you believe. Even though you're not going to be one of us, I'm telling you this, Hatem, because I feel like you're my lost son and a sheikh who will acquire learning but will find it hard to bear the consequences of your learning. Treat this as a summer trip, or an expense-paid month of Ramadan events allowing you to make some money along with the Quran readers. But the most precious thing you'll earn is the science of subjecting the miraculous to the inquiring mind, a training that might be useful to you, because this is how the Rifais lure snakes from their lairs calmly and submissively and how they persuade beasts to surrender. As soon as they show their heads, make them feel safe. There's no more effective weapon than making your enemies feel safe when they surrender.

"O God, with a talisman in the name of God the Merciful the Compassionate, remove the black bile that lurks in the hearts of our enemies and Your enemies. May the might of Your hand cut off the heads of the unjust with the swords of Nimshaq. Protect us with Your powerful amulets against their feeble gaze.

"Now talismans are for ordinary people, Hatem, but reason is for the elite. The Rifai is courageous, bold in his knowledge of all kinds of snakes. He has studied them and understands their strong points and weak points and their poison and its antidote. It's training, experience, clear thinking, and courage."

A little later Sheikh Zein decided to try him out with some new boys. They went to lure out some snakes and Hatem led them. It was the first and last time that Hatem failed at this task. When the first snake came out, one of the other Rifais had to step in to save Hatem, and then Hatem panicked and grabbed a big stick that was lying around the house and with the violence of a frightened man hit another snake that had eluded him. Then he threw away the stick and jumped in panic, and one of his companions lifted him up over his shoulder and quickly took him out of the house so that they could finish off the assignment. They told Sheikh Zein that Hatem had failed miserably and he hung his head in shame and trembled with fear. Sheikh Zein had laughed and told him that people who preach about death shouldn't wet their pants for fear of dying.

Hatem left when the sheikh dismissed him. He asked Hatem to pass by whenever he could, as if politely saying he was free to leave. Hatem avoided mentioning the Rifais for years, and maybe that was why the sheikh's ghost haunted him day and night.

Hatem was watching the guzzling that was going on in front of him, thinking back to those nights he had spent as a young Quran reader going to funerals with the other readers. The accusation that sheikhs had voracious appetites and could be bought with food still bothered him. In spite of his renown he still felt a dispiriting embarrassment whenever he met someone who boasted that he had known him long ago. Hatem would try to ignore him but sometimes the admirer would stick to him, proud that he had seen him and met him twenty or twenty-five years ago.

"Remember, Mawlana, when you were with Sheikh Abdel-Moneim el-Salmawi in Hadayek Helwan? You remember the house that was behind the old train station? There was a funeral tent there when my mother died, and you were speaking and you were so young and people were saying, 'Look how young that Azhar boy is, but his funeral oration is so good that people break down in tears and ask him to repeat it.'"

Hatem listened to this hasty outpouring without embarrassment, from a man who clearly relished the memory even if it was of the death of his mother. Hatem's presence in the funeral tent was enough to make his mother's death an occasion that brought back joy rather than sadness. But Hatem knew these orations by heart. Like everything else he had memorized, he could repeat them word for word in his sleep or even if he was lying drugged on an operating table. There was an area in his brain that controlled this rare gift for memorizing things rapidly, accurately, and permanently. Maybe he had a disease that he didn't understand and this gift was one of its effects.

He had been going to those events with Sheikh el-Salamawi, who discovered that Hatem could win the admiration of the mourners and would serve as an advertisement for Salamawi himself, ensuring the sheikh would be hired for other events. But whenever anyone mentioned one of those funerals Hatem felt embarrassed for Salamawi and other Quran readers because people made fun of them for their massive appetites. He was the only one who realized this, but he kept quiet. He had found it hard to eat at the homes of other people or in front of other people ever since someone called him 'the fat Quran reader who only thinks of his stomach' and he overheard the people of the house and those organizing the funeral giving instructions that the sheikhs get their dinner, with words such as: "Boy, give the sheikhs plenty of fat," "Now here's a hunk of fat worthy of your mouth, Mawlana," or "We want to see some meat in front of our sheikhs." Salamawi, as everyone knew, was blind, so Hatem stuck close to him in his comings and goings, and people saw them as father and son, especially as they both had the same fair complexion. Although when it came to their faces, Salamawi's unnecessarily large black glasses made it impossible to make a comparison.

All this talk about greedy sheikhs was an affront to Hatem's adolescent sensibilities, coming as he did from a middle-class home, the kind too embarrassed to talk openly about greed and that saw appetite as a private matter. He grew more and more reluctant to eat in front of strangers, and the relatives of the dead person took this as an insult. The only thing that would dispel this notion was for Salamawi and the other sheikhs to gorge themselves on all the meat and fat. From going around with them and becoming friends with them he realized there was some justification for the jokes that had long been made about the sheikhs' obsession with food.

People didn't understand the extent to which the responsibility of reciting the Quran created a suspense that ate away at the nerves. Some people thought it was an easy profession,

and that the readers just switched off and recited automatically, but most readers were driven to perform really well
in order to win admiration and applause, to maintain their
livelihoods and make sure they received regular invitations to
recite. On top of that, the field was highly competitive, which
created tension. Most importantly, these sheikhs operated
in a zone of conflict between the religious and the worldly,
between the divine and the human. They recited the Quran,
but at the same time they had human weaknesses, they were
trying to make a living and they were tempted to seek popular
rather than divine approval. One moment they were reciting
the word of God, and a moment later they would have to
talk about the things of the lower world, where people hag-
gled and things were complicated. Hatem had of course come
across men who smoked hashish between recitals to make their
voices resonate. This conflict led to a schizophrenic attitude,
which led to food, because a large appetite was the body's
response when a sheikh came down from the chair where he
recited God's word to where he sat on earth. He also had to
take on fuel to replace the nervous energy consumed in the
quest to perform well and in trying to find a balance between
the voice that carried God's words and the instincts that carried worldly desires. If most of the Quran readers accused of
being gluttonous sheikhs were blind, then it was a pleasure
that made up for other pleasures. Hatem hadn't forgotten that
these sheikhs would travel long distances for these funerals,
and travel is tiring and makes you hungry. After the travel
and the work and the nervous tension, food was a relief and
a reward for their efforts, so they would eat. Because many of
them were blind they didn't bother about the niceties of how
they ate, so they were messy and people misunderstood the
nature of their interest in eating at funerals.

They were seated in the air-conditioned hall, with
gold-colored sofas and chairs with carved wooden backs and
cotton cushions with covers of the same color. Khaled Abu

Hadid called it the Golden Hall. It was the kind of room that would be the pride of someone who has bad taste and is proud of it. The place radiated vulgar luxury on the part of a man who claimed that these gatherings were solely for the sake of God. With this in mind, Hatem pulled Khaled by his fat hand and installed him in a corner of the hall. People were coming in noisily and sitting down, some of them belching after the rich feast.

"Do you really think, Khaled Pasha, that God will believe you arranged all this to please Him?" Hatem joked. "If you want to please God you have to invite all these frauds to dinner?"

Khaled Abu Hadid laughed, buried his chin in his chest, punched Hatem in the side, then linked Hatem's arm under his own and dragged him off toward Sheikh Fathi, who was holding court in another part of the hall, on the alert against any sudden arrival that would undermine his ability to maintain his hatred for Hatem el-Shenawi. But Sheikh Fathi didn't intend to make this wish clear because it would undo the hard work he had put into projecting an air of solemnity.

"Help, Sheikh Fathi," said Khaled Abu Hadid, "Sheikh Hatem is casting doubt on my love for religious scholars."

"Sheikh Fathi thinks I'm basically a scholar of dreams and so I don't count," interjected Hatem, referring to his early work interpreting dreams.

"Do you really think that, Mawlana?" asked Khaled, probing to find out what was behind Fathi's quarrel with Hatem.

Now everyone was gathered in the hall on the sofas and chairs. They had taken off their shoes and were resting their feet on the thick carpets, taking cups of coffee or tea of various kinds, including mint or anise, from the trays brought around by Abu Hadid's waiters. They were too busy to notice Khaled Abu Hadid stirring up trouble between Fathi and Hatem. But Hatem did catch sight of Mukhtar el-Husseini following the situation with a smile and a trace of sympathy for Hatem as he negotiated the hazards and pitfalls of the reception. Khaled apparently wanted to see sparks fly between the sheikhs in front of the other guests. There were some members of parliament from the ruling party, who formed a circle in which they had brief conversations and exchanged snippets of information, then some of the police generals in charge of security in the province, linked to Abu Hadid by interests, influence, and money paid in the expectation of future favors. Whenever he made eye contact with the generals or approached them, he called on the sheikhs to listen.

"I swear, after God on High no one could possibly do me more honor than these men," he said, pointing to one or two police generals and some brigadiers sitting there.

"It's you who brings bounty and grace to the whole country, pasha," they would mumble in response. They knew how to answer flattery with flattery.

The question of how much good Khaled Abu Hadid really did the for the whole country was of course open to different interpretations by those present, but there was no doubt about the good he did these generals. Some of them were very upright and did not put out their hands for the gifts the man bestowed liberally on religious and security figures, but even they willingly and gratefully accepted jobs for their children and sons-in-law in Khaled Abu Hadid's companies at salaries everyone knew would not be available anywhere else. All of this could be in jeopardy whenever the interior ministry moved police officers around, because they might end up in a place where they had no influence in Khaled Abu Hadid's electoral constituency or economic empire.

Once during a reception, Abu Hadid had stood up and told a story about how the workers in one of his factories had gone on strike. He went to address them and told them he wouldn't be shaken by their senseless agitation. He said he knew who was inciting them to behave in this way, which would ruin the livelihoods of their colleagues and their families.

"I spoke to Kheirat Bey and he came himself with all the officers and the riot police trucks and criminal investigation department, and the kids in the factory shat their pants. The guy who five minutes earlier was on strike, was suddenly working away as if he owned the factory. I tell you, if I'd given way that time, they would have completely ruined me."

He went on to list the benefits he had brought the workers—the televisions he'd put in the dormitories so they could watch Egypt winning the African Cup of Nations, the food from the finest restaurants, the comprehensive health insurance that covered relatives even to the third degree, the compensation for injuries or illness, the annual and monthly bonuses he paid the workers, and a number of other benefits with which he almost broke the hearts of the audience. The only thing that marred the scene was Hatem's laugh and the remark he made, with obvious sarcasm.

"Not even Abdel-Rahman ibn Awf provided such benefits to the tribesmen who worked for him in Medina in the days of the Prophet, Khaled Pasha," he said.

Khaled Abu Hadid loved Hatem's cheek, even asked for it. Maybe there was something masochistic about it. He laughed heartily till his lips were wet with saliva.

"You're making fun of me, Mawlana," he said. "I'm nothing compared to a venerable Companion of the Prophet such as Abdel-Rahman ibn Awf, who financed the Prophet's raiding expeditions, spent money on the poor of Medina, and donated his caravans as alms to the Muslims."

Hatem knew how to play the game and stir the pot.

"It's true you're not a touch on Abdel-Rahman ibn Awf, neither you nor the whole Egyptian-American Chamber of Commerce, but your caravans don't feed Medina. They feed the whole of Egypt, Khaled Pasha," he said.

"Now you're talking politics, Mawlana."

Hatem laughed, along with others. Some laughed sincerely and others just for show.

"You can report me to the security people, Khaled Pasha, but you'd be wasting your time. They know I work for them and for my country and my government, and I'm also a coward and I have nothing to do with politics," he said.

He pointed to the group of generals, who were smiling and laughing. He put his hands up in a sign of surrender.

"President Sadat, may he rest in peace, used to say, 'No politics in religion, and no religion in politics,'" he said, "but my motto is 'No politics in politics, and no religion in religion.'"

Mukhtar el-Husseini knew this mission of Hatem's and Hatem knew that he knew, and although he didn't care what the other sheikhs thought, because he saw them all as compromised, he did care that Mukhtar should understand why he condescended to play this role with Khalid Abu Hadid. In the same place some years earlier, when he was not yet established and at a time when he was tired of jumping through hoops, he had discussed all this with Mukhtar.

"You know what, Uncle?" Hatem had said, looking deep into Mukhtar's eyes as if he wanted him to believe he was telling the truth. Hatem always called Mukhtar 'uncle' out of respect for his age and experience.

"You are my uncle, and anyone with an uncle has nothing to worry about," Hatem continued. "Did you know they're waging war on me? They're trying to keep me from earning my daily bread. Those programs are all I have to live on. I still have a job in the Ministry of Religious Endowments and my salary there is seven hundred pounds a month, which I leave for the accountant and the cleaners there. There's a war on against the programs and a fight between the television channels and the advertising agencies and they're all throwing accusations at each other, but Khaled Abu Hadid pulled a fast one on me. He trapped me in his cage and has been financing and sponsoring my programs ever since. At the end of the program you can see it says 'This program is sponsored by the Abu Hadid factories' and in the breaks in the program all the ads are for his factories and his companies. This has made a big difference to me. It's brought me millions in income and made me big, compared with all the other stations and sheikhs. That's automatically made me inseparable from Abu Hadid, and he's a pleasant man who loves to joke frankly with me and speak to the absurd and playful part of me. He just about has me by the throat, but I too have him by the balls, if you'll pardon the expression. It's true that he gets publicity and it helps to clean up his image, but he also gains something more important. He knows how much those in power admire me."

"Those in power or high-class people?" asked Mukhtar in response.

"No, not high-class people, Uncle," said Hatem. "I wouldn't suit them. People in power of course, people who live in palaces, from the Qubba Palace to the State Security palace and so on. The people who govern live in these palaces and they like what I say and the way I say it to people. Abu Hadid knows this and when he's around he acts as if he's one of my fans, though he probably doesn't watch a single one of the programs he finances and he doesn't know what they're for or what they mean, but that doesn't matter.

"You're my doctor and my sheikh, Uncle Mukhtar," Hatem continued sadly and slowly. "You're only five years older than me but you have a radiance that warms and lights up something inside me, and as long as I live I'll never forget that you brought something to life inside me. But Uncle, don't give these people the honor of coming here, because this place is like a nightclub without the alcohol, and the vested interests are the dancer that dances for them all."

Mukhtar el-Husseini roared with laughter, but then restrained himself. Hatem stood up, satisfied and smiling.

"Imagine if Abu Hadid brought in a fully dressed Islamically approved dancer right now!" he said.

*

Hatem now found Khaled Abu Hadid expounding on the question of adult breastfeeding, a source of controversy in Islamic law. He wanted to have fun and amuse his generals and other guests with a reality-show style contest between sheikhs who had personal disagreements, rather than disagreements over points of Islamic law—sheikhs trained to meet the needs of the shahbandar, the head of the merchants' guild. They were pursuing a profession that has existed throughout history—the profession of preachers to sultans. Khaled picked first on Sheikh Fathi, relying on his stupidity and rudeness.

"Mawlana," he said, "did you see Sheikh Hatem making fun of the fatwas on adult breastfeeding and saying that the sheikh who gave that fatwa needs suckling himself?"

Aware that Abu Hadid was playing the role of lion tamer in the circus, Hatem stood up.

"I never said that," Hatem said. "I said the sheikh who made the fatwa and said that adult breastfeeding was permitted was a man who was missing something."

Everyone laughed, apparently a sign that the bell had rung for the rival boxer to enter the ring, because Fathi's hackles had risen.

"What's it to you, Hatem? You give fatwas to adolescents that you borrow from sheikhs who are superior to you and more knowledgeable and could teach you a thing or two about good manners."

Sheikh Hatem stood up.

"Sheikh Fathi is mistaken," he said, with restrained contempt.

Sheikh Hatem knew what was behind this antagonism, from which poisoned well Sheikh Fathi had imbibed such hatred that he couldn't speak coherently or suppress his rage. Ever since they were together in lectures at college, where Hatem had sat listening to him, trying to memorize what he said, there had been a wall between them that grew higher and thicker. Fathi was a doctor because a doctorate raised your status, meant a higher salary, and was a source of joy in a family whose most educated member had been ignorant. He was an ambitious young scholar, the son of a humble stable-man in a south Egyptian village that wallowed in the mud of poverty. In southern Egypt poverty isn't just an economic reality that holds people down, deprives them of basic necessities, and restricts their ambitions to the level of subsistence. Poverty also weighs on the pride of the poor in southern Egypt, offending their dignity and reducing them in status to something close to slavery. Southern Egypt, forgotten and abandoned, works on the basis of cruel social divisions; those who are poor are low in status and treated as worthless. If a man is both poor and low-born, his grandchildren will reap the scanty harvest planted by their forebears. Ashamed of their poverty and mistreated by others, they produce children who are either rough and ready to explode against oppression, or malleable and adaptable enough to slip through the cracks and escape the stifling environment and the weight of poverty. Sheikh Fathi was of the second kind, or became so with the passage of time. At eighteen he came to al-Azhar in a city that seemed vast but at the same time claustrophobic and crowded to a boy who was alone. It had bright lights but it made him feel miserable. Most of the students at al-Azhar came from the same level of society as him—drained of wealth and of declining influence. Yet the limited inequalities between them were glaringly obvious; the difference between someone who has a monthly allowance of five pounds and someone who receives one pound might seem almost insignificant from a distance, but for the people involved it is a vast chasm.

One morning in the university corridors small groups of people gathered and linked up to form the beginnings of a demonstration. They caught the attention of Fathi, back then still a freshman, who publicly and in private hated people who talked about politics or took an interest in current affairs. He hated them with a vengeance because he saw them as extravagant wasters living in luxury. Why would a young man who could hardly pay his own keep be interested in anyone else? His world was a cruel and desolate place while colleagues lucky enough to receive financial support from their families were wasting time over a sheikh who had been arrested, and then it turned out that this sheikh lived in a mansion and owned cars and spent money lavishly. How could this wealthy man waste the money he had accumulated on opposing the government and arguing with those in power?

The demonstration was gathering and growing, to the surprise of the campus police and the faculty, who seemed aghast at this unexpected blow. In outrage Fathi stood defiantly at the top of a stairway and started to make a speech in his stentorian, melodious voice. It was an animated, enthusiastic though somewhat labored performance. At first the organizers of the demonstration ignored him, either in error or in the belief that he was on their side, but when it became clear what he was saying, they were seriously upset. Fathi had started urging the students to abandon the demonstration, which he called an abomination on earth. He criticized them for following the lead of what he called a decadent and deranged group and reminded them of the threats made by the university authorities. He tried to frighten them about being thrown in prison and throwing away their futures. When the organizers of the demonstration decided to respond, things were already out of control. People leaving the gathering to go home were pushing and shoving, and a trained group of students who were cooperating with the security and the police intervened, saying Amen to what Fathi said and cheering him. Skirmishes and fights broke out, the gathering broke up, and the demonstration came to an end.

After that Fathi was the darling of the university administration, especially the security officials. He had left his dignity at the gate where the campus guards and political police were posted, though in fact he had already abandoned it when he was growing up. He kept an eye on friends who were attracted to extremist ideas, which were rampant at about that time forty years ago. But Fathi had qualities that other informers in the university did not have: he had an excellent memory and a fine voice that projected strongly. He prospered, especially because he always flattered his teachers, wrote traditional poetry eulogizing the president of the university, and read poems at official events as a student representative. Then he had the genius idea of volunteering to give Quran lessons to the children of generals and brigadiers. He was invited into their houses and built up relationships with important people and their wives. Then came his appointment as an assistant lecturer in the university, a quick doctorate, and frequent appearances on the radio station that broadcast the Quran. Then he started to take part in religious programs on television and had one day a week in a program called Hadith al-Rouh, where a sheikh appeared alone for several minutes before the most important news bulletin. This won him special allowances, travel abroad, university assignments, bonuses, and the approval of his bosses. Fathi got married after several unsuccessful attempts to find himself a wife in his home village. Apparently the social equilibrium there had not yet changed enough for people to forget his origins, but he did manage to snag a wife who could help his career through contacts in the official hierarchy. She was the daughter of a late professor of his who came from an old family with a name that still resonated among those who moved in Azhar circles, though its fortunes had declined.

Dressed in his elegant Azhar vestments, he gave the impression that he was an established sheikh. He enjoyed official approval and regularly helped to issue fatwas that supported the government's laws and decrees with legal arguments based on watertight authorities in the works of recognized imams. As such, Fathi was comfortably seated in a better position than the sheikhs who tried to flatter and curry favor. He had an audience that really liked him, believed what he said, and followed him: they were the kind of people who wanted a version of religion that would serve their worldly aspirations and ambitions. But there was one powerful phenomenon that threatened to undermine Sheikh Fathi's privileged position—those preachers who didn't look like sheikhs, who took religion into the world of adolescents and women, and who shifted the focus of religious broadcasting from state television to the private satellite channels. He made fun of two or three of them in the beginning and launched a campaign of criticism and denigration against them. This served its purpose until a certain moment, the moment when his student, Hatem el-Shenawi, appeared on the scene, dressed as an Azhar sheikh but performing in the style of the new televangelists. As Hatem's fame spread, Fathi grew bitter. The competition drove him to revert to the traditional solemnity expected of sheikhs and to an uncompromising language carved from the rocks of the linguistic past. His fatwas were rigidly orthodox, perhaps because this was the only way he could set himself apart from the kinds of people who were making inroads into the field of religious learning. He set himself a target that would give him peace of mind. He thought that these new people like Hatem would never be able to compete with him in solemnity and gravitas and so the state would never think of giving them senior positions in the Azhar hierarchy or appoint them as mufti of Egypt. His real aspiration was to obtain that office, and he seemed very confident, acting as though the job was already his, until the storm created by his fatwa on adult breastfeeding.

"So you want to convince me, venerable sheikh, that Aisha, the wife and Companion of the Prophet Muhammad and the Mother of the Believers, told other Muslim women, who were devout and worshiped God, that they should bare their breasts—brown ones, white ones, red ones, small ones, or big ones—and sit down with men with mustaches and beards and eyes and whatever they have between their legs, and let every man suck their tits five times? Just so that the men could go and visit Aisha and sit and chat with her?" Hatem said. "Only someone who hates Aisha could make such a claim and only a madman would believe it."

Sheikh Fathi fumed with rage. He clenched his teeth and the veins in his cheeks throbbed. He studied the eyes of the people sitting around and realized that they wouldn't let him walk out grumbling or stay aloofly silent. They would read that as weakness and possibly as an insult, and he was of such a jittery and fragile disposition that he couldn't allow himself to stand on his dignity in the presence of officers, after spending years proving to them that he had abandoned it. Besides, his host was Khaled Abu Hadid, the lavish billionaire who had never begrudged him presents or money or jobs for his relatives and his in-laws. He couldn't deprive him of the entertainment that he wanted.

His fatwa on adult breastfeeding had ruined him as far as the important people were concerned. It meant a rapid and drastic reduction in his official credibility, because he became the laughing stock of the newspapers and the television channels. The experience taught him that when the media comes across a victim they don't check what they say or the allegations they make. On the contrary, the butchers work together, hastily and indiscriminately, to slaughter the calf that has stumbled or fallen. They don't read the classical texts or know anything about them, and their ears, which are their only source of knowledge, don't do research or make inquiries. They just listen and repeat. The fatwa had been lying in books and was tucked away in classical works that no one consults and no one has troubled to explain. It had been sealed in a little bottle for dozens of years, known only to a specialist clique of researchers, but when he opened the bottle the genie sprang up right in his face and dashed his dream of the promotion, which he had been about to pick ripe from the branch: the office of mufti of Egypt.

The present mufti had fallen ill and the state was looking for a successor. Fathi had been the frontrunner, based on the recommendation of the security services. Other officials were enthusiastic and they had old debts to repay, such as for fatwas that condemned terrorism, that called for obedience to the ruler, that banned dissent, allowed banks to pay or charge interest, and permitted commercial dealings with Israel and cooperation between Israeli and Egyptian businessmen. Fathi's fatwas were always ready to serve. He came up with them quickly and enthusiastically and they were so well-argued that no one could possibly pull them apart. They might dispute them or challenge them with counter-fatwas but Fathi didn't stray from the strict text of the Quranic verses, sticking to citations from the Quran and the Sunna, opposing anyone who appealed to the rules of analogy or of individual judgment. His strength was that he didn't offer his own opinion or even the opinions of the imams and jurists active in the early years of Islam, but based his arguments directly on explicit verses of the Quran and the hadiths of Bukhari, who was so revered by the public and the authorities that his hadiths were seen as uncontestable.

But Hatem el-Shenawi had made fun of him when, in an unfortunate slip at the annual Ramadan gathering in Hussein Square, he mentioned the fatwa on adult breastfeeding. It passed off peacefully that night and those who heard it were merely surprised and intrigued that the fatwa existed. But two days later, in his television program, Hatem el-Shenawi picked it up, showed a video recording of the event, and discussed the subject. Hatem thoroughly ridiculed the fatwa and the next morning masses of people from far and wide—friends and enemies, allies and rivals—joined in, ripping into Sheikh Fathi. They had segments on the fatwa in show business programs, it came up in scenes in the theater, and there were endless cartoons on the subject and commentaries in all the newspapers, with everyone acting like they were the top sheikh, defending and squabbling over the reputation of Islam. The administrators of his department at the university created an archive of 460 references to adult breastfeeding and the fatwa in Egyptian newspapers alone. His candidacy for the office of mufti was bound to suffer.

The head of the State Security Investigations department, who had been his friend since they were junior officials and who had risen through the ranks in parallel with Fathi, had told him at the time, "Mawlana, do you think the state could appoint you mufti at this juncture, when the whole country is making fun of adult breastfeeding? If it did, people would say the government wants women to breastfeed men in government offices and in schools, and we'd never hear the end of it."

He'd had to lower his expectations, especially after some mediocre sheikh was appointed to the office that Fathi saw as his legitimate right. This only added to his anger with Hatem el-Shenawi, whom he saw as the root of all his troubles, although Hatem had apologized to him in one of his programs and, in an attempt to placate him, had praised his learning and his legal expertise. But Fathi never forgave him, and when Hatem made another dig at him at Khaled Abu Hadid's reception, Sheikh Fathi stood up and, with a smile and a calm that concealed more sinister intentions, said:

"Sheikh Hatem, what did I teach you at university when I was giving you lessons on the sayings of the Prophet?"

Sheikh Fathi had managed to put himself in the position of a professor addressing his student. His sortie seemed to go down well with the crowd, judging from their faces. But Hatem had a quick retort:

"You taught me to say grace before eating."

He could see that Sheikh Fathi was shaken. Some of the people present tittered, which made him worried that Fathi might lose his cool and turn vitriolic. Hatem quickly made amends for his churlish quip with some more sober remarks:

"It's true, I swear, some of the most enjoyable and most educative moments possible are when you hear Dr. Fathi el-Maadawi explaining an eleven-word saying of the Prophet in intricate detail and with his vast legal knowledge, such as the saying, 'Speak God's name and eat the part that's closest to you,' which we all know by heart. Could anything be easier? You have the words of the Prophet, clear and direct, instructions that need no explanation. Why are you laughing, Khaled Pasha? I said explanation, not excavation, as everyone was doing when they were digging out the pieces of meat just now. Sheikh Fathi takes the hadith and deconstructs it, like an electrician when he takes the television or the radio apart in front of you, and then puts it back together again piece by piece after explaining how each piece works. That's what Mawlana Fathi el-Maadawi used to do."

Did that placate Fathi? Hatem thought that on the contrary it might have provoked him even more. Fathi brushed aside Hatem's attempt to appease him with flattery and hit back with a rebuke of his own.

"Apparently I taught you how to eat but forgot to teach you how to think!" he said.

This inflamed the atmosphere once again. Hatem decided it was war and there would be no retreat and no surrender.

"What do you think of Bukhari's book?" Fathi continued.

"The truest book after the Quran," someone said.

Fathi looked daggers at Hatem with his eyes, then turned his head toward those seated.

"But apparently Sheikh Hatem rejects many of Bukhari's hadiths," he said.

Hatem shuddered for a moment, for fear that Fathi might have access to something he had said in some private meeting. But he got his breath back when Fathi continued:

"I know Sheikh Hatem understood properly what I taught him in the course. I know he believes that when Bukhari cites a hadith it means he has checked it and has made sure that the chain of transmission is through people whose credibility is unblemished. Isn't that right, Sheikh Hatem? So what do you think of the adult breastfeeding fatwa, which is soundly sourced and in Bukhari's collection? I didn't make it up and I didn't even offer any particular interpretation of it. I just quoted it word for word. The ulema have taught us that Muslims must accept God's rulings obediently. *When a matter has been decided by God and His messenger, no believer, man or woman, has any choice in the matter: anyone who disobeys God and His messenger is on a clearly wrong path.* That's what Islam means, Sheikh Hatem. Muslims don't debate God's injunctions. They debate the evidence. Could the hadith be false even if it appears in both Bukhari and Muslim, simply because it's not to the liking of Sheikh Hatem?"

Sheikh Fathi then put on his prophetic voice. "It's correct and there's no doubt about it," he thundered.

"Are you sure it's reached the stage of 'no doubt about it,' Sheikh Fathi?" said Hatem.

Fathi ignored him and continued.

"I understand that Sheikh Hatem is fully aware that the hadith is sound, or else I and others would consider him to be contesting Bukhari and Muslim and other major scholars. But he has been carried away by the secularists who deny Islam and are full of hatred for it. He plays the role of the rational thinker who challenges sheikhs like myself who maintain the traditions. So he's the big brain and we're the ignoramuses who stick to the accepted books on the sayings and practice of the Prophet and who hold Bukhari in respect. I understand, folks, that people who are not specialists speak ill of people with turbans like us, but Sheikh Hatem's turban is too big for him and he dares to reject solidly attested hadiths lightly and to insult prominent imams with the same daring, might I even say impudence. You wouldn't expect this from someone who, as eminent scholars put it, has had a taste of learning and lived among learned men, either alive through their lectures or dead through their books.

"This hadith was not mentioned in just one book, or two or three," Fathi roared defiantly. "It wasn't recounted by just one or two Companions of the Prophet, or just one or two people from the generation that came after them. To quote Ibn Hazm, it was transmitted by everyone to everyone, through those of the second generation and then the third generation and then to the great imams who codified Islamic law after them."

Khaled and some of the generals laughed together at the sight of Sheikh Fathi getting worked up. Everyone ignored their cell phones when they rang. The audience was silent, although not because they were interested in scholarship—it was the kind of silence that occurs in the cinema during a sex scene.

"Why don't you tell us the hadith first, Sheikh Fathi?" said Khaled.

Fathi repeated the story in a clipped robotic way, like someone in a hurry who has memorized the text and assumes the others know it too, so there's no need to articulate it clearly.

They all laughed.

"We couldn't hear anything and we didn't understand a word," said one of the generals. He had proudly been fingering his prayer beads with an audible clicking throughout the session.

In an attempt to show that he wasn't upset and to needle Sheikh Fathi, Hatem decided to recite the hadith to them himself.

"Aisha, may God be pleased with her, related that Salim, the freed slave of Abu Hudhayfa, lived with Abu Hudhayfa and his family in their house. Sahla bint Suheil, Abu Hudhayfa's wife, came to the Prophet and said that Abu Hudhayfa was unhappy about Salim having free access to the house, whereupon the Prophet said to her: 'Suckle him and you would become unlawful for him, and Abu Hudhayfa's feeling will disappear.' She came back later and said: 'So I suckled him, and the feeling that Abu Hudhayfa had disappeared.'

"In another version Abu Hudhayfa had adopted Salim in every sense as far as his relationship with the rest of the household was concerned, according to Sahla, who said, 'O Prophet of God, we saw Salim as our child. He would come into the room when I was in my house clothes and we only had one room, so what do you think about the situation?' And the Prophet of God said to her, 'Breastfeed him five times and the milk will make him unlawful to you,' and she considered him to be her son through breastfeeding. She said, 'I breastfed him and the feeling that Abu Hudhayfa had disappeared.'"

"See, there you are, just as he said!" shouted Fathi with a wave of his hand. "And what's more, Aisha told her sisters and her sisters' daughters to breastfeed the men she wanted to visit her five times, even if they were old, and then they could come and see her. Umm Salama and the other wives of the Prophet refused to let any men be breastfed in this way."

"Go on then, deny it if you will, mister sheikh," he added, his hands outstretched as if to say 'over to you.'

"Forgive me, you're the expert, but anyway I don't deny the hadith, Mawlana. Don't misrepresent me," Hatem replied.

"My god," shouted Fathi. "You don't deny it when we're sitting here together, but on television in front of millions of people you treated me as though I'd found the hadith in my father's attic!"

"I know your father's house was a house of learning," said Hatem.

"You think this is funny! I swear by the life of your father . . ." replied Fathi, fuming with rage again.

"What's the big deal, folks?" chipped in Sheikh Sorour in his deep voice. "What's with this hadith on adult breastfeeding? Sounds like a good idea to me. At my age it's not often you get to suck a breast."

There was an uproar of laughter and outrage.

"See, Sheikh Fathi, this is exactly what I wanted to warn against," said Hatem. "This is a hadith for scholars and we shouldn't be broadcasting it to ordinary people. Now you see what happens. I didn't deny it, but I did explain the special circumstances in which it arose."

"What do you mean, special circumstances?" said Fathi. "Is this a hadith that's fully authenticated, endorsing the practice of adult breastfeeding, or isn't it? Go on, answer me."

"I haven't finished what I'm going to say, so don't rush me."

"Okay, but this is a subject where you can't be evasive."

"No, you can," said Hatem, "because evasion here means explaining the subject, Mawlana. Because the hadith covers only the case of Salim the freed slave of Abu Hudhayfa, and it was a case that was particular to the time and the period."

"If that was the case, why did Aisha treat it as a clear-cut ruling and have her nieces breastfeed men who wouldn't otherwise be able to visit her, so that they could come and go freely in her house?" said Fathi.

"Well, that was Aisha's opinion, but none of the Prophet's other wives did that."

"That's not true. Hafsa did it."

"Okay, but there was no consensus on it, and besides, for the breastfeeding sessions there had to be a child that was being weaned and the feedings needed to be large enough to fill the man's stomach."

One of the generals burst out excitedly, "That's right, Mawlana. How could a great oaf like me breastfeed from a woman in this way? There wouldn't be enough milk to feed me, or even to make my mustache grow."

Despite the guffaws from the audience, Fathi kept his cool and addressed the police officers. "Look, sir, is there a text or isn't there?" he said. "There is a text, and it has various interpretations. Yes, it does. Some people say it's forbidden and the case was closed with Salim, the freed slave of Abu Hudhayfa, who was breastfed by his master's wife, and there are people who say no, it's a ruling that continues and is still valid today, on the grounds that Aisha did it."

"But, general, mind you don't get the idea that breastfeeding means a mouth on a nipple," said Hatem.

They burst out laughing.

"Really? So what is it, if it doesn't mean a mouth on a nipple?" one of them asked.

"No, some people say she pours the milk into a cup and the man drinks it. That's what happened with Sahla," said Hatem.

"Sahla as well?"

"No, we're not going to make fun of the Companions of the Prophet."

"God forbid. You'll get us all into trouble."

At that stage, perhaps out of boredom, Khaled Abu Hadid wanted to change the subject, so he asked for Sheikh Said Sorour to sing a prayer, since by then he had had his fill of food and hashish.

After as much throat-clearing as you'd expect to hear during a whole night in a hospital ward for people with chest complaints, Sorour set to it. The amazing thing is that this wooden oaf of a man produced sounds from his throat that might have come down from heaven. All those sitting there—the corrupt, the debauched, the fraudsters, the flatterers, the servants, and the retainers—could still find space in their hearts for something pure and sublime. They stopped still to listen.

Muhammad, the Lord of the Two Worlds, Lord of Man
and the Djinn,

> Lord of the Two Groups, Arabs and non-Arabs,
> Our Prophet who commands and prohibits,
> No one is more truthful
> In saying yes or saying no
> He is the friend whose intercession is sought
> Against every fright that threatens

His voice came from the very depths of his chest, then he bowed his head in silence for a moment's rest. His singing had breathed fresh air into the hall. Al-Busiri's love poetry, addressed to the Prophet he adored, was like a soothing lullaby or a trickle of pure water. Then Sheikh Sorour resumed, giving Hatem a rope on which he could climb up to heaven, shaking off the folly of the world and the filth that came from being famous.

> He surpassed the other prophets in physical and moral qualities
> Nor did they approach him in either learning or generosity
> All of them sought to obtain from the Prophet of God
> A handful of water from the ocean or a sip from the continuous rains.
> They kept to their place with respect to him
> When it came to a drop of learning or a trace of wisdom.

Hatem, deeply moved, cried: "O God, O God, Our Lord the Prophet."

The prayer raised the spirits of the audience and some of them, spellbound, muttered the words to themselves. Others signaled their approval and admiration. For others the hymn reminded them painfully of their own failings and allowed them for a few moments to revel in closeness to God and the glory of the Prophet.

> For he is the one whose essence and outward form are perfect

The creator of life chose him as His beloved
Unmatched by anyone who shares his virtues
Because the jewel of goodness in him is undivided
Attribute as much honor as you like to his person
Attribute as much grandeur as you like to his power
Because the virtue of the Prophet of God has no limits
That anyone with the power of speech could put into words.

Hatem stood up, sad and moved. He turned to Sheikh Mukhtar.

"Bless our Prophet, the ancestor of Sheikh Mukhtar, the grandson of the grandsons of the Prophet and his family," he said.

There was something mysterious about Mukhtar el-Husseini that made Hatem like him. Although other Sufi sheikhs claimed to be simple and modest, in fact they looked down on people. They ensconced themselves in their zawiyas, aloof and supercilious. Their disciples willingly subjugated themselves, like slaves to their master or sheep to their shepherd. On top of that, important people, the rich of the community and people in high office, thronged at the feet of the head of the Sufi order they belonged to. All this made the sheikh, any sheikh, think he was more than just a normal human being. But Sheikh Mukhtar didn't have that covert snobbery or that arrogance that dressed itself up as self-denial for the sake of other people. Hatem often noticed this growing sense of privilege among the Sufi leaders that he met and it was not the privileged status of the kind enjoyed by film stars, artists, and soccer players, who had worked hard for their fame, which could rise and fall unpredictably. Their privileged status was temporary and piecemeal. It was also dependent on their conduct and everyone was watching them closely. But the fame of a Sufi sheikh in his order and in his narrow, limited world was deeper and had more influence on him and on his social milieu. The head of a Sufi order was not required to work for his fame; it was fame that came without the slight-est effort. His fame was part of him, and his privileged status didn't come through people choosing him. It came through the man's ancestry, his lineage. Some of them traced their descent to the family of the Prophet. Hatem was well aware that he and other well-known television preachers, and even the stars of television serials, might not always be treated as special in the rough and tumble of ordinary life, when they were with their families and within the four walls of their homes, for example. The head of a Sufi order, on the other hand, was privileged even when he was in the bath, because everyone treated him as if he had special gifts. A special aura surrounded him wherever he went and whoever he lived with and talked to. This meant that a Sufi sheikh wasn't a Sufi at all, but rather someone that people looked up to with expec-tations. He was molded by people and by the loyalty of his disciples. This created a massive barrier and made the man's Sufism suspect.

Sheikh Hatem didn't see Mukhtar el-Husseini in the same way as he saw the others, so he liked him, and he accepted the invitation he received on the evening of Khaled Abu Had-id's banquet. When the party was over and the gathering was breaking up Mukhtar came up to him and patted him on the back with a pleasant, shy smile. As people wished each other well, said their goodbyes, and gave and sought each other's advice, Mukhtar whispered in Hatem's ear.

"I need to see you about something very important at my place in the country, tomorrow," he said.

Quickly and with unfeigned enthusiasm, Hatem replied, "You give the orders and I obey, Uncle."

Hatem was struck by a sadness in Mukhtar el-Husseini, so he embraced him, not with the solemnity of a sheikh or the obsequiousness of an obedient disciple, but as if he were a brother, or a cousin whose mother has just died—firmly and sincerely, in sympathy and solidarity.

ON THE WAY TO SHEIKH Mukhtar's hometown the next day Hatem had some long and excruciating phone calls and Sirhan, his driver, bombarded him with news about production companies, television stations agreeing to new religious programs, a rival televangelist filming his Ramadan program, what another preacher said in his program the day before yesterday, and the number of calls he had received. Hatem didn't respond, although he was interested—this was the world that would transform you from a sheikh into a producer, from a preacher to a television star. There were dues he would have to pay to remain a star and to make sure he continued to get paid as a star. It sometimes occurred to him that what he called his "oil well"—the fatwas, the hadiths, the snippets of Quranic verses and his explanations of them, the stories and homilies about early Islam, the lines of devotional poetry—might suddenly run dry because of the glut of programs, lectures, and soirées with important and wealthy people. Keeping up with the others was tiring. It meant he didn't have time to catch his breath. So he thought about the décor in the same way he thought about fatwas. He took an interest in what his rivals' programs looked like and was worried if they obtained access to television channels that were wealthier or better known. When he reached Sheikh Mukhtar's place he slumped into an easy chair and cleared his mind after the ordeal of traveling. He could easily have fallen asleep in the chair.

When he had recovered, he said to Mukhtar, "Uncle, we race around like men of the world, not like men of learning."

Mukhtar laughed.

"Of course you don't think we're men of learning, or anything like it," Hatem commented casually, as if speaking to himself.

"Don't say that, Sheikh Hatem. You're a man of great erudition, of oceanic learning."

"Yes, Uncle, oceanic. But more like a lifeguard who stands on the beach and whenever a swimmer goes beyond the buoys he jumps in and brings him back, not like those who explore the secrets and treasures of the ocean depths."

He suddenly stopped speaking.

After a moment's silence he laughed and said, "Now I feel like eating fish."

Mukhtar replied with a relaxed laugh, despite his sad appearance.

"My mother insists on seeing you, Sheikh Hatem. You're like a son to her."

Mukhtar's house wasn't forbidding and didn't have the appearance one might expect from the house of one of the leading Sufi sheikhs. Hatem liked that. The house was neither grand and luxurious, nor simple and unadorned. The house was ordinary, without any striking architecture or furniture. It wasn't a mansion or even a house with a garden. It was in a four-story building that looked like millions of other buildings in Egypt, but it had a comforting and reassuring warmth and ordinariness, with no sign that the owner was an ambitious man who wanted his house to make a statement about himself. It was very obvious from the start that Sheikh Mukhtar wasn't at ease these days, but in his own home, away from the demands that his role imposed on him, he felt free to express his anxieties. When Mukhtar said that his mother wanted to say hello to him, Hatem realized that Mukhtar really did see him as a brother, because it was customary among some sheikhs that disciples didn't have anything to do with their sheikh's private life, as it would be an unacceptable invasion of privacy. Only close relatives of Mukhtar and his family could go into his house. The house that was set up and furnished for meetings with members of his Sufi order was in the city center, opposite the mosque that bore the name of Mukhtar's father, who was known as al-Sayed Mukhtar.

One of the things he liked about Mukhtar was that he had resigned himself to his fate with a willing spirit. He didn't resist or object, he didn't rebel or refuse to play his role. His name was in fact Mahmoud and not Mukhtar. His father was Mukhtar el-Husseini and when the father died his elder brother Ahmed was ill with kidney failure, needing dialysis three times a week, and had eventually died too. But they had long since preferred the younger son Mahmoud as heir to the leadership of the Sufi order. He had graduated from college a few months before their father died and hadn't yet made use of his education in the faculty of sciences. His name was changed to Mukhtar, his father's name, to maintain continuity and out of affection for the father, and he himself forgot his original name.

In his father's presence when he was a child, Sufis kissed his hand and placed him in a seat of honor. Oddly, throughout his childhood, no one had ever made any effort to ask what he felt or thought, or given him a proper education in the Quran or the Sunna. Some of the Sufis he met said that someone with his ancestry held his learning in his heart and did not need to memorize things in the normal way. They said he could understand by intuition and could see through the fog that blinded other people. He liked words and they had a deep impact on him, but when the time came for him to speak in public he felt that he would not be able to meet expectations. He was so at peace with the world that he said what he wanted to say without being devious or compromising the truth for personal advantage. He wasn't a scholar who could teach, he wasn't a leader who would take control, he wasn't a spiritual leader who gave guidance, he wasn't like his father in knowing how to strike a balance between religion and personal interests, and so he didn't speak much. He was silent most of the time. His silence made him seem dignified and mysterious. Then, when he met his wife, Suha Atef, it was as if he had come across his Aisha. She stole a part of his heart and gave him new life.

Sheikh Hatem shook hands with Mukhtar's mother, who was welcoming and attentive and said a prayer for him in a sentimental tone. Hatem knew that there were two women that mattered in Mukhtar's life. There was his mother, who was almost eighty but formidable and in robust health. Hatem knew what it meant when she appeared in his presence. It was a statement about the respect her son had for him. It was also a sign that she cared about him and had given her seal of approval for Mukhtar to bring up the subject he was going to discuss with Hatem and to ask Hatem to help. When she came in to see Hatem, it was more than a mere formality.

The other woman in Mukhtar's life was someone Hatem had never seen. If she had appeared, it might have signaled an even closer relationship. This was Mukhtar's wife Suha, the love of his life and the daughter of a member of the Sufi order. He had married her after a complicated love affair, after seeing her when visiting her father. He had married later than his brother and the other men in his family. The sheikh of a Sufi order couldn't remain unmarried, but he hadn't taken to any of the many women his mother insisted on proposing. His followers imagined spiritual and cosmic reasons why Mukhtar hadn't married, because Sufis see all of their leader's conduct as inspired, and they refrained from asking. Then he met pretty Suha, who was years younger than him. She loved the way he loved her and the fairy-tale world he lived in. She also liked the fact that he didn't ask her to wear a hijab or niqab or to change her way of life too much, though she was perfectly willing to play the role of first lady of the order, so she wore a hijab on top of the latest fashions and clothes so elegant that no one would have thought she was the Sufi wife of a Sufi.

The story that always made the rounds among sheikhs, both Sufi and Salafist, was that it was a love match, and Hatem had sometimes been intensely envious of Mukhtar and his wife in recent years. Their marriage gave him insight into his own eroding marriage and reminded him that he had failed to save his relationship with Omayma. When he and Omayma started life together, she could look forward to a comfortable marriage and an ordinary life, but his fame made her uneasy as much as it made her happy. She had managed to adjust to it, because it changed her, and through her ideas and her ambition Hatem's fortune had grown. They had moved from a small apartment to a spacious one with fine furniture and then to a large house in a gated community, but everything changed and deteriorated after Omar's accident. It was like being in a race and discovering yourself in the lead, and then finding that your partner can't keep up with you and cover the same distance at the same speed or with the same energy. There's a major difference of pace and it has a distorting effect and prevents the two of you reacting in the same familiar and concerted way to the same event. And then Omayma's grumbling made his life miserable in a way that was hard to explain. The things that gave him pleasure no longer gave her pleasure, and he no longer understood why she wasn't pleased. Perhaps she had fallen in love with the Hatem she needed and on whom she depended, and when he needed her, she was reluctant to help. Maybe being rich had made her more worried about him, and fearful of him, and as a result she dealt with him with increasing rudeness and hostility. She would ask skeptically why people liked him. She would have angry outbursts and would storm out saying, "If people knew the truth about their beloved sheikh!"

"What is the truth about their sheikh, Omayma?" he once asked.

"They think you're humble and godfearing in what you do and that you never do anything wrong."

"Okay, and what do you think I am?"

"You're average," she said coldly. "It's not like I'm living with Sheikh al-Ghazali or Mohamed Abduh."

"My dear, is anyone of the same stature as those two sheikhs?" he said, trying to make light of it.

"You pretend to be modest, but in fact you think you're something," she scolded.

Sometimes he shouted angrily, stormed off, or slammed the brakes on in the car.

"Yes, Omayma, I do think I'm something."

"Like what?"

"You tell me, what am I to you?" asked Hatem in desperation.

"A mosque preacher and a television evangelist."

"Very well, that's all very well and good. I thought you were going to say a mechanic or a carpenter."

Omayma used to watch his programs and listen to his sermons and lectures. She discussed things with him and disagreed with him and treated him as a teacher, but when Omar was in a coma and Hatem disappeared, she started to oppose and criticize his opinions sharply. She belittled his fatwas in the company of family and friends. For a while she kept talking about giving up the hijab and in the end she did take it off. He knew she had done it to annoy him so he ignored it. She dressed up, put on lots of make-up, and behaved outrageously, but then she tired of that. After one program in which Hatem attacked the niqab and said it was a custom and not a religious obligation, he came home to find her in a niqab— inside her own home, with Omar by her side. They had tried doctors, physiotherapy, medicines, reading the Quran, and giving alms in an attempt to restore Omar's memory and help him walk normally again, and there she was, giving Omar a distorted image of his mother by wearing a niqab in her own house. Once Hatem had got over the shock he started laughing, which annoyed her. Then he advised her to wear the niqab outside the house, since he was her husband and was allowed to see her hands and face. He said this with a laugh but she told him off and said there was a cook in the house and Zeidan the gardener in the garden. He laughed so hard that he started choking. He pulled himself together, sat down next to his son, gave him a hug and said:

"So, my love, what exactly do you think your mother wants from your father and his ancestors?"

Despite all this, or maybe because of all this, Hatem could sometimes be very sympathetic and solicitous toward her and apologetic about everything he did, because what he had done when he heard about his son's accident was no laughing matter. He had abandoned everything in the belief that his son had died or was going to die. He was in despair and fell apart. He was afraid of dropping dead himself and afraid he wouldn't be able to control his anger against God's will. "Why me, Lord?" he asked. "Why have you done this to me?" He had been devastated when his mother died, but he hadn't felt the need to ask why a woman in her sixties would die of grief after her husband took a second wife. That death was bitter and painful, but he took it in his stride and never questioned the divine decree. Two of his sisters had died young, so he came to know sudden death much earlier than a boy deserved, and he thought his mother was so long-suffering that she must have been descended from Job. His father had changed after his daughters' deaths and he married a girl the same age as they would have been. His two other sisters had been living in Saudi Arabia with their husbands, who were brothers, for the past twenty-five years. He didn't even know their children's names. The last time he had a phone call from them it ended in a silly religious disagreement over something he had said in a program and he expected his sisters' children would become members of the religious police in Saudi Arabia.

When Omar had his accident, Hatem lost everything—his fragility was all that was left of him. He wanted to protect himself from his weakness and his anger; those who are weak and angry are the most harmful to themselves and to others. He went to the Hussein mosque but didn't go inside. He spent twenty-two days in the restrooms there, or in the restrooms at the mosques of el-Sayeda Zeinab, el-Rifai, the Sultan Hassan, and some smaller prayer rooms and other mosques here and there. He cleaned the toilets and mopped the floors, getting rid of the pieces of shit left on the bowls and on the toilet seats. He mopped up the pools of urine left on the tiles and removed the dirt that had dried in the corners of the bathrooms. He washed the marble of the urinals with soap and sprayed the place with carbolic acid. He sat on the wet floor, lifted buckets, carried brooms, bathroom wipers, and rags on his shoulders from one toilet to another. His hair was unkempt, he was covered in dust, unshaven and barefoot, his clothes were tattered, and his eyes red. He was exhausted and the skin on his hands was peeling. His heels were cracked and his fingers were wrinkled. He grew as thin as if he had lost half his weight. No one would have recognized him in the crowd at such places when he looked like that. Neither his father, nor his driver, nor his secretary could find him, and the producers and owners of the television stations were about to announce that he had gone missing. He was later told that news of his disappearance had leaked out on several websites but had been contained because the person in charge of his Facebook page had been posting material in his name, giving opinions and even issuing fatwas, confusing those who believed he was missing. Omayma was almost as puzzled by what he had done as she was distressed about her son. She was angry with her husband because she had expected him to support her in this ordeal, but he had run off like a mouse. She never forgave him. Then, in the half-light of morning one day, Sheikh Mukhtar el-Husseini stood at the door of the toilets at the Hussein mosque and said, "O you who hear the call, answer your uncle."

Hatem felt a tap on the door of his heart. When he came out through the open door of a bathroom stall, he saw Sheikh Mukhtar and ran toward him, weeping as he had never wept before and would never weep again. Mukhtar went and asked the imam of the mosque for permission, grabbed hold of Hatem in his shabby state, pulled him off to the imam's prayer niche, and led the people in dawn prayers. After that Hatem reverted to how he had been. He went with Sheikh Mukhtar to the hospital where his son was lying and they went up to his room. Mukhtar told him that the boy was still alive.

"So get a grip on yourself, and thank the Lord by giving your wife some support," he added.

How did Mukhtar el-Husseini know that Hatem was there in the restrooms, doing penance for his pride, his anger, and his weakness? He later found out that one of Sheikh Mukhtar's followers lived in the Hussein mosque as a mendicant and had recognized Hatem after days of following him and making inquiries. He told his master, who came and took Hatem off. From then on, Sheikh Mukhtar was bound to have a special place in his heart.

Now that he was in Sheikh Mukhtar's house he was curious and impatient to find out what Mukhtar wanted to discuss, especially as time was short and he wanted to leave early enough to arrive in good time for a live program he was doing. He calculated the length of the journey and the rest time they would need and thought that after a good meal he would hardly have an hour. So he hurried things along. The servant brought tea and put it next to the sweet pastries, of which Sheikh Mukhtar recommended the basbousa.

"Is everything all right, Uncle?" Hatem asked.

Mukhtar began to tell him the secret reason why he had asked him to come: "I'm being subjected, Hatem, to a vicious war that's getting fiercer day after day. They are using a variety of methods—harassment, trying to freeze our activities, and even attempting to force us out of the country."

At first Hatem felt that Mukhtar must be exaggerating.

"Good heavens, why all that?" he said.

Mukhtar continued, a look of resignation on his kindly face.

"It's been going on for two years and it hasn't stopped, even as we're having lunch together now," he said. "As soon as you leave here, you'll see a piece of the picture. Imagine a family descended from the Prophet having to put up with this harassment and persecution, including criminal acts by thugs. They've set fire to houses, damaged private property, arranged traffic accidents, and deliberately cut off services such as water and electricity."

Hatem was stunned. He could hardly believe what he was hearing from Mukhtar, whom he considered a reliable source and a good friend. Mukhtar noticed that Hatem's expression had changed.

"Imagine," he continued, "when I came back from abroad with my whole family, as we were standing in line for the passport control, my wife and I were pulled aside and held for no reason. We sat in a small cold room all by ourselves and no one spoke to us or offered us a glass of water for two hours. They took away our telephones and a police brigadier came in and treated me very provocatively and arrogantly. In front of my wife he said, 'I hear that you Sufi types aren't interested in women.' I jumped up and he said, 'Okay, never mind, I guess they are.' Then he stamped our passports and said goodbye. I didn't know at the time that this wasn't the end of it, but when we came out we found ourselves in a long hall, then a corridor that branched into other corridors. It all seemed to be underground, and we got lost, I swear, for about an hour, from one corridor to another and from one hallway to another, and we didn't see or hear anyone and of course when they got bored of tormenting us someone suddenly appeared and said, 'Ah, you're lost.' He opened a door and we found ourselves in the airport car park."

"Did you complain to anyone or take it up with someone at a higher level?" Hatem asked.

"Yes," said Mukhtar, "I spoke to one of our members who works in the office of the airport manager, but the manager called me and swore he didn't know about it and that this was the work of the security people and not the airport staff. I was upset and I thought it was a message, from the Interior Ministry for example."

"Why? Why the Interior Ministry? And why a message?"

"Don't get ahead of yourself, Hatem. I know I'm boring you with my story but the airport part is the least of it because there's been a whole series of incidents. The Minister of Religious Endowments gave orders that a new preacher be appointed to the big mosque where our ancestors are buried, and the new preacher goes up in the pulpit every Friday, Monday, and Thursday after the sunset prayers, exactly the same time we meet our guests in the courtyard next to the mosque, and starts insulting and attacking Sufism and Sufis, and describing them as polytheists. We complained to the minister but that made matters worse and he insisted that the preacher would stay in office. Since when has a mosque preacher given sermons three days a week? We found out that the Minister of Religious Endowments had received direct orders from an unknown official that someone hostile to Sufism should be in charge of the mosque. Imagine! In the mosque where your father was the Sufi leader, a preacher comes along and condemns Sufism and Sufis and says they're not proper Muslims. Imagine how insulting that is, and then there's the damage to your prestige among your followers. It was a clear provocation designed to start an argument and make trouble, because our members, and the neighbors and the local people, wouldn't shut up when they heard things like that from the minaret of that mosque. That led to big confrontations between the local people and the Sufis on one side, and this sheikh and a bunch of Salafists who were brought in to pray in the mosque or, God knows, maybe they were plainclothes policemen or the police karate team, and a big fight broke out. In the newspapers there was a story, if you remember, about people breaking into a mosque and attacking the preacher. In fact that day it was our people who were beaten back when they tried to stop the preacher from preaching hate against us. So now I look like a Sufi sheikh who incites violence. And don't forget that we're constantly being followed, in taxis, pick-up trucks, or private cars, some of them without license plates or with false license plates, because we've asked about them and there's no trace of them in the traffic department. The drivers of these cars attack us or swerve their cars at us to cause us as much damage as they can, and every time the cars drive off. We've had four traffic accidents in the past two weeks, not counting the repeated harassment on the road wherever we go, whether at home or in Alexandria. Even in hotels and at the beach with our families, we're followed everywhere.

"At the same time the provincial governor issued orders that people should make use of the square where we've been holding our religious celebrations for the past hundred years, to set up a circus tent for example, or to display and sell goods, and for almost two or three months the place has been turned into a chaotic market that completely prevents us from performing our ceremonies on various special occasions. We've strongly objected to this but it looks like that official has more clout. Now the square has been turned into a marketplace for riffraff and peddlers and there are fights and acts of thuggery and muggings. Last year we put up a marquee in the square to commemorate the anniversary of the death of my father, may he rest in peace, who was one of the most important scholars of religion and Sufism of his age, and when the marquee was up and full of about ten thousand guests, the police came and surrounded the marquee and asked us to remove it. An assistant minister of the interior, who's the director of security for the region, was there in person, which is unprecedented. Yet we had all the necessary permits and had paid all the fees. The plan to undermine our reputation in the eyes of all those people was drawn up in cooperation with the National Council of Sufi Orders, which was ordered to intervene on instructions from the hidden hand. Everyone in the country wants to win the hidden hand's approval and avert its wrath at any price."

Hatem was alarmed by these revelations.

"And where are your followers who are generals and judges and other powerful and influential people, or the tens of thousands of other followers across the country?" he asked.

"My dear brother, what can I say to the members of the order?" said Mukhtar. "They look to me for baraka and miracles. They think that with a single glance I can change things. They believe I have secret powers and I can call them by telepathy when they're at home hundreds of miles away. They beg me to strike at those who treat them unjustly and to save them from oppression. The Sufi devotees imagine I'm one of God's saints and I can perform miracles like destroying the world and splitting mountains down the middle. They depend on my powers and rush to kiss my hand and do me honor, and now you're asking me to tell them that their sheikh, for whom they would be ready to die if I told them to, is completely powerless, that a policeman can push him around and intimidate him, that in the face of bureaucratic decisions or police brutality or harassment by a provincial governor or a police officer their sheikh can't say a word or do anything to stop them. If I said this to one of our members I would lose face and my prestige would collapse. Then he would say, 'Why don't you smite them with one of your prayers, or paralyze them or give them hell with your powers?' and I'd have to tell him that it was all a fantasy or wishful thinking on the part of followers and that doesn't work when God decides to try us with misfortunes."

Hatem bowed in deference to Sheikh Mukhtar's honesty.

"It's true you're a prisoner of the way people see you and love you and the ideas they have about you," he said. "You're supposed to be a miracle-worker but in fact you can't get yourself out of a detention cell at Cairo airport."

Mukhtar continued, as though his gallbladder had burst and he couldn't stop all the bile spilling out.

"In the oldest mosque in the province, which was built more than a hundred and twenty years ago, some of the descendants of the Prophet's family are buried. It's a place that large numbers of Muslims from various places often visit because the tombs produce certain fragrances and spiritual energy that only people with good hearts can detect. Then along comes a private charity created by someone we know nothing about claiming that he's submitted a request to the prime minister, who has issued a decree that the mosque be razed to the ground because it's about to fall down. This is a mosque that belongs to the Ministry of Religious Endowments. It's listed as a building of historical value and it has religious significance, and the ministry hadn't asked for it to be demolished. Yet someone came and got a decree from the prime minister and the ministerial committee on public services to demolish the mosque. Does that make sense? The antiquities committee and the ministry dismissed the decree as invalid, but mosques are now a toy the hidden hand is using to fight us. The guy has worn us down and rattled us with these ploys. We've wasted many months fighting this injustice and protecting the mosque from sabotage and destruction under cover of a decree from the prime minister.

"Then it got really out of hand and we had a gang of thugs suddenly turn up in front of our house to pick a fight. Out came the swords and the knives and the petrol bombs and the jerrycans of sulfuric acid. I swear, Hatem, sulfuric acid! Then there was a battle, with people who have nothing to do with the square where we live or the streets around us.

They were attacking each other and setting fire to car tires, which went on smoldering for hours after the fight broke up. In the middle of the fighting, when it was clear that calling the police was a waste of time because they never came, the thugs broke into the house, broke down the gate, and knocked down the fence and the railings and the guardhouse where the doorman sits. They were fighting with each other and trampling on everything in their way. They could have come to the upper floors where we live but it was obvious that they only wanted to intimidate us—they hadn't yet made the decision to go beyond frightening us and wrecking stuff in the house to humiliate us.

"And while we were away at one of our events, some low-lifes slipped into the house and tampered with the fuse box, which caused a short circuit and a fire that destroyed all the furniture and appliances in the house. The transformer caused massive explosions and if it hadn't been for God's protection we would have suffered even more serious damage. We brought an electrician and he told us that someone had played with the connections in the fuse box so that the wires would melt quickly and start a fire, and of course that was deliberate."

Mukhtar stopped and bowed his head.

"It's clear from these incidents that you're not up against someone ordinary," commented Hatem. "This is someone more important and powerful, someone people obey when he speaks, or rather when he whispers, not just speaks. He's the one behind all these incidents. Who could you have upset this much, Sheikh Mukhtar? You're an easygoing, good-natured person who prefers to be discreet. You don't talk about politics or government, if you don't mind me saying so, Uncle."

Mukhtar calmed down and regained some confidence when he heard the word 'uncle,' because he realized that Hatem still respected him and the stories had not changed the way Hatem saw him. So he didn't think too hard about what Hatem had said before 'uncle,' and continued with his story.

"Of course I know there are cameras spying on my house, even on my bedroom," Mukhtar said. "The strange thing is that when me and my wife are alone and being intimate with each other, there's a cement mixer under the bedroom window that starts up. It's a great beast of a machine and it makes a horrible noise that gives you a headache. They run it empty without any cement or anything else in it and there's no building site there, and it only runs under the bedroom and makes a noise at moments like that. When the kids go downstairs to ask the driver to drive it away they find a group of people around the mixer claiming that it's broken and they're trying to fix it."

Now Hatem began to have some doubts. Maybe Sheikh Mukhtar was suffering from paranoia and was convinced that someone was persecuting him. Perhaps Mukhtar, because of the pressure on him from being treated as a saint from an early age, had become simple-minded. They venerated him as a miracle-worker, whereas the only miracle he had really performed was resisting the temptation to exploit people's emotions for profit or personal advantage or sexual favors. But Hatem soon ruled out the possibility that Mukhtar was sick, because his mother appeared and corroborated what he said, and besides, there were bound to be witnesses to all his stories.

"Do you realize, Sheikh Mukhtar," said Hatem, "that you really are one of God's holy men?"

Mukhtar's spirits fell and he was worried Hatem might be making fun of him.

But Hatem continued, "A man in whom people see mythical powers, although he doesn't believe them himself, a man that people think is a saint, although he doesn't believe it and doesn't exploit it and doesn't want it and can't even live with it. A man who puts up with all that pain and all that harassment without kicking up a fuss really is a saint in my book."

"God bless you, Hatem," Mukhtar replied. "But I want to add something just to finish off my story. A while back we found out that the security agencies are using something called harassment patrols, which means vehicles full of thugs that surround us and play music so loud we don't get a moment's peace. Or trucks that come with their annoying engines and park in front of our house for hours on the pretext that there's something wrong with them, and there are trucks that dump rubble in front of the house to make it hard for us to get the car out. And we get notices that they're going to cut off the water and the electricity, just ours, and our telephones are constantly tapped blatantly to make sure we know that all our calls on the landlines and the cells are being monitored. It's done in a really intrusive way. They break into every conversation and then you get another call after the conversation to play back to you everything you said a few minutes earlier to the other person.

"You know, Hatem, everything I've told you and more has been reported to the police and to the prosecutor's office, including this incident—after which you won't need to hear any more. My wife and my mother-in-law were on their way back from visiting family in Cairo when the police stopped their car at a checkpoint. They took the driver and beat him up without any warning. They didn't even try to provoke an incident so they could claim he'd insulted them. Then they started verbally abusing my wife and her mother in an outrageous way. They forced them out of the car and threw the contents of their handbags on the ground, and then a senior officer turned up at the checkpoint in a police car. He got out and saw the scene and started shouting at the policemen as if he was their savior and God's mercy had descended from the heavens. He apologized to my wife and her mother, and even to the driver, and they went back to the car after being insulted and humiliated, and when the driver was about to drive off the officer came up to the window on my wife's side and said with a smile, 'Tell Sheikh Mukhtar that no one can save him from us. Goodbye, Mrs. Suha Abdel-Hamid Abdel-Mungi Ahmed Atef.' Her full name, right back to her great-great-grandfather, tripped off the officer's tongue. It seemed to be a double message—that I couldn't escape and that the target of their vengeance would be my wife."

Hatem was completely outraged. "Who's behind all of this, Mukhtar?" he asked.

"Your friend," Mukhtar replied, sadly but firmly.

The man in question was the president's son. He wasn't in fact Hatem's friend but Hatem was reluctant to deny the allegation and the idea had become widespread. He could sense the effect this had on everyone he knew, above him or below him. Some people thought Hatem even had influence over the security men who controlled the puppet strings and that had held the country by the throat for ages. Everyone was convinced that he had a friendly relationship with the president's son. Even the generals in State Security, who he assumed should know whether there was any basis for the story, were taken in by it. Although Hatem knew, like everyone else, that the world was fickle, for a long time he felt reassured by the idea that an influential sponsor was providing cover for his activities as he progressed up the ladder of fame in this lousy business.

One night at the studios he had gone into the green room where the guests sat before they went on air. He was his usual wise-cracking self and the staff were chasing him with questions that required quick-serve fatwas that were packed and ready to go so that their empty minds could handle them. He saw the actor Nader Nour, whose real name, he later discovered, was Shaaban Abdel-Samie el-Sayed. Nader jumped into his arms, showering him dramatically with praise, making it up as he went along in a way that showed he was an actor of modest talent when he deviated from the script he had memorized.

"Sheikh Hatem, I'm a great admirer of yours, a disciple. Whenever I see one of your programs I pray for you," he said.

"And whenever I see one of your programs, I curse you," Hatem shot back, punching him in the chest. "You've made me cry so many times," Hatem continued. "When I was watching you in that program when your mother, Inaam Salousa, died in the serial, I had tears rolling down my cheeks and my wife was laughing at me. Remember, the one where you threw yourself into her arms and said, 'Who have you left me for, mama?'"

Hatem's performance was masterly and members of the program crew burst out laughing. They were standing around watching the encounter between the sheikh and the actor.

"Amazing," said Nader. "That was a program that was broadcast in Ramadan four years ago. How come you remember that?"

"No, I stopped watching as soon as your mother died," Hatem replied. "And I heard that your film was a big hit, earning a million pounds a day. How did you do it? Did you offer people free steaks if they came to watch it?" he added.

With Nader's laughter Hatem began to open up and change into an actor playing the role of sheikh.

"Hmm meat, but there wasn't much meat on the heroine. She was just a skeleton wrapped in candy," he said.

Nader wouldn't leave him alone that night. After the program was over he waited and took him to the hotel suite that the producer of his new film had booked for him, and they had dinner together. Nader asked if Hatem would mind if he smoked a joint in his presence, and Hatem said that he honestly didn't mind, but then Nader laughed and said he was teasing and that God had persuaded him to give up hashish.

Hatem knew Nader was lying, but he liked his false modesty. A friendship between them developed and when Nader was around, his personality constantly took Hatem by surprise. But Hatem did start to grow wary of him because he was so persistent and would follow Hatem around for weeks on end, pestering him throughout with questions about religious matters. It gradually came to light that Nader (or Shaaban when he opened up and made confessions) was naive and inane. He was obsessed with religion but his knowledge of it didn't equal that of a child in the first grade of preparatory school in an Azhar institute. Hatem even discovered that he didn't know the Muslim profession of faith by heart but, like a child, struggled to get it straight.

Hatem would wake up to find Nader jumping on his bed. He had mixed in with the other people in the house so well it was as if he had been living there for years. He would drop in unexpectedly before dawn prayers and take Hatem off in his car to pray in the Hussein mosque or in the Sayeda Nafisa mosque. Months passed and Nader was very much part of his life. He never stopped giving Omayma films and CDs, and invitations to private screenings, festivals, and fashion shows, and computer games for Omar, and she put up with Nader's presence in Hatem's life because he was so generous and friendly and such a gentleman. He suddenly became the house manager, sorting out the car licenses, deliveries of gas cylinders, and the construction of a wooden shed in the garden. He hung lots of pictures on the walls and paid for all the workers to go to Mecca on pilgrimage. He starred at the parties at Omar's school and at the birthday parties of Omar and his friends.

"Hey Nader, don't you have a living to make?" Hatem often shouted at him.

In fact he didn't have a job, but he did have an income because his sudden fame and the success of his last three films, after four earlier flops, had made him a millionaire in two years and he was now earning millions of pounds a film. But his ambition had lost its bite and he didn't feel driven to go hunting for roles. He also had a problem knowing who exactly he was, because his personality was complex and nebulous at the same time. Hatem knew why Nader was an actor and why, in cinema circles, they said he had talents that went way beyond the limited roles he had played in his teen movies.

He had a personality that thrived in an intellectual vacuum. His mind was like a gas that assumed the shape of whatever vessel contained it. If he was let out of his box he would fall apart. He didn't have one clear personality, so he was always looking for characters to breathe life into his body. When he acted, the character took over and you could easily believe that he was that doctor in this film or the miserable weeping child in that series, or the bad-tempered officer that was chasing the gang. Naturally he was an excellent mimic who quickly picked up on the gestures, the eye and head movements, the smiles, and the hummings and hawings of people he met. Nader was running away from his own insubstantiality by acting, and when he had lost any desire to make popular films or to live the high life he had a compulsive urge to look for new characters—ones that really satisfied him, because those limited and superficial characters no longer tempted him.

Nader had passed the age of thirty without really intending to, because he was still a child at heart. He would pick up a toy and become obsessed with it, then get bored and break it. With his stories and his confessions he had given Hatem glimpses into the mansions of the country's famous and fabulously rich. He hardly slept because he had such a busy schedule of visits and social engagements it was hard to see how he found time for them. Hatem realized that Nader was looking for a conscience he could depend on. Nader had insisted that Hatem call him by his original name, Shaaban, if they were alone together.

"Why should I do that? Nader's a real enough name," Hatem asked.

"No, Sheikh Hatem, I feel that the name is fake and I want to be my real self with you," said Nader.

"Your real self is crap, whether you call yourself Shaaban or Nader."

"I'm not joking."

"Okay, and neither am I."

"Okay, enough, Sheikh Hatem."

"Okay, it's up to you. I could even call you Ramadan if you want."

Hatem was sure that one night Nader would tire of him and cut him out of his life. For a while, Hatem had been a godsend for this restless young man, helping Nader deal with his loneliness and fill his spare time. Hatem had come into his life at a precarious time when Nader was on the verge of depression and Nader clung to him. Nader's family had fallen apart when he was in elementary school, when his mother brought him back with her from Saudi Arabia after being divorced by his father, who stayed there and married an Egyptian woman twenty years his junior. His father's heart couldn't take the demands of his new marriage and he soon died, and Nader's mother stayed in Zagazig, looking after him in a joyless apartment. When he was leaving to go to the Cinema Institute in Cairo, she told him she was going to marry what she called a respectable man. He didn't take the trouble to judge how respectable he was. He just said goodbye and threw himself into Cairo, picking up crumbs of this or that: an education, some self-confidence, dreams, religiosity, and money.

His life was chaotic in his years at the institute, where he went into the production department because he didn't know what he really wanted from the cinema, other than that it offered him the only way out of the trials and tribulations of his years as a child and then an adolescent. He loved many of the characters from films and memorized the lines of the leading actors. He was an encyclopedia of knowledge about black-and-white films. When he imitated these characters in front of his colleagues his name spread among them, and some of those who had connections recommended him to other people who had connections and he started to act in scenes so short that viewers might miss him if they blinked.

But when he found out what he wanted to do, he showed talent, and as a younger generation came of age in the cinema he found himself moving unwittingly from seats in the third or second row to the ranks of the stars. His acting persona expanded to fit his body and his real personality caved in. The limelight and the extravagant lifestyle messed up his mind and when he found Hatem he saw him as a pillar of strength for his generation, so he parked himself next to him and leaned on him, and that was why he became so attached to Hatem.

As soon as Hatem appeared in his life, Nader stopped living in hotel suites and moved back to his abandoned villa in the suburbs. He filled it with servants and retainers and secretaries and drivers. Every Friday he organized a recitation of the whole Quran and brought together his acting friends and colleagues who were rising stars, along with their own associates—colleagues, secretaries, young producers, their own writers, and other film and television people. For the recitations he had famous Quran readers and Nader joined in with them. Although his religious knowledge was shallow, he was a fluent Quran reader in imitation of the famous sheikhs. Servants came around with incense and bowls of aromatic herbs and the tables were spread with food from the best-known caterers. By the end of the day everyone had held down copious amounts of hashish smoke—the equivalent of a month's hard work by a gang of smugglers. Then Nader, with one companion, got out his massive Jeep and wrapped up all the food tight in paper to keep in the heat and drove around the streets—streets he knew in slum areas such as the Pyramids, Embaba and Kitkat—giving out the food until it was time for dawn prayers. Then he drove back to Hatem, who was asleep, and woke him up to perform the prayer together in el-Hussein or Sayeda Zeinab. If Hatem complained or rebelled, he would make do with praying behind him in the garden of the mansion, but he insisted that Hatem say the dawn invocation in the second prostration. On one occasion, when Nader said the final Amen his voice could be heard throughout the neighborhood and Hatem had to control himself to keep from laughing. Nader felt it too and had to hold back a laugh as well. That made him fart and he collapsed on the lawn in fits of laughter.

Throughout their friendship Hatem had never seen any sign that his favorite actor had any interest in women. He never saw him with a girlfriend or in the company of an actress, or even heard him talking about women. Of course Omayma helped point this out to him and urged him to confront Nader.

"Why don't I see any women in your life, Nader?" he said. "I'm worried, God forbid, you might be one of two things."

"What two things?" Nader replied with a laugh.

"Either you're not interested in sex at all, or you're one of those bastards who like sex with their own kind," said Hatem.

Nader laughed till he cried.

"Good heavens, sheikh, why would you inflict that on me?"

"You know," said Hatem, "the way you laugh, much as it reassures me, it also makes me smell a rat."

"Don't worry, Mawlana, and get a cat for the rat. Yours truly is male and normal as well, but do you really want me to invite you to witness my love affairs? I'd be embarrassed, and besides you should be urging me to be pious and chaste."

"No, I do urge you to be chaste, but that means a nice girl and I want you to get married. I'm asking in order to persuade you to go out with Nana or Tata or whoever."

"Nana and Tata! No one has nicknames like that any more, sheikh."

A few days later, when they were together for dawn prayers in the Sayeda Zeinab mosque, Nader reminded him of his question.

"I couldn't possibly tell Sayeda Zeinab that you want me to fornicate," he said.

"I swear, you do seem to avoid women, Shaaban," said Hatem.

When they were in the car later, he suddenly said, "Yes, I do."

"Good God," Hatem replied.

"I do avoid women, that's a hundred percent true. First, I got fed up because it was all about sex without love, and second, I started worrying fornication might kill me. I once got a woman pregnant and she had an abortion and I despised myself and of course I despised her and so I lost interest. But for your information I have starting going with them again."

"With women?" Hatem interrupted.

"Yes, with women, as far as the bed. And then I pick up my clothes and leave without doing anything."

"You've got to be kidding me, Shaaban Abdel-Samie!"

"You don't believe me. I swear by Almighty God."

"By God I believe you. Get married then."

"It's too early. And who would I marry? After what I've seen and done I couldn't marry any woman. I wouldn't even trust someone as good as my late grandmother," said Nader.

Hatem wasn't in the least surprised when Nader one day asked him, earnestly and sadly, if acting was forbidden, or haram.

"Strange question," Hatem replied. "The question should be, 'is acting permissible?' 'Is it halal?' Why did you start with whether it's haram?"

"You're right. I never thought of that," said Nader.

"And does it matter to you to know whether it's halal or haram?"

"My God, why do you ask me this difficult question, Mawlana? You mean you think I could do something haram if I knew it was haram?"

Hatem smiled and slapped him on the shoulder.

"Yes, my friend, all humans are like that. We all know there are haram things that we do, and we do haram things that we know are haram, and that's very different. Someone who drinks alcohol and denies it's haram can be sentenced to death, according to some jurists, whereas someone who drinks alcohol in the knowledge that it's haram can only be flogged. In other words, it's the same act yet two different sentences."

"Really?" said Nader.

Hatem laughed.

"Really really," he said.

Nader, deep in thought, examined the pattern on the sofa covers and the paintings on the wall.

"Okay," he finally said. "Answer me as though I'm Shaaban Abdel-Samie el-Sayed and not Nader Nour. Is acting halal? There you are, see, this time I put halal first."

"Okay," said Hatem. "You want me to give you an answer as Shaaban and not Nader. Okay, but should I answer as Hatem el-Shenawi the sheikh at the mosque, or as Hatem el-Shenawi the sheikh on television?"

Nader was startled.

"Oh my God, does it matter?" he asked.

"It sure does," said Hatem, "because the sheikh in the mosque tries to please God, while the television sheikh tries to please the customer, either the producer or the company that sponsors the program or the audience, and if he manages to please God in the midst of all that, then all's well and good and it's a miracle."

"Is that what you're like, Sheikh Hatem?" asked Nader.

"Just like that."

"Come on now, there's no need for that feeble sheikhly humor. Tell me, on your honor . . ."

"It's haram."

"What's haram?"

"Acting."

Nader was taken aback, so shocked that he looked like a driver who'd just survived an accident on the desert highway and found out that all of his passengers were dead. Hatem felt that he had to explain.

"Hang on and don't just take the fatwa without thinking. In Islamic law there's a process the jurists call dissection, which means we take the subject we're interested in and break it down into pieces, exactly like Meccano, and then we can see what the pieces are made of and how they fit together and how they stand in relation to sharia law and what sharia law has to say about them. In this case we're talking about acting. For a start, in the time of the Prophet Muhammad . . ."

"May God bless him and grant him peace," Nader mumbled audibly.

Hatem gave a broad smile.

"May God strengthen your faith, but don't think that this blessing-the-Prophet business will make me change my opinion about you or about acting," he said sarcastically. "I tell you, even if you acted like Omar ibn al-Khattab right now in front of me my analysis wouldn't change."

"Sheikh," Nader replied affectionately. "You make me feel as though we're in the Center for Islamic Research. But we're just having a nice chat and I've just smoked a couple of joints, so take it easy on us actors."

"Okay, then perhaps you'd better ask me if hashish is haram or halal. That's a much easier question than the acting question."

"No, I know the answer to that one."

"Oh wow, such wide learning, such incisive legal expertise! Okay, tell me then, is weed halal or haram? And mind you don't tell me that if it's halal we'll smoke it and if it's haram we'll burn it, because that one's as old as your uncle's old boots, and because it's just wordplay, not a fatwa."

"No, I wouldn't give you such a cheesy answer," Nader replied sniffily. "There's another answer, Mawlana."

"Well spare us the wait," said Hatem.

"Okay."

"Go on, spit it out," said Hatem.

"It depends on why you're smoking weed, what it's being smoked for."

"Good Lord, so smoking weed is like drinking Zamzam water from Mecca," Hatem roared.

"Yes, if you smoke weed as a cure for depression or anxiety or tension, then it's treated like any other medicament, but if you smoke it for pleasure and to get high, then it's haram," Nader said.

Hatem roared with laughter.

"Who told you that, you son of a bitch?"

Nader jumped up.

"That's stumped you! You don't want to admit it's a good argument."

"Good argument, no way!" Hatem retorted. "Sit down, Shaaban, so that I don't waste your time or mine. Acting is a subject where it's right to use analogy, and what do we mean by analogy, my friend? We mean we compare. Simple, isn't it? When you ask me how far it is to such-and-such a place, I say it's like from here to the main street. Because they didn't have acting in the time of the Prophet or his Companions or the generation that came after. So this was something that was new to Muslims, but there was singing and music and what did Islam have to say about them? There are jurists who say that they're halal under certain conditions, and there are jurists who say they're haram and try to ban them. So much for music and singing, which existed in the time of the Prophet. So what about acting, where we don't have any relevant saying of the Prophet or, of course, any verse in the Quran? In this case the Muslim mind has to get to work, and this mind changes over time and with the various lives that people go through, and sometimes it's open-minded and tolerant, and sometimes it's stupid and narrow-minded. Get any of that?"

"No."

"But what do you think of the method?"

"Mawlana, without the joking, please."

"You idiot, what do you mean, joking? You think I'd joke about religion? I asked you what you thought of the method, I mean the intellectual methodology, but how could you understand what that is when you never got beyond reading children's stories? So anyway, the Muslim mind has to ask itself a number of questions and then deduce a clear answer, or the clearest answer."

"So is it halal or haram?"

"Why, Mr. Shaaban? Do you think I'm going to tell you it's halal for that pretty girl, what's her name, the heroine of that film with that hippie friend of yours who has his shirt unbuttoned throughout the film . . ."

"Oh please, Mawlana, spare me."

"Okay, sir. You want me to tell you that when he takes his shirt off and kisses her on the back of the neck and then pulls her toward him and kisses her lips in a shot that fills the 52-inch screen, that it's halal? You think I'm a sheikh from Las Vegas? Of course it's haram—nakedness and kisses and swimsuits and steamy scenes, and cold ones too, and all kinds of scandalous behavior. It's definitely all haram, haram, but is that all there is to acting? In fact from my own experience, no. Acting goes far beyond that, and by the way, I've seen several Iranian films in which all the women wear the hijab and even so the films were like magic. We're talking about stories and parables that are like epic poetry."

"So it's halal?" Nader ventured.

Hatem bowed his head pensively.

"The truth is I don't know," he said. "What's for sure is an actor assumes a character that's not his own and is treated as if he's the character he's playing rather than his real character. Of course that's deceit but everyone knows it's deceit, so it's not deceit. Then there's the allurement, which no doubt includes entertainment, playfulness, and showing off, but playfulness is important here and the entertainment is innocent and the showing off does no harm, so it's halal."

Then he turned to Nader.

"My God," he said irritably, "it looks as though it's halal, Shaaban!"

"Looks like it, after all that it looks like it," Nader shouted. "So what was all that complicated argument about?"

Hatem stood up and started hurling the sofa cushions at Nader with pinpoint accuracy.

"Do you think it's easy making up fatwas, you ignorant actor?" he said.

After finishing one of his programs, Hatem left the building with some of his team as usual. He found Nader outside with dozens of adolescents jostling around him. He held onto him with one arm as he waved to his fans with the other.

"Move back so that we don't get in the way of Mawlana the sheikh," Nader said.

"What's up?" Hatem whispered. "I feel like a blind man being dragged off somewhere. Where are you taking me?"

Nader got Hatem through the open door of his car and pushed in beside him in the back seat.

"So you're kidnapping me!" Hatem said.

He put his head through the window for the girls who were pressing against the window and the body of the car.

"Girls, I want you as witnesses that I've been kidnapped. You'll have to back each other up in court!" he said.

Nader pressed the button to close the window.

"Quickly, Saber," he shouted at the driver.

"Interested in soccer, Mawlana?" added Nader, suddenly acting serious.

"I support the Ismaili Dervishes of course, because of my profession," Hatem replied.

Nader laughed.

"We're on our way to an important match," he added.

"What? People play soccer at eleven o'clock at night? Are we playing by Brazil time?"

"Mawlana, I'm serious. It's a match in the summer league. We'll be playing together on the same side against a team including the president's son," explained Nader.

Hatem laughed sarcastically.

"No way. We're going to play against the president's son?"

"Would you rather play on the same side as him?" Nader replied.

"The truth is I'd rather go home," said Hatem.

"You're frightened, Mawlana," Nader jeered.

"What would I be frightened of? It's just that I'd be embarrassed to be running rings around the president's son. But if this goes on too late I'll have rings around my eyes in the morning."

Nader laughed.

"You're a hoot, Mawlana. That's why I love you," he said.

"No, I'm really serious, Nader," said Hatem, looking stern. "I don't want to make this trip, or play this match, or make this horrible acquaintanceship."

Nader was surprised.

"So you call it a horrible acquaintanceship if you meet the president's son and have a friendly chat with him?"

"It might work against me. And besides, what the hell would a sheikh in a turban be doing in a soccer league, prancing around with his belly hanging out in the presence of his honor the president's son? Who knows, the president might be up late and decide to come and watch the match."

"Look, Mawlana, I met the man a while back and I've come across him at the weddings of several respectable people," said Nader.

"Of course they'd be respectable. I mean, you're not very likely to meet him at a wedding in a shack in the slums."

"Once we went to the birthday of some billionaire in Madame Tussaud's in London. We went in his private plane and came back the same night."

"That was in some slum part of London?" joked Hatem.

"Anyway, he's a very polite man, well brought up and respectable, not at all a show-off or arrogant, well behaved and very modest. You'll see for yourself," said Nader. Hatem mulled it over and asked Nader several questions, such as 'Does he know I'll be there?' and 'Do you have any sports clothes that would fit me?' and 'Is it a long way?' and 'Does he know your real name is Shaaban?'

The answer to all the questions was yes, except for the last one, where it was no plus a 'mind you don't tell him.'

The car stopped at a remote spot in a new suburb for privileged people. As soon as Hatem reached such places, he understood that line of the miraculous Quran: *We gave orders to the townsfolk who live in luxury*. He liked the version that doubled the 'm' in the first word, making it 'ammarna' rather than 'amarna' and changing the meaning to "We made princes of the townsfolk who live in luxury," and princes didn't necessarily mean members of a royal family. They might also be members of a ruling family, ministers, or powerful people who gave orders and acted imperiously. That version no longer occurred in the readings by modern Arabs, the descendants of men who preached to sultans, who were worried the preachers might promote the version with the doubled 'm'. The sultans preferred the single-m version, which could be read as implying that God would order the rich to live debauched lives. What kind of idiot would believe such an interpretation? And what kind of even bigger idiot could hear it recited fourteen hundred years ago without preferring the real version over the sophistical version? Hatem kept such ideas to himself, except when he was fed up with feeling he was in chains, when he couldn't breathe because the people around him were in need and too weak to stand up to authority, influence, and money. He was as weak as they were but he drew some strength from his learning, in which he took refuge, and sometimes from humor. He tried to keep his conscience in good repair; whenever he felt that it had become too complacent he hurriedly set to work plugging the gaps and filling the holes.

As he and Nader went through the gate of the club with its high walls, Nader smiled and gave out pictures of himself to the strapping guards standing to attention in forbidding uniforms. The guards smiled back in delight and greeted Sheikh Hatem, whose arrival took them by surprise. They cleared a way for the car through the barriers of solid stone, which were carefully arranged to stop cars from driving too fast from the gate to the clubhouse.

Hatem greeted them, then leaned over to Nader and said, "I bet the High Dam in Aswan doesn't have a quarter or even a sixth of the number of guards this place has!"

Nader was surprised that Hatem was surprised.

"But why would you want guards on the High Dam?" he asked.

"You're right," said Hatem. "All the High Dam does is protect us from flooding or drowning, and provide us with electricity."

Nader ignored Hatem's sarcasm for a moment, then stopped the car and turned to him. "No seriously, why would we need guards on the High Dam?" he asked.

"Okay, I'm sorry. The High Dam can go to hell. I don't want it guarded," Hatem replied.

Hatem turned away and Nader started up the car again, driving down lanes that led to open spaces that loomed in front of them. There was a deep green soccer field and floodlights that were brighter than necessary.

"The townsfolk who live in luxury," Hatem mused. "And by the way that includes many sectors of society—me and you and him and them."

"Sheikh Hatem?"

"I'm just talking to myself, filling out an idea I had. Don't worry about it. Let's keep to the game."

Nader opened the trunk of the car and took out two sports bags of the latest fashion and the best-known brand and handed one of them to Hatem. He closed the car door and walked toward a corridor that led to a small one-story building.

"You seem to be in a playful mood yourself tonight," said Nader.

"No, don't worry," said Hatem reassuringly. "I'm just fine."

The building turned out to contain changing rooms, elegantly designed with everything inside suggesting cleanliness and regular maintenance. It had vast pictures of famous international soccer players on the walls and a private changing room with wooden lockers, a water cooler, and an en suite bathroom paved in marble and the luxury fittings you would expect in a five-star hotel. Speakers in the ceiling played soft music and there was a cupboard with clean towels folded up, each one marked with the club logo. When Hatem came out wearing his sports clothes, he ran into Nader wearing exactly the same uniform.

"Well, well, look at the sporty modern sheikh with an open mind!" laughed Nader.

Hatem pointed to his bare thighs and calves below the shorts.

"Sure, open everywhere," he said.

As they left Nader looked at his watch and told Hatem that the big man must be about to arrive.

When they went out on the floodlit field Hatem found himself in the middle of a group of businessmen he had met on many occasions and some of whom he was friends with. They were all in sports clothes, and although some of them were fat with large bellies, in their uniform they looked the model of elegant distinction, like the pampered few chosen to join the club. They greeted Hatem warmly and some of them seemed genuinely happy, though surprised, to see him there. They soon upgraded him in their hierarchy of important people because, if a sheikh like Hatem appeared here, it meant the president's son approved of him and had a friendly relationship with him, and so there would be an array of security agencies ready to protect him and make sure he was free to go about his business.

As the businessmen and members of parliament reassessed Hatem, some famous soccer players, impressed to see the sheikh, ran forward to welcome him. Hatem really liked them; he had met them in his mosque, in the studios, in the grand homes of the politicians and millionaires he visited, where he sometimes gave lectures on religion or attended parties. In all these encounters the soccer players were his favorites because they were innocently and absolutely ignorant in a way that Hatem saw as a sign of honesty. They were young men in the prime of youth, climbing the ladder of fame and glory through their boots, as God had denied most of them any intelligence or intellectual ability, concentrating all their talents in their muscles and their feet. Of course they would be greedy for money, dazzled by fame, and dizzy in the face of life's temptations, especially as most of them came from backgrounds of pure suffering and abject poverty, a hand-to-mouth existence and a culture of abysmal ignorance. When they started to climb, it happened suddenly and brought in its wake everything likely to lead them astray—money, celebrity, influence, the adulation of fans, the attentions of girls, and relationships with important people. Their lives were turned upside down and Hatem could see that they were completely shaken. He felt really sorry for them, because what they went through in three or four years would have been too much for a sane, balanced person to go through in twenty years, and one of the ways they kept a grip in the face of all these powerful pressures, whether wittingly or unwittingly, was by being religious. They mostly didn't know anything about religion, but they were very religious. Maybe that was how the whole country was—religious without religion. They hardly knew the basics of Islam, but they clung to the rites and the rituals like men drowning in the open sea. They didn't try to exploit religion but they really believed in it and it was their last line of defense, unlike the retired soccer players he sometimes shook hands with and embraced and who spoke to him at the end of his programs, saying things like "You really put that guy in his place" or "I watched you every day in Ramadan and if I missed a program I'd watch the repeat before dawn prayers." These retirees, who had grown up in an atmosphere of lies and deceit, had learned, along with soccer, how to play around, how to dodge and weave, how to trick the referee and win penalty kicks by devious means, how to cut corners with the rules, how to stir up the crowd, how to elbow opponents when the referee wasn't looking, as well as how to win rewards from businessmen who were fans or candidates in elections. They invested their celebrity status and stardom and made money any way they could.

Now Hatem was sitting on a luxuriously padded wooden bench of the kind that royalty might sit on. In front of him there was an icebox full of soft drinks, juices and bottles of water. Nader was warming up with the ball while they waited for the president's son. On the grass in front of Hatem sat a businessman in his early thirties from a well-known family that owned franchises from French companies.

"I really admire you," the man said, very politely, "because you're not a traditional sheikh, even if you sometimes appear with a turban and a caftan. But you speak in simple language that people understand easily. I'm very interested in religion. I've read several books but unfortunately they're written in difficult language and the way they explain things makes you feel like you're at school. I wish we could simplify religion."

Hatem had heard enough and he laughed.

"The problem is that if the sheikhs simplified religion, they'd be out of a job," he said. "They live by making it complicated."

There was a sudden commotion and the big man appeared at the far corner of the field, which was surrounded by wasteland with no neighbors or buildings. There was a screen of tall trees but when Hatem looked carefully he realized that the trees had been brought in and planted there when they were mature. The area couldn't have been planted long enough for the trees to grow so high. Even the grass was a brilliant green, but it didn't look fresh. People ran toward the president's son, the way you would welcome a friend, or maybe like messengers running after their master. The play stopped, a whistle blew, and the president's son came on to the field—slim and trying his hardest to be casual. He smiled at Hatem with a certain presumptuous humility as he approached. He gently waved some of the people out of his way, took hold of Nader's arm, and shook Hatem's hand warmly.

"Good evening, Mawlana," he said.

"Good evening, sir."

"It's a fine thing that sheikhs play sports. It's really great."

Eager to insert himself into the conversation, Nader replied.

"Teach your children how to swim, shoot, and ride horses. Isn't that right, Mawlana?" he said.

Hatem laughed.

"But they didn't say anything about five-a-side soccer," he said to the president's son with a smile.

The big man turned toward them.

"The sheikh's going to play on my team and bring us some baraka," he said.

"So exactly how many goals does baraka bring? So I can work it out," Hatem quickly replied.

The president's son smiled, apparently the strongest response he could muster to Hatem's humor. He took hold of Hatem's arm and said, "Mawlana, you're just as they told me you were."

Before he had a chance to explain who this 'they' were, a photographer popped out from underground and peppered them with flashes. He took another picture of them later, hugging after a goal. Hatem had blocked one of the retired professionals and passed the ball to the son, who dribbled around the defender and took a powerful shot at the goal, as if he were trying to prove to himself that he didn't need them to give him preferential treatment on the field. When the ball reached the goal, the keeper fumbled it and it whizzed into the net.

Hatem stopped, smiled, and shouted, *"We covered their eyes and so they could not see."*

Hearing the other players laughing, the president's son came up to him and hugged him and then headed to the substitutes' bench, where they were sitting drinking cans of soft drinks and wiping away their sweat with soft white towels. Some of them were talking about the national team's next match.

Sure enough, the team of the president's son won the match, after the international referee made a commendable effort to make a few calls in favor of the winning team. They went off to shower in their changing rooms, and when Hatem thought he was about to leave with Nader, they called him back to lead them in prayers on the field. Everyone stood behind him to perform the evening prayer, which he had in fact performed before he even came to the club, but when he saw how devout they were he had no choice but to perform it again. The photographer kept taking pictures, which gave new life to the rumors that he was friends with the president's son; they were responsible for the fact that within forty-eight hours Egypt thought they were best buddies—including his wife and even his son Omar, who didn't remember that Hatem was his father in the first place. Nobody knew that when he came out of the club in Nader's car the officers and guards stopped them and one of them came up to them and whispered in Nader's ear. Nader got out of the car and took Sheikh Hatem by the hand to a small building close to the soccer pitch. From the inside it looked like a luxury guesthouse.

"I tell you, I'm used to the sports center at the Citadel. This really is the first time I've seen a millionaires' sports center," Hatem remarked.

"What do you mean, millionaires? Billionaires, okay. The poorest of them is worth something like two or three billion," replied Nader, who realized that the president's son was waiting for them.

"There's no need to grumble," said Hatem. "Personally I've made more money out of religion than any of the early caliphs made, or Bukhari or Muslim, Ibn Kathir, Ibn al-Athir, al-Qurtubi, or al-Zamakhshari."

As Hatem murmured the list of names, an officer in civilian clothes, looking like a public relations official, appeared and asked them to come in. When they went in they found the president's son alone in the room in front of a large television screen, with a cup of steaming hot tea.

"Sorry, Nader, but could you leave me with Mawlana for a minute?" he said with a big smile.

"Of course, of course," said Nader, withdrawing from the room and closing the door obediently behind him.

The big man asked Hatem to sit down and went straight to business.

"Of course, Mawlana, you realize it was me who asked you to come. When I found out that Nader was friends with you, I told him to invite you here," he said.

"In fact I didn't realize that at all, because Nader didn't tell me anything," Hatem said candidly.

"I asked him not to say anything, and anyway I'm also asking you not to tell Nader why I wanted to see you, under any circumstances, and I hope you appreciate the seriousness of the situation."

Trying to act normally, Hatem smiled.

"The truth is I can see the seriousness, but I haven't yet seen the situation itself," he said.

The president's son showed no reaction.

"It really is a serious situation, and I think you're the only person who can help me with it," he said. "Not just the only person, but also the last. We've tried everything, but nothing has worked. In fact things have gotten so serious that we've thought of getting him out of Egypt just to limit the damage, now that we've failed to stop the disaster from happening in the first place."

Hatem was baffled and had no idea what this was all about, though he felt he was on the edge of an imminent calamity.

"Could you explain a little more?" he asked.

"Of course I'll explain everything to you, more than you might expect, but not now and not from me exactly. Tomorrow morning at nine the car will take you to my father-in-law's house and you can hear everything from my wife."

THE CAR ARRIVED RIGHT ON time, with an elderly driver of the kind that in the old days would have worked for an important person, and who, when that important person died, went on to work for someone new and even more important. He was dignified, taciturn, smartly dressed, and imperturbable, though his whole façade would no doubt collapse in the face of one friendly question from Hatem, who had woken up ahead of schedule. Not that Hatem really had a schedule. Gone were the days when he had specific appointments that meant rising early. They always say that Cairo never sleeps, but Hatem thought that it never fully woke up, that it had constant insomnia as the inhabitants breathlessly pursued a chance to rest that never came. Cairo had become very nocturnal. What with the crowds, the long distances, and the clogged streets, dinner invitations were for ten o'clock, appointments were made for midnight, and deals were done shortly before dawn. His social activities were sufficiently extensive and diverse for him to be quite sure that very few financiers, businessmen, celebrities, or famous sheikhs woke up as early as this. As he looked around that morning, something told him that this time of day was for drudges, while the dead of night was the preserve of the wealthy.

He sat in the seat next to the driver, who asked him proudly, "Would you like me to put the Quran on, Mawlana?"

"Which reciters do you have?" Hatem said with a smile.

"The car has a computer with every recording from Abdel-Samad to el-Tablawi."

"That's nice but, you know, I'd like to read myself."

"Wow, Mawlana, now that would bring us baraka!" said the driver.

Hatem felt a heavy cloud hanging over him that morning, a legacy of the previous evening. He hadn't said a word to Nader, though he knew the poor man must be insane with curiosity after the president's son had asked to meet Hatem alone. Nader hadn't dared ask him what the president's son wanted, and Hatem had tried to make amends by changing the subject:

"How many billions were they worth, the men on the pitch tonight?" he had asked.

Nader didn't answer, so he went on.

"So what's this club really called?"

"This is a new private club, Mawlana, and some of the people you saw tonight are members. Membership isn't open to anyone outside a limited circle."

"Ah, I see a narrow circle can come here, and it isn't possible to expand it," Hatem mused.

"I don't quite understand, but that sounds right."

Hatem laughed.

"Of course, as you know, what happened between me and the big man is a secret and he doesn't want me to share it with anyone, but if you want to know what exactly happened, I'll tell you anyway, right now."

Nader panicked.

"No, please. If he wants it to remain a secret and he doesn't want me to know what happened, then there's no need to say."

"So you won't be upset?" asked Hatem in surprise.

"Of course not."

Hatem slapped his fist on his thigh.

"Bare-faced liar!" he said. "You're dying to know but you don't want the responsibility of knowing and you're afraid he might be angry."

"It's true, Mawlana, and I'm worried for your sake as well."

"Mine too! Okay, Nader. But you're right, it is something worth worrying about."

Since early morning Hatem had been praying that the meeting would be to ask for a fatwa on something to do with the wife of the president's son: an oath of divorce the son had made, for example, or a foolish vow uttered in bed in a moment of anger, or one of those questions that pursued him everywhere, from people at both the top and bottom of society. He often felt much like a visitor who happens to be a doctor and when people find out there's a doctor in the house they start imagining illnesses. They remember old, insignificant pains that don't bother them in the least and describe them to him, or ask for a free check-up, just because they happen to have come across a doctor who is available for free.

In much the same way, he was like a religious doctor. As soon as people met him, they would ask him about trivial things, matters they weren't really interested in or bothered about. They were just taking advantage of the fact that a sheikh was around. They were making up questions to obtain a service that was there for the asking, though these days some people were crazy about seeking fatwas on anything. He was worried the driver might suddenly ask him, for example, "Are soap suds halal or haram?"

He remembered an exchange he'd had with another driver: "I have some money in the bank but I don't take any interest on it because people say that's haram."

"Okay, so what are you worried about?"

"No, but is it haram to keep the money in the bank?"

"Why would it be haram?"

"Because the bank deals in interest."

"But you're not taking interest!"

"Yes, but isn't it haram?"

"You mean you're worried it might be put in the safe alongside money that isn't ritually pure?"

In fact this driver didn't ask him for a fatwa on anything, a rare occurrence these days. But the driver was waiting for him to recite the Quran. He thought that Hatem was going to recite aloud in the car like a proper Quran reader. His ears and other senses were all at the ready. He slowed down and kept turning to look at Hatem, until Hatem realized what he wanted.

"Ah, you thought I was going to recite the Quran instead of the CD?" he said.

He laughed and the driver still didn't register.

"I meant I was going to recite it silently to myself," he added.

"Ah, now I understand," said the driver.

"But if you want us to recite, we can recite," said Hatem.

Without the driver asking him, he began reciting the Quran aloud. He was an experienced professional reader and so he could recite the Quran in the traditional style while thinking about something completely different—having a cup of tea or coffee, leaving the tent when the ceremony was over, the faces of the important people who had come to pay condolences, rival Quran readers, the wife waiting for him at home, even the meat he would be served after the recitation. He could do a complicated mathematical calculation in his head while reciting the Quran. But now this practiced professionalism annoyed and even sickened him. He knew fatwas by heart like someone who has memorized the technical manual for a fridge or a television: with all the instructions and operating procedures, the maintenance schedule, the specifications, and possible defects. These unusual talents of his gave him a bad conscience.

He tried to drive such thoughts out of his head as he stopped reciting and turned to the driver.

"You know the Quranic verse *and the morning when it breathes?*" he asked.

The driver was quick to show off how religious he was. *"By the night when it wanes, and the morning when it breathes,"* he quoted.

Hatem leaned forward, holding his prayer beads in both hands.

"'Wane' here means to fade, pass, go away, of course, and 'breathe' means to appear or begin, and breathing is when air comes out from the inside."

He looked out of the car window thoughtfully, and went on with a sigh:

"But when you hear the word 'breathe,' you get the impression that the morning has a smell, the smell of breathing, not the sound of breathing, because the sound of breathing is faint and, if it's loud, it's a sign of disease or a death rattle, so the focus is all on the smell. The morning has a smell, and you're a peasant like me so you know that. With 'the morning when it breathes' you can smell the morning right away."

"True, quite right, Mawlana," said the driver.

"You'll never hear that from any other sheikh. That interpretation is especially for you," said Hatem. "Exclusive," he added, using the English word.

"But, you know, the morning in Egypt now smells really bad," he went on.

They laughed together.

Although they were driving over the flyovers along the ring road that bypasses the congested center of Cairo, the roads were all clogged with the drudges for whom the morning symbolized hard work and the pursuit of a livelihood.

"People look really miserable in those crowded buses," said Hatem, "and even in the work buses and school minibuses with the crazy drivers, even if there are lots of fancy cars and cell phones and CD players in the cars. The misery embarrasses me, and it offends me too."

The driver didn't fully understand, but he was about to say something anyway. Hatem jumped in with a direct question.

"Do you think the people you work for understand the country and know how people suffer?" he asked.

The driver was taken aback. But, undaunted, he answered feebly, "Mawlana, those people like you very much."

Hatem laughed, humoring the driver's timidity.

"You mean I should shut up and not talk about such things," he said.

"No. Sorry."

"Sorry why? It's me that should be saying sorry. You think there's a sheikh under this turban!"

Now the driver was completely confused, and Hatem laughed again.

"You must be sitting there wondering whether the sheikh overdid it last night!"

The driver laughed and decided to take Hatem's remarks as a joke.

"Safely arrived, thank God," he said solemnly.

Hatem was surprised to find that the car had stopped outside an old building in Heliopolis. He had imagined the meeting would take place in a villa or mansion in some compound out of town, but here he was getting in the elevator in a building—an architectural gem with a hall that evoked the glories of the 1940s—flanked by a couple of bodyguards who smiled in silence. The lift stopped and the door opened into a large reception room. The guards left him and went down again, while Hatem was met by a woman in a smart gown and a scarf wrapped elegantly over her head. She welcomed him admiringly, delighted to meet a sheikh she had seen on television.

"I'm really pleased to see you, Mawlana," she said. "I'm a big fan of your lessons, and your learning. I watch all your programs."

"God preserve you. Thank you very much," he answered. He gathered that she worked in this vast, imposing household.

She led him from one room to another through an apartment that seemed to be endless. It was divided into several sitting rooms and reception rooms that suggested refined taste and costly old-fashioned splendor, with none of the frigidity or vulgar opulence of twenty-first-century design.

"What would you like to drink, Mawlana? Coffee, or tea with honey?"

"Why tea with honey in particular?" asked Hatem.

She smiled in confusion and said, "How about tea with milk, or anise, or Turkish coffee?"

"I like that coffee called 'Sultan Selim the First.' Make it Turkish, but authentic Istanbul-style, please."

She laughed and was still laughing when the president's son came in. "That's wonderful, you've made Fawzia laugh!" he said.

Fawzia stopped laughing immediately.

"Good morning, sir," said Hatem, standing up.

The president's son shook his hand and welcomed him.

"Delighted you could come, Sheikh Hatem. Please have a seat, please."

They sat down together.

The president's son gestured to Fawzia. "Have you asked the sheikh what he'd like to drink?"

"Coffee," she said.

"Fine, make that two," he said.

All Hatem's attempts to stop his courage from flagging in the face of this moment were a complete failure. He sat there helpless, in pieces, awaiting the inevitable surprise.

"Look, Mawlana, I don't need to explain that this is a serious matter, or point out the need for absolute discretion."

"No, there's no need to explain, sir," said Hatem.

"Were you ever in the army, Sheikh Hatem?"

"No, sir, but if you want me to join, I'll do so right away," answered Hatem.

Fawzia smiled, until the president's son looked at her disapprovingly, suggesting he was not in the mood for jokes. But then he smiled too, and said: "Okay, just consider it a military secret."

"As you say, sir."

A moment later, a woman in her late thirties appeared, wearing a dress that was simple, elegant, and modest. Her face was without make-up, and joyless. Her dignified beauty, though obvious, was swathed in a sadness that almost smothered it.

Hatem stood up to welcome her as the president's son introduced her. "Farida, my wife," he said.

"Good morning, Madam. It's an honor to meet you."

She sat down quietly, in a way that suggested a woman who was well brought up.

It seemed to be time for serious talk, especially as the coffee had arrived and Fawzia had put it on the table between them. The son stood up and brought the sheikh a cup in a gesture that put Hatem at ease because it struck him as unusually respectful.

"Sheikh Hatem, did you know that my wife is the daughter of Ahmed Kamel Mansour?" asked the president's son.

The name rang in his ears. How could he not know? Mansour was the richest of the rich in Egypt, in fact number twelve on the list of the richest people in the world, or so he had read and heard.

"I married Farida more than ten years ago," he continued, "and we have been blessed with twin daughters, Mariam and Reem."

"May God protect them, sir, and preserve them for you, Madam," said Hatem.

"My wife will tell you the rest of the story."

As soon as she started speaking, Hatem knew that the problem had something to do with her.

"My father brought us up to have principles and to be religious," she said in a frail voice, "and in our family religious didn't mean either narrow-minded or liberal and free of all responsibility. In fact Father was busy all the time and perhaps because he married late, he spoiled us slightly more than usual, but we all grew up with traditional values. I'm the eldest and then there's my sister Nourhan, who's married to Dr. Fathi el-Samadi. I think you know of him. He's the chairman of a bank."

Hatem nodded. He was well aware of him and knew that the bank was owned by Mansour.

"The last child was my brother Hassan. Mother had him after she'd had problems getting pregnant for some time, and the gap between me and him is about fifteen years. Of course you can imagine how happy a father of over fifty would be to have a newborn son after all those problems, and so he spoiled him even more than he spoiled us. Also, Hassan brought Father good luck. His businesses expanded and he went international, as you've no doubt read and heard, with oil fields, gas companies, banks, and contracting work, and he wanted his son to work with him and learn from him and manage all his businesses."

Hatem was interested in the story but it was hard for him to steady his nerves because of the host of questions he had about why they had invited him and what this was all about. He tried to maintain his composure by smiling incessantly, but this was bound to come to an end as soon as Farida finished speaking.

"The problem is that Hassan's recently started to have some strange ideas," she said.

Hatem sighed. Finally he understood.

"Hmm, he's become a religious extremist?" he proffered.

She looked away and tears began to well in the corners of her eyes, while her husband squirmed in his seat in discomfort. She raised her head and looked at Sheikh Hatem with doleful eyes. "No," she said. "He's converted to Christianity."

Hatem almost wet himself.

He had been distracted and had missed much of what Farida had said and the details her husband had added by way of explanation. They could tell what a shock it was by the way Hatem sat there immobile, staring at the design in the carpet under his feet. Now Hatem had to pick up the pieces of his nervous system, which lay scattered on the ground, on the sofa, and under the table, and reconnect the wires to the control board in his brain. Disaster has struck, Hatem, and it's struck you, not because of the mission that within minutes you will obviously be asked to carry out, and not because it's very possible that you will fail in that mission, but simply because you've been told. Just knowing means there's a dagger at your throat. But the question that pounded the loudest in Hatem's head was "Why me?"

When Hatem recovered from the shock, Farida was still speaking.

"He's always been very well-behaved and obedient and loving to his mother and father. Although he was pampered and spoiled of course from childhood, till recently he had never behaved in a way that was worrying. He had a generous allowance and plenty of credit cards. But even so he didn't party or drink too much, just the usual fun stuff you'd expect from his generation, and I don't think he ever smoked hashish or marijuana in his life. He studied business at the American University in Cairo after spending a year in England. He didn't feel at home in England although he had a Western education and spoke the language well and had friends there. He felt horribly homesick in England and went into a depression. So he came back early and didn't finish his course there. It never occurred to us to ask why a kid who spoke English fluently and was brought up in a very Western culture wasn't able to adapt to living in England. Then the psychiatrist told us just very recently that maybe he missed the sense of protection, being pampered, and the support that made him feel safe, so he got depressed. Besides, Mother and Father couldn't bear him being so far away, so he came back and finished at the American University. He graduated a year ago and worked for a while in one of Father's companies. Then some very strange things began to happen and he started behaving in a way quite different from the Hassan we knew."

"Are you following the story, Sheikh Hatem?" the president's son interjected.

Hatem nodded. "Absolutely," he said firmly. "I'm all ears."

The president's son turned to his wife and signaled that she should continue.

"I can't claim we've ever been a family that reads about religion or pays much attention to the details, just what you learn at school or see on television," she said.

"Do you know Sheikh Mohamed el-Ghazali?" Hatem suddenly asked. Even he didn't know why he had asked the question, so there was no reason why Farida and her husband should know. "I mean, have you read any of his writings or heard of him or ever seen him on television?" Hatem continued.

"I remember from childhood there was a very big library in the house and I think it had all the religious books, but none of us ever read any of them and I never saw Father or Mother reading one of them either. But of course we had newspapers and magazines in the house and Father was very interested in them and would comment on them in our presence, even though we didn't really pay attention and he didn't ask us to be interested in them. Our life was very full and we didn't feel we were missing anything and despite all the many changes the country's been through—Islamic groups, the spread of the hijab, and all the other things you know about—Father never worried that we might think about that kind of religion. He isn't religious himself. I've never seen him praying, for example, or going to Friday prayers, but he's very much a believer and always talks about God protecting him and helping him make the right decisions, with very many business problems. He used to say that God was standing by him. And he would never talk to us about so and so being a Muslim or a Christian or a Jew. Yet Hassan never had Christian friends despite the English-language schools and the American University. I just realized now that he didn't have any Christian friends from elementary school to the time he graduated, or any girlfriends. Even the foreigners he knew, he only knew them superficially, and they weren't interested in religion so I don't know if they were Christian or not. Oh yes, one of them was Buddhist, I'm sure. He met him in England and he was from India perhaps."

Her husband stepped in, perhaps from a sense that it was time to speed up the process. "Someone who works at the bank with my father-in-law noticed something very strange about Hassan's account. There's a monthly review of the charges on his Visa card, showing how much he spent where and when. The guy told his boss but the boss dismissed it, saying he didn't want problems. The next month the guy asked to meet my father-in-law, but he was busy and the meeting was delayed two or three weeks." He paused a moment. "Tell the story, Farida," he added.

"Suddenly we found Hassan had put a statue of the Virgin in his room," she said. "It took Mother a while to notice, and it didn't worry her. It was a beautiful, artistic statue. No problem. After a while she found many things changing or mysteriously appearing. He was playing hymns in the house, and pictures of Jesus were going up in his room. Of course she hid all this from us and didn't know what to do."

"She didn't understand what was happening," the president's son added.

"Mother was afraid to ask him or confront him," Farida continued. "She told Father, and of course my father travels a lot and is very busy. He was away at the time and he told her not to say a word till he got back. She started going into Hassan's room and ignoring the changes, such as the new Coptic icons and the fact that Hassan was sitting at the computer for hours on end. Then he let his hair grow to his shoulders and she concluded he was trying to look like Christ in the icons."

"My father-in-law had a call from his office saying that the guy at the bank wanted to discuss something important with him to do with his son," the president's son continued. "When he heard it was about Hassan, he told the guy to go to the airport and take my father-in-law's private plane that he was sending to Cairo to pick him up. I think he was in Dubai on business at the time. He came back on the plane after the guy at the bank told him that Hassan had written checks worth 160,000 dollars, all of them to a Coptic charity organization or another Christian organization based in Cyprus, and I think it was fourteen or sixteen thousand pounds on his Visa card to buy books from two church bookshops in Egypt.

"My father-in-law called Hassan from the plane and asked him to get ready and come to the airport to fly to Gouna with him. Hassan felt something was up and as soon as he'd said hello to his father and was sitting next to him on the plane he said he hated Islam and wanted to become a Christian. My father-in-law said there wasn't any point in the trip then and he told the pilot to turn around and land in Cairo. He went home with him in the car and didn't say anything, and as soon as he was home he told Hassan's mother. She asked for a glass of water and collapsed speechless. She had a stroke. That was about a year ago."

"She went for treatment in London," Farida continued. "Thankfully she recovered and has only a few problems moving, but she's much better thanks to the physiotherapy. Hassan was a little shaken by his mother's illness. My father couldn't take it and he went in and cut up Hassan's pictures and threw out the books, and broke the statues and the icons. As I told you, Your Grace, we've never been religious, either in the wider sense or the narrow sense, but when this happened with Hassan it was a big shock. Father built six mosques in five months, for example, and donated a million pounds to an Azhar institute in my grandfather's village, and my mother started wearing the hijab. My sister also took up the hijab and we started taking an interest in the religious programs on television. That's how we saw your programs, and my mother took you to heart because of your simple style and your tolerance and the modern way you speak. But Hassan became even more defiant, even though none of us had said anything to him about it since Mother collapsed in front of him. On the first day of last Ramadan—like all Egyptian households the whole family usually gathers for the first iftar—we were all invited to the presidential palace and, imagine, he stood up before the call to prayer at sunset and told us he'd decided to change his name and call himself Boutros!"

"Then two things happened," said the president's son. "I asked State Security to intervene and I asked for any information they had on the boy's movements, who he'd been meeting and who his friends were and everything to do with this conversion to Christianity. Of course there was one thing that had to be absolutely clear: that not a word on the subject should get out, because that would seriously alarm public opinion. It could create terrible unrest in the country if it was known my wife's brother was an apostate from Islam and a convert to Christianity. It would destroy all the good things we're doing in the country. Of course you know we're not against Christianity or fanatical, and we really do believe in equal citizenship for everyone. Religion is a matter between the individual and God while the country belongs to everyone. But this business is sensitive and dangerous and we can't just let it pass. Besides, people in the West and the racists will jump on the subject and make a big deal out of it, and the extremists and the terrorists, if they get wind of the story, they'll set fire not just to us but to the whole of Egypt. The second thing I said is we have to find a solution. If he's ill, we'll have him treated. If he's been tricked, we'll understand, and if he's been induced in some way we'll put an end to that. In fact the kid's been very open to any attempt to discuss things with him, and that was a surprise. He had a session with a very big psychiatrist—you must know him, Muhyiddin Kamel—and he's also had plenty of time with Sheikh Fathi el-Maadawi."

Oh my God, adult breastfeeding, thought Hatem. That sheikh will declare Hassan an infidel, and his mother too into the bargain!

"Of course, a great scholar that we all respect," was what he actually said.

"He failed abysmally," said Farida. "Hassan hated him and attacked him and almost insulted him. The sheikh thought Hassan was obviously bewitched or possessed by some demon—something retarded like that."

What she said set off major alarm bells for Hatem, warning him that he was destined for hell on earth if he failed with the boy. These people had taken Fathi's failure lightly because he was their sheikh, their man, whereas it would be no great loss to them if Hatem met a sticky end. He tried to move away from the subject of Sheikh Fathi. "What did State Security say?" he asked.

"They almost made it into an international crisis," Farida continued. "They arrested some groups they accused of trying to convert people to Christianity and they launched a security campaign. They gave the media instructions to start newspaper campaigns and to do special episodes on the issue on the television programs. It got to the stage where the country was in ferment and it all came very close to backfiring in our faces, at home and abroad. Maybe you yourself spoke on the subject in one of your programs, but there wasn't a scrap of information about what had happened to Hassan, even after they tracked down all the websites he'd viewed on the Internet. It turned out that for about eleven months he'd been spending many hours a day in Paltalk chatrooms and inter-religious discussion groups. We confiscated his computer and found he had downloaded hundreds of books and videos on the persecution of Christians and Christianity and the Gospels, and of course terrible attacks on Islam. But even so we didn't find a single name we could confront him with or that would help us understand what had happened."

"And the psychiatrist?"

"There were three of them in the end and they all said he didn't have a mental illness or nervous condition, and he was completely normal except for a little depression, which couldn't have led to this dramatic change."

Unconsciously Farida assumed a pleading tone, as if to win Hatem's sympathy. "We're in deep trouble," she said. "He's decided to apply to the courts to recognize his conversion and change his religion on his ID card," she said.

"Of course we won't let him," her husband added firmly. "And we won't allow any department in the country to approve his request. We won't let anyone find out in the first place. But the problem is the boy's very obstinate and he's become obsessed with the idea. We face several possible disasters. He might cause a world-wide scandal, and he's capable of that unless we lock him up in an isolated cell. Or something might be leaked by the organizations or people who converted him to Christianity. That would threaten a family that represents the very essence of Egypt and it would threaten the security of the whole country. Of course we couldn't deny it because the boy would dismiss the denial and play the persecuted Christ figure. Or he could go and live abroad in America or Europe, even under his new Christian name, but that option is fraught with the danger that he might go crazy in public or stab the country in the back, and that would be exploited by people who hate the country or have grudges against it. On top of all that, there's the trouble and anguish he's caused his family. There are only two solutions: either someone persuades him to revert to Islam or else, well, I'd rather not discuss that now.

"So we're placing our hope in you," he added.

Hatem didn't have it in him to flatter him by thanking him for his precious confidence, because he knew it was a deadly trap. Instead he said a silent prayer to God.

"Of course you're going to ask why we chose you," said Farida.

The words 'we chose you' had a comical effect. He sang them to himself: we chose you, we chose you, then thought to himself, "Because of my lousy luck."

"Mother was watching your program on television and you were answering a question from a viewer," Farida continued. "And while she was concentrating on what you said she realized Hassan was standing behind a screen in the sitting room listening to you with interest. She noticed you made an impact on him and in fact it was she and Father who suggested you sit down with Hassan in the hope that through you God might give him guidance."

They agreed on many of the details and the president's son took him to the lift to say goodbye. "You spoke about another solution you didn't want to talk about right now," Hatem whispered, "apart from me sitting down with Hassan. What might that be?"

"His father's from the south," the man replied calmly. "Don't be deceived by appearances. In the end he has south Egyptian blood in his veins, and the south Egyptian solution here is obvious. When someone brings shame on you, what do you do to him?"

"What do you do?" Hatem replied, making no attempt to hide the fact that he was only pretending to be stupid.

As Hatem saw it, the arrangements for his first encounter with Hassan were important and delicate. If he went to see Hassan at home, the boy would immediately feel that he was just another sheikh hired by his father or his sister's husband who had come crawling in on orders from his masters. The truth was, Hassan had already seen a considerable number of sheikhs who drooled over his father's wealth or his brother-in-law's influence. When they stopped acting like men of religion, they lost their prestige and credibility in the eyes of the boy. Hatem was seriously worried what might happen if he clashed with the boy in a setting he hadn't chosen, where he couldn't cut and run if necessary. It would also be dangerous if the boy came to visit Hatem. The boy might refuse to come and then they might force him, which could aggravate his hostility and stubbornness, of which he had plenty already, judging by what Hatem had heard. Or Hassan might decide that Hatem's house in the affluent suburbs didn't meet his expectations in some way, and that would then discredit Hatem, if Hassan gave him any credit in the first place. Then there was the question of what strategy he should adopt in the first encounter, which, if it succeeded, which it had to, would lead to other meetings. How should he begin? How should he proceed? When should he shut up and when should he act tough? When should he raise his fist and when should he smile? Hatem could think of nothing else on the two evenings after that damned meeting with the president's son and his wife. He went through the motions of his television programs: answering questions, handing out fatwas, telling stories from history and sayings of the Prophet. But he was like someone driving a car and watching the road while his mind was elsewhere, focused wholly on the meeting with Hassan.

He knew it would be a tough test and a massive headache. He would have to try out unfamiliar arguments in a debate with a young man who was saying goodbye to his old religion and moving on to another religion. Such people were often hostile toward their old religion and ecstatic about their new religion. Besides, he would be arguing with a young man and not a scholar who had already staked a claim in the world of ideas and religious law, and he sometimes found it harder to answer people who were ignorant and enthusiastic than to answer eagle-eyed scholars. On top of that, Hassan was related to powerful and influential people who could ruin him or have him thrown into a dungeon if he didn't find a way to make Hassan change his mind or if he inadvertently let out the secret of their hidden shame. He had no previous experience with such an assignment and he couldn't consult anyone, so he decided to put his trust in God and go into battle on the principle that he would have no one to back him up and no way to escape. He would say what he really believed without worrying about something he could do nothing about, even if he was worried. He decided that when he sat down with Hassan, or Boutros as he liked to call himself after Christ had shown him the light, as he put it, he wouldn't be afraid of the influence of Hassan's family, or the anger of State Security, or rival sheikhs, or the conditions set by his producers, or the demands of sponsor companies, or the instructions of the director or the rules for lighting or for cutting for a break. He decided to revert to the self he had lost and that he longed to be in his wildest dreams. He would go into the ring freely to ensure through his freedom—what a painful paradox—that he retained his celebrity status and his income.

Hatem sat waiting for Hassan at a table on the roof of one of the hotels overlooking a busy square. Down below he could see the vehicles and the pedestrians moving around—their paths crossing and diverging, similar and different, meeting and separating and moving in parallel or as opposites. It reminded him that we are just objects and that the world is too big for our thoughts to encompass. Hatem's heart skipped a beat when he saw Hassan. He looked about twenty-three, with a baby face. He reminded Hatem of his own son, and Hatem shuddered, stung by the thought of his son making him sit through a session like this or any other horrendous ordeal of this kind.

He thought about how he would feel if God or fate decided to test him by using his son against him. His son was the keystone in his psychological structure. Without him he would fall apart. God the Omniscient knows our weaknesses and might use them against us, he thought. It's bad enough to be ill or poor or to have one's feelings hurt, but if one's child plays a part in it, the effect can be devastating. And it's even worse when the child brings disaster, if you discover that he's a drug addict or gay or a thief, or maybe a murderer, or he might floor you by changing his religion. Whatever you are and whatever you imagined that you were, that is a moment you hope never to experience.

Hatem had called Hassan on the phone. When Hassan answered he said, "How are you? This is Hatem el-Shenawi."

"Pleased to hear from you," Hassan answered politely.

"I told your sister Farida that I'd like to see you and I told her you would agree."

"And how did you know I'd agree?" asked Hassan.

"I didn't, but you're a bold man. Someone who says what you say and does what you do and handles what you handle wouldn't be worried about meeting a sheikh who wants to see him. On the contrary he'd be eager to meet him."

Hassan liked what Hatem said, even if it was melodramatic and exploited his inclination to be defiant. "Of course, it would be an honor," he said.

So there they were, in a place that Hatem had chosen because it offered space and a view of the people in the square, as if he wanted to recruit them to his side against Hassan. It was also a place where it was extremely improbable that any bugging devices would be installed, because he was worried that the boy's family, with means not available to anyone else, would be monitoring him and Hassan, and he didn't want anyone to be able to hold anything he might say against him. Although he knew that some sophisticated devices could pick up voices from a distance and of course take pictures from even further distances, he felt comfortable sitting in this place, which even smelled reassuring.

"I almost died laughing when they told me what you did to Sheikh Fathi," Hatem said.

Hassan was surprised. "What did they say exactly?" he asked.

"No, please, you tell me. I'm dying to hear. I'd like to have the pleasure of hearing from you what happened."

Hassan laughed. "It was nothing," he said. "He sat down with me and it was as if you'd turned the television on or started playing a recording, something you've heard again and again. He was hostile and pathetic and he thought he was sitting opposite an idiot. And imagine, he was shaking. His fingers were shaking."

"Of course he was shaking. That sheikh's a creation of your sister's father-in-law and the regime you know from home, Hassan or Boutros or whatever you like to be called," said Hatem, deliberately joking and clearly slipping in the reference to reinforce Hassan's uncertainty and to suggest that his own attitude toward Hassan's conversion was not as decisive as Hassan might imagine. He waited for a reaction but all he saw was a clever smile.

"The sheikh was worried about his job," Hatem continued, "and the several thousand pounds a month he gets in bonuses and expenses and salaries. Besides, official approval depends on worldly things and he knew that if you turned against him, or if he failed with you, your family might give him a tough time and damage his career."

"I've known him for ages, ever since I was a kid," said Hassan. "I remember when he used to come to our house. The old duffer would act like he was Sheikh al-Islam. He'd sit and cozy up to my father and once he took a beach house on the north coast for his son as a bribe. Is that being religious?"

"That sheikh has little to do with religion," said Hatem.

"Yes, but isn't he the one who gives fatwas that people follow blindly and tells them what's right and what's wrong?" asked Hassan.

"Of course not. Good heavens! Look, Hassan, the first thing you need to learn when you're talking about religion is to make a distinction between religion and men of religion."

"Really?" said Hassan.

"Absolutely, a hundred percent."

The kid was smart, but still young and reckless.

"What kind of religion is it that makes its sheikhs slaves to worldly things, obsessed with money, hypocritical and cowardly?"

"I told you there's a massive difference between religion and men of religion, and that's true of any religion," said Hatem. "Take Islam as well as Christianity. I mean, okay, so you thought that sheikh was a total son of a bitch, with every possible vice, but on your family's honor, and they're good people, I bet you then went to Coptic men of religion, our brothers the priests. Did you find them to be brave, heroic, knights in shining armor? Before you say anything, I've found them just as cowardly as the sheikhs. If I went up to any pastor or priest in church or in the cathedral and told him, 'I want to convert to Christianity, Father,' he'd look around and be evasive and he might agree to risk the disaster of accepting the conversion of a Muslim. But if he knew that you're so-and-so, the son of such-and-such, and who your father's son-in-law is and who your sister's married to, then he'd start talking to you about the wonders of Islam as if he were Sheikh al-Islam himself. Right? Or are you going to deny it?"

"No, you're right. I've often been to the church in Heliopolis and I never said who I was. And of course I've spoken with people on the Internet and agreed to meet once or twice and I was very happy and felt I had found my way, but as soon as the priest found out who I really was he ran away from me. Everyone began to keep their distance so I started sending them messages complaining, then attacking them and accusing them of abandoning Christ and being cowards. But this drove me to continue on the path of light, and for me it was proof that Christianity and Christians are persecuted in this country. They're so frightened that they can't speak out against the injustices."

Hatem looked at Hassan's childlike face. He seemed relieved at the opportunity to express his suppressed emotions freely.

"I sympathize with the Copts' demands," said Hatem. "But for some reason I don't sympathize with the Copts themselves. Is that because I'm a fanatic or an extremist? I don't think so. But the truth is I don't have it in me to sympathize with a group of people who get knocked about while they feel sorry for themselves and act the persecuted victim. But Christianity isn't just the Copts. The world has billions of Christians and only six or eight million Copts. Christianity itself isn't persecuted anywhere in the world, not even in Egypt. The Christians are the lords and masters of the world, and they are destroying it. They don't act for a moment on the basis of Christ's teachings, and they're not persecuted. On the contrary, they pretty much persecute the whole world, not because they're Christians but because they're rich imperialist countries that rule the world according to their interests. In Egypt it may be the Copts rather than Christianity that is persecuted. There are the weak, poor Copts who look to the church for protection and who believe in the church, and there are the rich Copts, some of whom are corrupt and who are part of the corrupt autocratic class, rather like your father and his son-in-law and the group of rich people who fill your mansion for parties. The country's divided into rich and poor, corrupt people and honest people, not Muslims and Christians, but to make sure that the poor of both communities wallow in the mud and never get out, it makes sense to set them against each other, so that the Muslims treat the Christians as infidels who must convert to Islam, and the Christians treat the Muslims as infidels who are racist oppressors."

"What you say is politics, not religion," Hassan replied.

"Look, my boy, the day Christianity left Bethlehem it became politics, and the night the Prophet Muhammad died Islam became politics. It's idiots like you that we men of religion make fun of, in both religions. We delude them into thinking that it's about religion, but the whole story is politics, my dear."

133

"I'm not convinced," said Hassan, as if to end the discussion.

"Well, be not convinced then," said Hatem, as if relieved of a burden.

Hassan was appalled by what he'd heard. Just at that moment the waiter was taking away the juices and putting in their place a cup of espresso for him and the glass of tea that Hatem had ordered. Hassan glared at the waiter as if to tell him to clear off, and Hatem understood from the gesture that the boy was still unmoved, protected by his father's wealth and the clout of his brother-in-law. Hatem decided to strike.

"Do you think," he said, "that at the age of twenty-three you've learned all there is to know about this world and the next, that you've achieved all there is to achieve, that with your vast intellect and your genius insight you've understood the facts of Islam and the essence of Christianity? That arrogance is what Christ fought against, if I've understood his teachings correctly. If you want to know about Christianity, I'll tell you, or do you really think I'm just a television sheikh, with more to come after the break?"

The conversation was getting heated—all the more reason for Hassan to jump in.

"You'll make out that you believe in Christ and love Him and you'll say the usual nonsense about Muslims being required to believe in Christ and in all the prophets, and that the people Muslims like most are the Christians because they have priests and monks. But that's schizophrenic talk. You call them friends but you treat them as dhimmis and second-class citizens.[2] You say Christ spoke in the name of God but then you say Christians are infidels and will go to hell."

Hatem smiled.

"You know what? You're right," he whispered with a sigh.

Then Hatem sprang to his feet excitedly. Anyone who knew Hatem would have known he was acting, but Hassan didn't know him, so he assumed the man was angry and was leaving.

"I'll pay the bill and we'll see each other soon, God willing," Hatem said, adding to Hassan's surprise.

Maybe he wanted to arouse Hassan's curiosity, or give him the impression he had outargued a sheikh. Hatem himself didn't know the real reason why he had stood up and stormed off in this manner, but he recalled the scene later and said he may have been imitating the angry outbursts that musicians tried in negotiations—something he remembered from playing the lute in the old days before he played the cleric.

Twenty-four hours after the first meeting, Hatem called Hassan on his cell phone. He noted that Hassan picked up after a single ring.

"Are you into satellite channels or do you just make do with your laptop?" Hatem asked.

Hatem had succeeded in making Hassan confused and curious to find out what he was planning, so he answered straight out.

"I have a television in front of me," he said.

"Excellent, by the life of Jesus, watch the program that's going on air in five minutes. The first ten minutes are all about you. Concentrate and then we can meet, please," Hatem said.

He hung up. Hassan closed the pages he was reading online and turned the television on. He had to fiddle around with the numbers on the remote for a while because he didn't know exactly what channel it would be on. But that didn't work so he decided to seek help. He opened the door of his room to find his mother with some of her friends chatting about something silly and banal. He decided not to ask her, so he opened a window and called for the servant to come quickly. The servant appeared, dressed in the traditional costume that the household strictly insisted be worn to maintain appearances. "Do you know which channel Sheikh Hatem el-Shenawi's program is on?" Hassan asked him.

Surprised, the servant picked up the remote control and switched to the right channel. Hatem had already begun.

Hassan thanked him and pushed him in the back to get him out of the room so he wouldn't hear what Hatem said in the program.

Hatem was sitting in the same position as in the hotel, but he was wearing his turban and smiling earnestly, looking straight into the lens as if he were addressing Hassan directly. "My younger brother, Hassan Abu Ali, was asking me about contradictions in the Islamic religion, or what he thinks are contradictions," Hatem was saying. "Of course that expression will shock and upset some viewers, who might think it rather harsh."

The camera zoomed in on Hatem's face. "Before anyone gets upset, I'd like to say that our religion is strong and resilient, and so we shouldn't be afraid of questions and skepticism that might seem insensitive. Do you know why? Because our Prophet, peace and God's blessings be upon him, taught us that. This might not please Hassan. Okay, let's go and tell Hassan Abu Ali that we have more reason to have doubts than Abraham. Yes, the prophet Abraham doubted, yes, the father of all prophets doubted the power of God and maybe also the existence of God, but on top of all that the Prophet tells us we should be skeptical, even more than the prophet Abraham. Look at the saying of the Prophet narrated by Abu Hureira in Bukhari's collection of hadiths, number 4,537. In it the Prophet says, 'We are more entitled to be skeptical than Abraham because he said, "O Lord, show me how You bring the dead back to life." The Lord said, "Have you not believed?" He said, "Oh yes I have, but just for my peace of mind."'

"You'll find another version of the story with another number in the same hadith collection, number 3,372, and it says, 'The Prophet of God, peace and God's blessings be upon Him, said, "We are more entitled than Abraham to be skeptical because he said, 'O Lord, show me how You bring the dead back to life.' The Lord said, 'Have you not believed?' He said, 'Oh yes I have, but just for my peace of mind.' May

God have mercy on Lot. Certainly he wanted to lean on a powerful support. If I were to stay in prison as long as Joseph did, I would have accepted the offer of freedom.'"

"What does this hadith mean, Hassan? I know you can hear and see me now, unless you have a power cut at your place, and that's unlikely, or unless the satellite receiver is frozen, and that's even less likely. So what does it mean? It means the Prophet is patting us on the back and saying, 'Don't worry if you happen to have doubts or if some devil comes and whispers doubts in your ear or if your faith is shaken to the point of atheism, don't be too hard on yourselves, your ancestor Abraham had doubts, even Abraham wanted reassurance and wanted to be convinced that God exists and is omnipotent and could really bring the dead back to life and that there's resurrection and a Day of Judgment. Abraham had doubts and he addressed God in His heavens.' So how about poor humble mortals like us? In fact Hassan isn't poor at all. He's probably a millionaire, but there's no reason to be envious. What matters is that the Prophet himself, despite his unique status, says, 'If I were to stay in prison as long as Joseph did, I would have accepted the offer of freedom.' In other words, he might have cracked. Of course the Prophet was the target of assassination attempts and raids and he was besieged by the Meccan troops at Uhud and people tried to tempt him, and all this was harder to bear than imprisonment for Joseph, but he didn't compromise. But here he is, opening the gate of Mercy for us, offering us the chance to overcome our misgivings and rest assured that God will not judge us by what we think, but by what we do.

"Of course, Hassan, you haven't understood any of this! You're sitting there wondering when Sheikh Hatem will cut for a break. Okay, let's meet again after the break."

When the adverts started, Hassan realized that Sheikh Hatem really liked him, and he also realized that he would defeat Hatem.

When morning came, Hassan found a message from Hatem on his phone. "Do your homework properly and come meet me," it said.

"Where?" Hassan quickly replied.

He didn't get an answer for three hours and even thought of calling Hatem. Then he reconsidered and thought of breaking off contact with him. Then he reconsidered again, and when he went back to sleep, another message arrived. "In any fish restaurant where you can afford to take me to lunch," it said.

At first sight he knew that Dr. Muhyi, the psychiatrist who had seen Hassan, had lied to Hassan's family or was afraid to tell them the truth, or else they had misled Hatem, because Hassan did indeed have problems.

"Of course he does," Muhyi, speaking clearly, softly, and firmly, told Hatem in the garden of Hatem's villa.

Hatem had contacted him after getting his number from the people who produced his programs. He had had several chance encounters with Muhyi in the corridors at the studios and had exchanged the usual pleasantries. The phone conversation didn't last long. When Muhyi realized it was about Hassan, they both had visions of the president's powerful son and decided that meeting face to face would be safer and give them more space. They discovered they lived in nearby compounds, so Muyhi came to visit in the evening before going off to his clinic. They sat down together to have tea in the garden. They both knew how important it was that the other should understand their role in the affair.

"Psychological problems?" Hatem asked.

"Yes, psychological. What else would you expect from the son of one of the richest men in the world and a relative of the people who rule the country?"

"So it's his identity and background that are the key to his problems."

"See how complicated the human psyche is," said the doctor.

"You tell me."

"Well, I could tell you, though it's not proper for me to say anything, out of respect for the patient's privacy."

"No, don't get me wrong, doctor. I asked if he had problems and you said yes. But you didn't say he was ill. Is he ill or does he just have problems?"

"I'm not sure quite what you mean."

"Someone who's ill is ill, doctor. They have depression. They have obsessive delusions. They have psychotic schizophrenia. But someone who has problems, that would apply to you or me, my wife or your wife."

Muhyi laughed and his age showed beneath his hair that was dyed pitch black. "You've turned out to be quite the psychologist, Mawlana."

"Did I tell you, doctor, that I used to be a lutist? You know what a lutist is? It's someone who plays the lute at parties. That was when I was still pretty much a child, and at the same time I was a preacher and Quran reader at funerals. Anyone who has experiences like that deserves a doctorate in psychology, an honorary doctorate from the university of lousy life."

Muhyi laughed. "Of course the kid's suffering from severe emotional deprivation," he said. "And alienation from his family and community. On top of that he has a lively conscience somehow or other, and he's aware of the corruption and abuse of influence that surrounds him. I think this business of changing his religion is part of a psychological protest against society, but the kid's very serious about becoming Christian. He's studied hard and what he says about Islam is really bad and offensive."

As they said goodbye at the door, Hatem said, "To be honest, doctor, Islam won't be upset by the offensive things he says about it or even by his decision to quit Islam, but I feel sorry for the kid leaving Islam and turning to Christianity because he won't have done anything at all. The Ahmed who makes the pilgrimage to Mecca is just like the Ahmed who makes the pilgrimage to Jerusalem."

"You're joking of course, Mawlana."

Hatem bowed his head. "These days the people who hear jokes are sometimes more frightened of the jokes than the people who make them," he said.

Hassan came primed and defiant. He had a chain round his neck with a cross hanging on his chest, and wore a shirt with the words 'I Love Jesus' written in English. The meeting was at Hatem's office in the apartment that for years he had used for dealings with producers, his program team, and for meetings. He had wanted to insulate his private house from the intrusion of the ordinary people, saints or sinners, that he met in this office, which was small but stylish and neat. He had one assistant there, Farahat, an elderly man who was hard of hearing, and Hatem saw his deafness as his only qualification for the job. Khodeiri was the young janitor in his twenties and had the run of the place. His job description was to prepare drinks and clean the office—tasks he wasn't very good at. But he was a genius when it came to getting official papers sorted out for Hatem or dealing with the bank, reminding Hatem when payments were due or producers were dragging their feet, or letting him know there were technical problems with the lighting or the focus or the camera angles in yesterday's program or in an old program that had been rebroadcast. It was Khodeiri who maintained absolute possession of Hatem's telephone. It was he who answered it, berating people who called and getting rid of people who were too persistent, and it was he who arranged appointments for journalists and set up his phone calls to other programs. After a period of induction, Khodeiri started giving callers fatwas of his own on behalf of

Hatem, though he did have the good grace to inform Hatem of the gist of his fatwas in order to put his mind at ease. He was the only person who could bark at guests if they were boring or took too long to leave. Hatem saw him as his black box: if his plane crashed they would know from Khodeiri what had caused it. He made sure that Khodeiri would keep his hands off the guest that was coming this time, and would keep the office clear of unwanted guests while he was visiting. He was yet more careful to stop Khodeiri asking questions about the strange visitor with a cross on his chest who came to the office of an eminent and well-known sheikh, and luckily Khodeiri couldn't read the English words on Hassan's shirt. Hatem thought that for Hassan to come dressed like that was childish in a way that was natural for a young man who stubbornly wanted to provoke him, so he returned the provocation by completely ignoring Hassan's clothes. Hassan sat on a comfortable chair looking out through a large window with brown plastic blinds that broke up the sunlight coming from the street. Hatem sat next to him.

"By the way, I forgot to tell you I'm an admirer of yours," Hatem said.

Amazingly Hassan thought Hatem was being serious. "Really?" he said.

"Very much so," Hatem continued. "You're brave. Leaving aside the fact that I see your conversion to Christianity as reckless and ignorant, you're defying your father, a proud man with clout and heaps of cash, and you're also defying, very rudely I might say, your brother-in-law, who holds the country between his digitus annularis and his minimus."

Hatem paused a moment. "Do you know what they are?" he asked.

"No."

"My God. You don't know what the digitus annularis is and yet you think you know about religion and religious law and theology, and you're acting like Saint Peter the Apostle?"

Hatem took Hassan's hand and looked at the palm with a smile. Hassan was puzzled. "Can you see the life line?" Hatem said, and laughed. Then he grabbed the fingers roughly one after another and folded them over in turn. This is the pollex, he said with the thumb. And this is the secundus and so on down to the ring finger and the pinky, until he finally gave Hassan his hand back.

"So tell me then, why doesn't Your Excellency like Islam?"

"Are you making fun of me?"

"God forbid! Me make fun of you! How could I?"

Hassan stood up angrily. "Listen, if you think I'm a child when I'm with you then you're mistaken and you don't know who you're talking to," he said.

Hatem, still seated, took his hand and pulled him back. "Come on, sit down," he said. "You'll scare me. As soon as someone makes you angry you immediately remember that you're your father's son and that your sister's husband is the ruler of Egypt. Calm down and speak to me like a tolerant Christian who knows the worth of humble Jesus, not like an arrogant young man rebelling against his family to prove himself and burst the bubble they live in."

What he said was tough, honest, and shocking and Hassan, taken aback, shut up. He didn't walk away or sit down. He just stood there as Hatem launched the second stage of his attack.

"If you're just a spoiled brat who thinks it's a game converting to Christianity, then I'll be happy to see the back of you. But if you really believe you're right and you want to be a Christian and you're prepared to make sacrifices for it, then sit down and talk to me."

Hatem was applying with Hassan all the lessons at which he had failed with the Rifais—taming snakes and wrapping them around his shoulders. They might bite him at any moment but the sense that his whole future faced possible disaster made him play with the snake, so that the snake would play with him, especially as it was still a young snake, not a cobra like his father or his brother-in-law. Despite his good manners and his poise Hassan was proud of himself and his family and no one dared to shout at him or even raise their voice in his presence. He was used to people being obedient and servile toward his family, so it was important for Hatem to act tough and confident in order to change the balance of power.

Hassan was still standing there immobile. When Hatem realized that Hassan was confused, he spoke more softly. "Sit down, Hassan, or Boutros, if you like. Calm down and sit down," he said.

Hassan sat down in resignation and Hatem called out, "Khodeiri, bring some green tea."

"Tell me, Hassan, have you ever fallen in love?" he asked, turning to the young man.

"Why?" Hassan answered curtly.

"Why would you fall in love or why would I ask?" Hatem asked.

"Both!" Hassan said.

"I just wanted to know what you think of women," Hatem replied.

"Why women in particular?"

Hatem laughed. "Is that the kind of question a sensible person would ask—Muslim, Christian, or someone with no religion at all? The word 'why' just doesn't arise in this context."

"Of course. Because your religion is preoccupied with women."

"That assumes Christianity is preoccupied with what? With wind power?"

"It's Islam that allows a man to have four wives."

"No, even more. It allows concubines and slave girls and *'whatever your right hand possesses,'* as the Quran says, and your left hand too. By the way, Christianity had slave girls in large quantities as well, and a pious Christian can have a whole throng of women too, but is that what upsets you about Islam?"

"It's not a matter of what upsets me or makes me happy. It's what I've read and studied," said Hassan.

"When?"

"I don't understand."

"When did you read and study? And where? Who with? Do you think that if you read a couple of books then you've understood and amen, or that if you sit on the Internet for six months opening Muslim and Christian websites then you're a professor of comparative religion?"

"You're making fun of me because you're trying to avoid facing the facts."

"No, not at all. Bring me the truth and I'll face up to it. Let's agree on one fundamental thing on this lousy day."

Hatem stood up and called Khodeiri. "Where's the green tea, Khodeiri Bey, Khodeiri Pasha, Dr. Khodeiri?"

Khodeiri came in with a tray. "Were you planting tea in Sri Lanka, then harvesting and grinding it? Is that why you've taken so long?" he said.

"No, Mawlana. I was caught up in the conversation."

"Whose conversation would that be?"

"Your conversation. It was getting really heated and it's the first time I've heard anything like it," said Khodeiri.

"Eavesdropping, Khodeiri?" Hatem said, pushing him out again. "Okay, out you get, you and anyone else who's sitting out there eavesdropping too, and go off home right away, or perhaps it would be better if we went out, Hassan."

"As I was saying," Hatem continued when they were together in the car. "The fundamental thing on this lousy day, my boy, is that I don't want you to drop the idea of converting to Christianity because I'm worried you might go to hell. The truth is, I can't guarantee you'll go to heaven if you stay Muslim and I'm not certain you'll go to hell if you become Christian, because I believe that God in His glory and His greatness has compassion for all of humanity—Muslims, Christians, Jews, atheists, Buddhists, bastards, and sons of bitches."

"But you say that religion in the eyes of God means Islam."

"No, it's not us who say that. That's in the Holy Quran. That's God personally saying it, but what exactly does He say? 'Where God is, religion is Islam.' Where who is? Where God is. That's when we go to God then, but here on earth He Himself says, *You have your religion and I have mine, Whoever wants to, let him believe, and whoever wants not to, let him not believe.* And God said about Christ, *I am setting those who follow you above those who disbelieve until the Day of Resurrection.* In the Cow chapter of the Quran, He says, *There is no compulsion in religion,* and He says, *O children of Israel, remember the blessings I have bestowed upon you and that I have given you preference over all other creatures.* And God says, *There are certainly among the People of the Book some who believe in God and in what has been revealed to you and in what was revealed to them, and who bow in humility to God. They will not sell the signs of God for miserable gain! They will receive a reward with their Lord, and God is swift in account.* And you'll find in one chapter, *They are not all alike: among the followers of earlier revelations there are upright people, who recite God's messages throughout the night, and prostrate themselves. They believe in God and the Last Day, and enjoin the doing of what is right and forbid the doing of what is wrong, and vie with one another in doing good works: and these are among the righteous.*"

Hassan shuddered. "Okay, so what do you say to the Muslims who offend us by saying that Christians are infidels?" he asked.

"Look, what are you interested in: Muslims or Islam?"

"So Muslims don't know what Islam is?"

"The truth is that many of them really don't know what Islam is. Many of them are ignorant just like you and mentally deficient. In the same way, for a considerable number of Christians, the last thing they know about is Christianity."

"Why don't you say this on television?"

"Did they tell you I was stupid? If I said that I'd be out of a job. I need to live and have some peace of mind. If your father wasn't who he is, and if your sister's husband wasn't who he is,

I would hardly give you the time of day, because I'm focused on preaching and not on scholarship, on fatwas rather than jurisprudence. I'm interested in proselytizing, not in pastoral work. Satisfied, sir, now that I've confessed to you?"

Hassan felt that Hatem was being evasive, so he kept pressing. "But *If anyone does not seek Islam as his religion, never will it be accepted of him; and in the Hereafter he will be among those who have lost*," he said.

"Accepted where? In this world all religions are welcome," Hatem replied. "In the Hereafter God is free to do as He wants. So He won't accept anything but Islam, but what will He do with the other religions? We don't know. Perhaps some religions will have privileges over other religions. In the Hereafter non-Muslims might be losers in the sense that they go to hell, or maybe losers in the sense that they don't get the privileges given to Muslims. Besides, your criticism of Islam, that it says it's the only way into heaven, is exactly what Christianity says about itself, and also Judaism. If any religion didn't monopolize heaven for itself it would have lost a rationale for trying to win over followers. But the question here is, as far as Your Excellency is concerned, and listen to the question carefully because I'm saying it at 120 kilometers an hour on the ring road: Are you now angry with Islam because it says it's the best religion? Should the Quran say Islam's really good and nice but really, if you want to be Christian, then go ahead, be a Christian, or choose some other religion, never mind? Of course promoting a religion means saying 'My religion is the best, better than the others.' Anyway, Christianity says it's the best religion, and that's its right and quite natural. In fact it says there's basically no such religion as Islam, and if you fault Islam for being arrogant and calling other people infidels, then *a fortiori* you should find fault with Christianity for being arrogant and denying the Other too."

Hatem had confused Hassan. "Shall we go somewhere and have a coffee?" he asked.

"Well, I do have some work to do and I've been sitting here with you rather reluctantly, but I agree," Hassan replied with a smile.

Hatem parked the car in a distant neighborhood on the edge of a new suburb. They went into a quiet coffee shop with furniture and a seating arrangement resembling those of Western cafes. On the walls were pictures of giant coffee cups and of coffee beans, artfully sprinkled around, that you could almost smell. Hassan was grumpy when he saw the waiters advancing toward Hatem to say hello and express their admiration. The coffee shop owner came up to greet him too and stood to have his picture taken with Hatem on his cell phone. Then everyone joined in, starting a frenzy of picture-taking. Sporadic customers hovered around Sheikh Hatem to have their pictures taken as well, with enthusiastic help from the waiters.

When he finally had his cup of tea in his hand, Hassan found a moment to spring his question. "But isn't it a major contradiction that some verses of the Quran say that Christians are infidels and others say they're believers?" he asked.

Hatem paused and looked around at the pictures. "My dear brother, look. The Quran, whether you believe it came down from heaven or you think it's the work of a genius called Muhammad ibn Abdallah, has managed to convince billions of minds across the world that it's God's book, and not Muhammad's book. And whatever you believe about its origins, don't think that either God, from somewhere higher than the seven heavens, or Muhammad, with his exceptional genius and his amazing capacity to convince people, overlooked the fact that some bright-spark genius like you would read the Quran and come across points in it and say 'Hang on, this is contradictory.' Of course it would be very easy for God, who is omniscient and omnipotent, to know there would be a way of thinking that challenges the Quran, so He should have made sure it was free of any ambiguities or contradictions or loopholes or weak points so that it could stand its ground against highly talented and incisive minds like yours, or against the people whose writings you've read in some book or on some website. Muhammad too, he must have realized that there were people who would challenge him and attack the credibility of his book, so it would be natural for him to conceal any contradictions by not dictating them or not allowing them to be written down. So we can be quite sure that what's written doesn't contain any contradictions, because God, as we believe, or Muhammad, as infidels or Islamophobes say, would be too thorough to overlook the possibility that there would be rivals who would cast doubt on it. It's inconceivable that he would say in one verse that so-and-so is nice and fine, and then go back on that and say that so-and-so is ugly and horrible in another verse. Because he would know that a million goons would come out and imagine they had caught God making a mistake, or caught out a prophet who says that this is the word of God.

"So, Hassan, I suggest you go back and read the text of the Quran with respect for the divine mind, or even the human mind that received divine inspiration, and you'll realize that He wouldn't set traps for himself that would destroy His credibility. When God says in the Omran chapter of the Quran, *And God said: O Jesus! Lo! I am gathering you and causing you to ascend unto Me, and am cleansing you of those who disbelieve and am setting those who follow you above those who disbelieve until the Day of Resurrection,* it means what it says—that those who follow Jesus are above those who don't believe, until the Day of Resurrection. The Christians aren't infidels or polytheists. Not only that, but they're above them, in other words they have a different status and a completely different value when it comes to their belief, until the Day of Resurrection, so don't tell me that first He said that Christians are believers and then went back on that and said they're infidels. No. There's no way here he could have said they're infidels in the sense of polytheists nor in the sense of deviation from

148

monotheism, because the word 'infidel' has dozens of meanings and I'm not responsible for the way people interpret the Quran. I have the same Quran and the problem is definitely in the interpretation and not in the Quran itself. People fail to get to the heart of the matter and they just make do with the surface.

"You know what? It looks like I've given you an overdose of the deep stuff and I need to lighten up."

Hassan came out of his reverie and whispered, "Please stop insulting my intelligence and treating me like an idiot who can't understand complicated things like those things you were saying just now."

Hatem stopped to greet an admirer who had waved at him as he came into the coffee shop.

"On the contrary, I have the highest respect for your intelligence and your courage," he resumed. "I'm just being frank and sharing opinions and thoughts I've never shared before with anyone on the face of the earth. In fact I feel as if you're bringing me back to learning after years of pandering to the wishes of ignorant people."

Two days passed without sight or sound of Hassan, and Hatem busied himself with his daily life. He felt that something had lifted a weight off his shoulders, and he made a deliberate effort to tell God in person that he loved Him. He went to the Rifai mosque and performed the sunset prayer, surrounded by warm welcomes from the mosque sheikhs and other people who were praying. He lavished money and sympathy on the poor and the mosque servants, then set off on foot to his father's house. His walk became a procession of people seeking fatwas on matters that suddenly occurred to them when they saw a television sheikh. They wanted to ask him whatever they could while they had the chance. People who wanted favors clung to him, telling him stories about houses about to collapse or disputes over plots of land that needed a signature from the local council or the provincial headquarters. Suddenly prescriptions would appear, listing drugs that sick people needed, and people would press job applications into his hand as if they had been carrying them around in their pockets until the right moment came. The sight of his father cheered him up. He met Hatem in front of the house and went inside, greeting people and inviting them to tea in the hall downstairs. His father sent them a young man trained to deal with the situation, who gave them juice to drink and envelopes with some money inside, took their petitions and doctors' prescriptions from them and promised to meet their needs based on instructions from the sheikh. Meanwhile Hatem had slipped off his shoes and was sitting cross-legged. He heard his cell phone ring and started. On the other end it was Khodeiri, almost shouting in alarm and demanding that he come to his office immediately.

"What's up, Khodeiri? All's well, I hope?"

"Hassan Boutros is here," Khodeiri said gruffly. "He's not acting normal and he wants you. To be honest, I'm frightened."

Sirhan the driver set off, surprised that Hatem had come back so quickly from his father's house. Insensitively, he kept asking Hatem why he was in such a hurry. Hatem was in such a state wondering what had happened that he couldn't even hear the heavy traffic. Why hadn't Hassan called him from his phone? He thought of calling the president's son or his wife Farida but he decided against it because they hadn't spoken to him since the meeting at their house and they hadn't made any effort to find out if the meetings were going well or to ask what he thought of Hassan or whether he had any hope that Hassan would change his mind about converting to Christianity. Hatem felt that the problem was less alarming than they had made it out to be at the time and thought that Hassan was confused rather than determined to convert. (In fact he thought that Hassan might not even really convert but was only using the possibility that he might to attract attention and wind them up). Now he was anxious, but without knowing why. When they arrived at the office, Sirhan persisted in asking why the sheikh was so obviously and unusually tense, but Hatem was intent on ignoring him. His mind was all a whirl, but what he saw was the last thing he expected and definitely the last thing he wanted.

He went into his office, ignoring Khodeiri's noisy interjections, and pushed the door shut behind him. He found Hassan sitting at the desk, slumped forward with his arms hanging down by his sides. He wasn't moving, didn't make a sound, and didn't look up. The scene stopped Hatem in his tracks and he completely forgot all the questions he had prepared in his mind while he was watching the cars battling it out along the highway. His appearance alone was cause for concern but what he saw next concerned him even more. Hassan took his arms out from under the desk and lifted them up. Hatem was shocked to see drops of blood dripping from under his sleeves at his wrists. Hatem sat down speechless. There were cuts in the shape of a cross gouged into the inside of Hassan's wrists. The crosses seemed to have been dripping blood for some time. Thinking disjointedly, Hatem imagined Hassan holding a sharp knife and carving the sign of the cross into his skin. A smile of gratified vengeance appeared on Hassan's lips. Hatem finally stood up, shaken by this early defeat at a time when he thought he had won an early victory. He took a square soft white towel from the drawer in the bathroom next door and brought some bottles of aftershave from the glass shelf under the bathroom mirror, and walked toward Hassan, who submissively put out his hands. Hatem took hold of them forcefully and started to clean off the blood and spray Hassan's wrists with the aftershave. It must have stung, but Hassan didn't make a sound.

"That was a really stupid thing to do, but thank God you're intelligent," said Hatem. "You didn't sink the knife deep in your arteries or else you'd have killed yourself by now, and you'd be buried in the Muslim cemetery whether you like it or not. Please, tell me, why did you do this? And why did you choose my place to visit when you're dripping blood?"

Before Hassan could answer and before Hatem knew whether he would or wouldn't answer, his cell phone rang with a ringtone that Hatem recognized. It was the last straw. Hatem pulled the phone out of his pocket, stepped out of the office and turned his back on Hassan. "Hello," he said to the caller.

"Hassan's at your place and I'm sending some people over to take him away," the caller said excitedly.

"Is everything okay?" Hatem asked.

"What! Hasn't he told you?"

"We were just about to . . ."

"It's getting more complicated."

"To tell you the truth, as far as I'm concerned, it got more complicated just five minutes ago," said Hatem.

Hatem swung around and found Hassan covered in sweat. His face turned pale and then more and more bluish as the seconds passed. He grabbed the phone from Hatem's hand. "I will not come back and I will not see you and I will go to the monastery and become a monk whatever you do!" he roared.

Hatem, thwarted and robbed of his phone, could hear the answer loud and clear. "There isn't a monastery in Egypt that will take you in, or else we'll demolish it with everyone inside. Please, Hassan, don't force me to be cruel. I don't want that, for your sister's sake."

"I'm not Hassan. I'm Boutros!" he shouted back, his voice cracked, hoarse, and tearful.

Hassan threw the telephone down and Hatem rushed to pick it up.

"If you don't mind, sir," he said. "Could you tell your people to wait a while?"

"They're in the sitting room with Khodeiri, by the way," said the voice on the phone.

"Oh, so you know Khodeiri as well, sir?"

"What?"

"Never mind. Okay, I'd just like a chance to find out what exactly's going on."

He looked over at Hassan, who was cowering in the corner on the sofa, shaking and kissing the signs of the cross on his wrists.

"Do you know about the crosses?" Hatem whispered into the phone.

"What crosses?"

"Okay, let's stay calm and speak again in an hour, please."

"Okay."

He hung up and Hatem muttered to himself as he examined the message on the screen that said the call had ended.

"Without a goodbye or a word of thanks or a 'sorry to put you to so much trouble.'" Hatem said.

He turned to address Hassan: "Those relatives of yours are completely shameless."

Hassan smiled, despite the condition he was in.

Hatem continued: "And you're shameless too, in spite of the ketchup that came out of your arm a while back. Why did you decide to come to me, intent on being that bloody Boutros? Why did you call yourself Boutros? What's wrong with George or Michael or Tom Cruise? Fine, you want to be Christian, but what's that to do with my family now? I mean, instead of having a cross stamped onto your wrist in a church or in a tattoo parlor, you've gone and bloody injured yourself. You almost killed yourself just for the sake of a cross. And instead of saying 'I'll keep away from that sheikh who's always giving me a headache and pissing me off with the stuff he says about Islam,' you come all the way to my office and almost make Khodeiri piss and shit in his pants, and now we've got the death squad sitting outside with him. So what do you want from me?"

The incident was a powerful reminder to Hatem that he was part of Hassan's struggle with himself and his family, and the fact he had come to Hatem for refuge proved that Hassan was deeply divided between rebelling against his family, and the power and influence that it represented, and rebelling against his religion, which he hardly knew and on which he blamed his own lack of purpose, his depression, and the corruption around him. These were Hatem's thoughts as he tried to analyze why Hassan was now lying calmly on the sofa asking for something to eat.

"I'm worried the people outside might have brought some food, either to poison me or to poison you," Hatem said. "So we should ask Khodeiri to eat it first, but the problem is that Khodeiri isn't a normal human being, so the poison wouldn't affect him."

Hassan laughed. "After our last discussion I felt confused," he said. "What you said worked. It shook me, not so much that I had second thoughts but enough to make me worried. I went on the Internet and there's a website called 'The Home of Christian Converts' that brings together people who've converted from Islam to Christianity in Egypt. I look at it every day, but that night I was looking for an answer to my questions. I was seeking strength, through the things they write about the flaws in Islam and the power of Christianity, to keep me going through this phase. I found they were inviting all converts to gather in the park. They didn't say exactly which park of course because they know they're being monitored."

"Being monitored by who?" Hatem asked.

"State Security and Islamic groups that are against people who try to promote Christianity in Egypt."

"Is that really going on?"

"How come you let Christians become Muslims but you don't want us to convert Muslims to Christianity?"

"The truth is I don't want Christians to become Muslims, or Muslims to become Christians. I just want to go home," Hatem said with a smile.

"If you want my personal opinion," Hatem continued, "I'm against trying to convert Christians to Islam, on the sharia principle that preventing something that does harm should take precedence over doing something beneficial. If Muslims think that converting a Christian to Islam serves Islam they are mistaken. It arises from the sense among Muslims that they are less capable and less powerful in the world. It's a form of compensation. Particularly in Egypt it gives a sense of victory when reality is full of defeats. It's as if, when a Christian converts, it means the Muslims are better, as if they've won a battle and have proved that Islam is better than Christianity. Of course that's the feeling among poor Muslims of limited intelligence who see few victories in their lives, and besides, when everyone's wallowing in corruption, they see this as a way to purge oneself of sin and get close to God.

"The Christians, on the other hand, see the conversion of a Muslim to Christianity as a divine miracle that gives them revenge for the arrogance of Muslims who behave as if they're better, and as a victory for the minority against the majority, which inadvertently torments Christians—with loudspeakers bellowing the call to prayer into their ears, and with the Friday sermons and the lessons on television that call Christians infidels every day. So when the Christians manage to convert a Muslim it's a cause for celebration and they declare a victory. You don't see all that in Europe, for example, where Christians can convert to Islam and the world doesn't tremble and it doesn't affect their jobs or their family or social status, just as Europeans and Americans become Buddhists without anyone getting upset and just as Muslims convert to Christianity without any fuss and no Christians throwing a party. Why? Because it's not a broken society and it doesn't see religion or doctrine as a way to compensate for a lousy economic situation or restrictions on freedom or a political vacuum or a shortage of values or a lack of options.

"I tell you once more: if we were to suppose that the conversion of a Christian to Islam would do good, then the psychological, social, and political effects on the country would mean it also caused harm, and preventing that harm is more important than the good it would do. Do you understand me, or have you closed your mind?"

"No, I understand you," Hassan replied, "but you haven't considered the possibility that a Muslim might have read and understood about religion and discovered with his own intellect how inadequate, illogical, and contradictory Islam is, and then looked into Christianity and found in it a convincing answer to his questions, and then decided to convert, or the other way around."

"That's very objective of you, kid!" Hatem interrupted.

Hassan ignored the interruption and continued. "A Christian reads books and studies Islam and thinks it's better for him, so he converts to Islam. Not all converts are psychologically vulnerable or converting because of some situation. Of course your analysis of me is that I'm rebelling against my family because they're a bunch of corrupt oppressors and in order to assert my rebellion, I've rejected my religion and adopted Christianity."

Hatem turned his back and said, "Look, although I'm looking forward to hearing the details of the mess you made tonight before coming to my office and also hearing why you decided to come to my office in the first place, and although time's passing and outside this room there's a group of what I think are thugs that your brother-in-law has sent to take you away, I would however like to agree with you on two things: first, that there really are people who change their beliefs based on reason and without any compelling social motive, and second, I really do believe that your attitude toward your family is one of the main reasons for your alleged conversion to Christianity, along with ignorance and adolescence of course."

Hassan was irritated. "What do you mean, alleged? You don't believe me, even when I carved the sign of the cross with a knife to prove to you that I believe in Christ."

"Precisely because you did that, I think you're confused and hesitant and you're trying to prove it to yourself, not to me. Unfortunately I'm still not interested in what you decide, religiously speaking."

"You are interested," Hassan said defiantly. "You also think you're stronger than me with your learning and your intellect, and you're surprised I haven't broken down in front of you and reverted to Islam."

Hatem's phone rang but he rejected the call and put the phone on silent. "Hassan," he said. "I'm really not losing any sleep because you've converted to Christianity. You can be sure I don't spend the night dreaming about you reverting to Islam. The problem is that your brother-in-law is pretty much ruling Egypt and if he takes a dislike to me, he could get me in deep trouble or drive me into exile from my own country. So now we're in this together. I've really started to like you and feel very sympathetic toward you. It may come as a surprise to you that I see you as my younger brother and friend. I don't have any friends and the last person who claimed to be a friend of mine got me in deep shit—that goddamned Nader Nour, may God never let him see the lights of a studio ever again. Inside I have a strange feeling that I'm doing something for my son Omar, for his future, when I sit down and talk with you."

"I very much respect your candor," said Hassan, "although you're only candid with me. With the government, the state, and the police we don't hear you speaking out."

"So you're the opposition activist then!" replied Hatem. "You live off your father's wealth, which you call corrupt, and in the shadow of your brother-in-law's power and might, which you call despotic. It's true I conceal my real opinions, not only from those in authority but also from the authority of ordinary people, society, public opinion, and the masses, who

157

don't know anything but don't want to be exposed to learning. On the contrary they're delighted when their ignorance is reinforced. I sell learning, not so that people will learn but to improve the quality of their ignorance."

Hatem sighed and sat down on the sofa, devastated.

"Anyway, I'll go back and answer your question about people who convert based on reason and learning. I tell you, they're very exceptional. It might take years of research and study and poring over books and comparison and meditation and discussion and deep debate. All that's only possible for scholars who have the free time and are interested in the idea. But all the conversions we've seen in recent years, with Christians turning Muslim and Muslims turning Christian, have been the result of fast talk, hasty judgments, and half-truths, usually connected with social conditions, love affairs, or psychological crises. That's evident in your group of converts and in fact you personally. You made this decision in a month—or was it three, or even ten? And based on what? Hurried, superficial opinions and silly debates on the Internet. You want me to believe you sat down and read the Mutazila or the Muslim theologians? Have you read Ibn Rushd and his philosophy? Have you taken the trouble to read Abu Hamid al-Ghazali or Mohamed Abduh? Do you have the stamina to finish ten pages of the Imam Shatibi's *Reconciliation*? Of course not, and you don't know anything about these people in the first place, and I'm sure that the Christians who have converted to Islam haven't read them either and the Muslims who've converted to Christianity haven't read any Christian theology, or about the origins of the Gospels, the history of the ecumenical councils, or the decisions of the Council of Nicaea."

Hatem stopped and watched Hassan's eyelashes blinking. "Do you in fact know anything about the Council of Nicaea?" he added calmly.

"Of course," Hassan added, still tense and defiant.

"Clever boy! So what year was that?"

Hassan didn't reply, and Hatem didn't give him much time. "It doesn't matter," he said. "We're not on 'Who Wants To Be A Millionaire.' It was in the year 325, by the way, and the important thing is that the things we have in Egypt, even the religious things, are a complete mishmash. So tell me, sir, what happens when the Home of the Converts invites you all to meet in the park? That wouldn't be the zoo, would it?"

Hassan was taken by surprise. "How did you know that?" he asked.

"Are you serious? They meet in the zoo?"

"Yes. Of course we don't write that on the website, but there's a code on another website you can crack, especially if you're a regular visitor. The websites have a phone number you can call and you listen to a voicemail that says: 'The meeting is where we stand like lions in the jungle, taking refuge with Jesus when the sun is in the middle of the heart of the day.' 'Lions in the jungle' means at the lion cages in the zoo and 'when the sun's in the middle' means twelve o'clock noon."

WHEN HATEM WENT INTO THE room where they were being held, he realized at once that the guards at Giza police headquarters had put them there on instructions from on high. The bodies were curled up on the seats, and in the dark their faces were all a blur, like those ultrasound images of babies in their mothers' wombs.

Hatem told Hassan to sit down. He sat down next to him behind a small table with bottles of mineral water on top, along with white plastic cups with tea bags in them. On a piece of paper on the table there were pieces of bread, cheese, cold cuts, and, surprisingly, sesame halva with nuts. "Okay, guys," said Hatem with a smile he thought was sincere, trying to ease the tension. "They've brought you some sesame halva, seeing as how you're in detention. See how generous the Interior Ministry is—halva with nuts for five-star detainees!"

From the faces in the gloom the only response to Hassan's feeble attempt at solidarity was one of defiance toward what they saw as a sheikh in turban and gown who had come in the belief that he was a guide who could undermine their belief in Christ.

Hatem continued. "You know why we always hear people telling prisoners 'We're going to get you some bread and halva?' It's true and goes back a long time because sesame halva, especially in the olden days, keeps you warm, and in the deep cold of detention what the prisoner needs most is warmth. It also prevents diarrhea, so you don't need to go to the bathroom, I mean the toilet, because there's no way we could call the toilets in prisons bathrooms. This spares the prisoners the misery of using a dirty toilet shared with so many other prisoners."

There were eight of them. All Hatem could see of them was their bright eyes, looking him up and down inquisitively and with suppressed anger. As soon as Hassan told him about the arrangement to meet in the zoo, Hatem had known it was part of a trap, and his intuition had been proven correct.

When he arrived at police headquarters, he was met at the gate by the kind of escort that the police would provide only for a celebrity whose loyalty to the government was well-at-tested, such as Hatem. He exchanged quizzical glances with Hassan, who was sitting at the end of a large hall that had a large desk and a table big enough to seat the representatives of the member states of the UN Security Council.

"It was the investigations department that put out the invitations to meet in the zoo," said the police brigadier who met Hatem in his office. "It was a trap to draw the young converts. As soon as they felt that the kids were suspect they quickly surrounded everyone who was standing in front of the lion cages and arrested them. An hour ago they released six people who turned out to have nothing to do with it and who just had the misfortune to be there at the same time. Three others were so insistent that they were innocent and hadn't converted to Christianity that as soon as they heard the accusation they started assaulting the others. They were shouting 'convert bastards!' and hitting them in the ribs and the balls and the back of their necks and kicking them in the back. Hassan received a particularly vicious blow because he was insulting and provoking them and the policemen, and just as he thought he was going to be beaten to death he shouted, 'I'm Hassan the son of so-and-so, and my brother-in-law is such-and-such,' and to tell you the truth, Mawlana, we were worried the kid might be talking seriously and we weren't sure what to do. We spoke to the security chief and we told State Security and luckily we did all that before they went down to the cells, or else Hassan might have, how shall I put it, undergone a sex change down there."

"He would have been lucky to come out as a woman," said Hatem. "He might have come out with four legs. But tell me, general—"

"Brigadier, Mawlana."

"Who knows? You might be in luck and get promoted to general before we get out of the building."

"No, on your honor," said the brigadier. "I just don't want to be pensioned off because of this mess. How do you rate my chances of keeping my job now that I've met Hassan in person?"

He took another look at Hassan. "I don't know why the children of nice respectable people do things like this to their parents," he mused.

"I'm sure they're respectable, general, but 'nice' would require some detective work," said Hatem.

The brigadier laughed. "You'll get us into trouble that way, Mawlana," he said.

Hatem returned his laugh. "No," he said. "I'd like to assure you we've already been in trouble."

"I'm sorry to hear it."

"But before I go in to see the boys, I'd really like to ask you something: why did you arrest them? If they convert to Christianity, or even set fire to themselves, what's that to the Interior Ministry?"

"Oh my God, Sheikh Hatem!" replied the brigadier. "What's that to the Interior Ministry! Those kids, who only stopped wearing diapers a year or two ago, might set fire to the country. You've got the extremists, who might exploit the story and accuse the state of covering up heresy. You've got the church, which will conclude that it's free to act and will get itself into deep water, and you've got the forces that are hostile to Egypt that will treat the kids as heroes and use this against us. Besides the kids themselves are crazy and think they're prophets. They want to convert everyone and destroy the country."

"Brigadier," Hatem began.

The man looked up at Hatem in puzzlement. "So you've withdrawn my promotion, have you? Wasn't I a general five minutes ago?"

"Mister general governor, minister as well, do you think kids just a year out of Pampers, as you put it, could do all that to the country?"

"And more than that, Mawlana. My only fear for the country is from kids and from gays," said the brigadier.

"Yes, you mean boys and those who like boys."

Hatem was briefed on the plan: he would sit with the young men and give them some advice and then the police would set them all free unconditionally. The purpose was very clear: to make sure that Hassan wasn't upset or angry and that he felt guilty about the others, who were now expected to give vent to their grievances and their thoughts.

"Of course," Hatem told them, "don't get the idea you've been beaten and humiliated just because you converted to Christianity. The truth is that anyone who comes in here—pious Muslim, sheikh in a turban, Buddhist monk, Companion of the Prophet, either from Mecca or Medina— they'd all get slapped around because here there's complete equality between citizens. They all get a kick in the ass, and there's no distinction between Arab and non-Arab, whether you come from the slums or some fancy compound in the suburbs. It's kicks in the ass for everyone."

"And does Islam tell you to assault people and insult them and abuse them?" one of them shouted. Hatem was relaxed and listened with a smile, almost inciting the others to ratchet up the rhetoric.

"You're always saying how Islam is the religion of freedom and how it respects freedom of belief and how it invented human rights!" Hassan cut in excitedly, as if he had drawn strength from what the other convert had said.

"They brought us here because we're Christians, not for any other reason," added a third kid. "Just becoming a Christian makes you a criminal in the eyes of the state."

One of them stood up and grabbed hold of Hassan's arm roughly. "How did you get out, and why did you come back?" he said. "Are you a spy or an informer? And what's that guy doing here? Does he think he's the voice of Islam that'll show the way to the silly kids who've misbehaved and turned Christian, that we'll cry on his shoulder and go back to Islam?"

Hatem offered one of them a piece of bread. "Go on, eat," he said. "You look hungry." Then he pressed a piece of bread and cheese into the mouth of one of them. The kid resisted but chewed it in the end. He offered a cup of tea to another of them.

"For a start," he said, "I'm not in the least interested in the fact that you've converted to Christianity. You're free to do what you like and it won't bother me for one second or even one femtosecond what religion or denomination you are or, to be honest, whether you go to hell or you get burned at the stake, whether you become Muslims, Christians, Buddhists, or atheists, or whether you worship Satan or Iblis himself. You're free, and I don't want to convert you back to Islam anyway. I want to get you back to your homes or whatever dumps you're living in, and this session is a piece of theater by me and Boutros here (he pointed to Hassan, who seemed rather lost by what Hatem was saying) in which I pretend that I've had a discussion with you and given you advice so that you sign the piece of paper that the police will give you and go home to sleep and even catch the late-night movie on television."

Hatem stood up. "Okay, that's it. I've given you my advice and you're all convinced, so off you go to your homes, and goodbye, and hope to never see you again," he said.

Strangely, they dawdled, dragged their feet and generally hung around waiting. Hatem headed for the door, opened it, and shouted at the policeman standing there at attention. "Tell the brigadier we're done and the kids are going home if he wants to say goodbye to them, but it would be better if he didn't because they can't stand him," he said.

Then he went back and pushed one of them through the door and then another, and the rest started moving.

Hatem put his arm on Hassan's shoulder and whispered, "Looks like Christianity attracts all kinds of people."

He was going down the stairway with Hassan but the other young men, though emboldened by their rebellion against their religion, were still too timid to let him out of their sights. They walked right behind him as if he were in charge of a school trip and if they lost him they wouldn't know how to find their way back. They tracked his every step, although they found him irritating and suspected he was hiding something from them. They looked to him for protection, like frightened sheep following their shepherd. Two policemen and some security men in plain clothes were walking a little behind them, but they suddenly dispersed and disappeared into the dark. At that time of night the police headquarters was suspiciously and unnaturally quiet. Hatem preferred not to turn around. He felt that someone had their eyes on his distinctive gown and on Hassan, who was holding his hand like a child going to see the principal with one of his parents.

Hatem and the young Christians ended up together in the courtyard surrounded by walls with metal spikes at the top. The noise from the street nearby gave them a sense of security and there was a faint light from lamp posts inside the courtyard. Suddenly someone turned on searchlights aimed directly at Hatem and the little group, dazzling them. The Christians huddled around Hatem in fear and suddenly they found themselves surrounded by dozens of policemen armed to the teeth and dressed in tight-fitting black uniforms like panthers, ready to jump on their prey. The policemen, brandishing long, scary, gleaming weapons, were arranged in blocks like phalanxes on every side. Hatem and the confused kids almost died of fright. Hatem looked back and forth among the policemen for a senior officer who might be able to explain what was going on or call off the siege and let them go on their way. The eight kids, who thought that Hatem had secured their release, could see that he was trapped along with them. Now they were really worried. Then the police advanced on them, grabbing them and pushing them.

Hatem was almost knocked over in the melee but he found his feet and shouted, "What's going on, guys? I want to see Brigadier Wagih. There's been some misunderstanding. What in God's name has happened? Let me speak with a senior official!"

Some of the boys were crying and others were trying to protest, but then the police threw them down a staircase, one after another, to a small dark room with a steel door. The police pushed them violently into the room, and they lay prone on cold wet tiles. A faint light seeped through a window that was tightly closed except for a hole that was roughly circular. Apparently many people who'd been locked up here had scratched out the hole to let in a ray of light, and a glimpse of hope.

The kids were stunned. "What's going on, Uncle Hatem?" they muttered after a time of uncertain duration.

Hassan seemed to be recovering from the shock. "See how unfair it is, Sheikh Hatem?" he said. "You think you're dealing with respectable people, but they're savages who have no respect for people's freedom or religion. They set a trap for us, and for you. Didn't they give you an assurance that we could leave? Didn't you make an agreement with them?"

Hassan stood amid the tangle of legs and arms and exhausted bodies. "They're afraid of us," he said with the courage of someone who feels important. "They're terrified. We're the ones who have seen Christ and have realized that they are oppressive, loathsome unbelievers."

The young Christians rallied to Hassan's heated words and turned on Hatem, as if he were the target they had long been seeking. "We are ready for martyrdom!" one of them shouted.

Hatem was angry at what was happening and had been hurt in the jostling. "Don't get martyred or do anything else stupid," he shouted. "I assure you I'm not interested. How many times have I told you? How can I convince you that I'm not interested in whether you're Muslim or Christian. I just want to know why I'm here. Okay, so you've converted to Christianity and you're acting as if you're martyrs in the Age of Persecution. Fine. But I'm just a sheikh and a preacher, why should I be thrown in with you? Is it to punish me or to punish you?"

The shouting subdued them. Nobody had asked after them or brought them any news and they couldn't hear a sound.

"Can they apply the penalty for apostasy on us as apostates from Islam, Sheikh Hatem?" asked one of them, a young man of about twenty or twenty-one with a childish face. He had woken up the sheikh, who had dozed off from exhaustion and boredom.

"And where did you find out what the penalty for apostasy is?" answered Hatem.

Another young man intervened. "It's on websites all the time," he said.

"I'm sorry to ask, forgive me: does all your information come from websites?" asked Hatem.

"You know, you can find interesting lectures and debates and information on websites," Hassan added.

Hatem looked up at the dripping ceiling and the peeling paint and the damp beneath him as he lay on the broken, dirty tiles in a darkness that brought home to him what a mess he was caught up in.

"Of course," said Hatem, "but I told you, Boutros, that converting from Islam to Christianity or from Christianity to Islam is not an ordinary decision. It's a serious, significant decision, not in the sense that you're adopting a new religion or turning against your old religion. No, it's something more difficult than that. It's a decision that goes against human chemistry, that upsets the whole balance in one's life. Belief is just like love."

He paused a moment. "Have any of you ever been in love?" he asked.

Some of them smiled in the gloom. It didn't seem quite so dark now that their eyes had gotten used to it.

Hatem continued. "So you have been in love. Belief, like love, isn't driven by reason but by the heart. Reason in religion comes at the stage of interpretation, analysis, and corroboration, but the submission stage, which is fundamental, is centered only on the heart. Bring me any religion and I can offer you a critique of it, an attack on it. I can point out loopholes in it and ask questions about it and find mysterious elements in it, but the religion will continue regardless. Whether we're talking about two thousand years of Christianity or one thousand four hundred years of Islam—it's true there have been some conversions from one to the other but they've been very limited compared to the amount of belief passed down from father to son. Do you know why? Because religion has become chemistry. It's in the genes, deep in our psychological and nervous systems. If Muslims or Christians left their children free to choose whether to stick to the same religion or choose another one, the chemistry of the universe would be disturbed, because searching is confusing. It's tiring and it makes you tense, and looking for a religion is something that requires deep study and comparison and thought, and also free time. You can't be an engineer or a doctor or anything when you're preoccupied with choosing which religion you like most. Religion grows with you as part of your body and your way of thinking. When you're in middle school, it's different from when you're in secondary school, and that's different from when you're married and have children, and it's different again when you're old. Religion interacts with you, so you never stand at a point and say, 'Okay, I've arrived.' No, it never ends. You have inside you a bit of the pious Muslim, a bit of the good-for-nothing layabout, a little of the undecided, and a little of the resolutely indifferent. There's a back-and-forth interaction between you and religion. It evolves inside you as you make adjustments so that it suits you and you suit it. If we were all born to choose, life would be even bleaker than it is already."

Hatem paused a while. "By the way, I'm very hungry," he resumed.

Their eyes narrowed at the sudden change of subject.

"Let's shout at them to bring us some food," said Hassan.

"So they've thrown a famous sheikh in this dungeon, someone known and admired throughout the country, and they haven't asked after him or shown him any respect, and it's clear that the bosses have gone home and forgotten me completely, and yet you expect them to bring us some food?" said Hatem.

Hassan stood up by the solid door of the cell and peeked through a square hole someone had made in it. "We want to eat," he shouted, banging and kicking the door.

A few moments later a grumpy voice in the distance shouted back: "Eat your own shit."

Hatem couldn't help but laugh and the others burst out laughing with him.

Hatem took some bread and halva out of the pocket of his gown. They caught sight of it and a sense of triumph spread through the room. But then Hatem announced, "I told you I was hungry so that you wouldn't be upset if I ate this all by myself."

He wrapped the halva in the bread and was about to eat it, but then he smiled and started to break it into pieces, which he then shared out between them. They took the pieces gratefully.

Then he patted one of them on the back and said, "Were you asking me about the penalty for apostasy?"

"Yes."

"Okay, what's your name?"

"Bishoy."

"Pleased to meet you, Saint Bishoy. And what was your name before Bishoy, my son?"

"It was Dandarawi."

"No, Bishoy's nicer," said Hatem. "Okay, brother Bishoy, I'm giving you a fatwa that there's no such thing as a penalty for apostasy."

"Sheikh Hatem!" shouted Hassan.

"Look, boy, you and him. My fee for one show is three thousand dollars and yet I'm giving you a free show underground in the foulest dungeon in Egypt, so listen to me or else shut up and we can all settle down and go to sleep till someone remembers me and gets in touch with the people upstairs to let us out."

Hatem heard them muttering among themselves until one of them finally came up with a question. "That's the problem we have with Islam. We don't know who represents it. There are some extraordinary contradictions in it. You say there's no penalty for apostasy, but a thousand other sheikhs say there is. Then they call you an infidel because you say there's no authoritative text on apostasy."

"Clearly we're not going to sleep tonight," Hatem replied. "I'd just like to ask you ... er, what's your name?"

"Mutanassir."[3]

"What a great name! No mincing words with you. Just Mutanassir is better and easier and more expressive as well. Look, Mutanassir, my boy, we have to be clear here. We're not getting into a debate that ends with someone winning. Of course I probably see myself as the erudite sheikh, so I should feel that you're ignorant kids and not up to my level, and if you're not convinced by what I say, then it's a failure on your part. But on the other hand you probably see me as a Muslim sheikh who wouldn't be convinced by what you say because I don't understand and Jesus hasn't shone his light into my heart. So you should concentrate tonight on being rude about my family while I attack your ideas. Okay? Off we go. But I want Bishoy to wake up because I have a feeling he's asleep. And you, Mister Boutros, the bane of my wretched life, are you awake? Or do you commit your crimes and then settle down and sleep till morning? Of course you know you'll get out in the end."

Hassan was irritated by Sheikh Hatem making fun of them. He touched his injured wrists as if the pain was troubling him again.

"I have to ask you," Hatem continued. "Did you abandon Islam out of hatred for Islam or out of love for Christianity? Of course you can't hate Islam unless you're familiar with every aspect of it. Because at your age, with your experience and your culture, you're children properly speaking and you can only be familiar with ten percent of Islam, apart from what you're heard from sheikhs or from priests on the Internet insulting Islam. And besides, you can't understand Christianity without studying it for years, so you must be talking superficially. Of course you're free to talk about it any way you like, but you ought to know, when you lash out and attack Islam or even Christianity, that no one can really master all the details or even the basics of a religion. Now as for me, I don't represent Islam, of course, and that's the nicest thing about it—that no one represents it and no one can claim a monopoly over it. You're free in your relationship with God in Islam and in Christianity too, because the clerics have had a disastrous effect on religion—any and every religion."

Hatem examined their faces carefully in a light that was as meager as the prospect of mercy between those walls, which were bare except for lines and letters scratched into the plaster in an attempt at immortality. Tadros was standing on tiptoe to cut his name into the wall with the tip of a key on his keyring, followed by letters that looked like the beginning of a blessing that included the name of Jesus. There wasn't a wall in the country, Hatem mused, without something written or drawn on it, either in celebration or in sorrow, in prisons, on the trees in parks, in people's houses, and even in places of worship. Children were born drawing and scratching on walls, dating the events of their lives with letters and drawings on the walls of life. Here in this vault beneath a building designed to break people's spirits and put the proud in their place, the drawings on the walls showed that the prisoners were fighting back against being ignored by writing dates and names, recording their prayers and their grievances. While the young Christians watched Tadros drawing on the wall, Hatem tried to work out who they really were behind the façade of their faces. They didn't have any physical features in common but there were some psychological characteristics that they shared. The boy lying like a time bomb in his lap, although he came from a family of great wealth and influence, had almost the same facial expression as another young man who seemed to come from a poor family. When Tadros spoke, Hatem realized immediately he was right about the way they looked: there was a tense defiance behind their conversion, a defiance that wasn't based on religion, because for the most part they didn't know anything about the one they were abandoning or adopting. It was rather defiance of any authority or of all authority, including the authority that ignored them.

"Obviously, Sheikh Hatem, you think we're too dumb to see that you despise us and think we're infidels," said Tadros. "With you people everything is calling people infidels and claiming you're the best community, the best 'umma,' that ever existed. If your Quran is true, please tell me, sheikh, where is this best umma? Are the poverty, the backwardness, and the failure that's all around you signs that you are the best umma? Look at the scientific and medical progress across the whole world, look at the inventions and discoveries, no, forget about that, look at the justice and equality that prevail among people in America and Europe, the democracy and freedom, and then come and preach in the mosques with the retarded sheikhs and tell me you're the best umma."

Hatem's eyes opened wide at Tadros's outburst. The other young Christians took heart from his words and comfort against the biting cold and damp and the disgusting, putrid smell. They felt the strength of their pride in what they were doing. They felt honored to pay the price for the positions they had taken, and believed in their conversion to Christianity more deeply and more intensely when they felt persecuted. That was the sign that they were special, that they stood out, that they were opposing the status quo and fighting those in authority. Hatem felt they had converted in protest, the ultimate protest, or in order to attract attention, as much attention as possible—angry attention from the high and mighty, vengeful attention from the despotic. The young converts relished provoking the complacent, those in authority, the masters, those who were confident and self-assured. They delighted in jumping over obstacles and they tried to take their antagonism and their distinctiveness to the limit. Strangely Hatem was very sympathetic toward Tadros's enthusiasm and the questions he posed. If they were not expressed with so much hatred, they would be constructive questions that deserved to be answered.

"For a start, brother Tadros," said Hatem, looking toward Hassan, "the expression 'You're the best umma' is conditional on a duty Muslims have to fulfill, particular obligations that the Muslim community or the umma has to carry out. If it doesn't meet these conditions, it's not the best umma, or the worst. And be careful, the Muslim umma isn't the caliphate or a state that's governed by one president or king, or else what role in the umma would there be for British Muslims, or French Muslims or Muslims born in Brazil or Muslims in Senegal and Malaysia and Turkey and Indonesia? So what's meant isn't the umma in the Arabic sense of the word—which is what you mean when you say it's backward and in a terrible state. In that sense, it is a disgrace to Islam. If you want to confine the umma to the however many million Arab Muslims, then your question would be very logical and apposite. But if you broaden it out and include Muslims from China and India and Malaysia, taking in as you go Afghanistan and Iran and the Muslims in Russia and central Asia, as well as the Muslims in Brazil and Canada, then you're talking about Muslims who live within other nations, and who play a role in the progress or backwardness of those nations, just as non-Muslims in those countries do, which reminds me, Tadros, that the Christians and the Copts here play the same role as us in backwardness and cultural decline. And besides, in the Middle Ages, when the Muslims were the inventors and explorers, they were the best umma, and the Christians in Europe and the Old World were barbarians. Of course we shouldn't judge religions by their adherents, although we do judge people based on their religion, but I'd like to ask you, Tadros, and you, Boutros, and all you martyrs for Christ—"

"Are you making fun of us?" one of the boys interrupted, trying to counteract the effect his words might have on some of his colleagues.

"God forbid!" said Hatem. "But even if I was making fun of you, wasn't it a feature of the early martyrs and the prophets that they put up with ridicule from their enemies and turned it into prayers that their enemies might receive guidance and enlightenment? Anyway, the question is: have you read about religion or just heard about it?"

"Ever since we were born," Hassan replied, "we've been hearing sheikhs in mosques and on television and teachers at school and our parents at home, all talking about religion."

"Okay, Boutros, but does anyone else have another answer?" Someone else spoke up: "I'm Bishoy, by the way."

"Very well."

"Of course I've read about religion."

"What have you read and by who?"

"I've read a bunch."

"I don't mean to challenge you but I'd like to hear a sample of this 'bunch.'"

"Clearly, Sheikh Hatem, you think we're just ignorant kids tricked into converting to Christianity, and you see yourself as the one who's going to save us from going astray," Bishoy replied.

"I've already told you that I'm not interested in you in the least, and you can all go to hell together and it wouldn't bother me at all. I'm quite prepared to shut up and we can sit this out together till daybreak, though our miserable day together seems to be endless."

"We've read lots of books on the Internet," said Hassan. "Books that refute all the claims that Islam makes and show how feeble they are."

"I tell you," said Hatem. "If you read seriously and properly and then become Christians or Buddhists then that's your right, but the problem I have with you is that you're taking an enormous step in life without knowing anything. I'm not interested in what books or who you've read on Islam but I'm asking what you've read about Christianity. We're not switching allegiance from one club to another, but from one religion to another, and the question that most needs to be asked here is: 'Where will it lead?' Christianity may have most of the flaws that you don't like in Islam, for example, or maybe all religions are a big trick and they all come down to the same thing and it would be best to turn atheist and keep our distance from religions that are flawed but boast about being perfect."

"We've seen debates between sheikhs and priests, arguing about many things in Islam and Christianity," Tadros replied. "We came to the conclusion that the priests' point of view was right."

"The problem might have been that the sheikh didn't argue well," said Hatem. "Maybe his wife had annoyed him and he wasn't in the mood that day. Or maybe it was like one of those wrestling matches where they agree in advance who's going to win, but they get all worked up and angry anyway and one of them throws his opponent out of the ring and lifts up a chair and threatens the crowd, or hits the referee by mistake to give the impression of spontaneity and maintain the suspense. Then very often it happens that we sympathize with the one who's weakest in the match. We feel sorry for the short bald wrestler who faces the fearsome Big Show, so we root for the weakest even if we know he's bound to lose. And then the competition over who's the cleverest—Islam or Christianity?—is a game for freshman students, and has nothing to do with scholarship or ideas or culture. Especially on this point, I want to say that I'm not upset that you're leaving Islam, which you haven't read about, which in fact you've heard about from people most if not all of whom are ignorant, but I am upset that you're taking up a religion that you haven't read about and that you don't know about and that you haven't studied. It's as if you're repeating the same mistake, from a religion that's six of one to a religion that's half a dozen of the other."

The young Christians had fallen silent, overcome by Hatem's arguments or by fatigue. They also had to face the biting cold, the damp, the dirt, and the stink of sweaty bodies in an enclosed space underground. There were questions to be answered—not so much about who had persuaded them to convert but rather about who had decided to punish them for what they had done. The way they were treated seemed pointless. Harassment by the police would give them an added incentive to stick to their position, create a sense of solidarity between them, and probably postpone the process by which their conversions would cease to be personal dramas and just become a part of everyday life that they would be surprised to find was no longer surprising. If those sleepy faces were given some space to breathe, and if they were no longer made to feel that the universe revolved around them, then they could make up their minds about what they believed without anyone promoting them as heroes or accusing them of weakness.

Hatem was annoyed that the police were wasting his time and undermining his prestige.

He remembered one of the policemen who had surrounded them in the courtyard.

"Move back, Mawlana," the man had said.

The policeman was advising him to stay away from the fighting, but at the same time he was sending him the message that he knew who he was. Hatem wondered what people would say about Sheikh Hatem el-Shenawi if they knew he had been thrown into detention with a crowd of young men who had converted to Christianity. Had any websites got hold of the news and published anything? If only he had his iPad with him to find out. How would the editor of his Facebook page respond to the rumors that must be spreading about them being held in the Giza security headquarters? The oafish sheikhs who competed with him on television and in the mosques, and the journalists irritated by his success, by his very existence, might turn these scraps of information into big stories. There might be banner headlines on the front pages, asking questions under photographs of him chosen to match the scandal that their fertile imaginations came up with. God forbid they refer to the fact that he was with young men and got it into their heads that he was gay. That would be a godsend to those newspapers and scandalous television programs that would take up the suggestions with delight.

He refused even to think about the story leaking out. Would the president's son, who had so much clout, allow his reputation to be dragged irreparably through the mud? That seemed impossible, because the president's son needed him for his assignment with Hassan and wouldn't allow his efforts to be repaid with an attack on his reputation or his livelihood. The president's son knew, or imagined, that Hatem had agreed to take on this mission—as if he could have refused!—out of fear, or at least in order to win favor. God damn you, Nader Nour, it serves you right that your last two films flopped and you had to resort to presenting game shows that only lunatics would take part in because the production company was so poor and the producers so mean. But was it really possible that a scrap of information from a policeman would reach a journalist? Maybe the editor of the crime page in some daily newspaper was now on the phone with an officer in police headquarters looking for news, and the officer, keen to get his name in the paper as a hero, might say, "Do you know who we had in the building tonight?" and the editor would answer, "Who, Kheiri Bey?" And Kheiri Bey would say, "No, I couldn't possibly drop this bombshell on the phone," and that gets the editor's attention and in the end he wheedles it out of the officer and the conversation ends with a dramatic story in the newspaper.

Hatem was deeply resentful, and his resentment focused on Hassan, who had nodded off feeling safe, maybe a safety he didn't find in his bedroom in his father's mansion, or perhaps it was because he wasn't lonely or alienated here or because the group support had relieved his depression. Hatem, himself exhausted, could see that Hassan, unlike his colleagues, was sleeping like a cute little puppy, whereas the others in the cell—and surprisingly the young Christians were the only prisoners there—were either tired and bored, or upset and angry, or sleeping fitfully, though all of them were content with their fate and proud to be there. They kept themselves busy by writing on the walls—verses from the Gospels, the name of Jesus in badly formed letters and lines—determined to cut the words so deep that they would be hard to erase.

Hatem wasn't one of those sheikhs who grew big bushy beards down to their waists, and then shaved and even plucked their mustaches. He didn't cover his head with a light piece of white cloth, he didn't have bulging, staring eyes, and he didn't wear his watch on his right hand as a declaration of his Salafist commitment to sharia. Hatem had always been puzzled by that ridiculous obsession with wearing the watch on the right hand for religious reasons. For heaven's sake, the watches were Swiss or German or Japanese. Hatem could understand a sheikh showing off his watch on his right hand, but it wasn't as if it was an Islamic invention. Wasn't it the Christians, the Magi, the Buddhists, and the Jews who had invented all the devices used by this Salafist with his thick beard—his watch, the microphone clipped to the lapel of his gown, and even his gown itself, as well as the camera that filmed him, the broadcasting equipment, and the screen on which people watched him? Why didn't he wear all that on his right hand too?

That was the stereotype of the Muslim televangelist projected by the television stations that Hatem hated. But Hatem was very careful not to disparage them. In fact he flattered and complimented them, and when the owners of those stations came into a room, he greeted them and praised them. But they didn't really like him, because a large number of these garrulous sheikhs filled their television programs with hatred for him and for what he said. Hatem never debated a fatwa with any of those sheikhs, never challenged the opinion of any of the other preachers, never criticized their lessons or refuted any of their claims. Nonetheless they never stopped attacking him with ridicule and sarcasm. They declared war on the fatwas he issued, the ideas he suggested, and the stories he told. There was of course an underlying reason: the number of adverts that were broadcast during his programs, whether he was giving a lecture or answering questions from a presenter. He knew they were counting the adverts that ran just before the program began— six, seven, ten, sixteen. They were also riled by the names of the sponsors who financed and supported the program. They explained this largesse on the part of advertisers and sponsors by saying that Hatem promoted the kind of religion that ordinary people liked—the religion of pleasantries and anecdotes, of sentimentality and liberal fatwas, the religion of the women and the housewives who made phone calls to all his programs. They envied his adverts and tried hard not to be dependent on ads for cheap goods sold on the doorstep or with free home delivery. Their fees were lower, their audiences were smaller, and the women who watched were poorer. But the princes and Islamic organizations in Saudi Arabia and the Gulf preferred them and lavished money and gifts on them, especially when they were invited on trips to the Gulf to perform Islamically approved forms of ritual healing.

Hatem tried to stop thinking about the situation he was in and what he might have to do to get out of it. He resigned himself to listening to the snores from the disciples of Bethlehem lying beside him in the cell. When they slept, they still looked like children. They were no longer fighting back, pretending to be brave martyrs determined to convert. They seemed very weak and fragile and in need of their mothers' hugs.

Young men who turned Christian after abandoning Islam usually faced a massive backlash. They generally emigrated, because abandoning Islam goes hand in hand with disengagement from the country. That's what he had heard from Hassan about three converts who had traveled to Canada through a church in Helmiya or Zeitoun. He couldn't remember exactly, but Hassan was very proud of the church. He argued that the Muslims were throwing young Egyptian Christians out of their own country through persecution and discrimination.

"What do you think of Muslims who drive young Muslims out of their country too, through unemployment and poverty?" Hatem asked Hassan. "They get onto boats that take them to distant ports and drown in the sea or freeze in the forests and need to have their limbs amputated because of frostbite. They scrape together pennies to leave the country, lamented by their mothers. They have too many relatives and so few options in life that they can barely survive but they see a glimpse of hope for a world where food is plentiful and work is available, where you can live a decent life instead of the wretched life of poor people who are like the living dead, dressed in rags worth less than the box of tissues that you put in your car."

Hatem knew what the country was like. It had no time for poor people or people who changed their religion, unless they were from a minority, as if Islam acquired new strength or new energy when Copts in particular turned Muslim. He had seen people who were destitute and yet who jumped for joy when the wife of their Christian neighbor converted to Islam. He had often tried to understand the extraordinary happiness that these people felt, particularly amid the poverty of the south and the squalor of the Nile Delta countryside, where conversions to Islam made the most noise and were celebrated most enthusiastically. He'd never seen anything like that in the Citadel area, where he had grown up near the Sultan Hassan and el-Rifai mosques. It was only in the poverty belt, in the slums that surrounded Cairo, that he had ever seen a Coptic woman convert to Islam. It was usually a female—a young woman or a wife. There were very few cases he had seen or heard about where a Christian man converted to Islam. As soon as news spread that a Christian woman had converted to Islam, especially if she was married, crowds of people would turn up to ask questions and then spread the word. People would start dancing and shouting "There is no god but God" in celebration. Guns would be fired amid hysterical jubilation. Even the local toughs, the kids who did drugs and hung out at night with knives and waylaid passers-by and stole their wallets, treated the conversion of a Christian woman to Islam as if they were early Muslim warriors attacking Persian positions on orders from Khaled ibn al-Walid—the ultimate in faith and devotion.

Hatem still remembered the time when an old acquaintance by the name of Abdel-Basir invited him to a wedding party in the Nile Delta countryside. He thought it would be a banquet and he would deliver a homily. Hatem had visited the area before for a funeral and had won the admiration of the men of the village; he became well known there for his voice and the way he preached in a language that combined literary and colloquial Arabic, the historical and the contemporary. He spoke in a way that brought him close to ordinary people and that was also warmly received by people with an interest in religious matters. Religion has an audience, not necessarily of religious people but of people who admire a preacher's voice, even if they don't pay much attention to the meaning and intricacies of his words.

In this village, they wanted the superficial aspects of religion and were crazy about charismatic preachers and melodious voices that could move the listener. Most of them smoked hashish in generous quantities and were corrupt, but they liked to listen to sheikhs, attend religious celebrations, and judge Quran readers. Hatem used to go there with the Arzaqia sheikhs, who would never say no to a good dinner or turn down an invitation to a wedding that would end with some pancakes soaked in ghee or some mint banknotes just withdrawn from the bank, so sharp they could leave scratches on their fingers. Ever since Hatem had spent time with the simple sheikhs who liked their hot meals—at first obsequiously, then ingratiatingly, then hesitantly, and finally uncomfortably—and even when he spent time with the sheikhs who appeared on television, at official conferences and at the homes of businessmen—at first enthusiastically, then restlessly, then irritably, and in the end dismissively—he had never known a sheikh who came from a rich family. Perhaps that's what made them so cantankerous and competitive about making a living, their overwhelming sense that they had no security; the years of abject poverty had left their scars on them. Even when Hatem moved out of his apartment of seventy square meters to the apartment of two hundred square meters and then to the large house with the garden, he still worried that poverty would strike back and ruin him and his family. Many sheikhs were terribly naive when it came to business and people took advantage of them in all the ventures they took part in. At the very least, these ventures did not produce as much as they earned as men of learning. A ritual healing for an Arabian princess or for the wife of a wealthy man in some oil-rich country, or a visit to recite the Quran or prayers in the mansion of some businessman, would bring in more money more quickly and more easily, without compromising their reputation for piety.

An hour after he arrived, amid all the noise and the greetings, Hatem realized it was a wedding that Abdel-Basir was sponsoring. He heard people boasting gleefully that Nadia, who was a Coptic girl from a nearby village and worked as a nurse in Dr. Samaan's clinic in the health center, had converted to Islam and abandoned her family. Dr. Samaan had protected her when the family came after her, had put her up in his spacious house, and had decided to buy her an apartment and arrange for her to marry any young Muslim man, offering to make all the arrangements for the wedding. Naturally enough, there was competition to marry her, especially when it emerged that the girl was pretty with pale skin and blue eyes. A teacher in the village got engaged to her and the victory wedding was that night. He heard the story from the guests, including the children. People added details they had invented and others corrected them. When a man appeared in a white galabiya, with a green turban on his head, a long thick beard, and steel-rimmed glasses on his nose, Hatem realized that this was the local hero who had persuaded Nadia to convert. He was Gamal el-Naghi, who was proud to be the first Muslim pharmacist in the area, in a profession that was once the exclusive preserve of Copts. Some of the guests who fought to greet Gamal kissed his hands and slapped him on the shoulders and he seemed proud to be among the imams and Salafist preachers from the nearby mosques. The noise was unbearable and the women intermittently broke into a chorus of trilling noises that sounded like the screeching of fireworks.

Abdel-Basir confided in Hatem that he planned to stand in the coming elections, then grabbed Gamal's hand in the crowd to introduce him to Hatem and, with two loyal followers, pushed the two of them into a side room. When Hatem went in, it was a massive relief to have some peace and quiet. He sat on the nearest of the sofas arranged in the four corners of the room, which was clearly a reception room for guests. Gamal el-Naghi sat down beside him and they then shut the doors on them, though four of Abdel-Basir's followers had slipped in under his feet, some of them in case they were called upon for any purpose and the others so that they could boast of having sat with their hero and with the sheikh who had come from Cairo. Gamal was superciliously ingratiating: he had expected Hatem to congratulate him warmly and when that didn't happen quickly enough his confidence in the sheikh was immediately shaken. But Abdel-Basir's followers didn't waste the opportunity to start up a lively conversation, retelling Hatem the story of Nadia's conversion.

Hatem, irritated by their naive enthusiasm, turned to them in the middle of the story and asked, "But Nadia, *ma'aaha eeh*?" meaning 'What's the matter with her?' though the question might also have meant 'What does she have?'

The people in the room didn't understand the question. But after a moment, Gamal replied: "She has a diploma in business studies."

"You're a pharmacist, aren't you, Gamal?" Hatem continued.

Someone answered on Gamal's behalf immediately, repeating the story about him being the first Muslim pharmacist in town.

"Great," said Hatem.

As the noise of the wedding grew outside, Hatem was thinking that Gamal had probably spent years in Saudi Arabia and had then come back and opened his pharmacy. Gamal confirmed his expectations shortly afterward.

"I spent five years in Riyadh," he said.

"That's great," said Hatem. "Being a pharmacist is an excellent profession. I hope you manage to invent some medicines for us instead of these Western crusader medicines. I mean, when you go to the pharmacy and ask for some medicine, they say, 'Don't buy the local version. You'd best buy the imported one.' So you ask, 'But why? Doesn't it make more sense to buy the Egyptian one?' And they say, 'No, because this medicine is imported. It's made by a Christian man in Europe or America.' You say, 'And what's the difference?' And he says, 'The active ingredient in the imported version. Don't forget, 'imported' means it comes from the land of the Franks and the Christians, the sons of whoever. The active ingredient is bigger and more powerful, unlike the Egyptian version, the halal version that's ritually pure.' So Dr. Gamal, why don't you make us some effective medicines instead of sitting reading the Quran in your pharmacy day and night. You ought to be doing research and inventing better medicines."

The unexpected sarcasm stung Gamal.

"Are you making light of reading the Quran, Mawlana?" he snarled in reply. "Surely Muslims, whether they're doctors, engineers, mechanics, or farmers, are called on to promote Islam, Sheikh Hatem?"

Hatem nodded, reluctant to take part in a debate that he thought deserved only his contempt. He was always resisting the temptation to express ideas that people would not like to hear.

"I'm not making light of it, God forbid. I've memorized the Quran and I'm a Quran reader, but we shouldn't read the Quran in the workplace, in class, in factories, or even in fields. On the contrary, we should work, and not every Muslim is called upon to spread Islam, or else why would God have sent the Prophet Muhammad?"

"May God bless him and grant him peace," everyone intoned devoutly.

"That's what you're good at," Hatem whispered to himself. "The Prophet would have sent Muadh bin Jabal or Salim Mawla Abu Hudhayfa to teach people religion," he continued. "He wouldn't have sent Khalid ibn al-Walid or Bilal ibn Rabah for that task."

He didn't wait to find out whether they had understood or not, but turned to Gamal, asking, "But how did you persuade her to convert?"

"She used to come to the pharmacy because of her work, and I used to play the Quran all the time and she liked hearing the verses of the Quran. She asked me what they meant and I realized her heart was receptive to Islam and I explained things to her."

"You explained things to her?" Hatem asked, then stopped. Gamal didn't like the emphasis that Hatem had put on the phrase.

"Scholarship isn't the monopoly of sheikhs, Mawlana, it's in people's hearts and in books. I've read many books on the Quran and on the sayings and doings of the Prophet, as every Muslim should, and I've learned from our *major* sheikhs," continued Gamal, stressing the word 'major' as if suggesting that Hatem was minor, "so when I saw that Nadia was ready to find out about Islam it was my duty to provide her with books."

"Quite right," said Hatem. "A girl with a business diploma," he added to himself, "is going to read Zamakhshari and Ibn Kathir and Ibn Taymiya and understand and take it all in and believe it as well. It sounds unlikely."

"And I gave her tapes with lessons and sermons," added Gamal.

Hatem waved the idea aside dismissively. "Indeed, that's a good idea—Islam through tapes. It's novel. Like the 'Teach Yourself English' tapes. How old did you say the girl is?"

Several people joined in, eager to tell Sheikh Hatem the story. "The girl's young. She's twenty. But her father's a nasty guy and likes to drink. He's no match for any of the Muslims in the town and he beats his wife and abuses his daughter. The priest stepped in several times to try to make him mend his ways but it was no use, but I swear, Mawlana, her father's the best guy in the whole area when it comes to restoring furniture. The girl ran off once before and went to become a nun in a convent but her father acted all humble and cried in front of people in church."

"We don't have a church in our village," someone else interrupted, with pride in what he was saying. "That was the church in the main town."

"Her father went with the priest and they took her out of the convent," they continued. "But two days later he beat her and her mother."

Hatem was watching the way Gamal was following his clique of admirers in their spontaneous and spirited account of the psychological background that drove the girl to stand in front of Dr. Gamal in the pharmacy and show interest, or pleasure in his interest. With the remnant of logic that some Egyptians had managed to retain, Gamal could see that the story undermined the spiritual nature of the girl's religious transformation. It suggested factors other than his own powers of persuasion, his religious knowledge, or the idea that her heart was receptive to Islam. When Hatem saw again how

188

Gamal was looking around, he came to the conclusion that the girl had fallen in love with Gamal, and that Gamal had let her down.

Hatem struck while the iron was hot. "But why didn't you marry her, Dr. Gamal?" he asked.

The question hung in the air, unanswered. Just at that moment, Abdel-Basir came into the room, accompanied by the registrar, the teacher who was the jubilant bridegroom, and dozens of others who were jostling to get through the door. Abdel-Basir kept them out of the room with his back and invited Sheikh Hatem and Dr. Gamal to move through the other door to a reception room overlooking a large garden fringed with trees along the walls and massive vine trellises shading the entrance to a guesthouse. Beyond lay an expanse of greenery, which was now decorated with colored lamps and rows of wooden chairs stamped with the name of the businessman who supplied them. The wedding seemed to have kicked off, because the noise grew louder and the music bellowed out, interspersed with trilling sounds from the women. Hatem stuck his head between Abdel-Basir and Gamal and asked, "So guys, why didn't you organize a Muslim wedding? With no music or singing, I mean."

"Mawlana," Abdel-Basir replied, "we didn't want to arouse suspicions and have people calling us Islamists, and besides this is a victory we're proud of, so we can spite our enemies with it. It's not just any wedding."

Hatem wondered whether a drunk who restored furniture really deserved to be designated the enemy in the village.

A few minutes later Abdel-Basir rushed over and grabbed him by the hand. "Come along," he said, "we need to show you off to the important people and let me introduce you to the chief of police and his deputy and the State Security officer. They've just arrived."

"Arrived? What are they here for?" asked Hatem.

"To give their congratulations."

"God bless them," Hatem said with a smile.

That night he avoided looking toward the bride.

The mysterious man stood up to greet Hatem and came forward to embrace him. "Should we apologize or do you understand what happened?" he asked.

The man stood there waiting for Hatem to answer. "Sleeping in jail was very hard," Hatem said with a tired smile. "And the police were really brutal when they surrounded us and threw us in the cell. Note that word 'threw,' sir, because it's just the right word."

The man laughed and Hatem sat down in the chair facing him across the desk. "But I thought the guys here in headquarters had made a deal with you and you agreed they'd put you in the cell with the kids so they would trust you and you could get to know them better," the man replied.

Hatem began to take in details of the office as he struggled to overcome his exhaustion and indignation. These offices were always vast, to make you feel uncomfortable. It was deliberately a long way from the door to the official's desk, so that the official could assess you as you came in. Over many meters he had a chance to read the way you walked, how nervous you were, how confident, or how disgruntled. The fact that you can't take in the whole room in one glance helps to make you feel lost, even if only a little. Then there is the fear, the awe that a security official wants to create. He also has the advantage of a massive budget for furniture and other furnishings, probably including things specially commissioned for important people from the prison workshops.

The man who shook Hatem's hand and spoke to him as if they had been together in elementary school was not in fact the director of security. But he was apparently so much more influential that the director's office had been vacated for his use. He sat there in his well-cut suit, with a cigar in a holder, a gold lighter, and three cell phones that lit up constantly. One of them was vibrating, shaking the small table between them.

"We appreciate the fact you agreed to go through with this charade and I'd like to keep this meeting short in case the kids get suspicious. But I would like to hear your assessment of the situation as it stands," said the man.

Earlier that morning Hatem had suddenly heard the door opening noisily, as well as the sound of boots rubbing against boots, bolts sliding, and keys turning. The noise woke up Hassan and Tadros. Then it got even noisier and everyone stood up rubbing their eyes, looking around in confusion, and throwing quizzical glances at Hatem. A few long seconds later several policemen in civilian clothes came in. They got Sheikh Hatem politely to his feet, grabbed the kids gently, without the usual roughness, and led them out of the cell.

They went up some narrow, dark flights of stairs at the back of the building. There were no clues as to the time of day or to their whereabouts. Then they found themselves in another small room. But when they looked around they saw that Sheikh Hatem was no longer among them and, Hassan was surprised to find that he felt a sense of panic and missed the presence of the sheikh.

"Set them free immediately," Hatem told the man, whose name he still didn't know. "Those kids converted to Christianity for reasons that have nothing to do with Islam or with Christianity. When you harass them and detain them, you only give them an incentive to dig in their heels. To tell the truth, sir, even if they do convert to Christianity, is it the end of the world? Islam won't lose out and Christianity won't gain."

The man bristled and his face turned red behind the rings of smoke from his cigar. "Is that what you think, Mawlana?" he said.

Hatem smiled. "With all due respect. I'm saying that for your master's sake," he said.

The man stood up, as if he were recovering his strength and authority. He went and sat down in the chair behind the desk. "But those guys will cause trouble in the country," he said. "There'll be chaos. This affects national security, especially as there are foreign forces behind them."

"More obviously, they have psychological and family problems and they're ignorant and highly strung," said Hatem. He immediately regretted what he had said.

"You're talking politics, Mister Hatem!" the man bellowed.

So I've changed from 'sheikh' to 'mister' in a matter of seconds, Hatem thought to himself. "Well, you were talking religion so I thought I'd talk politics," he said.

The man smiled, as if to melt the ice that had suddenly built up between them. "Let's talk religion, especially as we have instructions to listen to your advice," said the man. He paused, as if for a comma. "On religion," he added, with a firm period. He looked at a telephone that was vibrating insistently, but decided to ignore it.

"We were thinking of getting a priest from the bishop's office and arranging a debate for the kids to watch. Don't worry, we'd arrange with the priest that you'd beat him," the man volunteered.

Hatem laughed. "You don't have confidence in me, or in Islam?" he asked.

The man laughed back. "Because they're a wily bunch and you can't be sure," he said.

"That would be doomed to fail," said Hatem. "Firstly, the kids would see it was set up and would be suspicious of everything about it, even if the priest seemed strong and straightforward in the debate. Second, those kids basically don't know anything about Islam or Christianity, and the conversation would go over their heads even if he and I really dumbed it down, and third, they are so stubborn and stressed out that a one- or two-hour debate wouldn't do any good."

"So what's to be done?"

"Let them out and tell them to go home right away."

"As simple as that?"

Frightened, on his guard, and exhausted, Hatem gave in. "That's what I think, but it's, it's up to you," he stammered.

The man got up and stood in front of Hatem, who also stood up, out of respect and as a precaution.

"Of course you realize that if we let them out we can't let Hassan go home till we get instructions from the big boss, and he's going to ask whether the boy's given up the idea of converting. We'll have to tell him the truth: that Hassan is still Boutros. He'll be angry with you, and angry with us while he's at it. Maybe you can take his anger but we certainly can't."

Hatem's fatigue got the better of his hesitation and he sat back down.

"Sir," he said, "if the boy was a soccer fan and supported Zamalek and we wanted him to support Ahli it would take us months, if we succeeded at all, and if he supported Ismaili and we wanted him to support Ahli, we would need eons and we still wouldn't succeed, and then you want me to reconvert him to Islam overnight?"

"You're right," the man said sympathetically. "But what should we do?"

Hatem showed signs that he had had enough. "Let him support Zamalek," he said.

He saw the man sneer menacingly.

"Just leave it to me. You release them all and I'll take Hassan with me," Hatem suggested.

"Where to?"

"To my place."

"Speak to the big boss," Hatem added after a long sigh, "and tell him I'll put Hassan up in my house temporarily, and hopefully God will come up with a good solution."

Hatem knew at the time that in this case he would need a clear definition of a good solution.

WHEN HE REACHED HOME HE knew he faced many arduous tasks. He and Hassan had arrived in a car driven by a police officer. Hatem shook hands with the officer and said good-bye, though the officer was clearly determined to come in with them and have a cup of tea. Hatem ignored him and the officer left before Hatem gave way and invited him in. Hatem took Hassan's hand and pulled him away from the car to the gate, which opened to reveal the Nubian doorman smiling and thanking God for Hatem's safe return.

Then Sirhan rushed over. "We were worried about you, Mawlana," he said.

"In you go, Hassan, please," said Hatem.

Hassan froze on the lawn outside the house. The gardener had clearly forgotten to trim the lawn because parts of it looked like an African jungle.

"What's wrong, Hassan?" said Hatem. "Are you shy?"

"We agreed that my name's Boutros," Hassan said, with all the petulance of a spoiled teenager.

Hatem laughed. "Wow, so that's what's upset you! Okay then, how about Peter?"

"Okay."

"Good, then please go in, Mister Peter. Or should I say Your Grace or Your Holiness?"

"No need for sarcasm," Hassan said emphatically.

"My boy, this is my house and I'll be as sarcastic as I like when I like," Hatem replied. "You can be sarcastic too," he added, putting his hand on Hassan's shoulder and pulling him toward him to embrace him. "Because this whole business is farcical," he added as he opened the door.

Only then, when he found that Omayma was out, did Hatem realize the immensity of the three tasks he faced: persuading Hassan to come with him, explaining to his wife why he had brought this problem home with him, and eventually finding a way to get the problem out of the house.

He had promised the president's son he would take Hassan home with him to stay with him so that he could bring him back to his senses, though Hatem was certain Hassan didn't have any common sense in the first place. The president's son had agreed, after consulting his wife, Peter the Apostle's sister, which took all of six seconds. The speed with which she agreed suggested she wanted to get the worry off her chest and throw the hot potato into Hatem's lap. They clearly imagined that Hatem was the grandson of Harut and Marut, the two magician angels, and that he had the power to cure idiots and imbeciles in the commercial breaks in his programs, just as he issued fatwas to callers in the program, who thanked him and the problem was solved. The way they saw it, it was as simple as that.

Several logistical problems remained. Hassan's clothes would come that evening from his father's house. Hassan would sleep in the guest room on the top floor, which was largely self-contained, with a fridge, a full-feature satellite television, an en suite bathroom, and a microwave, as well as a comfortable bed and a wardrobe. Thanks to his wife's foresight, guests could keep to themselves in their room without the permanent residents ever having to run into them.

Hatem took him up to the room. "If you find it's too much trouble to come up the stairs we could have an elevator installed," Hatem told him, with the levity of someone in despair at the task he faces.

Hassan received the sarcastic remark with as much seriousness as you would expect from a young man who wants to go to sleep immediately and avoid having a nervous breakdown. Hatem offered him some of his own fancy sports clothes.

"I've never worn them myself," he said, "and they're probably not my size. They were probably a gift from the owner of a sportswear store."

Hassan threw himself down on the bed, muttering things that would have made Omayma throw the two of them out of the house, had she heard them.

"Well, the room's better than that prison cell," he said.

As he was going downstairs, Hatem realized that he missed Omar. The feeling lifted him up and then slammed him down again. He missed going into Omar's room to find him playing on his PlayStation, oblivious of his father, looking straight ahead and answering his father's greetings with childish silliness. "Hi dad," he would reply, rapid and dismissive.

"Answer me nicely, my dear. Look at your father and tell him you missed him."

Omar would turn his head slowly toward Hatem and look at him for a few moments. "Missed you," he'd say.

"Okay, sir," Hatem would reply with a loving smile. "Thank you very much."

Omar's room had been empty since he lost his memory. When Omar came out of his coma, Hatem had been delighted. He fell to his knees and thanked God. In his happiness that Omar escaped death, he hadn't worried about the boy losing his memory, but as the days passed it became clear that he had lost some of his motor skills as well. Either he had forgotten how to move, or the brain damage had affected the motor centers in a way that made him walk like a young child. He didn't crawl but he didn't walk either. He stopped doing schoolwork of course and started physiotherapy sessions. Hatem was completely devastated. He was worried sick about whether his son could lead a normal life. He drew on all his reserves of patience and faith but couldn't get over the sense of defeat at seeing that there was no longer a sparkle in his child's eyes and that the words he spoke were twisted and broken like the speech of a foreign child learning Arabic. The fact that the boy had escaped the clutches of the angel of death and that Hatem had purged himself of pride and anger by cleaning the mosque toilets had given him some strength and taken away some of the pain, so when Omayma decided the boy had to go to England for further treatment, he agreed.

When Omar went away, Hatem was about the only father in the world who didn't have a telephone number for his son, who had relearned how to have a basic phone conversation. But Omayma had prevented Omar from taking his cell phone or the SIM card with his Egyptian number. She stayed there with him for a few weeks and then came back. The doctors promised her the boy could come home soon, once he recovered. Omayma didn't give Hatem the telephone number of Omar's room in the clinic and only allowed him to browse through photographs of the place on his iPad. The clinic had a garden on a stunningly green hill overlooking a lake in the middle of a thick wood of tall trees. The building was small and the rooms were very simple and practical. Hatem never missed an opportunity to tease Omayma by admiring the blonde nurses who would supposedly restore Omar's memory. He didn't know where Omayma found the strength to endure her son's absence. Maybe it was because she loved him so much and wanted him to be her bright-eyed boy again. Somewhere along the way she had turned hard and cold as stone toward her husband. Maybe this had started when he wandered off while Omar was in the intensive care unit and she sat alone on a plastic chair outside his room.

Hatem stretched out on the bed in his room overlooking the garden and caught a whiff of the mint that grew on the edge of the balcony. It relaxed him and brought him peace of mind. He remembered that he had to change his clothes, then he realized he needed to shower to wash away the dreadful night he had had. As he was preparing what he would say to Omayma, he saw her in their wedding photograph hanging on the wall. In the picture he was sitting on a chair in a dark suit that exactly reflected his poverty at the time. He laughed to himself when he remembered how much it cost. Omayma was standing behind him in her white wedding dress and a modest hijab under her bridal veil. Her mother had suggested she do without the hijab at the wedding but she had refused. She consulted him and he told her she was free to do what she liked, and his answer shocked her and she decided to wear it. Since then, he had grown fatter and she had lost weight and the gap between them had grown wider.

He couldn't pin down the moment when he realized that Omayma had changed, and he didn't like to ask himself which of them had changed first.

People are defined by their circumstances more than by their personality. Their circumstances and their interactions with other people affect them, and are affected by them. People create their circumstances and sometimes circumstances make what they want of people. He had married Omayma when he was an imam in a small mosque run by the ministry, and the term 'small' applied to him as much as to the mosque. It was a historic mosque but dilapidated, large but in a sparsely populated area. The term also applied to the world at that time: there was only local television, no Internet, no cell phones, and he never needed to go further than the Citadel. His income included his basic salary, fees for sermons at funerals, and gifts acquired through baraka. Omayma didn't have a job at the time, or ever. She had graduated from the faculty of commerce and heard him preach in the mosque next to her father's house every Friday. She waited to hear his voice, listened to what he said, and stood outside every Friday to see him. After the congregation came out of the mosque, he would shake hands with the people

waiting around outside with questions and with the shopkeepers who sought his blessings. He acquired a growing number
of admirers and his remote mosque started to get crowded. He
began to receive invitations to have lunch in the houses of people
who lived around the mosque where he preached on Friday. (Friday prayers themselves were banned inside the historic mosque
where he worked as imam and preacher, in case it became too
crowded and the building collapsed). Eventually he went to the
house of Omayma's family and she spoke to the young sheikh,
asking him about many points in his sermons. She seemed very
attentive and focused and definitely interested. After that he visited her a second and a third time, and on the fourth time he
brought his father to ask if Hatem could marry her.

He often wondered if she was religious at the time. The
same question could also be asked of him. It's true he was
a man of religion, a sheikh in a mosque and a preacher to
the public, but did he practice what he preached? People very
rarely practice what they preach, and Hatem was very busy
preaching. He also read voraciously, till knowledge oozed out
of him. He was ready and qualified to answer any question and
expound on any subject, but in his rush to become learned he
didn't stop to ask himself if he was acting on what he said. As
for Omayma, she was a typical young woman. It's true that a
typical young woman wouldn't get engaged to a sheikh or dare
to link arms with him in the Andalus garden on the Nile—
where you were forced to buy drinks from the juice sellers who
were more like highway robbers—because there was no such
thing as a romance with a sheikh. She was undoubtedly religious, but in a sense that didn't prevent her from memorizing
Mohamed Munir's songs, going to Adel Imam films during
Eid with her brothers, buying cheap make-up downtown, or
missing the afternoon or sunset prayers if she was visiting one
of her friends in Bab el-Shaariya.

After twenty years of marriage it couldn't be claimed that
she and Hatem had been passionately in love. Apparently love

was one thing and passion was something else. Passionate love was the Quranic expression that best reflected the sense of fusion through desire, but Hatem hadn't come across anything of that kind in his life and he didn't think Omayma was crazy about him in that way either. When they started living under the same roof and sleeping wrapped around each other in the same bed, their sexual encounters, and they were many in the beginning, would have been classified as intercourse—a precise term in Islamic law that required simply that penetration took place. But when you hear the term 'intercourse' it doesn't evoke a passionate or intimate encounter, with sighs, grunting, losing control, ecstasy, and earth-shaking orgasms. The word always sounds official, detached, and dry. What happened between him and Omayma was a marriage that was in fact a matrimonial contract, and the word 'matrimonial' itself conveys the level of restraint, formality, pragmatism, and materialism that marked the relationship between them.

Hatem would ask himself: "Has there been any affection or solace or compassion in these twenty years of marriage?" His answer was definitely that there had been, and there still was. When God spoke in the Quran about the triad of married life—"*And among His signs is this, that He has created for you mates from among yourselves, that you may find solace in them, and He has created affection and compassion between you. In this there are signs for those who reflect*"—he was laying down the basic elements without which a marriage cannot begin or survive. But there are many different levels of affection, solace, and compassion, and the degrees come and go, rise and fall, grow hot or cold, depending on many factors. On a scale of one to ten, the relationship between Hatem and Omayma was a level four at the beginning of the marriage. After that it was a long time before she became pregnant and they went to doctors and laboratories and had tests and X-rays, and there was the anticipation, the waiting, the anxiety, the feelings of inadequacy, the nasty remarks people made, the stupid questions, the idiotic advice, the excruciating frustration when Omayma's period came, the hopes that soared when her period was late and that then were dashed when it finally came. These painful experiences brought them closer together and took them up to a seven. After that the element of compassion outweighed the elements of solace and affection, and in many sermons in those days Hatem explained that he understood the elements in the Quran to be in ascending rather than descending order. In other words, solace was less important than affection, and affection was less important than compassion, while compassion was the broad, protective, and inclusive overarching element. On this same scale the relationship between him and Omayma now stood at about four and a half, because when God in His highest heavens said that these three elements are fundamental to marriage, He left it open to interpretation whether a marriage could be based on only one of these elements without the other two. Hatem was partial to the idea that it was compassion that kept his relationship with Omayma at four and a half.

What had happened was that Omayma no longer brought him solace. The peace of mind she had once given him, through her willingness to go along with his ideas and decisions and behavior, had diminished as his fame spread and his fortune accumulated. Circumstances had changed Hatem and made him more self-sufficient, but they had also changed Omayma and made her more acquisitive.

When Hatem earned a million pounds for his Ramadan program, all he cared about was being content and successful and continuing as he was. But it made Omayma ask why it couldn't be two million pounds rather than one million, and she developed an obsession for acquiring things. When Hatem once chanced to look inside her jewelry box (which didn't include the jewelry she wore ostentatiously on her hands and arms), he said, "If Abu Dhar al-Ghifari ever had a look in there, he'd give you a thrashing."

"That's why Othman bin Affan banished him from Medina," Omayma replied firmly.

Hatem turned toward her. "You . . . ! Where did you hear that story? Are you still watching my programs?" he asked.

"Do you actually tell stories like that on your program, Sheikh Hatem?" she replied sarcastically, tightening her head-scarf. "Now you wouldn't want the censors to get upset and say you were slandering the Companions of the Prophet, would you!"

"You've cut me to the quick, Lady Omayma," said Hatem, nodding his head in contrition and defeat. "But you haven't told me how you heard the story of Othman banishing Abu Dhar for warning people who hoarded money and silver that they would face hellfire."

"That was a long time ago, Sheikh Hatem. When we got engaged in the mosque in our street," Omayma replied.

The more Omayma took advantage of his wealth, the more hostile she was toward him. Something had snapped in this former admirer who used to memorize his sermons. She had grown older and was fed up and maybe bored, but she was also frustrated with this man who was and wasn't a sheikh. He tried to escape her by seeking renown. He distracted himself by making recordings, signing agreements, sitting with television producers, directors, and station owners, visits to foreign countries, conferences at home and abroad, press attacks, attacks from his rivals, expanding his other activities (such as sermons, soirees, invitations to mansions, private fatwas in the women's quarters of princes and millionaires), and giving his blessing at openings for new shops and companies, with his photograph under their names lit up in neon lights. Even at home he wasn't without his office staff, his program assistants, his producers, or uninvited delegations that would turn up, hang around, eat, drink, talk, and pass on whatever was said at his house. At first Omayma was involved in discussing everything, then she quietly withdrew from the scene. She saw him negotiating, getting angry, cursing and swearing because of some shortcoming or negligence or some other problem. She saw him making peace and on the attack. She saw him talking on the telephone and when the conversation was over he would say what he hadn't said on the phone, or the opposite of what he had said.

Once, standing behind the bedroom door when there were people in the sitting room, she said, "Hatem, I want to have my own bank account or a joint bank account with you, so that I can withdraw money like you."

He was surprised by the request and the timing, but he didn't discuss it for long. There was plenty of money and she was fed up with having to ask for money or having to remind him of the money needed for household expenses or for Omar, so he agreed. After that she surprised him by buying stock and managing her own tax affairs. He went along with these changes as part of the nature of things and as signs of God's bounty. Then she bought a farm and decided to move them into a larger house and send her son to a new school that was more expensive and classier. He found out by chance that she owned a store that sold clothes for women who wore the hijab and he scolded her gently.

"Why didn't you invite me to open the store, as I do for people that I don't even know?" he asked.

She said she hadn't wanted to draw attention to it, and he agreed and kept quiet. She bought another house on the north coast, then sold it and bought another one—he had hardly got used to sitting by the sea in the first house when she made him move to the next. She mixed with new friends that suddenly appeared in their lives, and took an obsessive interest in losing weight and radically changing the style of her hijab, from the traditional to the more modern. She didn't ask him what he thought, and although he was in favor and thought the new hijab was more stylish and more attractive, he didn't tell her so. The pace of the changes accelerated a few months after Omar fell ill. Omayma took Hatem to the weddings of her friends' children, and persuaded Hatem to employ some of her new acquaintances. A circle of helpers took shape around her and began to show up at the house. She remained religiously conservative, but her conservatism was now focused on formalities and superficial aspects of religion. It was remarkable the way she objected to any tolerant ideas that he had. Her life broadened and she became more narrow-minded. She wore the latest fashions but adopted ideas from the remote past. However, if he took a hard-line position on anything, she would take the opposite position, as if she had been born a secularist. She burned the bridges between them and took full control of Omar. Hatem had no right to decide anything as far as Omar was concerned. The boy was growing up in the home of a sheikh where there was no room for a sheikh's authority, at the hands of a mother who forced him to memorize the Quran one month, then banned the Quran teacher from the house the next month and decided that learning the short chapters of the Quran in school was quite enough. She would listen to Quran readers on television day and night and a few weeks later switch all the televisions to channels playing music videos.

There was a struggle between the young girl who fell in love with a sheikh's sermons and married him and the woman who got involved in business to fill the time, until the business filled her life and make her cold and unfriendly toward Hatem. He could hardly remember them sleeping together three times a year. He wasn't sure if she had lost interest in him or in sex. Maybe she had lost the ability to arouse him, or else he had lost the desire to be aroused. How could they go on living without sex? Fame took the place of sex, and the pleasures of wealth replaced sensual pleasures. But affluence created a demand for more affluence, a vicious circle. She didn't avoid him if he wanted her but she would be like a sack of potatoes lying passively beneath him. She might even look grumpy and what's worse, he once caught her looking at her watch when he was on top of her. Perhaps once in every twenty times he saw her take her bra off in front of him, he might be interested and get aroused. He thought to himself that that was a very reasonable average because sex was no longer on his list of priorities. Maybe his sadness arose because he had suppressed his sexual impulses.

They didn't complain about the situation but the gap was growing wider, and the fact that they increasingly ignored the gap made it worse. She never asked whether maybe he had taken a second wife in secret and he never suspected for a moment that she might leave him and ask for a divorce. So they didn't seek either to be far apart or close together. Managing their lives became more important than their lives themselves. How many other couples were like them, Hatem wondered.

Hatem dozed off a little and then woke up, thinking it was late. Omayma hadn't come home. He got up heavily, but not reluctantly because tonight he was filming an episode of his new program, in the middle of all the angst and hassle he had had to face since Hassan had appeared in his life. Under the jet of water in the shower he washed off the filth of the detention cell and his fatigue. He could almost feel his bones going back to their normal places. He had surprised himself and at the same time was pleased with how stoically he had endured the hardship. Nothing had broken his heart except Omar—worrying about him and the dark thoughts he had from time to time that undermined his peace of mind. He tried to dispel the images that came to him—Omar drowning in the swimming pool or swimming in his own blood, or bald from the effects of chemotherapy. He chased the images away by shaking his head rapidly. He hit his head with the hand that was holding the loufa, and the soapy froth became part of the images in his mind. He thought he might have heard foot-steps or a knock on the door, so he turned off the water and cleaned the rest of the soap off his ears. It was Omayma and he had no idea how she would react to him bringing Hassan to the house, especially when she found out that he was now a Boutros. Omayma could surprise him with strange reactions to very ordinary events and with calm reactions to events that were very strange, so she might shout in his face now or slap him when she saw the boy, or maybe the complete opposite: she might react very casually, as if he hadn't done anything that deserved any comment or attention.

He was also interested in seeing whether Omayma was obsessed with her weight and different diets these days, or whether she was in an easygoing phase where she hated strict diets and went back to being plump. Then she would hate herself for that and the wheel would turn full circle. Her weight fluctuated so much that he couldn't remember what she looked like when he last saw her.

But when he came out of the shower this time, she went straight to the point.

"Who is this person?" she asked.

"Oh, the mercies of God!" he exclaimed, parrying her attack. "Which person?" he added quickly, before she could get upset about his initial response.

"Ali el-Kaaki," she replied stridently.

He was taken aback. "Kaaki!" he exclaimed.

She sat down, stood up, turned, then came up to him and looked him straight in the face.

"On my way back I found the streets suddenly full of adverts for a new program of yours," she said.

"Since when did you take an interest in a new program or adverts all over the place?" he asked quickly.

She ignored what he said and continued. "I found out you've been working with Kaaki, Sheikh Hatem," she scoffed.

"I don't understand why you're upset that I work with this person," he replied, taken aback by the reason for her scoffing, not by the scoffing itself.

"He's a charlatan," she said.

Hatem roared with laughter as he looked for his clothes. "The problem is that Ali el-Kaaki wouldn't even know what that word means," he said.

Standing in front of the wardrobe, Hatem mumbled to himself, trying to remember. "Now is this the program where I wear my turban and caftan, or is it the Italian suit job?" he said.

"Can you remember how I was dressed in the adverts?" he asked, turning to Omayma.

"Italian, Mawlana."

"So it's the suit then."

Omayma was in one of her featherweight, shapely phases so she was nimble enough to outsmart him with jittery movements to accompany the words she spat out.

"Kaaki, Hatem, is a dubious character," she said. "He suddenly appeared from a job in Saudi Arabia as the partner of a police general in a company that does television ads. Then suddenly he started throwing millions around here and there and no one knows where his money comes from, so everyone says he's laundering drug money."

"How do you know all that?" asked Hatem, as he fastened the rest of the buttons on his shirt. "Since when were you interested in people who own advertising agencies in Egypt?"

"For a start, many of my friends know him well," she said.

"Friends!" he said, emphasizing the word by drawing it out slowly.

"Women friends, and I'd rather not tell you what women say about him being not just a charlatan."

"God forbid, Omayma. It's wrong to make false accusations against people."

"I tell you, this man runs his agency from the offices of the State Security Investigations department and he's so close to the Interior Ministry he might as well be a senior police officer."

Hatem sat down in silence and rested his arms on his lap until he had his breath back and his anger had subsided.

Then, deliberately calm although he doubted she would reciprocate, he asked, "Might I know right now what your relationship is with this man?"

She hit back with the violence of a cat when someone has stepped on its tail.

"Have you gone crazy, Sheikh Hatem?" she said.

"Choose your words carefully, Omayma."

"I will choose my words. What do you mean—relationship? How could I have a relationship with that lowlife?"

"Very well, let me rephrase the question and apologize for the way I phrased it the first time. Why so much interest in this man firstly, and second why so much anger?" Hatem asked.

"Because the woman he divorced is a friend of mine."

"Omayma, the last place to find accurate information about anyone is from the woman he divorced."

"On the contrary, they have accurate information, simply because they're divorced. Women who have accurate information about their husbands are bound to end up divorced." Omayma paused a moment, seated on a chair by the bed. "A happy marriage can't survive accurate information," she added.

"That's a new theory. But I'm not interested. Ali el-Kaaki might be the most disgusting man in Egypt, and I suspect that might be the case, but he has a monopoly on advertising across the country and he's the person who produces and finances my program and he's going to sell it to the stations and the program has cost him a good deal. He's a crook and I can't dispute that, but he's paid me three million pounds in fees for thirty programs, up front and in cash in a bag that I took from his office straight to the bank, so what's the problem? And besides, is he going to talk in the program, or am I? Is this about what I say or what he says? He may be a bigtime son of a bitch, a thief, and a cheat but in my program

I'm going to say things that are beneficial to people in their lives and that are good for me financially. Besides, since when have I refused to deal with people like Kaaki who work with the security services? For your information, the whole country works for them, and everyone I work with at the television stations gets permission from them before they even breathe, and they obey them like the guards who stand outside their office doors. And thank the good Lord and there's no need for you to have accurate information about your husband!"

After a conciliatory pause, Omayma resumed. "Do you work with them, Hatem?" she asked.

Hatem had tightened his belt but now he let it out crossly. "I'd work with them and more if they asked, but I hope to God they never ask. A two-bit officer who doesn't even know the Maun chapter of the Quran can force you to stay home and deprive you of millions of pounds in earnings, and I wouldn't rule out them throwing me in jail on any old trumped-up charge, and then you wouldn't find a single television station that would condescend to offer me a three-minute program. Omayma, I keep the truth to myself and I thank the Lord when I don't say the wrong thing."

She calmed down and seemed persuaded, then she sighed. "So what can I tell Shaimaa?" she asked.

"Which Shaimaa?"

"Kaaki's former wife," she shouted.

"Omayma, if Kaaki were to give Shaimaa three million pounds she'd kiss his hand and say the opposite of what she's saying now. So calm down and tell her that her former husband, the big bastard, has bought your husband for three million pounds and she'll sympathize with you immediately!"

"You don't know Shaimaa."

"The truth is I'd like to get to know her," he said with a smile.

Omayma decided to drop her bombshell. "Did you know he imports slave girls and sells them to millionaires in Egypt?" she said.

The problem was that Hatem had already heard this rumor. But right at that moment they heard a voice calling from outside the room. "Sheikh Hatem!" it said.

Hatem knew at once who it was, but Omayma was taken by surprise.

"Who's that?" she screeched nervously.

"I'm Boutros," came the answer, hesitant but still loud.

She turned to Hatem with her mouth open in a stunned stare. He had finished dressing and he responded to her reaction with a broad smile and nodded. "Would you rather shoot me now or wait till I come back from the recording session and poison me at your leisure?" he said, confident that disaster was imminent.

In the studio that day Kaaki deliberately hung around with Hatem and insisted on giving Hatem a lift in his car. In fact Hatem was surprised by how grand and luxurious the car was, but he had trained himself to be indifferent to the behavior and material wealth he came across, although a man like him should have spoken out against the greed he encountered. Being impressed might lead to envy or imitation or indignation or frustration with the power and arrogance of money. He didn't trouble himself with comparisons between, on one hand, the abject poverty of the millions of people who lived along the road from his house to the studio and, on the other hand, the wealthy people who were bingeing and carousing with all the dismal and disgusting wealth they had. He had given up making comparisons because it was all relative. Everyone at each level of society saw the next level up as the ultimate end, and there were people who would be envious and competitive toward other people at the same level, because there were distinctions and differences within that level. "*We have raised some of them by degrees above others.*" He often found peace of mind in this verse of the Quran when he went to places where he used to live and met crowds of people seeking alms or wanting

211

recommendations for jobs, or he had to deal with the people who rushed to the television studio doors to wait for him and ask him for help. Some interpreters of the Quran talk about these "degrees" as if they are degrees of piety or closeness to God. Others interpret them as meaning degrees of knowledge. But Hatem was inclined to believe that there wasn't one single scale, but many different scales. Someone might score 1 out of 10 on the wealth scale but much higher on the faith scale, for example, or 8 out of 10 on the health scale but very low on the knowledge scale, because they were ignorant. And over time people could move up and down the various scales. Hatem imagined the scales having colors to distinguish them: green for faith, say, and red for wealth.

There were poor people who would consider Hatem a millionaire, while Hatem himself thought he was poor compared to the people he met. For every man of learning there was someone more learned and for every rich person there was someone who was richer. For every car there was a newer model, even though you could get into an accident and die in any of them. There are no limits to ambition and those who can never have enough will always be hungry, however much they eat and however much they think they are full. Hatem very much liked the concept of judging a car by its condition, not by its model. Applying this to people had an interesting effect: you would judge people by their health, their knowledge, their faith and their happiness, and not by external features, such as whether they were rich or poor, important or insignificant, famous or unknown.

Hatem was deep in thought because throughout the one-hour journey Kaaki never stopped talking on his cell phone. He made decisions, cursed, flattered, humored, whispered, shouted, paused, and exploded twenty times, and when they reached the studio he was still talking as he got out of the car. One of his staff had been waiting for him and opened the door of the car. When three of Kaaki's employees welcomed Hatem, Hatem took one he knew by the hand and said, "Wait a moment."

Hatem turned to Kaaki, who was smiling at him as he chatted and who waved him into the studio. Hatem grabbed the phone from Kaaki's hand. "We regret the technical fault," he intoned gravely to the person on the other end of the line. "We will contact you after the break." Then he hung up to laughs from everyone around and put the phone in the hand of the employee.

"Keep your boss's phone well away from him or else I'll commit a felony in the studio," Hatem told him.

The studio was equipped with the most up-to-date and most expensive equipment. They went in together to where the studio set was. Kaaki was talking to him about the set designer and how so-and-so was the most expensive and the most famous. Kaaki was pleased that the program was based on his idea, even though it wasn't a new idea, but with his money and with the staff he had around him they thought it would be an international television event. The idea was that Sheikh Hatem would stand in the middle of the set and would occasionally sit in a chair on one side of the frame. In front of Hatem there would be chairs arranged in a semicircle or a horseshoe shape where the audience of young people would sit. Hatem would move around among them with five cameras covering all the angles, giving his condensed lecture. Then he would listen to what they thought, answer them, and comment on their questions, which could also be asked by text message or on Facebook or by email. Hatem had seen it a million times in many programs and he didn't believe there was anything new in it but he agreed to it because it was a new format for him. As they admired the set, which was overwhelmingly green (on the grounds that green was the favored Islamic color, without anyone really knowing what green had to do with Islam), a tall, well-built young man slipped in among the group. He came up to embrace Hatem and Kaaki introduced him as "the film director who's going to direct our programs, Mawlana."

"You're the one who directed that film with that really pretty girl, aren't you?" Hatem asked him.

The director and Kaaki couldn't think who Hatem was talking about. "Which one was that, Mawlana? They're all really pretty," said Kaaki.

Hatem gave Kaaki a friendly push. "You don't know anything about women, Kaaki," he said.

"You're the artist," Hatem added, turning to the director. "So tell me, are all women really pretty?"

The director was unsure how to answer.

"You look confused. Look, all women are pretty but there are different types of pretty—there's even pretty plain and pretty awful."

"But we still don't know who the actress is," said Kaaki.

"It was the girl who starts wearing the hijab at the end of the film," said Hatem. "Why would anyone do that anyway, make that girl wear the hijab? Putting a hijab on her is a crime!"

Everyone laughed, but Hatem would probably pay a high price for that moment.

Kaaki then asked him to come over to the horse stables he owned nearby to discuss something important and urgent, and since the money had been decided and the contract had been signed and Hatem had received his millions, Hatem didn't understand what important and urgent subject they needed to discuss in the shade of the lime trees and to the sound of the horses neighing. Hatem wasn't surprised to discover that Kaaki owned horses, but when they reached the stables he realized that the man was more interested in acquiring all the trappings of wealth and high social status, regardless of whether he liked horses. The stables dated back to before Kaaki became rich and it was the first stable Hatem had ever been in where the owner wasn't impatient to show off his horses and boast of their pedigree and their beauty.

Hatem felt immediately that this was a man who didn't deserve his horses, but he didn't say anything. The money in his pocket was still warm from when he had received it from Kaaki and the program hadn't started yet, let alone finished. In the absence of Kaaki's staff, who usually clung to him through all his disastrous doings, and with the door of the large office in the annex to the stables closed behind them, Kaaki ambushed him with a question Hatem couldn't possibly have foreseen.

"Mawlana," he said, "why did God say it's okay to buy and sell slaves?"

Hatem almost said, "What the hell does that have to do with you?" but he changed his mind when he saw Kaaki's face, which was serious with a hint of evil.

The question took Hatem by surprise, although the subject was scattered throughout the history books like goods on the pavement that people had tired of buying and selling. But given that the question came from Kaaki, the owner of a famous advertising agency, and that he asked it with such impatience and so secretively and with a mysterious flash in his eyes, it suddenly struck Hatem as significant. He hadn't put much stock in the vague rumors discrediting Kaaki because the intense rivalries, inevitable when hundreds of millions of pounds were at stake, undermined the credibility of accusations involving anyone in the television business. It was true that ever since he had met him, Hatem had known deep down that Kaaki was just a clever conman—not clever in the positive sense, but clever as the word might be used to describe a thief. He was also very influential, perhaps by sharing his profits with senior officials, or as Khodeiri put it when he brought Hatem tea in the office after Kaaki had gone, after having handing over the bag with the three-million-pound fee for the program, "That man, Mawlana, is laundering money, either his own money or the money of important people."

Why did Kaaki insist on giving Hatem the money in cash rather than by depositing it in the bank or by making a bank transfer? Hatem thought it was showmanship. He wanted you to see his millions in front of your eyes, not just a number on a piece of paper coming from a bank, or else it was a display of his financial might at a time when fraud and evasion prevailed among producers like these, but unfortunately Khodeiri's logic was the soundest. Rationally the three million pounds should have been handed over in installments, not all in advance like that, and in the form of checks or bank drafts. But putting the money in front of him in the form of thirty thousand one-hundred-pound notes in a bag was the kind of scene you'd expect in a gangster film. Hatem's suspicions about Kaaki never made him consider refusing to do the program and he thought he had plenty of arguments to justify his position: he reckoned he was giving people knowledge and religion, for a start. But when Kaaki asked him about buying and selling slaves Hatem realized that he was even more of a lowlife than he had suspected, and he tried to avoid the question by asking more questions.

"Why do you ask?" he said.

"Do I have to have a reason for asking? Suppose I just want to know!"

"Know why?" Hatem asked stupidly.

Kaaki tried to be clever. "Isn't it just an accusation made by the West and by people who hate Islam, that the Prophet permitted slavery and the slave trade?" he said.

"And you're suddenly interested in Islam's reputation?"

"What's up, Mawlana? Why are you so stingy with your knowledge?"

"Okay, you want knowledge, you can have it. When we say Islam didn't ban slavery, that is more precise than saying Islam allowed it, because slavery, like alcohol, existed before the Prophet Muhammad began his mission. Then Islam came and alcohol was banned, and please don't ask me whether hashish and weed are halal or haram."

Hatem expected Kaaki to laugh. But instead Kaaki said seriously, "For your information, Mawlana, I never go near alcohol and I never have sex outside marriage."

"You only buy and sell slaves," Hatem said with a laugh.

Kaaki's face turned various shades. There was a long silence, interrupted by Kaaki muttering and recovering.

"Could you continue, Mawlana," Kaaki finally said.

"Continue what?"

"Your fatwa on slavery."

"I'm not giving a fatwa on it, because it doesn't call for a fatwa. The truth is that Islam didn't in fact outlaw the slave trade or slavery, and you'll find dozens of religious scholars trying to defend the position of Islam on this."

"And does Islam need to be defended, as if it's been accused?"

"The underlying principle is that Islam is a religion of freedom, justice, and equality. One of the aims was to free Muslims from slavery to anything and anyone other than God. We are slaves only to God. Besides, humans are free, and if a religion with this message didn't say that no human being should be a slave to any other human being, then this is something that calls for thought about how far this is compatible with the message of freedom that Islam brought. In fact no religions ban slavery. It looks like God accepts and approves the existence of slaves among His creatures on Earth, and this is something that believers might not be able to understand. Why indeed didn't Islam ban slavery and the slave trade? Since the Prophet died"—Kaaki quickly mumbled, "May God bless him and grant him peace" though Hatem himself hadn't used the formula—"a million people have explained that Islam says that slaves should be well-treated. Even the Prophet"—Kaaki slipped in another "May God bless him and grant him peace"—"said, 'My friend the Angel Gabriel advised me to be kind to slaves and I even thought he was going to set a deadline for setting them free.'

"You'll find people who talk about the explicit verse of the Quran that urges good treatment for slaves, or *what your right hands possess*, as the Quran puts it. *Worship God, and do not ascribe anything as partner to Him. Show kindness to parents and near kin and orphans and the needy, to neighbors who are kin and neighbors who are not kin and friends by your side and wayfarers and what your right hands possess. God does not love those who are proud and boastful.*

"It tells you to feed slaves with the same food that you eat, dress them in the same clothes, not to make them do more than they can bear, and to help them. It urges you to marry off widows and slave girls, and male slaves if they are virtuous, and not to break up families that fall into slavery. There are many verses that recommend emancipating a slave as a way to atone for sins, but none of this challenges the indisputable reality that Islam did not ban the slave trade and did not take a stand against slavery. In fact the spoils of Islamic wars included prisoners and slaves and there are very many stories about thousands of slave girls and slave boys living in the houses of the Companions of the Prophet and the generation that came after and in the palaces of the caliphs of course, and of princes, and in the mansions of Muslims. And there was an enormous amount of activity in the slave trade, so much so that there was government oversight of the sector by the Islamic state. The slave traders had a government official who supervised their operations with the title 'superintendent of slaves' because there were special markets for slaves in Muslim cities. In the reign of the Abbasid Caliph Mutasim it got to the stage where they set up a special government department for slaves, the equivalent of a ministry today, called the Diwan of Mawali and Ghilman."

"That was the same Mutasim as in the expression '*Waa Mutasimaah*.'" Kaaki cut in. "The caliph in the story about the woman who appealed to him for help when the Byzantine merchant hit her."

"Yes sir, the *Waa Mutasimaah* guy. He had a government department for supervising slaves. Any objections?" Hatem asked.

Yet again Hatem stopped and waited to hear where this intense and sudden interest in slavery was leading, but Kaaki just waited for Hatem to say more.

"And of course there are books with stories about slave girls," Hatem added in desperation. "Would you like me to tell you a few slave girl stories with lots of sex and music and wild parties?" he continued, warming to the theme. Then he stood up, pretending to be startled.

"What's up, Kaaki?" he said. "There's something weird about this conversation and I'd like to know what this is about."

Kaaki smiled for the first time since they'd arrived. "Calm down, Your Grace," he said, "just sit down and tell me what Islam says about right hands possessing things."

"I've sat down, sir," Hatem said, "but I won't say a word about right hands possessing things, or left hands for that matter, until you answer my question. What's all this about?"

"It's a new film, a historical series, and I'd like to know what you think about the sharia aspects," Kaaki said. Hatem listened to his hasty explanation and took it with a large pinch of salt.

"Look," Hatem said. "It's modern law, which many of our sheikhs don't like, that outlawed slavery. Slavery came to an end as humanity progressed and societies evolved. After slaves had ruled Egypt, for example, for five hundred years—in the Mamluk state, as you learned at school, owning slaves became a criminal offense, but not a religious offense unfortunately, and that means that I, with my inadequate intellect and my limited knowledge, can't understand God's logic in not stipulating that slavery is haram. There must be a reason but I haven't been able to find it and I suspect that no one else has either. It's a gap in our understanding. People have filled the gap by banning slavery, but only after hundreds of years of misery that was inflicted with the support of holy books and religions. Whatever people tell us about Islam imposing limits on slavery or mitigating the effects, what's undeniable is that Islam didn't ban it or stop it and it never told us what the logic was in that, or if it did I've never heard it or come across it."

Kaaki looked pleased for some reason. "Okay, I'll fill you in," he said.

Early in life, he explained, he got a job in a public relations and advertising company in Saudi Arabia through a recommendation from a relative of his who was working in State Security and later retired. He got in touch with someone, who spoke to someone, and he received a contract offering him an insignificant job with derisory terms, as you would expect given the distant relationship between him and the man who recommended him. The company was not very active or successful and it didn't have extensive dealings with television stations or newspapers, for example, although it appeared to be wealthy and showed signs of opulence. He worked as a clerk in the office of the Lebanese manager, Michel Abu Maalouf, a Maronite and one of those Lebanese who had helped turn Lebanon into a playground for Saudi princes and sheikhs by transferring assets, buying real estate, arranging holidays in Lebanon, and buying shares in companies. The man had considerable influence in the company and Kaaki noticed right from the start that Abu Maalouf was the big shot, so he curried favor with him the Egyptian way, just as you'd expect from an outsider who has neither money nor influence nor morals. After a few months Kaaki was the chief clerk and Abu Maalouf's constant companion. He moved into a room in his large house on the Jeddah seafront and at that stage he found out that the company's advertising activities were just a way to keep everyone looking busy and the real money was pouring in through the spoiled, good-for-nothing son of one of the princes. Because he was the fourteenth son, the prince wasn't bothered that his son was useless and wasn't upset that he was frittering away his share of his father's fortune.

So far the story seemed very normal and Hatem was getting bored, though Kaaki's attempts to be mysterious were very obvious. He was like a child trying to hide a balloon behind his back and asking "Do you know what I'm hiding?" when the balloon was clearly visible over his shoulders. It was obvious that Kaaki had got involved in something or that Abu Maalouf would turn out to be the leader of a gang at the end of the film.

Finally Kaaki said straight out that the Lebanese man was responsible for supplying women to the prince and his sons and that his activities extended far beyond just the household of that prince.

"Mawlana," Kaaki said, "you know the Saudis who come to Egypt and marry young girls for pathetic dowries that go to the father, who's poor or greedy or handicapped"—"or a beast," Hatem added, and Kaaki didn't object—"and then take them off to Saudi Arabia, where the girl finds she's just one of the man's wives and the man soon starts to ignore her so that she doesn't know whether he's divorcing her or keeping her on. Those men are the poorest and the lowest of the low in Saudi Arabia. When it comes to the rich and wealthy types and anyone from the princes on down, they have all dealt with Abu Maalouf, who brought them 'what their right hands possessed.' Once we were in a hotel in Beirut where there was a big hall that only guests and some of their trusted staff could enter, and Abu Maalouf was anxious to make sure there was more than one customer present in order to play on the competition and envy between them. It wasn't so that he could jack up the price of the girls because there was never any bidding. Abu Maalouf got his money from them in the form of gifts and presents, with no prices set or fees calculated. But it was important to liven things up, so that every customer felt he had won a girl by snatching her from someone else. The girls would appear wearing long gowns that covered their whole body, then each one would start revealing what was underneath, turning and walking and bowing and standing up and bending over, stretching and dancing and shaking, sticking out their bottoms and lifting up their breasts until one of the men pointed at a woman and she would go over to him and be his property instantly.

"So where did these girls come from? Abu Maalouf kept that a secret as if his life depended on it. But he chose very carefully because his customers were unforgiving. If one of the girls turned out to be diseased or disobedient or rebellious, the consequences would be severe. And when the man was fed up with the girl he only had to tell Michel and Michel would take care of it."

Now Hatem understood everything, but what did Kaaki want? He leaned back in his chair.

"Very well," he said. "What do you want from me now? I've got the message that you were assistant to a highly successful slave trader in the Arabian Peninsula."

"I'd like you to reassure me."

"Reassure you that God will forgive you? Do you think we're in a Catholic church, and I'm going to take your confession and forgive you?"

"What do you mean, forgive me!" Kaaki said indignantly. "Am I doing anything wrong?"

Hatem picked up on the tense Kaaki had used and was taken by surprise.

"Doing? Doing? That's the present tense, Kaaki, not the past," he said. "Are you still doing it, or you used to do it?"

"I left Saudi Arabia ten years ago, Mawlana, and then Abu Maalouf himself died, and the princes and sheikhs there were too much for me—they had become too much for Abu Maalouf himself a long time back—but the truth is Egypt has people who are so rich they're never satisfied. Most of them are people who pray and give alms and are religious and make the pilgrimage to Mecca every year, and they don't want to have anything to do with illicit sex and other such horrors, because they bring bad luck. I've met quite a few of them who handle it through short-term marriages, which isn't in our version of Islam. Maybe the Shi'a do it, but we're Sunnis, thank God. Some of them got involved with some European bastards who ripped them off, and so I decided to relive the days of Abu Maalouf as long as it's all halal. God laid down the law on slaves, and anyway, who was the second best Muslim ever?"

"Who?" asked Hatem.

"I mean after the Prophet, may God bless him and grant him peace. So who would it be?"

"Please, tell us who it is and spare us!" begged Hatem in exasperation.

"Let's suppose it was Omar ibn al-Khattab, may God be pleased with him."

"Okay."

"He had slave girls and other slaves and 'what his right hand possessed,' and he was the most ascetic man ever. Ali ibn Abi Talib had them too, and even Hassan and Hussein. Is there anyone better than Hassan and Hussein? Absolutely not. But they had good-looking slave girls and I won't say anything about the caliph Othman or the other caliphs and their harems, yet they were the great men of Islam. I'm not doing anything that would make God angry. Women sell themselves or traders buy them in Europe or from Latin America and even from Africa or Asia. The businessmen and rich people here don't have a market where they can buy them. When you buy a slave girl, she'll do anything for you. She'll make you feel good and give you a really good time without any responsibilities or any heartache. She's there in a house or a hotel and they call her an employee in a company or a hotel or a night club but in fact she's a slave girl at your beck and call. For your information, Mawlana, it's true there's a lot of money in this business but I don't have more than ten or twelve girls in the market. I only buy as much stock as the market will bear."

"You know what the problem is here, Kaaki?"

"What, Mawlana?"

"In your case the difference between slave trading and pimping is impossible to see with the naked eye."

"So I'm a pimp?"

Hatem ignored his surprised indignation and continued: "I have a feeling you don't earn much from this business but you find your true self in it. You really love it."

"Haven't you asked yourself, Mawlana, why I told you the story?" Kaaki asked in earnest.

"I asked you two minutes ago and you didn't give me an answer," Hatem replied.

"I asked you because I wanted to be sure that slave girls are halal, and that you couldn't say they're haram in the least—and you can't. Anyway, the main thing is that I found out that Khaled Abu Hadid told you about me and about the Ukrainian girl he got pregnant and he asked you what he should do with her and you advised him to marry her."

Omayma's restrained reaction had convinced Hatem that she was confused. He had expected her to throw a fit or explode when he told her who Mr. Hassan Boutros was. He had no idea what she would do when he went on and said that Boutros was going to stay in their house for God alone knew how long. Her moods were unpredictable and her reactions could swing from one extreme to another.

In fact she was delighted when she saw Hassan and, surprisingly, she called him Boutros. By accepting him she won his heart immediately and his initial reserve faded away. He sat next to her on the sofa like a child in middle school taking orders from a teacher. She asked him questions Hatem hadn't asked, which led Hatem to admit that his wife's brain was not completely frazzled and what was left of it was perfectly adequate for a person to live by. She asked him about his birthday and discovered that he was the same sign as Omar, and she began to list ten things she predicted both of them would do in the same way. She asked him which school and university he had been to and whether his boss at work had been a man or a woman, about his roots in the country and whether he went to the family's hometown or not, about whether he knew so-and-so who was at school with him and so-and-so who worked in the same company. She grilled him on whether he had had a girlfriend as a student and told him about Omar and the adventures he had had in nursery school and later at school. Hassan answered her questions with the pride of an adolescent when his mother realizes that his voice has broken.

"Do you like your room, Boutros?" she asked. Hatem noticed that she said the Christian name as naturally as someone who had long been used to saying it.

"It's very nice, Mrs. . . ." He stopped and stumbled on his words, not knowing how to address her.

"You can call me Omayma," she said, trying to help him out. Hatem wouldn't have expected her to answer that way on other occasions.

"Omayma," Hatem interrupted, disapprovingly and in a hurry because filming time was fast approaching.

She ignored him and turned to Hassan.

"By the way, I used to love my Coptic school friends in the old days, and my friend Demiana was one of my best friends before she emigrated to Canada with her husband, who was a pharmacist," she said.

Hatem was amazed. He no longer knew if this was professional lying or consummate acting or whether it contained a grain of truth about something he had never heard in all his married life.

Omayma continued. "And Salwa Abdel-Malak was my neighbor and my friend. Her mother used to make us the best rice pudding I've ever tasted, and I went to church with her often and the priest once told me he could see the radiance of the Virgin Mary in my face."

"The priest was probably flirting with you," said Hatem, interrupting again. Then he turned to Hassan and said sarcastically, "Is this national unity spiel having any effect on you?"

"To tell the truth, no," said Hassan, embarrassed for Omayma but in collusion with Hatem. Hassan and Hatem laughed, and Omayma joined in belatedly.

"As for me, Hassan, or Boutros so you don't get angry with me after my virtuous wife has baptized you, I've never really known any Copts. In the neighborhood where I grew up I hardly ever came across a neighbor who was Coptic and I never dealt with any Coptic pharmacists in a drugstore for example, even by chance, and of course I was an Azhar student and so there weren't any Christians in my school life right through to graduation. Then I was in the Ministry of Religious Endowments and you know about that. Then in the world of satellite channels and television I might have come across one or two, colleagues or technicians, but not colleagues or friends close enough that we would visit each other at home and so on. I now realize that's been negligent on my part, or perhaps a strange turn of fate, that's gone on for forty-five years. Everything I know about Christians comes from books about Christianity. But I've always felt uneasy when I hear a Muslim talking about his friendships with Christians, or a Christian talking about his Muslim friends. When Omayma was making up those stories for you now, or dragging them out of some forgotten region in the memory center in her brain, she wanted to prove that she was good and not prejudiced, or that she was normal, but it's not normal that just because someone's Muslim they should be required to prove they're not prejudiced against Christians, or because they're Christian that they're supposed to talk about their Muslim friends, to prove that they're tolerant. We're all defensive here. We're defending ourselves against an accusation that no one has specifically made against us, but now it seems to become a wound that we all keep touching. So anyway, I've never in my life knowingly met or made friends with a Christian, I've never had a Christian neighbor, and there was no Uncle George that was my father's friend and no Umm Rizq that was my mother's friend. I never went to a Dr. Jeannette to have my tonsils treated when I was young. If one of the requirements for being tolerant is being neighbors with a Copt, does all this make me prejudiced?"

Hatem stood up, feeling nervous. "Okay, Boutros, I have to go on air," he said.

"Why the hurry?" asked Omayma. "It's only five minutes to the studios."

"This is the first program in the series and I'd like to be there early. Besides, I got dressed here for a change, because I haven't sat down with the production people and the director for days and I don't know what we'll be talking about in the first place. So off we go."

In the car, as they were about to drive through the gates of Media Production City, Hatem spoke to the driver. "Sirhan, could you go deaf for a minute?" he said.

"I've been deaf since I was born, Mawlana," replied Sirhan, happily compliant.

"Sirhan?" said Hatem.

"Yes."

"Come on, how can you be deaf when you heard your name?"

Sirhan laughed, and Hassan too. Then Hatem whispered in Hassan's ear.

"In the studio you're Boutros, okay? But everyone will treat you as a Christian who wants to turn Muslim, and I'm persuading you to convert or I'm teaching you about Islam. But if they find out you're Muslim and you want to be Christian or you've already converted and I'm trying to persuade you to revert to Islam, I guarantee you they'll pulverize us. We'll take a beating that'll crush our bones and turn them into dust."

*

When the red light on the camera facing him came on, Hatem recited the Fatiha and put his trust in God. He heard the song that had been composed for the program sung by a famous young singer that made the girls swoon. Kaaki had decided that, to give the program more appeal, he would drop the sad, soft music that dominated religious program after religious program and grab people's attention with a song by the most famous young singer in the country. It was a chance for the singer to associate himself with religiosity, especially after some well-publicized relationships of his had tarnished his image. The singer had decided to set this straight with a song that he called a gift to the program, although Kaaki claimed he had paid half a million pounds for it. In Hatem's view, the song was an accurate reflection of how children behave when they try to get involved in adult conversations, but Kaaki and the production staff around him were delighted with it and thought it would be a big hit. Hatem was sure it came from a different world from the one he knew. The rhythms of the music faded out with the singer's voice in Hatem's earpiece and then the director said, "Over to you, Mawlana, we're on air."

Hatem was standing in the middle of an incomplete semicircle surrounded by young people sitting on wooden tiers. Their faces and clothes suggested that Kaaki had chosen them himself. He gave each of them a respectable amount of money for taking part in the program, so they were carefully chosen to be smart and well-dressed. Hatem could well have been meeting the public relations team from Thomas Cook. He had asked for the girls not to be separated from the boys, while leaving a clear distance between any boy and girl who were sitting next to each other.

"Mixed but not cheek by jowl," as Hatem had put it clearly.

Kaaki objected, arguing that it was too late to change the plan. Then he revealed his real motive: Saudi stations might refuse to buy the program if the boys and girls sat together.

"Mawlana, I barely managed to persuade them to let girls be present without the hijab," he said. "Leave the format to me, Mawlana."

So Hatem left it to him and cleared his throat, abandoning his ideas about being the enlightened preacher if that was a threat to marketing the program.

"Peace be upon you and the mercy and blessings of God. How are you all?" he began.

None of them answered and he realized they had not been given instructions to speak, except for the ones they had agreed would ask questions. The production team had assured Hatem that all the questions were phrased in a way that looked spontaneous and the questions were safe. Kaaki himself had reviewed them for censorship purposes and they had offered to brief Hatem on them so that he could prepare his responses. He smiled confidently and turned the offer down.

"Return the greeting. Don't you know that if someone greets you, you should respond with an even better greeting, or at least return the greeting?" Hatem said.

There were murmured greetings from the ring of seats, in compliance with signals from the assistant director.

"Very well, that makes me ask what could be better than saying, 'Peace be upon you and the mercy and blessings of God.' The instruction is that we should respond with something better, or at least with the same greeting. Is there anything better than 'Peace be upon you'? God says, *Their greeting will be "Peace."* See how beautiful that is. So what's better? What's better might be in the manner of the greeting and not in the words, the warmth and sincerity and enthusiasm of your response. In the countryside you find that after 'Peace be upon you' the man replies 'Please' and the other man then says 'God preserve you,' and the first man insists with another 'Please' and the other man then says 'God bless you.' Being insistent when greeting others goes with the beauty and the enthusiasm of the greeting. And after the greetings we have to remind ourselves that we're in a forum on religious knowledge so don't be misled by the lighting and the cameras, the sets, and this nice spacious studio. You all look like you're going out for dinner after the filming anyway."

Some of them laughed, angrily or cheerfully. Hatem sneaked a smile at Hassan, who was sitting at the end of the upper tier of seats. Hatem was moving around among them, trying to breathe some warmth into them. In a mosque the congregation looks unnatural. They're clearly making a show of being respectful and devout, as if that's what required by the etiquette of sitting in a mosque, while a mosque is also called 'a gathering place.' In other words the sense of people gathering there is important. Warmth, presence, sharing, and listening, not silence but movement, internal movement that shows in people's eyes when they are listening attentively and with interest. Friday sermons are a golden opportunity for people to doze off, out of boredom, so it's important for the preacher to keep people awake. But that doesn't mean shouting and screaming, because that makes people tense and tension doesn't make people listen or wake up. It just makes people annoyed. All the successful sheikhs, regardless of what Hatem thought of their learning, were the ones who succeeded in moving the crowd, in stimulating the listeners by engaging them in the sermon or the lesson interactively, by smiling or crying. He hated that acting that the audiences in television programs went in for, and the worst kind of acting was pretending to be interested. Several times he had tried to persuade the producers of his programs to let him take on a random audience that hadn't been selected so that he could get rid of the artificiality, but they were too worried about who they would get or they rejected the proposal on the grounds that the production process would be too chaotic.

"Muslims must never stop asking questions," Hatem continued. "To be truly religious you have to question things, because questions lead to knowledge and knowledge leads to faith. That's why you find God commanding us to ask questions. *Ask those who possess the Message*, it says in the Quran, defining both the person asking and the people asked. You'll find eminent sheikhs persistently warning against debate, while the truth is that we have been ordered to debate things. God says, *And argue with them in ways that are best*. Of course what our eminent and learned scholars are criticizing is debate that serves no purpose. Remind me to speak to you some time about learning that serves no purpose and ignorance that does no harm, but now for your questions."

A young man came forward, clearly a school prefect that the production people or the assistant director had chosen. He came down the steps and headed for the microphone set up in front of a camera that transmitted a picture of the questioner to a screen behind Hatem.

"Peace be upon you," he began.

"And the mercy and blessings of God."

"Mister Hatem . . ."

They had agreed that on this program he would be 'mister' and not 'Your Grace' or 'Mawlana.' The supposedly youthful nature of the program, the fact that Hatem was wearing his suit rather than his gown and turban, and Kaaki's orders—all these were reasons for giving the audience strict instructions to address Hatem as 'mister' rather than 'sheikh.'

"What's your interpretation of the Quranic verse in which God Almighty says, '*We offered the trust to the heavens and the earth and the mountains, but they refused to accept it and were afraid of it. And man assumed it. He has been unjust and ignorant.*' Do the heavens and earth and the mountains hear and understand? Are they conscious and can they choose to refuse or accept anything? Then it says God gave the trust to mankind. Does it mean He gave it to Adam?"

Hatem was impressed by the production person who had helped the young man memorize the question. The face of the questioner, as he appeared on the big screen that Hatem was watching with an expert eye, looked so casual and theatrical that Hatem assumed he was as a young actor practicing on the program.

The camera turned and followed Hatem as he moved from one corner to another. "The question is excellent," he said. "It goes straight to the heart of the matter. It's a question about basic principles, but what's missing from the question is more important than what's in it. What is this trust? God offered something to the heavens and the earth and the mountains. How and why and where? Okay, but the 'what' is more important here. What is this thing, this trust?"

In the gap between thinking about the answer and coming out with it Hatem relied on standard phrases that he knew by heart, giving himself a moment to choose how to proceed. Should he answer the question in a way that would be appropriate for the audience of adolescents that surrounded him, or for the much broader television audience? The broader audience would have limited knowledge, it would only understand ideas superficially and wouldn't have the ability or the desire or the patience to delve any deeper. Or should he address those rival sheikhs who were waiting to pounce on him? Crouched over the keyboards of their computers, they had closed their minds against anything they didn't understand, if they understood anything at all, that is. Hatem didn't ask whether he should reply to satisfy his conscience or to remain true to his scholarly profession because he didn't intend to lie. Instead he would say only the part of the truth that was fit for television consumption. He was a businessman addressing his customers, and his answer—both the content and the way he delivered it—was responsible for bringing in advertising revenue, not charitable donations, to keep the producer and the program sponsor happy. As for keeping God happy, well, God would judge him by his intentions. He hated himself at those moments—the moments between when he started speaking and when he decided what he actually wanted to say. It's true that he wasn't going to lie or mislead people, and he came out of the tunnel so quickly that no one noticed that his eyes were roaming and the camera didn't catch the seconds of hesitation.

"Do the heavens and the earth and the mountains understand? Can they hear and speak? This is a question and the answer is: very possibly, but not in the way humans, for example, speak and understand. So God asked them and offered them the trust, and most of the early Muslims, when they were explaining this verse, said that it's 'When God asked the heavens and the earth and the mountains if they could accept this trust, with everything that implied,' they said, 'and what does it imply?' and God said, 'If you do good, you will be rewarded, and if you disobey, you will be punished.' Okay, so they understand like humans. We have to remember that all inanimate objects are subject to God Almighty. They obey and prostrate themselves to Him, as God says in the Quran when he addresses the heavens and the earth: *'Come ye together, willingly or unwillingly, and they said: We come, obedient,'* or when He spoke about rocks, saying *'And indeed there are rocks which fall down for the fear of God,'* or when He says, *'Haven't you seen that those who are in the heavens and on earth bow down to God, and also the sun and the moon, the stars, the mountains, the trees, and the beasts.'* So they worship differently from human beings, and so their speaking, hearing, understanding, and feelings are different from what we are familiar with as humans, but there are some scholars who say that God, very temporarily and to a very limited extent, equipped them with reason and understanding when he offered them the trust, so the heavens and the earth and the mountains understood and came up with their decision to turn the offer down."

Hatem went up to a girl sitting in the stands. When she realized she was on the screen, with everyone looking at her, she started to play up to the camera.

"Understand anything?" Hatem asked her. He laughed and the audience laughed and the girl was flustered.

"You watch cartoons, don't you?" Hatem continued.

The question took her by surprise. "Yes, when I was young," she replied.

"But not now that you're old!" Hatem said, walking in front of her, heading to the other side of the set and looking at another section of the audience. "Anyway, when you see animals and trees speaking in cartoons, for example, or in science fiction films you might find mountains talking, all these ideas are derived from the stories that are found in all religions."

Unconsciously he glanced over at Hassan, who was captivated by the scene.

"If we go back to the Quran, we find God saying '*And ask the town where we were.*' Does it mean 'ask the town in the sense of its hills, the sun, the shade, the ground,' or does it mean 'ask the people in the town'? So when He offered the trust to the heavens, the earth, and the mountains, was He offering it to the people who were there, and who were they? They were the angels. So it was the angels, and they were afraid of the trust, because the angels can hear, yes, and they can understand, yes, and they can speak, yes, but they turned down the assignment. In other words the mountains, the earth, the sky don't understand. They're not conscious, they can't hear, and they don't speak. What's meant is the angels. God created two kinds of beings: mankind and angels, and an offshoot of the angels is the devils, of course, the descendants of Satan and his helpers. He offered the trust to one group and they turned it down. So he offered it to another group and they agreed to take it on, and what does God say about mankind? 'He has been unjust and ignorant.' Unjust to himself and ignorant about God's ways and the trust he was taking on."

Hatem went up close to a young man in the audience.

"But didn't God offer you this trust?" he asked.

With a smile Hatem answered his own question to the surprised young man.

"No, He offered it to Adam, and it was Adam, may God reward him, who accepted it and landed us with this horrible job."

Hatem was in full control of his audience, both those in the studio and the people in front of their televisions at home, but he decided to send Kaaki a message to show that he hadn't thrown his three million pounds down the drain.

"Okay, but what is the trust that was offered?" he said. "The books that try to explain the Quran say it was the duty to perform prayers, to give alms, to fast in Ramadan, to make the pilgrimage to Mecca, to tell the truth, to pay debts, and to be honest with weights and measures. But note that God offered the trust to humanity and not to Muslims, so we shouldn't take it for granted that it means the detailed obligations of Muslims, because the question at the time was 'okay, and what about non-Muslims?'

"You know the explanation of the trust I'm most partial to? That the trust that God offered to the heavens and the earth and the mountains, and that they refused to accept and that humanity did accept, was in fact the reproductive organs."

There was a deafening silence as everyone fell speechless in shock. Through his earpiece Hatem heard the producer's reaction: "Oh God!" Hatem couldn't help smiling, almost laughing, as he continued.

"Yes, the genitalia, according to the explanation of Abdullah ibn Amr ibn al-As. Now there's no need to get embarrassed. I know you didn't attend the lesson on the reproductive system in biology class when you were in year three of middle school, but if you think about it you'll find that the tiresome trust, this ordeal, is the genitals or the reproductive organs of human beings."

He could hear the rumble of voices from the control room through his earpiece and then the producer shouting, "Cut to the ads, Mawlana."

"And at that we'll take a break," said Hatem.

When the red light on the camera went off, Hatem laughed.

"A break, right?" he said to the producer.

"Strong stuff, Mawlana," said Kaaki through the speaker in the ceiling of the set. "An adults-only program."

Hatem ignored the youth in the audience, who were unsure whether to admire him or disapprove of him, whether to take him seriously or make fun of him. He whispered into the microphone so that the studio audience couldn't hear him, as the make-up person wiped off his sweat and powdered the shine off his forehead. The hairdresser straightened his hair and pumped bursts of spray onto it.

"So what's the moral of the story?" said Kaaki, who was sitting in the control room to monitor the first program of the series. "When we say everyone should take care of his trust, what does it mean? It means he should take care of his dick."

The audience could hear roars of laughter through the speaker. Then Sheikh Hatem appeared, coming back from the break.

Hatem couldn't in the least claim that he felt at peace. On the contrary his success, his fame, and his confidence that he could trade profitably in religious learning had not made him feel less anxious or more secure. His unhealthy anxiety about Omar meant he could never claim he had peace of mind. On top of that, there were of course the potentially explosive implications of having Hassan in his life. The competition and the battle for ratings and adverts left him feeling vulnerable, but what made him feel really fragile, like a rickety car that might fall to pieces at the next big bump, was the gap between what he said and what he wanted to say. Inside himself and in his private meetings and in what he said to those closest to him there was another Hatem, different from the Hatem who sold a superficial form of learning that people loved. But he would face disaster if he challenged the popular preference for ignorance, if he said something that didn't please those who owned the television market, if he disobeyed State Security or made the government nervous. He would be disowned by the satanic television machine that called people to paradise through religious directives. The millionaires would deny their stations and companies to him, the distributors would be wary of him, the advertisers would avoid him and the producers would run away. They were all gangsters who thought they were respectable. Their interests lay with the religion of the prince or the president, not with God's religion. There was to be no talk about freedom, only about obedience. No appeals to reason, only to tradition. No going back to the ideas that appear in the classical books on history or legal theory, only stagnation based on the ideas found in religious pamphlets that are free or subsidized, such as summaries of the material in school curricula, offering paradise in the form of question and answer.

Hatem had been struck by a pretty girl in the audience, although he didn't yet realize what an effect she would have on him or where it would lead. She hit him somewhere vulnerable without realizing it. Or maybe she did realize it and there was someone behind her who wanted to take advantage of his vulnerability.

The camera focused on the girl's face when she stood up to ask her question. "Mister Hatem," she began, with a disapproving look of skeptical defiance. His heart raced.

"You've said we're not under orders to imitate the Prophet, may God bless him and pray for him, in everything he did. But that opens the door to denying the sayings and practices of the Prophet, rather than following them, whereas we all know that the Sunna is what explains the Quran and Islam in general. What Your Grace says"—hadn't they told her to say 'mister' and not 'Your Grace'?—"supports the line taken by the Mutazila, a group that many early scholars condemned as heretics, so I'd like to hear Your Grace"—again!—"explain what I heard you say."

Hatem heard Kaaki shouting through the earpiece: "Who brought this skank in here, and why isn't she asking the question she was told to ask? Whoever let her in is fired. Tell Hatem"—no 'mister' or 'Mawlana' here—"to totally humiliate her," he added, addressing the director. "She's going to get us all in deep trouble."

In the control room it hadn't occurred to anyone that the girl's question could be that serious. They were drinking tea, smoking, and joking around, giving and taking orders. The question seemed as ordinary as any other. It's true it was a little over their heads but when Kaaki started screaming and shouting, getting wound up and shaking and smoking voraciously, a vague sense of apprehension morphed into an inexplicable anxiety.

By that time Hatem had recovered his poise and had started speaking. "Excellent question," he said. "What's your name, you clever girl?" he added languidly.

The question took her by surprise. She was still standing there, rather stiffly and nervously, and Hatem hadn't asked her to sit down. He went up to her smiling, awaiting her answer.

"My name's Nashwa," she said, overlooking the condescending 'clever girl' comment. Her jaw quivered, suggesting she was ready for a fight.

"Spiritual nashwa, I hope," Hatem replied, playing on the fact that her name meant 'ecstasy.' He felt drawn to her, bowled over. She had suddenly thawed the frost that had built up inside him.

"I've no idea, Nashwa, where you heard me say that about imitating the practice of the Prophet." Before she had time to reply, he continued. "That isn't important now, because we are short of time."

He knew he had said it and that it was what he thought, and when he wasn't under pressure, he would try to find out whether she really had heard him say it or how she had found out about it. He would ask Kaaki to cut out the references to the Mutazila and the denial of the Sunna from the question when they rebroadcast it, and then get rid of the tape that included those words. At that he concentrated and resumed.

"God says, '*You had in the Prophet of God a good example for those who look forward to God and the Day of Judgment.* That means we are commanded by God Almighty, Nashwa (he went up to her again), to emulate the Prophet, may God bless him and grant him peace. And what does 'emulate' mean? It means take him as an example, that we act as he acted. He is a model for us. So far so good. But then the question is: do we have to emulate the Prophet in everything he did? Or only in the things he told us to do?

"The early Muslim scholars"—he took a long look at Nashwa—"differed on this. Some said we could break the things the Prophet did into three categories: obligation, delegation, and authorization." Kaaki in person came through Hatem's earpiece, apparently very upset. He had pushed the director aside and taken charge of running the program.

"Enough of this big boring talk, Mawlana," he said. "Simplify it, loosen up, and finish it off for God's sake."

Hatem complied immediately and smiled.

"What matters, guys, is that the Prophet only does good deeds and things that are halal." Then he lightened up. "The Prophet had up to nine wives at a time but we're not going to follow his example in that respect, because that was something that was limited to him. Okay, so what did the Prophet fight with? With swords and spears. Should we copy him and pick up swords to fight our enemies now? So when the enemy has tanks and planes, we'd have swords and spears. Of course not. So can you tell me, Nashwa, if that means we'd be violating the requirement to follow the Prophet's example?"

Nashwa was about to reply but he stopped her by raising his hand and with a look that mixed admiration and warning.

"The Prophet used to eat without spoons or forks, with his hands. Is that what we should be doing now, to follow his example? The test is whether the Prophet, if he'd had knives and forks and spoons, would have said, 'No, I'll eat with my hands.' The Prophet used to wear a gown that was cut short so that it didn't get covered in the dust or the mud on the ground. But did they have suits and trousers and shirts and ties in the days of the Prophet, and did he refuse to wear them? The point here is that the Prophet asked us to be clean and neat and smartly dressed, but he didn't tell us to wear a gown or anything else. If we imagine that instead of camels outside the Prophet's room there were Land-Rovers and Mercedeses"— he could hear the director passing on hurried instructions: "no brand names because of the adverts"—"and other big fancy cars, would he have told us to forget about the cars and ride the camels in order to follow his example?"

"Wrap it up, Mawlana. You've got thirty seconds left."

Hatem glanced at Nashwa and then looked up at Hassan.

"I leave you in God's care and protection," he said.

The program's theme song faded away from somewhere over the studio set and some of the lights went out in the corners, above the tiers of seats and on the backdrops behind where Hatem was standing. The television screens went dark, turning into rectangular expanses of black. The lamp in the ceiling that had been on throughout the program went out and the place came to life with chaotic, random activity. The young people came down from the stands, some casually, others in a rush. The cameramen wandered away from their posts behind their cameras and the sound technician came up to Hatem to remove his microphone and earpiece. Then Kaaki rushed in, together with his men from the program team and his staff, beaming and smiling happily at the first program in the series. He heard cries of 'congratulations,' 'awesome,' 'well done, Mawlana,' 'it'll be a big hit,' and so on in the distance from assorted flatterers and time-servers. But Hatem's eyes were looking out for the girl with the pretty face, the athletic physique, and the feisty temperament. He was listening for her voice, which still rang in his ears and made his heart race. Nashwa had disappeared into the crowd or into the darkness. Several girls in the hijab went past, lingered, and stopped, but she wasn't one of them.

Kaaki grabbed him, embraced him, congratulated him, and turned him toward the studio door, shouting, "Quickly, people."

They did act quickly. A team in the uniform of a famous store appeared, pushing a table on wheels carrying a large cake decorated with sparklers lit in celebration of the occasion. The crowd gathered around the table, pretending to be celebrating, but the mood was somewhat marred by the tense way Kaaki looked at and whispered to his assistants and the way Hatem was checking all the faces that came and went around him. People wrapped their arms around Hatem and grinned into flashing cameras. Then Kaaki pulled Hatem off by the hand, followed by the director and the man in charge of production, apparently under a prior agreement to meet. They went into a room next to the studio that had large, low chairs, and as soon as they had sat down Kaaki let out all the anger he had been holding back.

"I want to know right now who let in that bitch who asked about rejecting the Sunna and the Mutazila and all that talk that'll cause trouble. Who's responsible?" he asked.

"It all worked out fine in the end," Hatem volunteered.

"What do you mean, Mawlana?" Kaaki retorted. "Please, I may not know much about religion. I may have only one percent of your knowledge, but I do know about business and dirty warfare, and that girl had been planted to wreck the program and tarnish the reputation of Sheikh Hatem or start malicious rumors about him. I have full respect for the sheikh, who's a learned man, but I translate it into money, into millions, and when the yellow press, or the green press or whatever, comes out with headlines about the program, with the sheikh saying 'Don't do what the Prophet did,' no offense, but I'll be screwed and we'll be ruined. It's true Sheikh Hatem hit back hard when he answered, but the trap was set and there might be some spillover, so I want to know right now who the girl came with and who she's working for."

Kaaki's team was tense, frightened, and uncomprehending, especially when more of his assistants came into the room, drawn by his loud shouting. The smiles on their faces turned to absolute silence and smoke filled the room from the cigarettes they dragged on nervously.

Sparks started to fly when no one answered Kaaki.

"What?" he said. "You clowns don't know who brought her or who she is?"

"To be honest," said the director. "I saw all the girls and boys the production team chose and I ruled out a few of them, but that was all about the way they looked and the ratio of boys to girls, but I wasn't responsible for the questions or the production and preparation."

The producer quickly summoned his assistant, who was responsible for the audience. While he was on his way they pleaded with Kaaki to calm down.

While Hatem admitted that the fuss that Kaaki had made was entirely legitimate and that the danger he mentioned was real, he was more interested in musing on the girl's face, which had a distinctly calming effect on him. He suddenly remembered Hassan with fondness and called him up to find out where he was. He was told that Hassan was waiting for him in the car with Sirhan the driver.

Kaaki leaned over toward Hatem quizzically, as if he wanted to set his mind at rest.

"But tell me," he said, "who are those Mutazila, Mawlana?"

"They're a group of soccer players who used to play for Ahli, and when they retired, they formed a team called the Mutazila," Hatem quickly replied, playing on the fact that 'mutazila' could mean 'retirees.'

Everyone laughed, after waiting for Kaaki to laugh first.

"You're kidding, Mawlana," Kaaki said.

Hatem smiled.

"Okay, let's deal with the retirement you're planning for me before we play," he said.

The production official accused of bringing Nashwa arrived, looking as though they'd dragged him out of the bathroom. He was wet and trembling, and he soon admitted that one of the girls he knew on Facebook had told him about a friend of hers that would like to take part in Sheikh Hatem's program. Clearly the guy had been boasting on Facebook that he was working on the program, and he told her the time and place of the event after checking that she was pretty and wore the hijab.

"How did you check?" asked Kaaki.

"I looked at her Facebook page and saw her picture. She turned up and I gave her one of the questions from the production unit when she said she wanted to ask one."

As Hatem got into his car next to Hassan, he asked Hassan what he thought of the program.

Hassan handed him his phone. "My sister wants to speak to you," he said.

Hatem picked up the phone, surprised and exhausted by the strain of the evening's activities. He thought about the ordeal that God had sent to try him and realized that he felt indifferent.

"Good evening, Madam," he said.

"And good evening to you, Mawlana. I thought I'd congratulate you on the program. It was great. We benefit greatly from your learning, Mawlana."

"God bless you, Madam," said Hatem.

"How's Hassan doing with you? We're really imposing on you."

"Not at all. It's an honor to have him. He's a great guy, a fine young man."

"Is there any hope, Mawlana, that you can show him the right path?"

"God is the one who guides us, Madam."

Apparently her husband was with her on the same line.

"Sheikh Hatem," said the president's son. "Of course we know it's God who guides us, but if that's the way it is we could have kept him at home and waited for God to guide him while he sat in his bedroom."

Hatem was disarmed by the rude interruption. "You're right, that's true," he said, regaining his strength. "But even if he sat by the Kaaba in Mecca every morning, there'd still be no guarantee that the good Lord would show him the way, sir."

Farida stepped in to mitigate her husband's nonsense and reassure Hatem.

"We have high hopes that the good Lord will guide Hassan through you," she said.

"It's all in God's hands, Madam."

He said goodbye, then threw the phone into Hassan's lap. Hassan laughed vindictively.

"He treated you badly," he said. "He's arrogant and bad-tempered."

Hatem denied it completely but he felt that Hassan was aware of his weakness when faced with his sister's husband. He tried to act composed.

"Look, your sister's husband is the son of the big man, the son of the president, and not just that, the inner workings of the whole country are under his control, so you can be proud you've given him such a hard time," he said.

Hassan grinned, which seemed odd when he was so depressed and unemotional. "It's true, and this happened after he gave you personally a hard time," Hassan continued, "but look on the bright side, he doesn't matter to you either way."

"So does he matter to you?"

"I don't know if you'll believe me or not, but it's you that matters to me now."

And Nashwa too, he whispered to himself. Now how did she get hold of something he'd never said in public?

"But what does 'Mutazila' mean, Sheikh Hatem?"

"Nothing important. They were a group that was put in quarantine at Quraysh airport," said Hatem, taking from his pocket a slip of paper with Nashwa's telephone number on it.

Hatem found Omayma in the garden having breakfast with Hassan. He realized she was interested in him, that this young man had aroused her curiosity. As he went down to join them in the sunny calm, Nashwa's face popped up in his mind. He tried to ignore it, but all night he had been wondering how a face he had seen only fleetingly could have found a way into his heart of stone.

"Excellent. Before long I'll come down and find you two in the swimming pool together," he said with a laugh as he approached them. Hassan didn't understand what he meant, and Omayma just ignored the remark.

"What are you going to do after what happened on the program yesterday?" Omayma asked.

Hatem sat down and tried to relax.

"Thank God you saw it. What did you think?" he asked.

"Do you know that girl?"

"Nashwa?" he asked, with a sigh he failed to conceal.

"How did you find out her name?"

"So you didn't watch the program. You only heard about it from others. What did they tell you?"

"No, I watched it."

"Well, my good woman, I asked her what her name was and I said it several times. But what I really want to know is how your friends reacted to the program."

Silence.

"Come on, I know you stopped watching me some time ago," said Hatem.

"By the way, I saw the repeat early this morning," Hassan interrupted.

"Did they do what I asked and cut out the bit about the Mutazila and denying the Sunna?" asked Hatem with interest.

"They certainly cut out the word 'Mutazila.'"

Hatem smiled and nodded. "I believe you because that word Mutazila had a big effect on you," he said.

"In fact the people who told me about it just said that the girl was obnoxious and they didn't really understand the stuff about accusing you of denying the Sunna," said Omayma.

Suddenly she lost interest in how Hatem might answer her question and turned to Hassan.

"So, Peter, have you become an Orthodox Christian or a Catholic? Or have you decided to be a Protestant?" she asked.

"You're amazing, my dear wife," Hatem said. "It's a very good question."

Hassan was at a loss, and he dealt with it by being argumentative: "You have Sunnis and Shi'a too!"

"That's right," said Hatem. "That's why she was asking you how it is with your lot."

"There are plenty of Westerners who've converted to Islam," said Omayma with maternal tenderness. "And some of them have become Shi'a. I heard that myself. And besides, when you're starting on something new and everything's on offer for you to decide for yourself, then it's a real opportunity to make a fresh start and choose based on what you think and want and how you feel."

"The truth is I haven't thought about that at all."

"Do all those who convert become Orthodox like the Coptic Church?" asked Hatem.

Apparently Hassan hadn't yet accessed that part of his brain, and Hatem continued: "Didn't I tell you some people convert to Christianity here out of sympathy for the Copts, especially if the person converting is sentimental or sensitive or rather naive. So those people go straight to the sect that's closest to them, and not to the sect they've studied and understood and are convinced about. Even the Christians who convert to Islam in Egypt operate on the basis that Islam means Sunni Islam. By the way, the Shi'a more than anyone else promote the idea that they're committed to the Sunna of the Prophet. But which sunna? That's the question, because we disagree over the authenticity of hadiths. It's much the same in Christianity, where there are various sects as a result of ideological and religious and political and sometimes military conflicts, and bloody ones too. You come and say 'I'm going to convert to Christianity.' Okay, you're free, convert. But wouldn't it make more sense to know what you're leaving behind and where you're going?"

Omayma had ordered a breakfast especially for Sheikh Hatem. The servants took away dishes and brought other dishes as he was speaking, and when he was ready to eat he shut up and Omayma took over.

"In fact," she said, "the Coptic Orthodox priests we have are very much like the Salafist sheikhs who appear on television, with long bushy beards that aren't trimmed, and they henna their beards yellow rather than let them turn gray from old age. They all have square faces without mustaches and their faces are so hairy you can't see their features clearly. Their faces start at the nose and end at the eyebrows. The Salafists put a white piece of cloth on their heads, not a turban or a skullcap, and what the priests wear is rather like that piece of cloth but with crosses printed on it. The Protestants, on the other hand, are really smart—no long beards, or short beards either, and their clothes are dignified and neat, with the white collar standing out against the neck of the black suit."

She turned warmly toward Hassan.

"Protestant is much nicer, Hassan," she said, "so that you can be different from your fellow converts and stand out from the crowd."

Hatem laughed at the reasoning, and Hassan laughed too.

"So he should choose his religion based on the cut of the suit," said Hatem.

"In fact being well-dressed does make a difference," Hassan said. "The priests and the Salafists are just as Auntie Omayma described them."

Hatem thought it was cute when Hassan called Omayma 'auntie,' but Omayma disapproved. "Auntie!" she said. "Is that what we agreed? My name's Omayma."

"Madam Omayma," Hatem said. "Sectarian distinctions are especially common in Christianity and Islam because the two religions were widespread and open to everyone, in all their geographic, social, and cultural variations, unlike Judaism for example, a religion that's confined to its adherents and has a horrible attitude to anyone who disagrees. Christianity came from Bethlehem and Nazareth but it spread as far as the English counties, Spain, and the backwaters of the Roman Empire. Islam was born in Mecca and Medina but it went to Persia, Byzantium, Sindh, and India, and political disputes over government and the struggle for power were undoubtedly the root cause of the disagreement between the Sunnis and the Shi'a. Then culture came along and added to the mix, but the big cause was politics."

"Why don't you say that on your programs?" asked Omayma.

He had a good laugh, then replied. "Because we want to sit in this garden, with the swimming pool in front of us and Omar in Europe, and have drivers and waiters and put up brother Hassan, sorry Boutros, in our house. We want to meet his sister's husband, the real ruler of the country, and not the head of the prison service. There's an audience for superficial religion and people willing to finance it, whereas no one understands serious religion and no one will fund it."

The only sounds for a while were the sipping of tea, the clatter of spoons and plates, the rustling of the leaves in the trees, and the tinkling of the water in the swimming pool.

The friendly conversation had taken the edge off the cold, depressing reality, and their courageous confessions had swept aside some of the barriers between them. They enjoyed a safe silence for a while.

Then Hatem asked Omayma, "Can I speak to Omar?"

Omayma turned to Hassan. "Have you seen any pictures of Omar?" she asked him.

"I saw the pictures on the walls," he said.

"He's sweet, isn't he?"

"I just want to check on him," said Hatem. "Stop being so difficult. I miss my son."

"Shall I tell Boutros?" she said firmly.

Hatem was angry and reproached her.

"For a start his name's Hassan. But go on and have done with it. What are you going to tell him? That you're hiding my son's phone number from me so that I can't speak to him and check up on him when he's ten thousand miles away?"

Omayma defended herself. "I'm in the wrong," she said. "But I just want you to toughen up and learn how to deal with your son as a son, and not as a reason for having a nervous breakdown."

He shut up in defeat and she continued.

"Your morbid worrying about him is wearing him out, and wearing you and me out too."

"But in fact, Auntie . . ." Hassan interrupted.

"Auntie. Great. Carry on," said Hatem.

"I would have liked my father to take an interest in me, and ask after me," said Hassan.

"My dear," said Omayma, "Sheikh Hatem can go a week without asking after Omar but he never stops worrying that, God forbid, something bad will happen to him."

Then, turning to Hatem, she added, "Should I tell him, Your Grace?"

"That sounds like a threat, Omayma," replied Hatem. "Look, Mister Boutros, I've had panic attacks because of my son since he was a child, and when Omar had an accident . . ."

"He had a heart attack," said Omayma.

Clearly she didn't want to disclose Hatem's wanderings around el-Hussein and Sayeda Zeinab and the fact he had walked out of the house and the hospital out of weakness and fear and anger, in case Hassan had doubts about the soundness of his intellect and mental health. With grateful looks, Hatem thanked her for her courtesy and good sense.

Omayma looked up at Sirhan, who had suddenly appeared. Sirhan, his hand over the mouthpiece of a cell phone, whispered to Hatem.

"It's Sheikh Mukhtar el-Husseini on the line," he said, offering him the phone.

Hatem heard the name and quickly grabbed the phone. His cheerful smile began to fade within seconds of listening.

"Hello there, Mawlana. God bless you . . . You too, we've really missed you . . . Of course . . . Really? It would be an honor and a privilege . . . Where? . . . Really? . . . That's good news."

Hatem then stood up and started walking toward the door of the house.

"Open the gate for Sheikh Mukhtar, you guys," he ordered those around him.

Just as they opened the gate a car drove up. It stopped to let out Mukhtar el-Husseini, who was still holding the phone in his hand, as was Hatem, who hung up and opened his arms for the sheikh.

Mukhtar asked to be alone with Hatem, who took him into a room furnished with arabesque furniture and carpets and pictures on the walls. It smelled of incense and the sharp aroma of coffee from a little brass coffee pot on a small gas ring where Hatem himself made a cup of coffee for Sheikh Mukhtar.

"I'm very sorry," said Mukhtar, genuinely apologetic. "And I'm embarrassed to have turned up so unexpectedly."

"By your ancestor the Prophet, never say that again," said Hatem.

"God preserve you and bless you, Mawlana."

"God is our master on earth and in heaven. I'm to blame and I ask your forgiveness," said Hatem. "I meant to speak to the son of the big man about your problems with the security people and with him, but I didn't get around to it and other things distracted me. To tell the truth, Uncle, I was worried, because if I had asked for something on your behalf I would have hated it if he had sent me away disappointed and I would have been embarrassed—what could I have said to such an eminent descendant of such a noble lineage?"

"Don't worry about it, my friend. It's God who relieves our sorrows," said the Sufi sheikh. "I came to you in a hurry today because I heard they were about to do something major against me and I don't know exactly what it might be. As you know, we have friends everywhere and one of them told me it was serious and imminent, so I thought I'd go abroad temporarily. Some friends in Saudi Arabia invited me to stay there and now I'm on my way to the airport."

The news deeply saddened Hatem.

"So you came to say goodbye to me?" he asked.

"To say goodbye and to ask you to keep some things safe for me."

"Of course I will."

"Firstly, there's my mother. The old woman refused to come with me and decided to stay at our house in the country. I'm asking you if you'd be so kind as to keep an eye on her and make sure she's safe."

Hatem had tears in his eyes as Mukhtar continued with his request.

"There's something else I'd like to leave with you," he said. He took a flash drive from his pocket, along with a small pocket notebook and a closed envelope sealed with a strip of transparent Scotch tape, and gave them to Hatem.

"The notebook explains everything that's happened to me recently, in my own hand, and there's the text of threats I've received and the letters I've sent to all the senior officials about this. The flash drive has some audio files and pictures of some very important things we obtained through God's grace and by His testing of us. I'm leaving them with you until, after hardship, God brings relief and hopefully joy."

"I can't believe this is happening. I'm sorry, Uncle, but I don't understand. Are they harassing you this way because you once said something about the president's son? Is all this hatred and persecution because of one word or one sentence? Isn't that rather excessive? Might there not be something bigger than you think behind all of this?"

Mukhtar stood up, calm and smiling.

"May God bring relief after torment, in the name of my Lord and Master, the beloved Prophet," he said.

"May God bless him and grant him peace," echoed Hatem.

Next to the car, Hatem asked him, "Are you rewarding my negligence by trusting me with these things for safekeeping?"

Mukhtar nodded as he got into the car.

"Why not say I'm punishing you for your negligence and adding to your troubles?"

When Hatem was back in the house, he took a piece of paper out of his pocket, picked up his phone, and dialed Nashwa's number.

He didn't think of opening Mukhtar el-Husseini's envelope, he didn't take out the notebook that Mukhtar mentioned, and he didn't put the flash drive into his computer. He never thought of doing so. In fact he looked at the envelope with unease. He flicked it with his finger and made it spin like a top. He didn't put it in his little safe, saying he'd wait till he could remember the code. He decided to avoid thinking about it and speak to Nashwa instead. His heart was beating and he couldn't think straight. It was the same slight dizziness he had felt in the past when things happened so fast that he couldn't keep up. He had often thought it might be the first sign of diabetes, but he had grown used to it over the years and just put it down to aging.

She answered in that same beguiling voice.

"Hello," she said, politely but coldly.

"Hello. Miss Nashwa?"

There was a puzzled silence and then an inquisitive voice.

"Who is this?" she asked.

"It's Sheikh Hatem el-Shenawi," he answered, firmly but impassively.

The silence was longer. He was waiting for her to answer, while she was waiting for him to say something more.

"I'm sorry to trouble you," Hatem continued.

"Not at all, it's an honor, Mawlana," she replied, as if worried he might back off.

Hatem acted even more formally. "I got your number from the production people," he said.

"Production?" she asked, unfamiliar with the term.

"I mean the producer of the program. I wanted to thank you for taking part."

"Do you usually get in touch with the audience and thank them for taking part?" she asked.

It wasn't clear whether she was acting dumb or was genuinely curious.

"No, this is the first time," he answered recklessly. "On the contrary, I usually avoid speaking to the participants."

"So why have you granted me this honor?"

Now he was sure she was acting dumb.

"Because your question suggested you have strong views but you misunderstand my ideas and opinions, and so I'd like to clarify and explain," he said.

She abandoned the attack.

"Please do," she said.

"Thank you," he replied. "But if you agree, I'd like to meet you in my office."

Before she had time to ask any questions, he added quickly, "And by the way, when I meet participants or my followers I always do so in my office, and there's nothing special or unusual about it."

She agreed, he thanked her, and they arranged an appointment.

THE STREET WAS PACKED TIGHT and people in the crowd were reaching out to shake hands with Sheikh Hatem. Tawhid Abdel-Qadir, with his vast frame and his long arms, was waving to his men and his aides to keep people from harassing Hatem, who was surrounded by bodies. Loudspeakers in front of the shop were blasting out religious poetry at high volume, and the contractors had arranged rows of chairs on the pavement and on half the street, completely blocking the traffic, although there were policemen standing around to greet him too. Hatem realized that Tawhid was throwing velvet bags containing dozens of pound coins into the crowd. This attracted more people and created chaos as they scrambled to pick up the money. Hatem had a splitting headache as he cut the ribbon to open the enormous store, and the video cameras pursued him everywhere he went. The noise almost burst his eardrums and dozens of people raised their cell phones above their heads to take pictures. Others came up and took pictures of themselves standing next to him. When he was pushed into the store by the crowd and the chaos, he found young people in uniform with fixed smiles on their faces waiting to greet him with religious anthems like the ones taught to elementary school children. Some of the people in the crowd pressed pieces of paper and envelopes into his pocket and he was sure they were requests for jobs and for financial help from people who saw him as someone famous or lucky or successful who could give them help. With Tawhid he inspected the clothing section, including the underwear section and the women's and children's departments, the shoes, the perfumes, and the electrical appliances, as well as a section for the special clothing that pilgrims wear, with a large model of the Kaaba in the middle.

"Tawhid, you have succeeded where Abraha failed!" joked Hatem, an obscure reference to a Yemeni ruler who attacked Mecca before Islam. No one understood it.

At every step there were pictures with the crowd and the noise. Hatem had come all the way from Cairo to this small town a few kilometers from Kafr el-Zayat in the Nile Delta as a favor to Ahmed el-Faisal, a senior officer in the branch of State Security that specialized in monitoring religious activities. In fact Hatem fell under the authority of two branches of State Security: one of them, called Religious Activities, had probably been monitoring him since he was a preacher employed by the Ministry of Religious Endowments. The imams of mosques had to have security clearances vouching for their good conduct, to prevent them from deviating from government instructions, which were essentially instructions from the security people. The process began with a plainclothes policeman assigned to the mosque, and if the mosque was important it would be assigned to the officer in charge of the department, and if the sheikh was popular and succeeded in attracting a large congregation then the State Security officer for the whole area oversaw and monitored the mosque and the preacher. But when Hatem moved into the world of television, he came under the responsibility of another branch of State Security for the satellite channels, which had officers assigned to each station and each channel. The senior ones had direct access to the owners of the stations, who were of course already being monitored by the branch that kept an eye on the activities of businessmen, because there wasn't a television station owner who wasn't a businessman, and every businessman had a file and had been covered by the security people ever since he started doing business. The relationship might take the form of coordination, subordination, or even blackmail, in varying degrees of benevolence or severity depending on the businessman's relationship with those with political influence and whether the businessman had carried out favors in the past, such as giving a job in his companies to a retiring officer or to the sons of police generals, or contributing to the cost of building an office for the branch in a new city, or providing gifts at the feasts of Eid al-Fitr or Eid al-Adha or New Year or Police Day or the spring festival of Shamm el-Nassim, when they might send salted or smoked fish wrapped in ribbons tied with bows like birthday presents. The junior or younger officers had relationships with the directors of the television stations and programs, and there were program presenters who were the direct responsibility of senior officers because they were well-known and successful, and the agreements with them superseded any agreements the station owner or manager had with anyone else.

Hatem kept Ahmed el-Faisal sweet to avoid any problems with the security people. Throughout the fifteen years since Hatem had started to appear on the scene, insignificant at first and then moving up the scale and expanding, he had managed to maintain a good and secure relationship with the security people, without working on their behalf. He wasn't one of the clerics who were completely under their patronage and who didn't try to hide it or feel any shame when they openly admitted their relationship with some senior official in the Interior Ministry. At the many gatherings organized by Khaled Abu Hadid, to which he invited sheikhs and preachers and police generals and other officers, the officers were always careful not to state an opinion or to give instructions. They saw the gatherings as social occasions that brought them good luck and were not part of their official duties. They preferred to summon the sheikhs to their offices in the ministry, which meant getting through the barricades and checkpoints and past all the guards. Then you were met by an officer who took you up in the elevator with a policeman and you had to go along complicated, winding corridors till you reached their vast offices. The presence of flags and people in uniform everywhere and people repeating the words 'pasha' and 'bey' and 'your excellency' all the time created an aura that might impress the guests. But the security people did not always welcome publicity about these contacts. On one occasion Sheikh Safwat, the star performer on a station where all the men had the kind of beards that troubled Omayma, received a scolding from a general for what he had said.

"Sheikh Safwat, how can you say in the newspapers that you sit in the lap of State Security? Do you think statements like that make us happy? I swear, I told General Adel we ought to lock you up for that statement. Keep up appearances in public, sheikh. We want you to do what we tell you, that's very true, but people have to believe you if you're going to be important to us and to yourself. Now say what you want, for the love of security and stability, because true Muslims want to save their country from chaos, and obedience to authority is part of obedience to God. You might say something really good and proper, but then someone might come along and say, 'Oh, he's a government man. He sits in the lap of State Security.'"

The funny thing was that in the program immediately after this conversation Sheikh Safwat came out and spoke about the Jews and Israel and jihad against them in Gaza, to give the impression he was a big militant and a dreaded opponent of the government. This made the State Security man even angrier and a few days later the television station had to close down on the grounds that it hadn't paid some money it owed to the authorities. Hatem was eager not to work for security and made do with working for the Ministry of Religious Endowments, which itself worked for security. He didn't do meetings with officers, though he ran into them by chance through Khaled Abu Hadid or other businessmen who had links with both security and with sheikhs and preachers. He spoke to them on the phone and gave them presents and helped them get on subsidized pilgrimages to Mecca. He congratulated them when their children and relatives got married and gave them his condolences when someone died. One way he was able to keep his distance from them was through their sons and daughters, because of all preachers Hatem was the one who had won the hearts of young people, and this trip to open a store two hundred kilometers from home was one way he could get close to the Interior Ministry people, so that he could in effect safely keep his distance. He had seen no sign that Ahmed el-Faisal and Tawhid were related in any way, but the event clearly mattered to Ahmed because he had insisted that Hatem attend.

Hatem leaned over toward Tawhid's ear in the midst of all the noise.

"Tawhid," he said, "I'm going to play a trick on you, but it's well-intentioned, I swear."

Tawhid smiled amiably and supportively. He didn't understand or take in what Hatem said, but he was definitely welcoming. In the meantime Hatem took out some of the pieces of paper stuffed in his pocket and read two or three of the names of the people asking for financial help. Then he asked someone for the microphone they had prepared so that he could give a short homily to celebrate the opening. Hatem stepped up onto the platform overlooking the open space outside the store.

"I ask God Almighty to bless this store," he began. "May He bless its owner, those who work in it, those who have dealings with it, those who visit it, those who buy from it, and those who sell to it, and may God in all His glory have us work together to ensure that the store fulfills God's purposes, doing good deeds that undo evil deeds, earning the owner of this store a place in paradise alongside the martyrs and the prophets, the rivers of milk and honey and dark-eyed houris—sorry, Umm Abdel-Rahman, if you can hear us."

Everyone roared with laughter and Tawhid himself laughed so hard he nearly choked. Umm Abdel-Rahman was Tawhid's wife and was in fact there, with several other women on one of the balconies of the building, all of them wearing the hijab or niqab.

"And on the occasion of the opening," Hatem continued, "Mr. Tawhid has decided to offer presents from the store to some recently married couples. He has awarded a 12-cubic-foot fridge to Mr. . . ."

Hatem read out the name from one of the slips of paper, to the consternation of Tawhid and to cheers, shouts, and cries of 'Allahu akbar' from the crowd below. A vast hulk of a man suddenly came forward, with coarse features and tattered clothes, and everyone realized he must be the man whose name Hatem had read out.

Hatem leaned over toward Tawhid.

"You should get a mortuary fridge ready for this guy, not a regular fridge," he joked.

With Hassan in tow, Hatem went into the large hall that Tawhid had prepared for the dinner. Guests had already started pouring in, competing to say hello to the guest of honor, the famous sheikh, to have their pictures taken with him, and hopefully to receive some of his baraka. Hatem had decided to bring Hassan along on the trip to show him how interested he was in him. Although bringing Hassan along was no bother, especially after Omayma's reaction, Hatem couldn't forget the grave responsibility he had taken on, trying to reconvert to Islam the son of just about the richest man in the country and the brother-in-law of the president's son. Hassan was wearing pieces of leather around his wrists so that no one would notice the crosses he had cut into the skin. No one asked about Hassan and how he was related to Hatem, though he was too old to be Hatem's son and too young to be a colleague. They settled for the idea that he was the sheikh's student or disciple but definitely not a member of his staff. This was evident from the quite different way in which Hatem dealt with Khodeiri, who seemed eager to know the minutest details of the schedule for the trip and who took on an importance shared only by Sirhan on a trip of this kind.

Hatem felt a tremor in Hassan's hand, which he was holding for fear he might get lost when people pressed around Hatem to say hello and embrace him. Hatem turned and saw a priest in his black ecclesiastical robes and tall cowl, sitting in the corner of the hall. He glanced at Hassan and then at the priest, who then caught sight of Hassan. The priest looked closely at Hassan's face as Hassan approached, and Hassan's hand shook even more. The priest took an even closer look, clearly perturbed, and began to stroke his thick, coarse beard with his hand. Hatem headed straight for the priest, dragging Hassan by the hand after him. But Tawhid suddenly appeared out of nowhere and took Hatem by the arm. The priest stood up to greet them.

"This is Father Mikhail, Mawlana," said Tawhid.

"Sheikh Hatem el-Shenawi," he added, turning to the priest.

"Of course, there's no need to introduce him to me," said the priest.

"Nice to meet you, Father. It's a great pleasure," Hatem said warmly.

"So here we are in national unity," said Tawhid, from behind. "No fanaticism or sectarianism. Father Mikhail has been the pastor of the church in the town for the past three years. And for your information he has a doctorate from America."

"Fantastic," said Hatem. "In theology?"

"No, in chemistry," said Father Mikhail.

"Really? And yet you decided to go into the church. The more we know, the closer we are to God."

Hatem wasn't speaking to Mikhail as much as he was watching Hassan. Hassan didn't shake hands with the priest, which added to Hatem's suspicions. They didn't look at each other, though they were only a few inches apart. He was increasingly convinced that something was up, but then people came up and dragged Hatem away from the priest to say hello to him. Tawhid finished off introducing him to the important guests, then invited everyone to have dinner, telling them all that Sheikh Hatem had blessed the store that night, not only by opening it but also by shifting the first goods as a charitable gesture—a fridge, a washing machine, and six fans. The guests said prayers for Hatem and Tawhid and murmured admiration for the roast lamb placed in front of them, while Hatem kept his eyes on the apprehensive Hassan and the oblivious priest.

After dinner, although it was late, Hatem made up his mind to go and visit Father Mikhail. Sirhan and Khodeiri were reluctant to go along with Hatem's plan, while Hassan was silent.

"Are you into making bets?" Hatem asked with a half-smile mixed with a trace of defiance.

The question was addressed to Hassan, who was sitting withdrawn next to him in the car. They were driving along an unpaved road, kicking up clouds of dusts and running into potholes that took Sirhan the driver by surprise. Sirhan cursed the potholes, then restrained himself, trying to act professional and so that he wouldn't upset the sheikh. Then more potholes rattled him and he shouted out again, and Khodeiri put his hand over Sirhan's mouth to silence him.

"Let him shout," Hatem commented irritably. "It only proves he's an inexperienced driver."

The journey was unexpected and a mystery to them. Why had Sheikh Hatem decided to visit Father Mikhail in his church? Anyway, here they were following the priest's car toward a small town deep in the remotest countryside. Behind them came two cars full of admirers, sent by Tawhid to keep Hatem company and help him if needed.

"They're the backup team," said Sheikh Hatem.

Hassan finally replied to Hatem's original question, very much in Boutros mode.

"Do sheikhs make bets?" he said.

"Oh yes," said Hatem. "But in this case I'll make a bet with you as Hatem the citizen, not Hatem the sheikh. Are you on?"

"What's the bet?"

"That the mosque in front of the church we're going to now is newer than the church, and built many years later. In other words, if the church has been there for fifty years, the mosque will have been there about twenty years."

Hassan was amazed. "How could you tell that?" he asked.

Hatem smiled triumphantly.

"Clearly you know there's a mosque next to the church there," he said.

"What do you mean?" said Hassan, stumbling over his words in his confusion, half defiant and half friendly.

Hatem stretched his legs. The strain of the journey showed on him, as well as the pain of knowing what to expect.

"Nothing special. When you have a town like this that has a church with a priest who's well known and conspicuous in the area, then it provokes the local Muslims, despite their claims of tolerance. They can't bear being outdone, so frictions arise with the Salafist and fundamentalist preachers in the mosques, and in the parliamentary elections one of the candidates buys a piece of land next to the church from heirs whose house has been demolished after the father dies. To outdo the candidate from the ruling party he then decides to donate the land and have a mosque and a Quran school built on it. People in the town are invited to contribute to the building costs, and the mosque gets bigger and bigger and the minaret goes up and up, higher than the domes and the crosses above the church. And although the fundamentalists

are against minarets in principle because they think they con-
travene the practice of the Prophet, they approve of them
when it's a matter of showing off and intimidating the infidels
by putting up taller buildings, and those mosques are the
ones that draw the largest crowds every prayer time, and the
preachers start giving sermons saying that churches shouldn't
ring their bells close to mosques.

"Then the problems heat up after the Muslims who come to
pray complain that Christian girls are walking past the mosque
on their way to the church, so the priest makes some modifica-
tions to the church entrance, but the Muslims reject them and
the police have to step in, and in return they get a commitment
from Father Mikhail that he won't ring the church bells. Then
the Muslims decide to play recordings of the Quran all the
time, and the priest and his congregation complain, and they
all hold a meeting sponsored by the State Security officer in the
area and the members of parliament and some of the sheikhs
from the mosques. The meeting decides that the loudspeakers
at the mosque will operate only for the call to prayer and during
prayer times, in order to be respectful and tolerant, but some
people reject the decision as a concession, and State Security
has to intervene and the protests die down."

As Sheikh Hatem went on with his story, disrupted by the
lurching of the car as it battled over the potholes, the church
loomed in the distance, next to the mosque, just as he had
explained. He could see in Hassan's eyes that he was impressed
and inquisitive.

Hatem checked his clothes and his appearance before getting out of the car, then put his hand on Hassan's shoulder.

"You know, I've understood from this trip that you really
are enthusiastic about Christianity," he said. "From the fact
that you came all this way and made such an effort, it's clear
you're really determined. But the question is: Why did you
come here? What does this church have that others don't
have? And what is it about Father Mikhail in particular?"

Hatem's candor bowled Hassan over like a left hook and left him shaken. Hatem hurried off and stood by the car. In the distance he could see Father Mikhail heading toward him.

"See how big and grand the mosque is from the outside," he said. "They took great care to ensure it would inspire awe, in a show of strength toward the church. It has a minaret like the Cairo Tower, in a town that's more like a village, and a round dome that hides half the nearby houses, and verses of the Quran inscribed along the mosque walls. The church, on the other hand, is very austere, as if it's trying to project the same simplicity and spirituality as the Christians themselves.

"And I bet you that on the inside the church is a master-piece of splendor," he added, advancing toward Mikhail, who was coming to meet him.

"Good evening, Father," he said, embracing the priest.

Once they were in the church he gave Hassan a dig in the ribs. Hassan knew what he meant. He might have said, "Didn't I tell you how grand it would be, what with the carv-ings and the paintings, the ceilings, the wooden panels, the icons, the statues, the stained-glass windows, the candles, the lamps, the carpets, the curtains, and furnishings?" There was even a large library with shiny beechwood tables. Nothing in the church suggested it was rustic or neglected. On the con-trary it was richly endowed with donations from the pious, either out of rivalry with the mosque or because, under the priest in charge, the church had a mission to perform.

The other visitors stayed in the hall, while Hatem and Hassan followed the priest to his office upstairs. Hatem had asked to be alone with Mikhail—a request that had made the priest feel vulnerable.

Hatem sat down, determined to find out what those around him knew, or what he thought they knew.

"I'm sorry to trouble you, Father," he said. "I know I'm imposing on you, though I'm exhausted too. But this visit will be the talk of the whole area, which will set an example for tolerance and cooperation and show that we are all part of the fabric of one nation, without bigotry or sectarianism. The bigots on your side will find out how tolerant we are and the bigots on our side will realize how tolerant you are."

Hatem paused a moment and let the priest say some nice words in return. The priest, with sweat on his brow, stroked his beard and threw tense glances toward Hassan.

Then Hatem took the bull by the horns and asked straight out, "Are you the great-grandson of Sheikh Mikhail Mansour?"

The question took the priest by surprise and struck him dumb, but the impact of the question on Hassan was so mysterious that it struck Hatem that maybe Hassan didn't know who Sheikh Mikhail was. He was surprised.

"Do you really not know Sheikh Mikhail?" he asked Hassan.

"Is that really possible, Father?" he added, turning to the priest. "I doubt there's a single convert who started out on his journey without knowing about the life of Sheikh Mikhail."

Father Mikhail smiled at last. He thought the sheikh was teasing him, to be honest, and he decided to take it one step further.

"How did you find out, Mawlana? From State Security?" he said.

Hatem roared with laughter, pleased that the priest was so sharp.

"Father, I'm not one of those and you know them very well. Don't they have meetings with you and negotiate with you and make requests and give orders and sometimes plead with you? Could you survive in this church of yours without their approval, without keeping them happy? But you seem to be much more intelligent than them, because I doubt they know about your family or your great-grandfather, or else they wouldn't have approved you. In fact I'm sure they don't know about your private meetings here with young men like Mister Boutros."

With that, he pointed to Hassan, who was following every word, every gesture from either of them.

"Clearly you're different from the other sheikhs," said Mikhail, surrendering graciously. "In fact, different from how you are in the programs we see. But tell me, how did you know?"

Hatem looked around the room.

"From your office," he said. "You're obviously more interested in evangelical books than in theological books. You feel safe that your visitors are ignorant so you've splurged on books. On this shelf in the bookcase there's a book about Mikhail Mansour and there's Kamel Mansour's book about his brother on another shelf, and there's that same book again in several corners, which means that you give away many copies of it."

Hatem reached out and took a copy of the book from a pile on the priest's desk. On the cover there was an old photograph of Sheikh Mikhail.

Hatem put his finger on it and said, "The same eyes, Father, with the same name."

Mikhail smiled the same disciplined, formal smile and his voice sounded less strained.

"I'm impressed by your detective skills," he replied.

Hatem laughed. He detected a trace of sarcasm.

"You put our humility to shame, Father."

"If I told you I wasn't the great-grandson of Mikhail Mansour," said the priest, a touch of coldness in his voice, "what would you say then?"

"I'd say you're the great-grandson of Kamel Mansour, his brother."

Mikhail slapped his hands on his thighs, making a loud crack.

"You're quite something, Mawlana!" he exclaimed.

Hassan stood up, stunned by what he was hearing.

"Are you really the great-grandson of Kamel Mansour as he said, Father?" he asked.

"For shame, boy. Of course he is," Hatem cut in.

And then, after winning on points, Hatem asked Mikhail to tell Hassan the story of his grandfather. When Mikhail began Hatem realized that the priest knew his grandfather's book about his brother by heart because of his reverence for the man and for what he had done.

Hatem picked the book up, held it at chest height, and skimmed through the pages while glancing up at Mikhail as he spoke. Hassan was listening, embarrassed at how little he knew. Hatem realized that the boy hadn't read anything about Christianity, hadn't done any research, and didn't know anything. Hassan's conversion, he was now sure, was a psychological compulsion that had been unsuccessfully treated by an incompetent doctor who didn't understand Hassan's aims in becoming Boutros. Hatem welcomed the chance to go over the story of Sheikh Mikhail again, because his knowledge of it was very cursory, from books or things he had heard here and there, and now the story had caught his interest to such an extent that he would stop Father Mihkail to correct something that didn't quite match what was written in a line of the book he was holding in his hands. He could see from the seal on the inside cover that this luxurious bound edition of the book was printed in a church press and not through an ordinary publisher or a publishing house that specialized in Christian books. It was clear that someone didn't want the book to give rise to any problems with religious institutions, or in any other way. It remained an internal publication that circulated in secret and was passed only to those who believed in its contents and could be trusted with it.

After a restrained preamble, Mikhail started to get enthusiastic as he narrated as much as he could of the details of the epic of his family. His great-grandfather had been writing about his brother Mohamed Mohamed Mansour, who came from the southern town of Girga in Sohag province at a time so far back in history that Hassan who was now Boutros couldn't grasp how far back it was or what significance that distance in time might have.

"Mohamed Mansour, who became Sheikh Mikhail Mansour, was born in March 1871," Mikhail said. "As usual, his family enrolled him in the elementary Quran school for him to memorize the Quran. That was in the al-Aref Billah mosque in Sohag under a Quran reader who was well known in his town at the time, Sheikh Massoud al-Azazi. Mansour memorized the Quran within a few years, like all of his generation."

Hatem turned to Hassan. "Notice carefully, Boutros, that at the time memorizing the Quran in childhood was normal," he said, "but that doesn't mean that the people who memorized it remained believers or never rebelled. The Quran schools produced ulema who served their communities as well as thieving bastards. In those days the Quran schools were more like elementary schools. Going there was no proof of belief, no step toward Heaven. I apologize for the interruption, Father. Carry on with the account of your venerable great-grandfather, sir."

Mikhail tried to give them the impression that taking pride in his ancestors was beneath him, but he failed. He paused for some seconds and tried to cut the story short. Hatem dissuaded him by brandishing the book and Mikhail continued.

"Mohamed Mansour's father sent him to a town near Sohag called Balasfoura to be educated since it had a mosque that was equipped to teach Islamic learning. At the time students came there from all over southern Egypt to study under Sheikh Ali Badr, who was a Malikite and a Sufi. Mansour spent ten whole years in the institute, working diligently and very enthusiastically. Under his sheikh he completed courses in the legal precepts of the Imam Malik and was taught the main works of Quranic interpretation—al-Kashif, al-Baydawi, the two Jalals, the main books on the sayings and doings of the Prophet and his Companions—al-Nawawi's Forty Hadiths, the Sahih of Bukhari and the Sahih of Muslim, and many books on the theory of monotheism, on the Arabic language, morphology and syntax, rhetoric and logic, poetry, literature, philosophy, history, law, and a large number of books by Sufi masters. He excelled in all of this in a way that amazed his colleagues at the time, and his sheikh was also very impressed."

Hatem closed the book and turned to the priest.

"But Father, as the great-grandson of his brother," he asked, "don't you think your great-grandfather exaggerated a little when he talks about his brother's genius and mastery of Islamic learning? For the story to end in triumph, when Mohamed Mansour turns into Sheikh Mikhail Mansour, does he really need to be an eminent and devout scholar, so that his conversion is a crushing victory for Christianity?"

"Firstly, there's a consensus on his Islamic learning in all the biographies written about him, even by his Muslim colleagues," Mikhail replied. "Secondly, Mawlana, he was called Sheikh Mansour. In other words he acquired this title, which means that he led people in prayer, preached in a mosque, and taught in a school. In fact he and some friends of his opened a school."

Sheikh Hatem opened the book and began to read: "In 1893 he had the idea of researching Christianity, prompted by his zeal and desire to promote Islam. He studied a book called *Truth Revealed* by Rahmatullah Kairanawi, which responds to Christian criticism of Islam, and he asked Sheikh Ali Badr for permission to try to convert Christians to Islam and to debate with them. Sheikh Ali Badr didn't approve of the idea and quoted the expression: 'We are bound by promises not to harass Christians and Jews.' He was worried his disciple might become arrogant and conceited. Mansour discussed it with him, arguing that spreading Islam and debating non-Muslims who disagree with Islam were the duties of all Muslims, based on the Quranic verse: '*Call to the way of your Lord with wisdom and fair counsel, and debate with them in the fairest manner.*' Sheikh Ali Badr said, 'Yes, that's true, but I'm worried you might waste your time on things other than improving yourself and purging yourself of flaws. We have to be tough on ourselves and on our inclinations, and carry out what God has commanded.' Mansour did not like this reply, so he remained silent."

Hatem put the book on his lap and addressed Hassan didactically.

"There are three points to note here, Boutros," he said. "First, his age. He started looking into Islam and Christianity at the age of twenty-two, which is a very young age. It's true that in the old days men used to mature early but Sheikh Mansour, although he had acquired much learning, was still inexperienced.

"The second thing is that he had a very arrogant attitude from the start, when he tried to convert Christians to Islam. It's very possible that his brother added this aspect for dramatic effect, since it suggests that Mikhail had discovered Islam's Achilles heel, but, generally speaking, arrogance undermines learning and that holds back a young man who has convinced himself that he knows everything.

"So what's the third thing, Boutros?"

Hassan didn't answer, though it didn't take much effort to see that he was upset that Hatem was making fun of him.

"Okay, Father, what's the third thing?"

The priest looked irritated, as if he wanted the evening to end.

"What is it, Mawlana?" he asked.

"Sheikh Ali Badr, his teacher, knows very well that the kid isn't mature enough or knowledgeable enough to venture into the uncertain world of comparative religion. The sheikh's worried he might get confused. He realizes that he's alarmingly enthusiastic and that his learning is not well grounded. Besides, he himself is reluctant to turn religion into a contest."

Hatem turned to Hassan and said: "I tell you, people really should obey their teachers."

Then he turned to the confused priest.

"Okay then, Father," he said, "tell me how Sheikh Mikhail found out about Christianity in Sohag?"

"The first person he spoke with was a dyer called Mikhail, but when he brought up the subject the man told him he didn't know anything about religion. He told him to go and ask one of the priests who would know, and he directed him to an Orthodox priest called Dean Menkerios, who wasn't very convincing. Menkerios sent him to a blind cantor but the cantor didn't want to talk to him. He told him the only person who could answer his questions was the Evangelical priest. Then he started asking around and going to the Evangelical church in the evening, especially to hear a priest called Mikhail Abadir, who was the pastor of the Evangelical church in Alexandria and came to proselytize in Sohag."

"That was the second Mikhail he'd met, Boutros."

Neither the priest nor Hassan paid any attention to Hatem's remark, and Mikhail resumed the story, helped along by brief glances at a copy of the book that he had pulled off a bookshelf a little earlier.

"Then he often mixed with Christians, and his bookcase filled up with Christian books," the priest continued, "and some Muslims began whispering that he was sympathetic toward Christianity. They couldn't say this in public because it wouldn't have been believed of someone like him—an accomplished scholar who was a devout Sufi who fasted by day and got up at night to pray.[4] Then many people became suspicious of him and kept an eye on him. They condemned him for mixing with Christians and going into their homes. He was as discreet as possible and always secretive about going to Christians' houses, which he usually did under cover of darkness. Then he asked the Evangelical Church to baptize him, and the church prevaricated out of fear. It finally accepted his request but he hadn't expected the church to be so unenthusiastic. He explained the situation to the Coptic Catholic priest there, who was an acquaintance, and the priest said he could arrange for the Coptic Catholic Church to baptize him right away. The priest wrote to the Catholic patriarchate in Cairo to tell them about the case, and the patriarchate asked the priest to send Sheikh Mansour to them. Mansour handed his school over to his partner, left everything, traveled hastily to Cairo, and joined the Coptic Catholic Church there. That was in late 1894. He chose to be called Mikhail and was baptized."

"All that took place within just a year," said Hatem. "That's much quicker than I thought. And of course Sohag was in uproar and his family was devastated, and it was a big disaster and a scandal."

"Definitely. His mother started wailing and screaming and sobbing and weeping, as well as his sisters and his aunts, as if he had died, and the house filled up with men and women paying their condolences. His father went to Cairo to look for him and found him in the Coptic Catholic Patriarchate. He told him the rumors about him in Sohag, and Mansour replied that everything he had heard was no doubt true. This struck his father like a thunderbolt: he was crushed by grief and almost went crazy with anger. He threatened him, and he implored him with tears, but this only confirmed Mansour in his faith and made him more committed to Christ his redeemer.

"In August 1895 he traveled to Rome with a Catholic delegation and, dressed in Islamic dress, he had an important meeting with Pope Leo XIII. The pope called him forward, blessed him, and asked God to strengthen him in his Christian faith. He gave him a collection of valuable pictures and other gifts. The visit impressed everyone in Rome who saw him or heard of him and a posse of journalists sought him out in the hotel where he was staying in Rome. He was also photographed several times on his way to the Vatican, wearing his turban and caftan."

"Of course it all became a big show," said Hatem. "And Mohamed Mansour realized that his visit to the Vatican in his caftan, his turban, and his Azhar uniform would turn him into a dashing hero, with his conversion striking a painful blow in this religious struggle. We've often seen that scenario in our own lives, Father."

He threw a copy of the book onto Hassan's lap and said, "That's a picture of him on the cover in his turban and caftan! In other words, his importance lies in the clothes he's wearing, not in him seeing the light and converting to Christianity."

"Of course what you say is hurtful, Mawlana, but understandable in the context of your own position," Mikhail replied.

"Father, that might wash with our young friend here, but it won't wash with me or with you. There are hundreds of stories, and no one knows how true or accurate they are, but they're about monks and priests who have converted to Islam, and there are hundreds of them, not just one. That doesn't prove anything. Arguing about whose religion is best, and whose religion can win over more people of the other religion, is enough to drive anyone crazy. It's the kind of thing that religious adolescents care about. It doesn't need to be a reason to feud. Besides, in your great-grandfather's book about his brother it says that he switched from being a Catholic to being an Evangelical, doesn't it?"

The priest took it as a rhetorical question and didn't answer. But apparently Hatem was expecting a reply, so he replied after a pause.

"When he came back from Rome, he didn't find in the Catholic Church the teachings and principles he had found with the Evangelicals when he started exploring Christianity. So he decided to go back to the Evangelical Church, which had its headquarters in Ezbekiya," he said.

"So he remained undecided even in his new religion," said Hatem, "because people who chop and change from one sect to another are undecided and they counteract their uncertainty by being extremely enthusiastic, to convince themselves rather than convince anyone else. Let me read you what your great-grandfather said about him. Listen."

With that, he opened the book and began. "He once visited me in a house where I was living near al-Azhar with a group of Azhar students. They gathered around him and talked about many things. One of them said, 'We are are very distant from the Christians. Do you really believe that Christ was a god?' As soon as the student finished his sentence, Mikhail Mansour stood up straight and made a speech that was so full of enthusiasm and so defensive about the divinity of Christ that I was worried that he might be in danger.

"His brother speaks about his enthusiasm and his sincerity with pride. But as far as I'm concerned this suggests someone who is troubled, not someone pious who has seen the right path and is at peace. The man was obsessed with spreading his new faith and with confrontation, and not a confident believer. In fact, he saw himself as a man with a mission, and this clearly involved an unhealthy dose of mania. That doesn't mean I'm knocking him, because I think he should be free to do as he likes, but to turn his story into an epic of heroism is quite unjustified. His brother, who was Your Grace's great-grandfather, wrote this: 'Another time he came to see me with the late Atiya Hanna, who was editor of the magazine *al-Murshid*, and they met me with a group of students who were coming out of al-Azhar, and one of his acquaintances asked him, "Don't you ever regret what you did when you converted to Christianity?" And he replied, "No, but I did regret the time I spent far from Christ and His grace, before I converted." And one night when the church had a meeting in Ezbekiya, about seven hundred people gathered outside, including many of the country's worst criminals and thugs, and shouted that they wanted to kill him and that they wouldn't leave till they had killed him. The missionaries were afraid for his safety and advised him to escape through the back door of the church but he refused. He stood on the pulpit, bared his chest, and shouted, "If anyone wants to kill me, they should step forward, because I am no better than the one who died for my sake, and I have no idea why these people have turned up outside.'"

"Your grandfather is proud of his brother in this scene, but the question is: Why did those criminals, as he put it, go there? Of course, they weren't exactly criminals. They were Muslim extremists and fanatics who wanted to teach Sheikh Mikhail a lesson—counter-extremism in response to Sheikh Mikhail's extremism. Do you know why? Because the man wasn't content to live in the spiritual peace he said he had found through Christ, his savior and redeemer. He turned his conversion into a battle against his old religion. He held meetings in the Ezbekiya church with Muslims by the dozens, it's said, or by the hundreds, to promote Christianity at a time when he was still studying Christianity in the Catholic schools.

"Read what your grandfather said about his brother: 'When the newspaper *el-Liwa el-Masri* attacked missionary activity and missionaries because of him and suggested taking tough measures to silence people promoting the Bible, he went himself to the offices of *el-Liwa*, met the late Mustafa Kamel Pasha and asked him to put an end to *el-Liwa*'s campaigns. Mustafa Kamel Pasha replied, "We are resisting you by writing and if that doesn't work we'll do it with fire and steel." Mansour replied, "You can't force us to be silent and to stop evangelizing, and we will meet your fire and steel with Christ's love and we will overcome you." Once a group of people from al-Azhar also attacked the evangelical movement and he wrote an open letter to the Sheikh of al-Azhar and the Grand Mufti of Egypt that was published in the newspaper *Misr*, saying the ulema should be prevented from slandering and libeling, and pointing out that spreading the gospel was one of the most sacred obligations in Christianity and that it could not be ignored. He signed this letter "Mikhail Mansour the convert."'

"This suggests to me that he was looking for a religious war because he was uncertain and maybe even sick. He wasn't seeking the kind of spiritual peace that he would have found as soon as he felt he had made the right choice. In this he was like dozens of other people who have switched from one idea to another and have become more hostile to the original idea than they are supportive of the new one."

Hatem turned to Hassan. "Do you understand what I'm saying, Hassan?" he asked.

"You've got it in for Sheikh Mansour and you want to make him out to be sick because he converted to Christianity," Hassan replied, trying to argue back with equal force.

"Indeed," Hatem quickly retorted, "but I'd also like to say that there are plenty of sick Christians who've converted to Islam, and mind you don't think that I don't respect the suffering and torment the man went through, but at least he had studied both Islam and Christianity and had worked hard to find out what was true from what was false. Whereas you, Hassan, what have you done to become a real Christian? Have you studied or did you just come and see Father Mikhail here?"

He looked at the priest, who had premonitions of scandal and a nightmare if Sheikh Hatem decided to expose him.

"So tell me, Father, do you know who this young man is, sitting with us tonight?" asked Hatem, looking toward Hassan. "I mean, he came to see you with some other young men who wanted to convert, for you to encourage them or lecture them, or teach them something that you obviously didn't teach them because Hassan's as ignorant about Christianity as he is about Islam. But do you know who he really is? Or did he come through other people or through a website, and you don't know who his family are?"

The priest tensed up. He felt he might be in grave danger at any minute. But Hatem took him by surprise and changed tack completely.

"How did your great-grandfather come to convert after his brother?" he asked.

"He gave him the Bible and he read it," said Mikhail. "His heart found peace in belief in the Redeemer and Savior."

"As simple as that!" said Hatem.

Hatem stood, picked up some of the Bibles that filled the bookcase, and put them all on Hassan's lap and in front of him on the small round table, knocking over the brass teacups that were sitting there. A church servant had brought the cups in when they were deep in loud conversation some time earlier but no one had paid them any attention or drunk from them. Hatem ignored it when the tea spilled on the floor and neither Hassan nor Mikhail seemed to notice the tea or the cups.

"Off you go then. Read the Bible and we'll see what you've understood, Hassan. Nothing at all, would be my guess. Just like the only parts of the Quran that millions of Muslims know are the parts they need to say their prayers, and they don't understand what the verses or even the words mean. Faith isn't in the Quran or the Bible. If we gave a copy of the Quran to a Christian and they read every chapter, do you think they would end up Muslim? Faith is in your mind or in your heart, and if you're not very intelligent or if your heart is sick, then there can be no faith, but just obedience, imitation, and submission, or else it comes down to madness or something done for material gain. The problem with your grandfather, Father, and with those that were with him, was that he continued to describe his brother as Sheikh Mikhail, as if his value didn't lie in his Christianity but in being a sheikh when he converted at the age of twenty-two."

As the priest came out to say goodbye, Hatem thanked him cheerfully for putting up with the strain and the nervous pressure. He said that he had no intention of blackmailing him or disclosing Mikhail's secret, and that he had his own reasons for wanting to keep it a secret. But he suggested Mikhail stop meeting young converts in the church, in case the meetings led to conflict in the town as Mikhail could end up in serious trouble if people found out what he was up to.

"But Sheikh Mikhail was a Catholic and then an Evangelical. So how come you, the great-grandson of his brother, became Orthodox?" Hatem asked the priest.

"In my early youth, Mawlana," he replied. "So who is Hassan's family then?"

"The best thing that ever happened to you in your life, Father," Hatem said, "is that you don't know who his family are. Keep it that way, I beg you."

HATEM WAS BACK IN HIS office, usually the place where he unwound before he stepped back into the world again. But now, sitting in his lair, Hatem was trying his hardest to play the television sheikh, as if the cameras of the world were trained on him. He was sitting in front of Khalil el-Nahhal, who owned factories making cleaning products and was the main sponsor of his new Ramadan program. Khalil was a conformist and very traditional in religious matters. Hatem realized this when they first met at the man's factory. He had gone to see Khalil at the insistence of the program producer, an enthusiastic, very well-educated young man from a wealthy family. Hatem thought Khalil was honest and was delighted at the considerable amount of money on offer when Khalil suggested they cooperate on a new program at a time when he wanted to break free from Ali el-Kaaki and his advertising agency. So he was going to work with someone else in Ramadan, so as not to put all his eggs in the basket of one slave trader. But apparently his new producer's only motive for financing the program was as a vehicle for the advertising campaign that his companies were mounting.

Khalil el-Nahhal was not the smiling type and his voice was soporific. In conversation he kept quoting sayings of the Prophet and repeating memorized texts that he had read or probably heard from sheikhs from the Arabian Peninsula.

Hatem knew that Khalil's father, Mohamed el-Nahhal, had been a Muslim Brotherhood leader about fifty years ago, and he remembered clearly how his teachers at al-Azhar had spoken well of Mohamed el-Nahhal, as good company and a man who was open-minded. He didn't have a beard and he never wore a galabiya to work. He used to preach at a mosque in Manyal and at the time neither his wife nor his daughters wore the hijab, but only small scarves that covered some of their hair. Khalil was his youngest child and when the Abdel-Nasser government launched its campaign against the Muslim Brotherhood, Mohamed el-Nahhal was briefly imprisoned. When he came out he moved to Saudi Arabia with his family, died the following year, and was buried there. The family stayed on in Riyadh and Khalil's mother married a Muslim Brotherhood widower who was also a refugee in Saudi Arabia. Khalil was brought up by his mother's new husband, who washed his hands of politics and worked in the world of finance and commerce there.

When Khalil reached university age, President Sadat had opened the door to Brotherhood members who wanted to come back to Egypt. Khalil was the only person in his family to do so, while his mother and her husband stayed in Saudi Arabia and even acquired Saudi nationality. His two sisters married an Egyptian and a Kuwaiti and lived in Kuwait, and it was said that Khalil's factory, which he set up in the early 1980s when he was twenty-five years old and which succeeded despite his youth, was financed by money from his stepfather and his brothers-in-law. His products became well known and he was a pioneer in the field of cleaning up the country, as Hatem liked to put it. He teased the man by saying he was cleaning the whole country, not just ordinary kitchens but also the corridors of power. Khalil never smiled back at Hatem, nor did he show any sign of annoyance, as if he didn't understand what Hatem was saying. Once Hatem got this, he abandoned his usual jovial demeanor and adopted a character that he didn't often adopt even on television—the dignified, serious sheikh. On his first visit he felt no enthusiasm toward Khalil; he thought he was impervious, like a pane of glass. When you throw water on glass, the water just runs across the surface.

After that visit, he asked his new producer, "Are you sure this surly man wants to sponsor my program?"

"What he told you, Sheikh Hatem, is that he hopes that he and you can cooperate fruitfully for the sake of God," the producer replied.

"I bet you he hasn't seen a single one of my programs, because the man has nothing in common with what I say and the way I say it."

"What do you mean, Mawlana?"

"Ah sorry, I forgot you went to the American University and were educated in an English school. Anyway, we'll see what happens with our friend who washes whiter!"

Hatem was surprised when Hassan tried to insist on going back to his sister's mansion at exactly two o'clock in the morning after they came back from Father Mikhail's church. He didn't take pleasure from the fact that a responsibility would be lifted from his shoulders, at least temporarily. On the contrary, he didn't want Hassan out of his sight because he was worried that if Hassan went off unexpectedly, without good reason and with unpredictable consequences, he might find himself in serious trouble with the family of the president's son. So he asked Hassan to calm down and stay. Just then he heard his cell ringing; it was his producer telling him that Khalil el-Nahhal wanted to sit down with him the following morning. He was surprised but he agreed, provided the meeting took place in Hatem's office so that he could sleep an extra two hours. Then he remembered that he had an appointment with Nashwa. For God's sake, he wondered, how could a devout woman have such a name?

With difficulty, as if he were dealing with an unruly bull-ock, Hatem persuaded Hassan to stay the night at his house and in the morning God, "the dispeller of darkness and the splitter of date stones," would sort things out. In the morning he offered to kiss Omayma's hands and feet for her to per-suade him to wait until Hatem came back from the office so that he could have a word with what he called "this idiot that I might be tempted to finish off." She turned down his tempting offer but agreed to do her best.

"Hello, Khalil, please come in," said Hatem, hoping the meeting would be short and the mystery would be explained.

"Praise the Lord, whose every act brings good, even if peo-ple deem it bad," said Khalil.

When Hatem heard this, he was worried the man had withdrawn his financing.

"I'd like you, Your Grace, to promise me two things," Khalil continued.

"Of course."

"Everything is in God's hands and always has been. I was watching an episode of the program you're doing at the moment and I heard you say many fine things in it, praise the Lord."

"May God preserve you," said Hatem.

"But there were two things that caught my attention and so I'm asking you to do a couple of things."

"The first?"

"The first is, given your extensive erudition and the impor-tance of simplifying that erudition for the masses, I hope you'll uphold the dignity of religious knowledge, in the sense that you will maintain the atmosphere of a lecture and go easy on attempts to trivialize the material."

Hatem understood instantly that Khalil was the real pro-ducer and not just the man who would finance the adverts and that the polite young man from the American University was just a façade.

"The second point was that in the program I heard some remarks by a young woman who accused you, sorry, asked you about the Mutazila and who thought you were a Mutazilite by doctrine. Is this true? I would have thought better of you than that."

Hatem smiled. He could do without this arrogant lesson from a man who thought himself knowledgeable about religion and God's ways, when all he really knew was the piety he'd been force-fed while he was being suckled by his widowed mother and the canned ideas that his stepfather had bought in a Riyadh supermarket and taught to him. But he was worried that this might be the start of a rift that could widen. He didn't know whether Nashwa had spoken spontaneously or at the instigation of someone else, but her words beat like a hammer on the window of his fame and his livelihood.

"Mr. Nahhal," he said, "I think you know that al-Azhar follows the Ashaari school and we study the Ashaari curriculum, so it might be said that we are Ashaars, but in fact for hundreds of years no one has asked the graduates or sheikhs at al-Azhar what school they belong to, because the knowledge they are taught comes from a pure spring."

"But Sheikh Hatem, you know that these schools have polluted that spring, and that the Mutazila and even the Ashaaris are not qualified to make pronouncements on Islam. It is Islam that is qualified to make pronouncements on them." Khalil said, showed off his learning and denting Hatem's confidence.

"That's great, but who here can say what Islam is, Mr. Nahhal?"

"The people who follow the practices of the Prophet and the consensus of Muslims."

Hatem knew he faced a choice between, on the one hand, continuing the discussion and losing his sponsor and producer and about two million pounds in fees for thirty hours of programs and, on the other hand, curbing his desire to punch the man in the face and thereby keeping his sponsor despite the mistrust that had now arisen between them. Hatem immediately started operating on the basis of the second option, even before he had made his decision.

"Look, Mr. Nahhal," he said, "I'm sure we agree, to start off with, that the Sunna and the pious early Muslims stand above everyone and that our task as preachers who appear on this amazing box, this world stage called television, or online too, is to bring religious knowledge into people's homes—useful knowledge that sustains this world and the world hereafter— and not to get bogged down in theoretical debates or get carried away with things that cause divisions or dissent. Second, I must make it clear that we don't disagree on any idea or opinion, but if you feel you could enlighten me a little by asking questions or making remarks or comments, then feel free, and I'm very happy that you watch the program so that there's some interaction between us. It's very important to have someone who's sensible, mature, devout, and familiar with religious knowledge, such as yourself, to watch the program and make observations. That would be a useful contribution. For example, why did I reject Ali el-Kaaki's offer to work with him in Ramadan even though, I swear, the man offered me twice as much as I'll be earning from our programs here? Because I want to work with people who show an interest that complements my efforts, but are not intrusive in a way that distracts me from my objectives—as happened when they let some young woman, God alone knows who brought her along and persuaded her to ask a question that was really an accusation, or rather throw an accusation in the form of a question, as you heard, Mr. Nahhal. Isn't that negligence in the selection process? Aren't the producer and the program creators responsible?"

Hatem could see Khalil's face cheer up and his knitted brow relax. His fingers played less frenetically with his prayer beads and his face was less flushed.

"This story of the Mutazila is all because the ulema are envious of each other," Hatem said. "If you're going to move into the field of religious programming, Mr. Nahhal, you'll have to get used to envious ulema and understand what rivalry will do to some people, however learned and pious they might be. God protect us from mistaken pride and pernicious envy."

Khalil said something brief about how relieved he was by what he had heard, and that he knew all this but he wanted to check for himself because he liked him and thought his work was good for the promotion of Islam and for young Muslims. Then he took out of his pocket three booklets, with fine bindings, expensive paper, and colorful covers dominated by the color green. He presented them to Hatem. "This is an anthology of quotations that I collected and arranged myself. They're from *The Meadows of the Righteous* and *The Victory of the Creator* and they're sayings of the Prophet, may God bless him and grant him peace. The first is on the subject of self-improvement, the second is on Muslim women, and the third is on the special qualities of the chapters of the Quran. I had it privately printed by a friend of mine and I give it out to my staff and the workers in my factories. I was thinking of selling it through bookshops at a nominal price so more people could benefit from it. In it you'll find my point of view on the kind of religious knowledge that should reach people."

Hatem flipped through the booklets and smiled happily.

"Thank you," he said. "I see they even have hadiths that only a really diligent researcher would dig out. I swear, Mr. Nahhal, you really have proved to be a missionary for Islam and scholarship. I'll soon have a rival, especially with your smiling face and your eloquence."

Khalil lapped up Hatem's flattery with such enthusiasm that when he said goodbye he told him openly that he was indeed the sponsor and producer of the program and he would raise Hatem's fee because sheikhs of his kind deserved to find backers.

Khalil left. Hatem hoped with all his heart that Nashwa wouldn't turn up on time because he wasn't in the right frame of mind to see a young woman who had almost put an end to his television career and might have turned his life upside down in ways that God alone knew. When he saw her and spoke to her something in his heart opened up like a flower, but right now he preferred his heart to stay closed up like the junk room in an old house. He might have vented his anger by insulting Sirhan and Khodeiri in turn, but she was already standing at the door.

In she came, her bronze face set off by a hijab wrapped tightly around her head, her loose gown—it couldn't be described as a dress—trailing behind her as she walked, making a swishing sound like the wind in the trees. Behind her stood Khodeiri, to introduce her to the sheikh. "Miss Nashwa says she has an appointment," he said.

She came in without waiting for an invitation from Hatem, who stood up and moved toward her. Then he had a thought and stopped.

"You don't shake hands with men, do you?" he said.

She shook her head nervously without answering, though he took that as answer enough. He sat behind his desk again and pointed her to a chair, but she sat on another chair, the one that Khalil el-Nahhal had been sitting in moments before. Hatem decided that after she had gone he would order Khodeiri to throw the chair out of the window.

Hatem looked at Khodeiri, who seemed to be asleep on his feet.

"Would you like something to drink, miss?" droned Khodeiri.

"You'd prefer 'sister,' wouldn't you?" Hatem corrected, looking at Nashwa. "Would you like some tea?"

She ignored both questions.

"Bring two teas with the sugar on the side," Hatem told Khodeiri.

Khodeiri took hold of the door and mumbled, "The sugar's always on the side."

Hatem heard him and let out a laugh that he then tried to cut off politely.

"Good to see you, sister Nashwa."

She nodded silently.

"Tell me a little about yourself."

She didn't speak and Hatem paused too, wondering to himself what he liked about this damned woman with her nervousness and restlessness. She had hidden her claws in black silk gloves that he had to admit looked better than those gloves that hung loose from the fingers, the kind he often saw on the hands of women like her who were anxious to hide the parts of their body that God hadn't even asked them to hide. Some of them then add insult to injury by wearing rings on top of the gloves.

"I'm sorry I haven't taken any lessons in sign language," Hatem said. She was surprised by this comment, and her face tensed up even more. "Because if you're planning to stay silent like that throughout the meeting, I really won't understand you. I don't have the right qualifications for dealing with the dumb."

She laughed, but after three bursts of laughter she regretted laughing. Something in her aborted laugh upset Hatem but he got over it when she finally spoke.

"Thank you for the invitation, Mawlana," she said. "The truth is it was me who wanted to hear some answers."

Now Hatem was worried.

"That's fine by me," he said, "and you can ask your questions later, after you're spoken about yourself. Tell me, are you a college graduate or are you still studying?"

"I'm not as young as you think," she said defensively.

"Ah yes, you really are old."

"No, really. I graduated six years ago from the Faculty of Humanities, English Department, and got a diploma in missionary work from the Institute of Missionaries. I'm applying to do a master's at the Islamic College for Girls."

"Excellent, and what's your master's on?"

"The freedom of women in Islam, a study of the practice of the Prophet," she said.

"Very good. And do you think that women are free in Islam, based on the practice of the Prophet?"

"Of course."

"Good, so why are you doing the master's?"

"To prove it."

"And who said it hadn't been proven?"

"There are Western and orientalist claims that Islam doesn't treat men and women as equals," she said.

"Are you going to write your dissertation in English?"

"Why?"

"Since it's designed as a response to the West."

"It's not just the West that claims that. There are secularists who claim that Islam doesn't treat men and women as equals."

"And does Islam treat them as equals?"

"Of course."

"What do you mean 'of course'? What about inheritance and as witnesses in court?"

"There are reasons and justifications for not treating them as equals in those cases."

"So there isn't equality."

"There is, but . . ."

"Okay, so if someone came to you, not an orientalist or an occidentalist, and asked you how you interpret the hadiths like the ones in Bukhari, for example the Abu Hureira hadith that quotes the Prophet as saying, 'If a woman spends the night away from her husband's bed, the angels curse her until she returns.' I remember it precisely. It's hadith number 67 in the section on marriage and number 85 in the section on when a woman spends the night away from her husband's bed. Come on then, how would you respond?"

Was she silent out of embarrassment or ignorance?

"So, if a woman's tired and fed up and comes back from work in the factory or the office or she's exhausted from housework or helping the kids with their homework and her husband gets it into his head that he wants sex or he has an argument with her and she walks out, does she deserve curses from the angels till she goes back home? Okay, suppose her husband's an idiot and a brute, does she have to submit to him passively like a plastic doll or a prostitute in the red-light district? And why should the angels take the husband's side? I mean, if the husband is useless and he leaves, why don't the angels curse him? I mean, why's the woman always to blame?"

He felt he had shocked her so he took a break. But she bristled and replied, "Do you deny the Sunna, Mawlana?"

"My dear pretty Nashwa, you're always turning our discussion of hadith into denial of the Sunna. Couldn't I reject just this one hadith? Why do you always want to get me into trouble by trying to make me deny the whole Sunna outright?"

"You say it's a hadith from Bukhari."

"Yes, and in Bukhari there's a hadith in which Abu Hureira quotes the Prophet as saying, 'If it wasn't for the children of Israel meat wouldn't putrefy, and if it wasn't for Eve, no female would ever betray her husband.' It's hadith number 60 in Bukhari's chapter on prophets, and number one in the chapter on the creation of Adam.

"Do you know what it means for meat to putrefy? It means it rots. And what's meant is that, just as meat rots, women betray their husbands, as a fact of nature. So either the Sunna tells us that women are treacherous by nature, or else we face two other options: either we deny this hadith and then you tell me that it's in Bukhari, as if Bukhari is untouchable and as if he didn't collect hundreds of hadiths that are strange and poorly attested, or else we do something else, and that is to look at it rationally. We can either agree that the hadith is sound and then interpret it in a way that doesn't lead to the conclusion that women are treacherous by nature, and if others disagree, so be it, as long as they don't say that their interpretation is more correct than our interpretation. And what do you think of the hadith related by Abdullah bin Omar: 'I heard the Prophet say, "Three things bring bad luck: mares, women, and houses."' Bukhari cites this hadith in the summary, number 60 in the chapter on jihad. Is it equality in Islam that women should bring bad luck like mares and houses?"

He was worried he might have gone too far in offending her with his vehement and mocking intrusion into areas that, to someone of her background and as religious as she was, might appear to be a challenge to the Sunna, but he could see that she had recovered her composure and was in fact even more stubborn and defiant. Okay, then she deserved to be treated harshly.

Hatem continued. "For a start, I'm not being selective. On the contrary I'm quoting hadiths in full, with their numbers and where they are in Bukhari. Second, your ulema, with all due respect, see no contradiction in this because they're inclined to believe the text when it occurs in Bukhari and they're told it's genuine. Well, let them think that way, no problem. The problem is I don't accuse them of ignorance or of being wrong or troublemakers, whereas if they heard what I think, they wouldn't dismiss me as just someone who disagrees with them. They would accuse me of disputing the Sunna and, as you heard from someone or other, of being a Mutazilite, and I bet you don't know who the Mutazila were in the first place or what they believed."

"I studied them in the Institute of Missionaries," she said, raising her voice and showing how young she was.

"Great. So you read maybe a two-page tract by some Salafist sheikh that insults and defames them. You probably read a hasty, cursory account by someone who hates them. You've read about them, but not what they say themselves. Suppose you heard, for example, another hadith that's in Bukhari. It's hadith number 17 in the book on marriage and number 10 in the book on marrying women who've already been married, and the source for it is Jabir ibn Abdullah. He says, 'I got married and the Prophet of God, God bless him and grant him peace, said to me, "What kind of woman have you married?" And I said, "I married a woman who's been married before." And the Prophet said, "Why? Don't you have a liking for virgins and playing around with them?" I mentioned this to Amr ibn Dinar and Amr said, "I heard Jabir ibn Abdullah say, 'The Prophet of God, may God bless him and grant him peace, said to me, "Why didn't you marry a young girl so that you could play with each other?"' Nashwa, do you think . . ."

He paused and then asked,"What's your second name, Nashwa?"

She didn't answer and for a moment he suspected Nashwa wasn't her real name, but he continued, "Do you think the Prophet was really interested in hearing from Jabir ibn Abdullah, the man who narrated the story, whether his new wife was a virgin or a woman who had been married before? Then the Prophet in all his glory talks about fondling virgins, and the expression 'playing around' here in the hadith means being naughty and flirtatious, and the way the girl behaves. Can you imagine the Prophet trying to turn a man against the woman he's just married and advising him to marry a particular kind of woman? And then this incomprehensible intrusion by the Prophet ends with the Prophet feeling sorry for Jabir for having married a woman who's already been married because kissing a virgin is completely different from kissing another woman. For heaven's sake, isn't this hadith, which is cited in Bukhari, really insulting to the Prophet, who was always modest and proper in the way he spoke? How could he take part in such a conversation and ask such a question?"

She tried to argue back, like someone who won't admit how hopeless their cause is.

"But there's nothing to be embarrassed about when it comes

to religious learning, as long as the Prophet wanted to give Muslims something that would be useful to them in their lives," she said. His phone was flashing with an incoming call and the name Omayma appeared on the screen. Hatem had already ignored two calls from her but at the third he felt she must be listening to his talk about virgins and previously married women.

"Oh right! So the Prophet was interested in giving us a lesson in the merits of marrying virgins rather than non-virgins!" he said, commenting on Nashwa's answer.

He swiped the telephone screen with his finger and answered Omayma with a sigh, anxious not to mention her name.

"And peace be upon you," he said.

He looked flustered and his face was strained. Nashwa noticed how nervous he was, despite her own nervousness.

Omayma was telling him that some security people had been with her in the house for some minutes and they had told her that the president's son and his wife were on their way right now, and the security people were asking about Hatem and where he was so that he could be there to meet the president's son.

Hatem looked over toward Nashwa, who was busy playing with her phone. Somehow her face helped him think straight.

"Okay, I'll be right with you," said Hatem, trying to calm down Omayma, who had raised her voice. "But tell Hassan his sister and her husband are coming, so that the surprise doesn't upset him."

"The thing is that Hassan's disappeared. He's not in the house," Omayma replied.

"What?" said Hatem, standing up and slapping his gown. "Okay, okay, I'm on my way right now."

He turned to Nashwa, who looked at him in a way you wouldn't expect from a student of religion who was arguing stubbornly with someone like him. She looked more like a woman defying a man who thinks he has overcome her and tamed her. He ruled out the possibility that she was anything more than a stupid but attractive young woman to whom he was drawn by something in himself, rather than by something about her.

"There's even plenty of doubt about the story of playing around with virgins," Hatem said, "because it's experienced women, women who have been married and had sexual experience, who know how to play around with men, but an inexperienced virgin, an unfledged kitten, who would she play with, for God's sake? You might spend the whole of your honeymoon trying to persuade her to get over her shyness and her fear."

Nashwa smiled and he suspected that behind her master's she was hiding a doctorate in some other specialty.

"Shy virgins belong to another age, Mawlana," she said.

"Right, a time about fourteen hundred years ago, so playing around with her would have been really difficult."

He clearly faced a puzzle but he was in too much of a hurry to solve it now.

"I'm very sorry. Some people have suddenly descended on me for some silly visit, an unexpected one no less. It's more like a raid than a visit, I tell you, but I would be interested in pursuing this conversation with you. Will I see you tomorrow at the next program?"

She nodded enthusiastically.

Hatem stood up, walked toward her, and waved her to the door, where they stood face to face.

"So tell me, Nashwa, how did people discover God?

"They discovered him through reason."

Hatem laughed triumphantly. "That, my lady, is the Mutazila's whole theory—that people discovered God through reason!"

He opened the door for her. Khodeiri and Sirhan stood up immediately and followed him and Nashwa to the elevator. Hatem and Nashwa went down together while Khodeiri went back to the office and Sirhan walked down the stairs to get the car ready.

In the elevator Hatem could feel her breath on his face. For a moment he thought it was deliberate and he was cautiously surprised. But she was behaving so normally that he tried to dismiss the suspicion that it might have been deliberate. In the silence that was hard. Finally, when the elevator reached the ground floor, she said, "I'll read up on the Mutazila so I'll be ready for you."

"I'm always ready," he said with a laugh. "I'll always be waiting for you."

There was definitely something between them at this moment, he told himself as she shuffled along in her loose gown and he followed on behind. He could still make out the shape of her tight young body beneath the folds of cloth and he completely forgot for a moment the disastrous reality that the president's son had come to his house to check up on the progress he was making with Hassan. Not only had he made very little progress but now his charge had gone missing as well.

It wasn't in fact the president's son who was waiting, though all the hullabaloo and commotion strongly suggested he was there. It was only his wife Farida, who Hatem called 'The Lady' because she reminded him of the grand, dignified ladies in furs and black evening dresses who used to appear in the audience at Umm Kalthoum concerts broadcast on television late at night. Farida had apologized for arriving without an appointment, then apologized doubly because Hatem wasn't at home when she arrived and had had to drop everything to get there. She was sitting at one end of the sofa, bolt upright on the edge without leaning against the sofa back. Hatem couldn't tell whether this was out of politeness or nervousness. Without saying anything, he glanced at Omayma, thanking her for sitting with Farida with all the graciousness she knew how to summon when necessary and without indulging in her hobby of undermining his image as a sheikh. It was clear that the two of them hadn't said much, since neither of them knew what the other knew. Omayma opted to talk about how heavy the traffic was, while Farida praised her good taste in interior design. Hatem was still thinking about Nashwa and how, behind the hijab and the loose skirt, a sexy young woman might be hiding. Omayma took her leave on some nonsense pretext that Hatem didn't understand, but he appreciated her good sense in leaving him alone with Farida. Now that Omayma was gone, Farida suddenly looked sad. He realized she was really exhausted and urgently needed to confide in him. He pre-empted her.

"You're worried about Hassan, aren't you, Madam?" he said.

Her resistance collapsed. "Something very upsetting happened and it's kept me awake the last two nights," she said.

"All's well now, I hope?"

"Did you hear what happened to the son of that famous Hamas leader?" she suddenly asked.

The question took him by surprise. He hadn't heard anything about the man, didn't even know who he was, although he was apparently famous. He only just understood that she meant the Palestinian group Hamas.

"I'm not sure quite what you mean," he replied.

"A couple of days ago we were at dinner with one of the leaders of the Palestinian Authority, someone from Fatah. To tell you the truth I wasn't really interested in what Fatah and Hamas mean or in following Palestine and Gaza and the Hamas government from a distance, but I found out many things at that dinner. The man was staying with us and he was an old acquaintance of my father. They'd done business together long ago in Ramallah because the Fatah leader was originally a businessman or he took advantage of his important position there. But anyway my husband also likes him, and both of them hate Hamas like poison, as was clear from what they were saying over dinner, but the Fatah man told a story that he said was a scandal we should use to attack Hamas. Although he said he didn't like to get into personal matters, the subject from his point of view had an important political aspect and showed that Hamas had been infiltrated, because the son of a Hamas leader had turned out to be an agent and spy for Israel and had told the Israelis where to find several leaders, who were then assassinated because of his betrayal."

Hatem couldn't see what this had to do with anything related to anything he knew, but he listened patiently out of respect for Farida.

She continued her confession: "The scandal, as he put it, wasn't just that the son of the Hamas leader was working for Israel but that he announced that he was converting to Christianity and renouncing Islam."

"Ah."

Now he understood what a deep impression the story had made on Farida.

"The kid's name was Musaab. He started calling himself Joseph and completely washed his hands of Islam. A while back he said something really horrible on an American television channel about Muslims and Islam, and attacked his father and Hamas and called them terrorists and said Islam was a terrorist religion and that he had found himself through Christ, had been baptized in a church, and had fled Palestine and traveled to America."

She cleared her throat before continuing.

"Apparently the kid attacked Islam really viciously and of course the Israeli press picked up the story and it was a big scandal despite Hamas's attempts to dismiss the story as a personal matter. But our guest, the man in the Fatah leadership, said some members of Hamas had attacked their own leaders, especially the father of the kid who converted to Christianity because he hadn't had his son executed for apostasy, and this showed the double standards of Hamas, which always kills spies, and this damaged Hamas's prestige even among its own supporters."

"But this is all very remote from us," said Hatem, trying to give her a little reassurance.

"Not at all. It's very close, closer than I thought," she replied in surprise.

"How so?"

"Because the Christian evangelical sites on the Internet have started presenting the story as a victory and as having infiltrated the Hamas leadership, and they've been promising other conversions in the most important ruling families in the Muslim and Arab world," she said.

"Ah, that would be quite a painful coup. But it could just be bluffing and bluster."

"It may be, but my husband looked very tense, so much so that the man from Fatah sensed that something was afoot, and he shut up after saying that the Fatah people hadn't exploited the scandal, which might ruin any Palestinian or Arab politician."

Hatem could see that she was growing increasingly anxious. "So you're worried about the news getting out and creating a scandal for your husband?" he said.

"No, I'm worried about Hassan," she said. Strangely she spoke calmly, staring into space.

"My husband's very kind, as you know," she added after a pause, but before Hatem had time to ask her to explain.

He kept his reaction to himself. Besides, he certainly wouldn't have expected the wife of the president's son to say anything different, even if she had seen signs that Hatem was skeptical about her husband's character or intentions.

"Maybe many people who don't know him as he really is or who disagree with him politically say the opposite, because no one can please everyone," added Farida.

"Of course, of course."

"The truth is that he's kind, but his political ambitions are enormous and he has high hopes of governing the country. I've never said this to anyone, even to him. Although he loves his family, there are lots of things he wants to do for the country that his party hasn't yet managed to do."

"And of course," said Hatem, anxious to put an end to the spiel about her husband's altruism, "if it leaked out that his wife's brother had publicly converted to Christianity it would do a lot of damage to his reputation."

"He won't let anything leak out," she answered firmly. "I'm quite sure of that. It'll remain a secret, and that's what makes me terrified for Hassan."

What she said was clearly mysterious. He looked at her face for clues. She lowered her eyelids and whispered, "I'm frightened for Hassan's life."

The revelation was a slap in the face.

"Are you serious?" he said.

"I love my husband very much and I can't think ill of him, but there are people around him who might advise him to do something, or might do it on their own initiative, to serve his ambitions by getting the problem out of the way."

They both stopped, especially as Hatem thought he too might be a target, along with Hassan, since he knew the secret, and also because he was being asked to protect and go around with a young man who was in imminent danger.

Farida broke the silence. "Is Hassan an apostate, Mawlana?"

He wanted to tell her that Hassan was disturbed and not an apostate but he was worried it might sound too harsh for such a sensitive woman.

"Given that Hassan says he's a Christian and has abandoned Islam," he said, "the term 'apostate' does apply to him under Islamic law, but Islamic law gives him a chance to return to the faith. But Hassan is basically confused and he isn't thinking straight and I don't think his conversion is serious yet, although he's making an enormous effort to prove to you and to me that he is serious."

"So the penalty for apostasy would apply to him?"

Hatem leaned back and answered calmly. "Well, madam, if you were to ask the opinion of the sheikhs who have sprung up all over the country these days, then it does apply, but I'm convinced there is no penalty for apostasy in Islam."

Farida pricked up her ears but she wanted to be sure. "You know, what worried me most was that I found my husband researching the penalty for apostasy on the Internet. He left his laptop open on the bed one morning."

She stopped and bowed her head. Perhaps she was thinking he had left it open deliberately. Then she continued: "And I Googled it and found ten sites with articles about the penalty for apostasy."

"Madam, what I'm going to tell you now I wouldn't dare say openly, on television or in an interview or a discussion, but I'm convinced that the two incidents in which the Prophet, may God bless him and grant him peace, is said to have killed apostates are not properly attested and the people who narrated those hadiths were not reliable, incontestable sources. In his book *Nayl al-Awtar*, the imam al-Shawkani, who is a very important imam, madam, and his book is a major reference, says these hadiths have weak chains of transmission. Do you know what chains of transmission are?"

He didn't give her a chance to reply, but explained anyway.

"It's where the hadith says that so-and-so heard this from so-and-so who heard it from so-and-so, who said the Prophet said this and that and so on. That's called the chain of transmission. The hadith is based on what someone quoted the Prophet as saying or doing. The chain is weak here in the sense that it doesn't come from any of the Companions of the Prophet who were known for telling hadiths, or it could be that it comes from someone who told lies about the Prophet or was known for making up stories or from someone who's just a bit dodgy. So it hasn't been proved that the Prophet ever punished anyone for apostasy. There are some relevant hadiths in Bukhari and Muslim, which are the most important compilations of hadiths for Muslims, although I've just had an argument about whether everything in Bukhari is correct.

"In Bukhari and Muslim there's a Bedouin man who pays homage to the Prophet, may God bless him and grant him peace, and who later asks the Prophet to release him from Islam, in other words to let him renounce Islam, which would clearly be apostasy, but nevertheless the Prophet didn't penalize him but let him leave town peacefully. Bukhari also cites a hadith from Anas—Anas was one of the Companions of the Prophet and a servant of his—that says that a Christian man converted to Islam and then reverted to Christianity, and that was during the lifetime of the Prophet. But the Prophet didn't punish him for his apostasy. Also during the life of the Prophet a group of Jews apostasized after becoming Muslims to lure Muslims away from their new religion, and the Prophet didn't punish those apostates. But you will find a thousand sheikhs or preachers who'll tell you we have to cut their heads off or slaughter them or apply the penalty for apostasy, although there isn't a penalty for apostasy in the first place. Recently society has wanted there to be a penalty and people see this as being religious and committed to Islam, and they've forgotten all the concepts of freedom in Islam, things like 'Those who want to can believe, those who don't want to don't need to' and 'You have your religion and I have mine.' Now the slogan is 'I have my religion and I'll root yours out.'"

Farida let out a laugh despite the way she felt, then went straight back to feeling miserable.

"Is there any hope that Hassan will turn Muslim again any time soon?" she asked.

"To be honest, madam, I can't even tell you whether Hassan will come back to my house soon, so how could I tell you whether he'll go back to being a Muslim soon? As for there being no penalty for apostasy, that's my view, but apostasy exists of course, and it applies to Hassan, despite the deep mystery about his motives. Hassan is a mysterious young man. But there's definitely hope that he'll return to Islam, plenty of hope, especially as I still believe that Hassan hasn't yet fully abandoned it. Roughly speaking, he's in a kind of limbo."

"And where is Hassan?" Farida asked, and Hatem didn't have an answer.

"But what's your father's position on this problem?" asked Hatem. "I thought he was with you at dinner when the subject of Musaab and his conversion came up."

She bowed her head and looked mortified. "My father's the quiet type. You rarely hear him angry or shouting. His answers to questions are vague and sometimes rather like the clues in a crossword puzzle. That's why Hassan, being young, has grown very distant from his father, and Father has been very busy too, of course."

She looked up and added innocently, "My father would frighten anyone who could hurt Hassan, but he could hurt Hassan himself if it affected the family."

Hatem understood something he didn't want to understand, but he promised her that everything would be fine, perhaps to reassure himself rather than to reassure her.

Hassan's cell phone was "unavailable." Hatem realized that the phone was the only link he had to Hassan. He was trying to find a way out of the trap, although he had already eaten the poisoned bait at its entrance.

Hatem summoned Sirhan from where he was sitting in the garden room and asked for the telephone number of Father Mikhail. When Sirhan said he hadn't saved it, Hatem jumped down his throat, shouting and ordering him to obtain it instantly from any of the people he had met on the day they opened the store and visited the church. He had promised Farida he would find Hassan that night. The kid's absence was a serious blow and, even if he did turn up now, the two of them wouldn't be out of trouble. He felt that he and Hassan were in the same shoes. They might both be in mortal danger and God alone knew which of them might take the bullet.

When Sirhan came up with his cell and put it to Hatem's ear, Hatem was muttering, "God is the only source of power and strength."

"Speak," said Sirhan.

"Who is it?"

"The priest. Didn't you want to speak to him?"

Hatem felt his hand trembling and he tried to steady his nerves.

"Good afternoon, Father Mikhail," he said. Mikhail's voice sounded devious though apprehensive.

"Good afternoon, Mawlana. What an honor, to see you and hear your voice two days in a row!"

Hatem decided to get straight to the point. He didn't have the luxury of time to be cunning.

"Where's Hassan, Mikhail?" he asked.

Mikhail didn't speak for a moment as he absorbed the question, but Hatem had no time to wait.

"I'll be quite upfront with you. The kid's disappeared and you know I could make tonight the last night you remember what your name is. I won't say anything to State Security or to the government. I'll just express my misgivings about you and your church to the janitor at the mosque next to you. Notice that I didn't even say the sheikh of the mosque, no, I said the janitor. Let me put it this way, Father. If I don't find out where the kid is within one hour, Father, I'll turn the church upside down on you."

Mikhail got his breath back after the succession of verbal assaults.

"By the living Christ, I don't know anything about him," he whispered.

"By the living Christ you'll know something about him within the hour. Make some phone calls and find out and give me a call." Hatem hung up without saying goodbye. He looked thoughtfully at the phone; he had run out of patience. He ran through the names with his fingers and found the one he wanted. He pressed the key to call him. When he heard a voice on the other end, he put on a little act.

"What an angelic voice!" he said. "Anyone would think it was one of those famous Quran readers! I tell you, Ahmed Pasha, you could work as a broadcaster, when you retire from the Interior Ministry, after you've served as minister of course."

"And what can I do for you, Mawlana?" asked Brigadier Ahmed el-Faisal.

"Nothing really. I was calling just to say hello and ask whether you're satisfied with us," said Hatem.

"Mawlana, after the lady came to see you at home, you ask me if we're satisfied! I should be asking if you're satisfied with me," Ahmed replied enthusiastically.

Hatem was speechless for a moment, but he was soon back to his ingratiating routine.

"So the satellite was taking a really close look at our house then!" he said.

The officer smiled, "We've got you covered in more ways than one, to tell you the truth."

"In fact I was calling just to ask after Khalil el-Nahhal."

"What about him?"

"Not much. He's the sponsor of my Ramadan program but I wanted to make sure he's a good guy and you're happy with him sponsoring the program," said Hatem.

"Any reason to think otherwise?"

"Not at all. But I wanted to check for myself."

"He's a man who's seriously Saudified but, as you know, those Saudified types aren't interested in politics, so they don't bother us and we don't have any trouble with them," said the officer.

"You mean he's fine?"

"Happy Ramadan, Mawlana. Enjoy your iftars."

"You too."

He hung up, worried that he might have paid a price for worrying about Hassan and being anxious to find out whether the security people knew anything about his whereabouts that might have come to the attention of Ahmed el-Faisal. The pretext he had given for calling was ridiculous because neither Khalil el-Nahhal, nor indeed the month of Ramadan, could move an inch without prior approval from the security people. But Hatem decided against asking him directly about Hassan when he realized they knew that Farida was at his house.

Hatem looked around the house wondering who the informer was.

He went back and examined the guava tree, marveling at the structure of the leaves. Who knows, he thought. Maybe they found out from Farida herself or from her bodyguards. The whole country leaks like a sieve.

He found Omayma, who had sat down next to him some minutes ago without him noticing.

"By the way, Omar says hello," she said. It was as if she had breathed new life into him.

"I want to speak to him. Please, Omayma!" he said.

She stood up and walked away.

"There's no need for me to remind you of things we don't like to remember, Hatem," she said.

The tension was unbearable. He felt a sharp pain in his stomach and sweat began to run off his forehead and drip down his nose. He took his turban off. He hadn't taken it off since he had gone in to meet Farida. He put it on his lap, sunk in thought about visiting Omar in the hospital. Omar's doctor, a friend of Hatem, had assigned a pretty Ukrainian nurse to look after Omar after he came out of his coma, and she thought Hatem was the local priest, come to be alone with the child and give him spiritual comfort. She fell in love with the voice the sheikh used exclusively for reciting the Quran to Omar. The place was rather like a luxurious morgue and his angelic child was sleeping there, tearing at all his heartstrings with his blank stare and his lost memory. He couldn't remember who Hatem was. They were at the stage where Omayma, the doctor, and the Ukrainian nurse were all trying to teach Omar that she was his mother and that Hatem was his father. Sometimes Hatem would weep so much that they chased him out of the hospital.

His phone rang and he shuddered. He answered the phone when he read the name of the caller. Sirhan had given the number the misspelled label "the preest." Speaking more calmly and less angrily, Hatem said, "Yes, Father. Have you found out where Hassan is?"

"I have," replied Mikhail, exhausted. "But that's all I've managed to do."

"Why? Where is he?"

"In the Vatican Embassy in Cairo."

As night fell Hatem didn't know what to do now that Father Mikhail had told him Hassan was in the Vatican embassy.

"By the way," Mikhail had continued, "that kid is crazy, Mawlana, and he'll be the ruin of us all. Apparently he heard the story of my grandfather and he got it into his head to convert in the Vatican, so he went to the embassy in Zamalek and asked to meet the papal nuncio. Of course he didn't meet him, but he sat with the consul there and told him he was seeking political asylum in the Vatican because he was being persecuted after converting to Christianity. The man didn't know what to do and of course he suspected that the boy was deranged. They explained to him that it would require lengthy procedures and he could come around in a week after leaving all his details, but the boy insisted and said he wouldn't leave. The nuncio was told about it and in fact the man was very sensible and was worried that the boy might get into trouble if he contacted the Egyptian foreign ministry or the police, so he told them to let the boy stay. The boy refused to give them any details about his family and just showed them his passport."

"How did you find out all this, Father?"

Mikhail was being deliberately evasive.

"A friend in the embassy called a friend in the church and asked him for advice, then the friend in the church called me to get my opinion a few minutes after you spoke to me, and I asked him the boy's name. He made a call and found out and told me the name, and I advised them not to agree to his request and to wait for me to contact them," he said.

Hatem realized that there were networks of relationships at play here and for the moment he wasn't interested in finding out about them. He asked Mikhail for the telephone number of his friend's friend in the Vatican embassy.

He hung up and called the number. A man picked up and answered in formal literary Arabic. Hatem said he was calling on behalf of Father Mikhail and he wanted to speak to Hassan or Boutros.

"Tell him it's Sheikh Hatem el-Shenawi," he added.

The man from the Vatican shuddered at the name and didn't speak for a moment. Then he asked for a few minutes and said he would call back.

After one ring, Hatem picked up and found Hassan on the other end.

"Was it my sister's husband who told you I'm here?" he asked.

"Come and spend the night at my place," Hatem said calmly, "and I'll take you to the Vatican in Rome myself."

Hassan didn't answer.

"You do realize," Hatem continued, "that I could tell your sister or her husband, or forget them, I could speak to your father, and the papal nuncio would come out now and announce in front of you that he'd turned Muslim so that you'd get out of his face. In less than an hour you'll find Sirhan waiting in the car opposite the embassy gate. Come out and come here immediately."

*

Sirhan came in first and announced he was back.

"And where's Hassan?" Hatem asked.

Sirhan didn't answer because Hassan appeared right behind him. Hassan stood in silence in front of Hatem, who was sitting on the ground-floor patio that opened onto the garden. Hatem looked at him; he was pale with bloodshot, glazed eyes. His eyelids were drooping as if he was exhausted. Feeling sorry for him, Hatem stood up and sat Hassan in a nearby chair.

"Thank God you're safe. You look completely wrecked," he said. Hassan didn't speak. He just stared into the garden.

"Are you hungry?" Hatem asked. "I could make you lunch, or has the Vatican invited you to grilled prawns?"

Hassan didn't respond to Hatem's attempt to be funny.

"Would you like some tea?" Hatem tried. "Sirhan, make some tea with milk quickly," he shouted to the driver.

Hatem sat up straight to face Hassan.

"Look, Hassan," he said, softly and sympathetically, "you and I are now trapped in a sealed box at the bottom of the ocean, and we have to find a way to get out and escape drowning. You want to officially convert to Christianity for a reason that can't have anything to do with either Islam or Christianity, because you don't understand Islam and you don't know much about Christianity. But you're free to do so, as I've told you a thousand times. At the beginning I imagined that this idea had nothing to do with religion and now I'm sure of it. Your family thought I could convince you, and in fact I don't know what to convince you of anyway. But the issue's now very much bigger and more complicated. Your sister's frightened for you, not for your religion or your mind or whether you go to heaven or hell, but for your life. And I'm frightened for myself and for my future because apparently I'm not allowed to fail in the mission I've been assigned. Did you notice how many times I said 'frightened'? Now let's get back to the box

309

under the sea. No, I said the ocean, because it's deeper, and by the way it's the Atlantic and not the Pacific, because the Pacific is pacific and predictable. I have one last suggestion, a solution that might pay off, but I'm not going to tell you now. First I want you to drink your tea."

He gestured to Sirhan to put the tray he had brought on the table in front of Hassan.

"Tell me, Hassan, have you ever taken drugs?"

Hassan was taken aback by the question and blinked. His pupils narrowed and he shook his head.

"You've never tried weed, for example?"

Despite himself, Hassan's lips widened with a smile but he quickly suppressed it.

"No," he said.

"Okay, have you ever drunk beer?"

"I never touch it."

"So why are you alive, for God's sake, if you don't take drugs or smoke weed or drink beer?" Hatem snapped.

Hassan finally let out a short laugh and his face relaxed.

"Great. I know you don't drink coffee and you only like tea with milk. So I'm going to put in a clear request to you, so that I might present to you the proposed final solution."

Hatem stood up and patted Hassan on the shoulder.

"Go upstairs and have a hot bath, then swallow this tablet," he said.

He took a strip of tablets out of his pocket. He opened one of the tabs, took Hassan's hand, opened the palm, and put the pill in the middle.

"Don't worry. This is Calmepam, a tranquilizer. In a case such as yours, with no alcohol or caffeine, you'll fall asleep a quarter of an hour after taking the tablet and sleep for ten to twelve hours. Tomorrow, you'll wake up exhausted, feeling a little heavy-headed and dizzy, but your mind will be completely empty, as if pumped full of air. Stay at home, relax, play Xbox, and forget everything about everything. Then later in the day

I'll be back from recording the program and we can sit in the garden here and I'll tell you the solution, provided you don't tell anyone else. Not the Pope in Rome nor the Coptic Pope in Alexandria nor your father or even your mother. You can speak to Omayma if you like, though I'd rather you didn't."

Before getting up to leave, Hatem added, "Hassan, are you sure you've never taken drugs or smoked weed or drunk beer?"

"I'm sure, Sheikh Hatem," Hassan replied cheerfully.

"By the way, you sound like a Buddhist," said Hatem as he turned to go. Then he looked back, took the strip of pills out of his pocket, and threw it into Hassan's lap.

"Anyway, take two pills just in case, because I don't believe you," he said.

Omayma woke Hatem up with a rough push on his shoulder.

"Please get up and go to see the girl."

He slipped out of his sleep with difficulty and tried to put some words together.

"Girl? What girl?" he said.

Omayma scowled, unable to appear indifferent.

"She says her name's Nashwa and she's been waiting for you since seven o'clock in the morning. The guards had to let her into the office since we didn't answer and she was insisting. She said she was a relative of yours and when I woke up they told me about her. I didn't go down because I wasn't ready to receive anyone, especially a girl who's come so early in the morning and without an appointment. I said I'd wake you up so you could go down and see her."

Hatem mulled over the surprise and pushed the cover off his body. He got up and went into the bathroom.

"You know her. She's the girl who asked me about the Mutazila," he shouted through the half-open door.

Her tone changed. "Oh, now you tell me, so she must be mad!"

"Since she came to our house at seven o'clock in the morning and found out the address and decided to wait till I woke up, then your description of her resonates with me," he said.

He came out of the bathroom with wet hair, puffy eyes and his sleeves rolled up, with a towel around his neck.

"The possibility that would be most reassuring is that she turns out to be mad. It's the other possibilities that are worrying," he said.

"Such as?"

"God alone knows."

"That she's mad about you, for example?"

He laughed out loud, gruffly and with a bit of a cough.

"That would make good sense," he said.

He found the last thing he expected when he opened the office door on Nashwa. He found her lying on the sofa with her legs stretched out and her shoes off, fast asleep. He could hear the muted but regular whistling sound she made as she breathed in and out with her nose buried in the cushion. He saw an exhausted young woman preoccupied by thoughts much too weighty for her to bear. Her head was wrapped tight in a hijab tied expertly to her loose, shapeless gown. Her fingers were buried inside gloves of some silky material and she was wearing military-style boots that reached up her calves. Nashwa had covered her face in make-up—kohl, lipstick, powder, and eyeliner—but it had all gone to waste when she fell asleep on the sofa. Strangely, as soon as she heard him come in she stood up and pulled herself together and then sat down like someone caught red-handed. She excited him, aroused him, although he had slept little, and restlessly at that, and was tense and annoyed by her visit and worried that Omayma might react angrily, but her sleepy eyes were so seductive that he felt refreshed despite his misgivings.

"Would you like breakfast?"

"No, thanks, I had breakfast ages ago."

"What do you mean, ages ago? It's only half past eight in the morning."

"No, seriously, I've had breakfast, thank you."

"Okay, coffee or tea?"

"No, thanks, the guard already brought me some tea."

Hatem looked at the half-drunk cup of tea and smiled.

"The tranquilizer he put in it must have had a very powerful effect."

She laughed, conniving in his attempt to banter flirtatiously. The look she gave him wasn't that of a student of religious learning, and the way he looked back at her wasn't the way the teacher would look at a student.

"I haven't slept all night," she said. "I've read masses about the Mutazila on the Internet. It's true that most of it was the same stuff repeated, but I read it carefully and I can say I didn't understand much of what I read, but from what I understood I'm sure that they reject the Sunna, as the Salafists accuse them of doing."

Hatem was calm and not in the mood for defiance.

"I like you saying you read about them on the Internet," he said. "Aren't there any printed books left in this day and age?"

He looked at the books on the shelves that covered the walls in his office. The ones that stood out were the ones with gilt bindings and the titles written in Kufic script with arabesque decoration. She looked at them too: apparently she hadn't seen them when she came into the room earlier.

"You won't find a single book here about the Mutazila or by the Mutazila because I wouldn't put them here," said Hatem. "But a number of well-known history books or biographical works are by Mutazilites, either overt or covert."

He looked at her carefully.

"You read all night and then you couldn't wait to meet at the studio or in the office, and so you came to my house around dawn. Isn't that rather strange?" he asked.

Flustered, she apologized. "I'm really sorry but I didn't feel like sleeping until I lay down on the sofa, and then I told myself you were bound to get up early. I've disturbed you, haven't I?"

"Why do you care so much?" he asked with a smile.

"Because I'm a fan of yours!" She didn't say it in a way that suggested she wanted to talk about theology.

He cleared his throat and said, "By the way my wife's upstairs and she was having trouble sleeping and if she doesn't get back to sleep it'll be a bad year for me, as well as for you and for the Mutazila."

Nashwa smiled in a way that seemed at odds with the way she was dressed.

"I mean a fan of the way you explain things and address the audience and simplify religion, but I'm very upset by the campaign against you on the Internet and on Facebook. They're accusing you of lots of things," she said.

He was surprised at what she said but he was cautious about how he replied. He stuck to the conventional.

"But what made me very angry is that you really are a Mutazilite," she continued, shooting the accusation like an arrow into a target.

He sighed.

"You're the only person I've ever heard this from," he said, "and I've never seen any trace of these accusations on my Facebook page. In fact my many fans on the Internet, and those who contribute to my Facebook page and my website, have never mentioned these accusations on the Internet. But I sometimes say things to my fellow sheikhs and ulema that the Salafists on the Internet can't understand. Besides, the only people who would understand this story about me being a Mutazilite would be people versed in Islamic schools of thought and I don't think there are any of those among the wider audience you're talking about. It's very true that the Salafists don't see me as authentic, but I have never appeared in any public forum, let alone on television, and said anything on which people disagree. Nashwa, I don't display my learning in interviews and on television programs. I say things that shock people only a little, to spare them any distress and to make my own life easier."

Nashwa was shocked by what he said, but he continued: "I'm speaking to you frankly, but I want you to be completely frank in return. You can't stick a label on me for things I've said in interviews and meetings that might offend people's thinking. I'm well aware of my own best interests and they could deal my interests a deadly blow if I came out with opinions or ideas that are different from what everyone wants to hear. Everything I say in public is what I believe of course, but it's on the margins, on the surface. I give people moral guidance, remind them of God, tell them interesting historical anecdotes and give them fatwas for daily life that meet their need for piety. But the fatwas don't change anything in their lives or even in their souls. The difference is that I speak in language that's simple, as I said, and connects with people, and isn't complicated and heavy or traditional in an old-fashioned way. I'm a sheikh in a turban but, in my style and manner, I'm not like many others who wear turbans— people see me as modern, like the young preachers who wear suits and shirts and who act all reverent on camera and speak like the Muslims spoke in the film *The Dawn of Islam*. And by the way, some people think that the way we look and the way we talk are modern, but what we say comes from the museums of thought, preserved, text-based, old, and recycled. The preachers who are my competitors in the marketplace may not know any other way of speaking but I have studied and I have learning that I have found convincing, fell in love with in fact, but I don't make any effort to deviate from the television version of religion."

"You mean that what you say in public is not what you think in private?" asked Nashwa.

"No, you idiot. That would be hypocrisy, but I don't make public everything I think and feel. I don't tell lies, but I say superficial stuff."

Nashwa was moved by this candid outburst. "But that means you might not be the man I thought you were," she said.

"That's why I'm telling you what shouldn't be said, but I can say it because you're an idiot and enthusiastic and you woke up early to listen to what I think, and most importantly because I expect to hear the truth from you in return."

"Why are you suspicious of me?"

"Who said I was suspicious? Anyway, forget the reason and concentrate on the answer."

She looked at him in a way that asked for sympathy and trust.

"I saw you a while back in several programs and in fact I wasn't concentrating very hard, and then a few months ago I watched two of your programs and I was very interested and I admired you. I started following the things you did and your programs and interviews and I asked Sheikh Fathi about you because I attended all his lectures at the Institute of Missionaries, and he told me you were a gangster, not an Azhar sheikh!"

Hatem laughed till he cried.

"I thank him for his opinion, and you for your honesty," he said.

"What he said really shocked me, but I like him and respect his opinion and I've memorized many of his fatwas," Nashwa said.

"Wow!" said Hatem. "So there are people who memorize fatwas? When did you take up this hobby?"

"As soon as I made a commitment."

"A commitment to what?"

"Sheikh Hatem!" she said with a laugh, looking at him disapprovingly, with eyes that were not in the least committed.

"Nashwa!"

"No, really, you must know what it means when someone says they made a commitment."

"In fact I do know but I'm just acting dumb."

There was no longer any doubt that they were warming to each other.

"Then I asked the preacher Yasser Abul-Ezz and he told me you were a respected sheikh, but he was uneasy about what he had heard about you from major sheikhs, which was that you don't like the Salafists and that several times you had attacked Abdel-Aziz bin Baz, the mufti of Saudi Arabia. So I went and asked Dr. Mohamed el-Alami about you after his meeting in the mosque and he just said he didn't follow you and that really annoyed me and I concluded he was arrogant."

"But you know, Nashwa, I don't follow him either, but I hear he's a good eye doctor. He's a physician, as you know."

"He's a useless eye doctor," Nashwa said firmly. "He almost blinded the daughter of a friend of mine."

Hatem laughed.

"A friend of mine from the institute," Nashwa continued, "told me she met you at a seminar and after it she asked you about the hadith that goes: 'The grave is either one of the gardens of Heaven or one of the pits of Hell' and you answered her by saying, 'Is that grave in Old Cairo or on the west bank of the Nile?'"

"Your friend must have been very ugly or very pretty for me to reply like that," Hatem said.

"She wears a niqab."

"Oh dear, now I've put my foot in my mouth."

"I think you met her before she started wearing the niqab."

"In that case my answer must have been the reason she started wearing the niqab."

"No, it was because she got married. She started wearing the niqab after she got married. Anyway, her husband, who was her fiancé at the time, told her he knew some Salafist sheikhs who said you spoke about the Mutazila at a seminar as if they were religious reformers, whereas they thought the Mutazila were heretics. They also said that in discussions with sheikhs in private sessions you rejected some sayings of the Prophet. I decided I had to confront you because I like you."

She blushed and Hatem blushed with her. He looked around despite himself, as if to see if anyone was watching them.

"Like you in the Platonic sense of course, and then I came to see your program," she continued.

Then she went back to speaking like a girl in secondary school.

"I was given the runaround and everyone and his uncle gave me hell before I could attend your program and, to tell the truth, when I was in the office at your place I couldn't hate you, though I was quite convinced that you do in fact reject the Sunna."

He slapped her on the head disapprovingly without thinking what he was doing or about the consequences of touching her head with his hand. But she didn't resist. In fact she smiled.

"My dear, there isn't a Muslim in existence who denies the Sunna of the Prophet. How could we live and pray and worship God without believing in the Prophet and the things he did and said? The Prophet couldn't possibly have spent twenty-three years carrying out his mission as prophet without teaching his companions, talking with them, explaining things, giving them advice, telling them what to do and what not to do, but because what the Prophet said and what instructions he gave is so important we have to make sure that these acts and sayings really are the Prophet's. For example, after the Prophet died, Abu Bakr al-Siddiq gathered the people together and said people were telling dubious stories about the Prophet, and that in the future people would disagree even more about which ones were true. So, he said, don't tell any stories about the Prophet and if anyone asks you, say, 'We have the Book of God to settle any disagreements. If the

Quran says something is halal, then treat it as halal, and if the Quran says something is haram, then treat it as haram.'

"And through the caliphate of Omar the ban on hadith continued. His ban didn't only apply to Abu Hureira and Kaab al-Ahrar, though he did accuse them of narrating hadith and threatened to expel them to their original homes if they didn't stop it. His orders also applied to important Companions of the Prophet, including Abdullah ibn Masoud, Abu Darda, and Abu Masoud al-Ansari. To them he said, 'You've told too many stories about the Prophet,' and he confined them to Medina. In other words he banned them from traveling and so from spreading these sayings of the Prophet. And of course the decision also applied to his military commanders and, when he was walking along with them to see them off, he made them give a pledge to avoid telling stories about the Prophet, may God bless him and grant him peace. Then he told them he had come out with them to give them this advice: 'You will meet the people of a town where they recite the Quran like bees that are buzzing. Don't distract or divert them with hadiths. Don't complicate the Quran by adding hadiths or stories on the side. Don't tell too many stories about the Prophet. If anyone insists, refuse and blame it on me.' And when some of the commanders arrived in Iraq, they met new Muslims who were impatient to hear anything about the Prophet because they had never seen him. They hadn't been Companions of the Prophet or even contemporaries. And the new Muslims said, 'Tell us about the Prophet.' And the commanders said, 'Omar has forbidden us from saying anything.' But with the death of Omar things loosened up and everyone felt quite free to tell stories about the Prophet, and for hundreds of years hundreds of thousands of sayings of the Prophet appeared, very many of them fabricated, attributed to the Prophet by people who wanted to flatter the Umayyads or the Abbasids, or just to entertain. The difference here is over how to handle the hadiths, and that leads us to the Mutazila, but did you understand what I said before we move on to the Mutazila?"

"Wow. You do trust me!" said Nashwa.

At this point Hatem invited her into the garden so that they wouldn't be behind closed doors too long and to have breakfast with Omayma while they were at it.

"But I tell you, it's good to be committed," Hatem said. "I mean, if you can wear the niqab for an hour or two that would be great too."

Omayma treated Nashwa as any wife would when subjected to an unwanted visit to her home by someone she doesn't know who sits with her husband without asking his wife's permission and without the visitor apologizing to her. But Nashwa, by playing with great expertise the role of a strict and committed Muslim woman who also happened to be in a foul mood, managed to mitigate Omayma's annoyance, especially when Hatem began a speech she hadn't heard before.

"It always begins with politics. All these ideas and schools of thought and different and contradictory opinions arose under the barrage of politics. When the Prophet Muhammad set up an Islamic state, Islam wasn't a religion with denominations or theories. But as soon as he died, political disagreements arose over who should succeed him and who should govern. Since the Companions of the Prophet, who had great prestige, all lived under the same sky and in the same circle, the disagreements remained under control because everyone knew how much weight and authority and knowledge everyone else had. But when the Companions of the Prophet left Medina during the reign of Othman and the Muslims grew more powerful and wealthier and the empire expanded and they became the center of attention for the masses, other phenomena started to intrude into Islam. Then disaster struck in the form of the first civil war with the assassination of Othman, then there was the conflict with Muawiya and his rebellion against Ali, ending in Ali's son

Hassan ceding power to Muawiya, and then Muawiya turned the Islamic caliphate into a hereditary monarchy. There was a heavy price, paid in the blood and the belief of Muslims. Movements sprang up in opposition to Muawiya and the hereditary monarchy he set up. The opposition needed a theory and some religious basis, and the Umayyad regime under Muawiya and his successors likewise had to find a theoretical religious basis. Because the Quran doesn't provide much scope for politicians to mess around with interpretation or for the rulers or their opponents to twist the Quran to their liking, they made use of the sayings and doings of the Prophet by making up a vast number of hadiths attributed to the Prophet to justify or support one point of view or another. So Muslims have been inundated over the years with hundreds of thousands of fabricated hadiths. And don't forget, the Sunna only started to be properly written down in the third century of Islam, about two hundred and fifty years after the Prophet died. In the meantime, people found their rulers were openly violating the sharia and the Quranic injunctions. So the Umayyad rulers and the jurists and preachers who worked for them were in a fix, so they came up with an idea called 'deferral.'

"Do you know what 'deferral' means here? This is where a distinction arose between action and belief, rather like saying that marriage is one thing and love is something else."

The analogy drew a discreet smile that flashed like lightning across Nashwa's lips, while there was a hint of thunder in Omayma's eyes.

"If someone does something bad and unjust," Hatem continued, "that doesn't mean that the person isn't a believer. That's from the point of view of the rulers and their preachers, because faith is in the heart and is not affected by sin, so we defer judgment on sinners and people who do wrong until the Day of Judgment, when God can judge them personally. That's what they mean by deferral, and the deferral school of thought was favored and promoted by the Umayyad regime against the Kharijites, who thought that an unjust ruler was a prima facie infidel, but amazingly after a time the Umayyads' opponents became advocates of the deferral doctrine. Their demands were that rulers should again consult the people and that governors and police chiefs should be dismissed. Along with the idea of deferral came another idea, which was that of determinism. This idea also came about as a result of political repression. The Umayyads and their preachers didn't want to admit they had mistreated people, so they came out with the theory that all acts, good or bad, are determined by God, and human beings are compelled to do what they do and don't have free will, so we have to forgive the bastards who abuse us because it's out of their hands. In other words they're compelled by God to give other people hell. The theory worked a dream in the Umayyad period and the two most important pillars in their world became deferral and determinism. But although this approach was widespread and was adopted by the state and its ideologues, many thinkers didn't like it, including someone called Wasil ibn Ata, who was a disciple of an important character called Hassan of Basra, the head of the justice and monotheism group. Wasil dissociated himself from Hassan, which is why his school of thought became known as the Mutazila, or 'those who dissociate themselves.' Wasil ibn Ata said there are five principles. There's justice, meaning that all of us are fully responsible for what we do and we can't say we acted under compulsion or that it was God's command, because God doesn't do wrong and you can't drag Him into the argument by saying that you had to mistreat me because God wanted it that way. No, God does not do wrong, so this is something wrong that you have done. That's justice, the first principle. Then we move on to the second."

Hatem stopped and looked at the two women. He was relieved to see that they looked interested. Each of them was holding her cup by the handle and resting it on the palm of her hand, paying close attention.

"Do you have time to continue after the break?" he said with a smile.

"Do you want to haggle over your appearance fee, Sheikh Hatem?" Omayma said teasingly.

"You know what sheikhs are like, my love," said Hatem. "As soon as they finish their work, it's straight to the buffet for dinner."

Nashwa found the exchange mildly offensive. Both remarks struck her as demeaning to Hatem and his vocation.

"The second principle was monotheism," Hatem continued. "At the time there were groups that said that God had a body, not like our bodies, but that he had organs and limbs. They based that on the fact that there are verses in the Quran that talk about the hand of God and the word of God. Then the Mutazila came and said God transcended such things. The third principle was 'the promise and the warning,' which means that those who obey God go to Heaven and those who disobey Him go to Hell and it is only our deeds that determine our fate in the afterlife. The fourth principle is 'the intermediate position,' which was aimed directly at rulers. It said that people who committed grave sins were not infidels, as the Kharijites claimed, or sinners, as others said, but they were in an intermediate position between the two. The fifth principle was 'promoting good and preventing evil.' The hadith people said it was wrong to use force or violence to prevent evil acts, while the Kharijites were in favor and the Shi'a made the use of force conditional on the coming of the long-awaited Imam. But the Mutazila said that the way to prevent evil acts was 'by the tongue, by the heart, and by the hand bearing a weapon,' so they were the leaders of uprisings against Umayyad and Abbasid rule and strong supporters of Shi'ite opposition movements at that time. That's why there was so much anger against them, so much so that their ideas were banned and they were ostracized and prevented from teaching their ideas, and anyone who disobeyed was banished or imprisoned or killed. The Abbasid rulers, for example, ordered that the Mutazila be cursed from the pulpits of mosques, their books destroyed and burned, and anyone who possessed them punished. The Abbasid state made persecution of the Mutazila official policy with a law approved by the mainstream clerics, circulated in the provinces and in government offices, and read from the pulpits. But despite all that their ideas remained, and by the way there were Mutazilite thinkers in all Muslim sects, Sunni and Shi'a. They set up a secret organization that was strong and widespread but of course over the years the attacks on them and the persecution destroyed the organization. They remained oppressed and condemned, although they were the freethinkers of the Muslim world. But the most important reason why the preachers and sheikhs wage war on the Mutazila even now is because of their position on reason."

Hatem turned to Omayma and laughed.

"By the way, Nashwa here is an authentic Wahhabi Salafist. There's no one like our Salafist friends for hating reason. As soon as you say the word 'reason' to them, they start rummaging in their bags for fatwas to declare you an infidel."

Then he turned to Nashwa, who resented Hatem attacking her in front of his wife. "Calling people infidels is the enemy of thought," he said.

"Mawlana, that's a slander on me and the Wahhabis," Nashwa replied irritably.

"I'm trying to place you," Omayma suddenly cut in, squinting and examining Nashwa's face carefully. "Have we met somewhere before?"

"I've never had the honor," Nashwa replied tensely.

Before the conversation between the two women could get out of control, Hatem continued.

"The Mutazila were rationalists and, compared to them, all the others are traditionalists. Reason is the principle that underlies all their ideas and the way they deal with texts, whether it's the Quran or the Sunna. Everything incompatible with reason was wrong. If it was a Quranic verse they found a way to interpret it and if it was a hadith they dismissed it."

"But does it make sense to let everyone use their reason when they're interpreting religious texts and saying this is right and this is wrong, and they just say, 'that's how my reason sees it'?" said Nashwa.

"See, she just said something very Wahhabi," said Hatem with a glance toward Omayma.

"Reason here doesn't mean the reason of anyone walking down the street or writing a comment on some website. It means the reason of people who have studied and done research and who know how to use the tools of reason, not uncontrolled reason. But the Salafists want submissive minds that hear and obey and imitate, whereas the Mutazila want rational Muslims who think and choose, and that's why a deep rift developed between the Mutazila on one hand and the rulers and their preachers on the others."

Hatem leaned his head back, took a sip of tea, and pointed at Nashwa to answer, but she didn't.

"But this is all about politics and not about religion," he continued. "What's happened is that politics has been permeated by religion, and religion has been politicized, and that's what the Mutazila tried to tackle by the use of reason, and their attitude toward sayings of the Prophet was often skepticism about their authenticity and sometimes rejection of the sayings because, as they put it, they judged hadiths by rational principles, and didn't twist reason to make it conform with what they found in hadiths."

He paused a moment, then asked Omayma if she was going out today. Omayma was surprised by his sudden silence and his unexpected question. "Yes, I have a few appointments," she replied.

"Because Hassan is asleep upstairs and I gave him a sleeping pill to calm him down because last night he was giving us hell. Anyway it looks like we won't be here if he wakes up, so try to get home early because I have filming this evening and I don't want him to disappear."

Omayma was surprised that he seemed to have abandoned his earlier caution and was talking about Hassan openly in front of Nashwa, a visitor they hardly knew. She said she had to go right away. Nashwa stood up immediately and took her leave too, and Omayma tried unconvincingly to persuade her to stay.

"Make yourself at home, my dear," she said, but her "my dear" of course made it clear that this was the signal that she had to leave, and so she left.

Hatem went back to bed, but all he could think of was the way she looked, her laugh, and the way she flirted discreetly when they were sitting together. In the evening she was waiting for him in the studio and she attended the filming of the program, in which he deliberately talked about expressions such as 'Praise the Lord' and 'I beg pardon of God' and the importance of long, moving, tearful prayers.

He described the program to her as "gentle on the heart and cathartic for the soul, rather like a perfumed lotion that they massage into your muscle before they give you an injection." When he asked her what she thought of it, she replied, "It was beautiful, and you were very sensitive."

He couldn't remember being particularly sensitive, and they went back to their conversation about the Mutazila.

"The consensus among the Salafists is that reason and individual judgment rank third after the Quran and the Sunna as sources of sharia law," he said. "But the Mutazila disagreed with that consensus and put reason at the head of the list because it is by reason that we can tell good from bad and it is by reason that we know that the Quran has authority, along with the Sunna and the consensus of scholars.

"The hadiths are divided into those that have multiple chains of transmission that are all in agreement and those that have only a few narrators. The Mutazila dismissed even those with multiple chains if they were incompatible with reason, so you can ignore accounts by an enormous number of people as long as they're not holy men and as long as they don't include anyone who's infallible.

"The Mutazila reject hadiths that have come down to us from only a few narrators. They certainly don't recognize a hadith with only one source as the basis for any legal rulings, because doctrine must be proven definitively and convincingly, not by conjecture based on a single source. They didn't distinguish between hadiths that were seen as sound and other categories of hadiths. The fact that hadiths were irrational or implausible was enough to reject and not to use them."

They were in the car and she had sat next to him. Sirhan was driving, peeking at them in the rear-view mirror. Hatem noticed him looking in the mirror.

"Understand anything of what I said, Sirhan?" he asked.

"Nothing, Mawlana, I was daydreaming."

Hatem turned to Nashwa and whispered, "We're almost at the house. Where are you going to get out?"

"I'm coming with you," she said.

She put her gloved hand on his hand, which lay on the seat in the gap between them, and he shuddered. She tapped him lightly on the back of his hand and pulled her hand back.

"Why do you switch so easily between being a preacher and being a scholar?" she asked.

"I'm a Rifai and I know how to charm snakes," he replied, trying to get over his tenseness. He was surprised to see her face contorted in fear and her lips trembling.

*

Nashwa soon got over the shock of hearing that Hatem had been a Rifai. She pulled herself together and laughed.

"You're pulling my leg of course," she said.

"Not at all. When I was young I lived with the Rifais for a time and learned some of their powers but I realized I was a fake and a failure. I didn't go beyond elementary level with them. I did play with snakes, but don't worry, I left the Rifai order before I learned how to play with wily women."

He heard what sounded like the beginnings of a vulgar laugh but she quickly held it in check.

"Is that how you see it?" she asked.

"That's my little fantasy," he said.

Nashwa took him by surprise by changing her mind about coming home with him. She decided to spend the night with an aunt who lived in a compound nearby and said goodbye at the gate.

When Hatem and Sirhan reached home, Sirhan got out first to knock on the door for the guard to open up for them. Then Hatem got out too and the two of them started up the short flight of stairs that led to the inner gate.

"Sheikh Mukhtar el-Husseini's wife called, by the way," said Sirhan. "I told her you were on air and she asked me to tell you that Sheikh Mukhtar didn't arrive in Saudi Arabia."

Hatem felt as if he had swallowed a burning piece of coal and it had slipped down into his stomach. The pain was like an earthquake in his heart. He could hardly believe he had been normal a few minutes ago, even relaxed, looking at Nashwa's face in the back seat of the car.

He stumbled up the stairs, fumbled with the key in the door, and bumped against the edge of the steel door as he walked past it. He almost fell over as he passed the sofa in the reception room.

He sat down and stretched out his legs, breathing heavily. What does this news mean, he wondered.

Sheikh Mukhtar had visited him a few days earlier and told him he would be leaving for the airport within hours.

Sheikh Mukhtar thought he was always being followed and harassed. There was the story he had told Hatem, when he asked him to mediate, and then there were the things he had left for Hatem to look after.

Hatem stood up hurriedly and felt the blood rush to his head. His head felt heavy, as if it were pulling him down, so he sat down again.

The things that Mukhtar had left—the flash drive, the CD, the notebook, and the envelope he had given him that day. He had asked Hatem to open them if anything bad happened to him. Did he really tell him to do that? He had asked him to ask after his mother and he hadn't done that either. How many times had he let the man down? But where were the things Mukhtar had left him? When Mukhtar left had he put them in the small safe in the cupboard in his office, or had he forgotten them and left them on the small table outside the office? Had he taken them with him to his other office?

He was torn between getting up now and looking for them, or calling Sheikh Mukhtar's number and asking after him, or looking for the telephone number of Mukhtar's mother and asking her what she knew. He felt something in his fist, which was clenched so tight that his fingernails had left marks in the palm of his hand. He opened out his fist with difficulty and found a piece of paper with a telephone number written on it in Sirhan's terrible handwriting. Sheikh Mukhtar's mother, it said. Sirhan had probably handed him the piece of paper and told him she had called, but he was so tense he hadn't realized it was in his hand all this time. It was too late to call the woman and disturb her. But wasn't it possible that Sheikh Mukhtar had gone to a country other than Saudi Arabia? But even if he had done that, he would definitely have told his mother.

Had something unpleasant happened to him on the way to the airport? If that had happened, how come he, or at least Mukhtar's mother, hadn't heard about it?

The only possibility left was the one he was avoiding: Mukhtar el-Husseini had been the victim of something he had long feared, something he had tried to protect himself against by asking Hatem to intercede with the son of the president and the men around him. Was it possible that they hated him that much? Had they killed him? That wouldn't be easy, because Sheikh Mukhtar was the sheikh of a Sufi order and his followers were neither few in number nor people without significance. And besides, what could Mukhtar el-Husseini do to them that would make them want to kill him? Even if he had spoken ill of the president's son and had been difficult or given offense, he was basically harmless. In fact he was someone who called for love and tolerance.

Hatem didn't dare to get up and look for the things Mukhtar had left in the library. Maybe he was afraid or anxious or incapable of doing it, he didn't know, but he explained his reluctance by saying he had no right to examine the things Mukhtar had left until he found out what had really happened to the man. Might he not be fine and Hatem was blowing it out of proportion? And what business of his was it? Might they harm him too? What did Mukhtar's fate matter to him? Would they penalize him for liking Mukhtar el-Husseini? Oh yes, they might want to punish him because Mukhtar trusted him and they may have found out that Mukhtar had told him a secret. But what secret? Hatem thought and said to himself: "Many secrets, in fact." Then he reassured himself, saying he had the approval of the ruling family, which had handed over their lost son for him to guide, and what confidence could be greater than that honor? But at the same time he knew a terrible secret about them that would shake the country if it leaked out, and he was one of the few people in the country to know it. Did that make him strong, or weak? Could these people stand it if Hatem held two secrets about them, and not just one?

He decided to go to the office and open the safe. No, he wouldn't do that until he had spoken to Sheikh Mukhtar's mother, but how could he speak to her? Wouldn't her telephone be under surveillance if something bad had happened to Mukhtar? In fact, surely it was always monitored—if not her phone, then his.

This fact suddenly stared him in the face. How naive he had been all this time in dismissing it whenever it occurred to him—his own phone was being monitored, without a shadow of a doubt.

My God! Do they know about the relationship between me and Nashwa? Are they recording my conversations with Nashwa?

But what was there between him and Nashwa? What had he said in his phone calls? Nothing. So why did he feel there was something between him and Nashwa?

Before the night was out he would have to swallow one of those pills he had given to Hassan.

The next morning he didn't need to get in touch with Mukhtar el-Husseini's mother because he received a text message from a number his phone didn't recognize. It was just one line: "Sheikh Mukhtar el-Husseini arrested, charged with leading an Iranian organization promoting Shi'ism in Egypt." Hatem had already completed his morning rituals, which included waking up late and asking after Hassan. Omayma had told him that Hassan had woken up very early and, according to the cook, had stood by the fridge for an hour eating everything he could find straight out of it. He then went up to his room and when Omayma called him a while later he didn't answer. She was worried and asked the cook to go upstairs to see if he wanted anything, and the cook told her he was asleep. Hatem was anxious when he heard that Hassan still hadn't woken up, so he went up to Hassan's room and found him fast asleep and covered in sweat. He wiped some of the sweat off Hassan's forehead after checking that he was breathing regularly and audibly, and that he hadn't died. He shook his shoulder, called his name, first in a whisper and then louder, but Hassan just mumbled in response. Hatem rummaged around for the strip of pills and found it on the pillow. There were three pills missing. He decided it was best to leave Hassan asleep. There would be more to worry about when he woke up.

Hatem couldn't bear sitting at home in the anguished state he was in. Omayma clung to him and begged him to stay at home, but he resisted. She had received the same message and when she tried to tell him, she realized that he already knew and she pitied him the way he looked because he was as pale as a ghost and she was worried he might have another nervous breakdown.

"Please, Hatem, there's no good reason to go out. Sit here and relax and let your nerves calm down," she said.

"I'm going to see my father," he said, speaking like an angry child.

"There's no need for him to see you in such a state, and besides, you have to tell me what this news means. Has Sheikh Mukhtar really gone mad and done such a thing?" asked Omayma.

His cheeks were soaked in tears and he couldn't stop crying.

"They're bastards, Omayma!" he said.

She was startled. "Who are they?" she asked.

"May God punish them. They've destroyed the man."

"I don't understand. Do you know anything about what's going on, Hatem?"

"What I know is that I've grown old and very tired and I haven't a friend in the world," said Hatem. "How many years have we been married? More than twenty. Have you ever seen me have a friend? Never. Why am I so alone? Why isn't there anyone I can speak to and consult, someone who can give me advice and who I can trust and listen to? All these years, Omayma. The people I've known best have been people who cozied up to me for work or because it suits their purposes for a month or two, or maybe longer. I remember I was close to Muhsin for about a year and a half, and Sabri for a little under a year, and Sharif who lived in our neighborhood in the old days, you remember him. I meet him about once a year and we're like lifelong friends, though we can't have spent more than five hours talking in the past thirty-five years. I'm very much alone, Omayma."

With difficulty she had made him sit down and given him a glass of water. He held it in his hand but didn't take a sip. She was very sympathetic but, more than that, she felt responsible and inquisitive.

"I'm sorry, Hatem," she said. "But what does all this have to do with Mukhtar el-Husseini and this terrible thing he's done?"

Hatem jumped up.

"No," he said, "he hasn't done anything terrible. It's just that they're bastards."

"Okay, I get the idea that there are some bastards out there, but what does your loneliness and not having friends in your life have to do with Mukhtar el-Husseini?"

He looked at her indignantly, as if he had given up on her. "Did I say there was any connection?" he said.

"But it was you made the link when you said . . ."

Hatem walked out. She tried but failed to grab him and hold him back.

On his way to his father's house he read the message on the screen of his phone again, then again, and then a fourth time. He turned on his iPad and opened up a website. "The office of the public prosecutor," it said, "has received complaints from lawyers accusing Sheikh Mukhtar el-Husseini of insulting the Companions of the Prophet and Sayeda Aisha, may God be pleased with her, in lectures in various places in Egypt. Investigations revealed that the places were husseiniyas that Sheikh Husseini set up to attract young people to convert to Shi'ism, travel to Iran, stay in the city of Qom, and study Shi'ite jurisprudence under the ayatollahs in Iran."

Hatem realized that he hadn't given much thought to the things that Sheikh Mukhtar had left with him for safekeeping—either to look for them, because he was unsure where he had put them, or to read what was in them and see what they contained. The news made him even less inclined to deal with the contents of Sheikh Mukhtar's secret cache. What would it be, he wondered. Was it a handwritten letter about his harassment by State Security? But that wasn't very serious and Mukhtar had already told him the basic story anyway. Or did it go further? Was there something there that Mukhtar would normally reveal only under exceptional circumstances? Or maybe it was conversations, in writing or recorded, with people who were threatening him. Okay, but what did Mukhtar el-Husseini want him to do, he wondered. To publicize it when something bad happened to him? Did Mukhtar think he was brave enough to do that? And who would listen if he did try to publicize it? Maybe the things Mukhtar had given him included details of what he wanted Hatem to do for him, which would at least save Hatem from the temptation to be cowardly.

He reached the street where their old house stood. In his anger and frustration, he saw the place with new eyes. In the past it had been a poor area, no doubt about it. But it had been clean. It had been simple, but neat and tidy, or at least that's how he remembered it as he turned into his street, crossed the road, and looked at the houses and the shopfronts. He saw vendors on the pavement, people hanging around and wandering aimlessly about, metal posts with chains between them to reserve parking spaces, dusty, crumbling walls with torn election posters and advertisements, a clash of crude and garish colors, chaos, and a jangle of people shouting over one another, songs coming out of the televisions set up at the entrances to shops, and the sound of the Quran broadcast at high volume from other televisions in adjacent shops. The shopkeepers struggled to compete with each other, but sat together over waterpipes amid the clutter of tea trays from the coffee shops nearby. It was all chaotic and dispiriting. Hatem asked Sirhan to take the car to his own house and stay with his children until Hatem summoned him by phone. He didn't want anyone to see the car in the street and know that he was at his father's house. If people found out, uninvited guests would flood the place. He told Sirhan not to tell anyone where he was. He made his way through the crowd of passers-by, hiding his face with the loose end of his turban and with big dark glasses. He hurried in without even saying hello to anyone. His father was surprised when he saw him, then he greeted him and took him into his arms. After a brief hug, his father pushed him away and said, "What's up? Is there something wrong?"

He could tell from Hatem's appearance and behavior that something was amiss.

Hatem denied every possibility his father mentioned. His father found it hard to imagine what the problem might be, and his suggestions didn't go beyond a slight illness or an argument with Omayma. Hatem didn't understand why, if he was ill, he would have come to see his father. Why wouldn't he have gone to the hospital or stayed in his own home, which was well equipped for resting? And if he had argued with Omayma, why would he have come to his father's? His father would only ask him questions and shower him with advice, or his father's wife would have fun gossiping about him. Hatem insisted he just missed him so he had come to visit and he begged him not to tell anyone so that he could have a little relief from the crush of people and petitioners asking for things.

"See, didn't I say you were hiding something?" his father said.

Hatem smiled. He knew how stubborn the man was getting, now that he was close to ninety.

"And suppose I did have something to hide from the world. Would I hide it from you, Father?"

335

"Of course, a good son like you, or a reclusive one like you, hides his weaknesses or his fears from his father and from his wife."

Hatem laughed. "Is that a recognition of reality, or a piece of advice I should follow?" he asked.

"Your mother, may she rest in peace," said his father, patting him on the shoulder, "used to say, 'That boy Hatem keeps his cards close to his chest and you can't get a secret out of him unless he wants you to know it.'"

"May she rest in peace." As he said the words, Hatem half-expected her to come out of the kitchen with a plate of basbousa and hot tea and a fresh story about her niece or her brother-in-law.

"She worried you didn't have enough friends. She used to say, 'Hatem my son is a good boy. He's funny, he never stops talking, he speaks well, he's religious, and he has a cheerful face, but nonetheless he doesn't have any friends.' Then I'd say, 'Really woman, don't be unfair. Half the people in the street are friends of his.' Then she'd say, 'They're all friends like anyone else, but he doesn't have a real friend. Hatem is friends with himself.'"

Hatem's father stretched out on the bed in the inner room, which no one had tried to tidy up for ages. He asked his father about the latest calls from his sisters and their children and was told that the sisters were angry with him because he never called them. Then Hatem announced, "I'm going to take a nap."

Perhaps Hatem wanted to be alone with his thoughts, or maybe he didn't want to rake over old memories. His father left the room muttering something Hatem didn't understand about something he was going to fetch. Hatem thought it was a cup of tea, for example, so he didn't pay attention. He was about to put his cell on silent when the screen lit up with a message from a number he didn't recognize. He read the message. "They've arrested your friend, the infidel Shi'ite sheikh," it said. He was surprised by the harshness of the message. Then he had a call from the same number but he didn't answer. He let it ring and when it stopped he found a new message from the news service of a well-known newspaper: "Sheikh Mukhtar el-Hussein detained for ten days for questioning in the case of the Shi'ite organization," it said.

Had they had time to arrest the man and obtain a detention order? Another message from a news service arrived: "Insults to Companions of the Prophet and attacks on Sayeda Aisha in voice recordings of Mukhtar el-Husseini, the sheikh who adopted Shi'ism, among the evidence in the case of the Shi'ite organization."

Hatem's father came back as Hatem was shutting down his cell phone and putting the iPad next to the bed with his keys, his cell, and his wallet. His father offered him a stack of evening newspapers.

"I usually buy them for the sports," he said, "but today I thought you'd definitely want to know about Sheikh Mukhtar. They've written two whole pages about him. Is it really possible, Hatem, that he would say such crazy nonsense?"

He looked at the picture of Sheikh Mukhtar on the front page.

"Although Mukhtar el-Husseini, the sheikh who adopted Shi'ism, has been arrested and is currently being questioned by State Security prosecutors on charges of contempt for religion and receiving funding from abroad, the accusations against him are still coming in while he is in detention. A group of lawyers has submitted a complaint to the public prosecutor accusing Mukhtar el-Husseini of deliberate contempt for religion, propagated through recordings that include disparagement of the first three caliphs, Abu Bakr, Omar, and Othman, and the rest of the ten who were promised entry to Heaven, and Sayeda Aisha and Sayeda Hafsa. With their complaint the lawyers included copies of CDs of lectures in which Mukhtar el-Husseini made these remarks. Arrested on charges of working against Egypt's interests by passing on instructions from Iran to Shi'ite cells with the intent of damaging Egypt's security and economy and doing harm to the Egyptian people, it was only to be expected that he would also exploit religion. One only has to hear these lectures to discover a number of facts, primarily that the tapes prove his links with Iran. Most of the lectures were recorded in husseiniyas in the Iranian city of Qom, considered holy by the Iranians, where they arranged for him a program called The Najaf Pageant, which has taken place for years in the month of Ramadan. Behind him banners can be seen that identify the place where he was lecturing. More importantly, and this was not mentioned in the complaint by the lawyers, there are lessons in which this convert to Shi'ism insulted the Egyptian state and people as well as Egyptian history, an offense no less grave than slandering the Companions and wives of the Prophet. Contrary to reports on some websites that Husseini visited Iran only twice, he in fact visited the country often. After declaring allegiance to the Imam Ali and adopting Shi'ism in the mid-1990s, he started to exploit his Sufi order in Egypt to spread this doctrine. Sources said that when some of the man's disciples discovered the truth about him, they made statements and gave startling confessions, with details of the mission Mukhtar el-Husseini was carrying out for Iranian intelligence.

Now Hatem was even more confused and anxious.

"Was Mukhtar a spy for Iran as well, or just a sheikh who went mad and turned Shi'ite?" his father asked. "And tell me, Hatem, is it true that the Shi'a have a Quran that's different from our Quran that they call Fatima's Quran?"

Hatem pushed the newspapers toward his father. Exhausted and trying to get a grip on himself, he replied, "Father, *If a wicked man brings you news, check it carefully.*"

"What do you mean, 'wicked man'? That's the public prosecutor's office and the newspapers and there was an announcement on one station just now about a program tonight about Mukhtar el-Husseini and his Shi'ite organization, and Sheikh Reda el-Masri was speaking about him this morning on the Medina channel, and he said terrible things about him. Why don't you have a program on the Medina channel? Everyone at our mosque and the whole street watches it. You know, my wife once bought one of the blankets they were advertising on their programs and she was really delighted that they delivered it right to the house, and after that she bought three abayas for the price of one."

Hatem's father then stood up and walked out, after taking the newspapers and putting them under his arm.

"Sleep a while, Hatem," he said. "You seem very upset about your friend Mukhtar."

"Who told you he was my friend?" Hatem snapped back irritably.

His father left without answering.

Hatem couldn't get to sleep. He had visions of Mukhtar el-Husseini, policemen, Hassan, Mikhail, the president's son and his wife, and Hassan's father, all appearing in weird forms that made it hard for him to breathe. Nader Nour turned up with his vulgar stage smile, then Khaled Abu Hadid and Kaaki and Khalil el-Nahhal, and the faces of sheikhs who taught him in his childhood and gave him warnings and punished him and praised him, then a scene of Omar lying down and going naked into the scanner. The visions filled his sleep with horror and his chest wheezed. He shivered and his whole body began to sweat. He didn't know if he had really fallen asleep, as his father had advised, or if he was still awake and really seeing these ghostly figures. Had much time passed, or was it just a few seconds and time had stood still for him? He got up and had a drink, then turned the main light on, then turned it off again. Nashwa appeared in front of him and he shivered in surprise. In the half-light, part of her face was in shadow and he was frightened. He stammered but couldn't speak. He fumbled but couldn't move, and then she pressed the light switch and made the room light again, and there she was in front of him, looking at him affectionately and flirtatiously.

Then he realized she was real, not a ghostly figment of his imagination.

"What brought you here?" he shouted at her. "How did you know where I was? Who let you in? And where's my father?"

Before he had finished his father came in with a tray of tea and some homemade, rock-hard biscuits, in honor, he thought, of his guest. His father seemed delighted and puzzled at the same time.

"You're welcome, young lady. Please help yourself," he said.

As she took the tray from him, Hatem yelled at him.

"How could you let her into the bedroom?" he asked.

His father laughed, in complicity with Nashwa.

"My dear sheikh, this is Nashwa," he said. "How could I stop her?"

Hatem was surprised but gave in and looked at Nashwa.

"Do you know her?" he asked his father.

"She's a good girl. She's religious and she has a will of her own. She visited me a few days ago and said she was a television producer and was making a program about you and collecting information about your childhood and your family."

Nashwa finally spoke. "And I sat with your father and we chatted and drank coffee, and after that we cooked lunch, me and your stepmother, and I made some zucchini with bechamel sauce, and rice with vermicelli. Then we had another cup of tea and we bought some dessert from Mungi at the end of the street."

"So where's my stepmother?" Hatem asked his father as he was leaving the room.

"She's visiting a relative in the kidney unit in Mansoura and she should be back tonight."

He turned to Nashwa irritably.

"So what brought you here?" he asked.

"I was worried," she whispered.

He tensed and hesitated. He didn't get off the bed. "Worried what might happen to who?" he asked.

He noticed the powder on her cheeks, the kohl around her eyes, and her lipstick.

"Worried about you," she whispered, flirtatiously this time. "And the story of Sheikh Mukhtar," she added.

"What's Mukhtar got to do with me?" he asked, so frightened now that he could hardly put a sentence together and get the words out of his mouth in the right order.

She had been standing in front of him, watching him with interest, but now she sat on the edge of the bed.

"First, you like him. Second, you're shocked at what's happened to him. Third, you're worried about your reputation in case your name comes up as one of his fans. Fourth, you don't believe a single word that's being said about him, and by the way I heard there are six or seven programs on the satellite channels this evening all devoted to his case, and they say they have recordings of him that they'll play."

Hatem was frightened for reasons that he couldn't explain.

"How do you know all this?" he asked. "And by the way, no one knows I'm here in my father's house, so how did you know to come here?"

"I'm very interested in you," she said with a smile, trying hard to appear sympathetic. "I told you I was an admirer of yours, so why wouldn't I know what's upsetting you? But if Sheikh Mukhtar really has turned Shi'ite and said these things about the Companions and wives of the prophet, and insulted them in this horrible way, why should you feel sorry or sad for him? But if you're worried about being associated with him, then why don't you go on television tonight and give him hell?

That way you can dissociate yourself from him and stop anyone suspecting you."

He looked at her in silence, surprised, and even warmed to her suggestion for a moment. His face relaxed and she looked back at him mischievously. When she stood up and went to the door, he could see her from behind. Her clothes were close-fitting compared with the loose clothes she had worn before. He could make out the shape of her body, and his body thrilled with desire for her. She pulled the key out of the keyhole on the outside, then closed the door again and put the key back in the keyhole on the inside. She double-locked it, turned, and leaned back against the door.

"By the way, I spoke to Sirhan and found out from him that you were here," she said.

She took a step forward from the door, raised her hand, set her fingers to work undoing the knot on her hijab, then let down her hair in all its brown softness. She looked perfect and he would do anything for her. But he didn't know what to do so he just lay there waiting for her to act.

She went to the chair opposite where he was lying. She sat down, crossed her legs and started to take off her shoes, looking at him seductively, as if she were testing his capacity to resist. She took off a long sock and bared her thigh. She threw the sock toward him and it fell on the floor before reaching him. Then she took off her other sock, raising her smooth and slender leg and baring her other thigh and her knee, then her calf and her foot. He was transfixed, on fire with lust for her. Then her fingers unbuttoned her blouse down to her cleavage and the swell of her breasts. She jumped onto the bed on top of him, embraced him, and kissed him in a frenzy of passion. Within seconds Hatem was spent, overwhelmed by the thrill.

HATEM SAT ALONE IN A large cold room with almost no furniture. There was a small sofa that could seat only two people, if they were thin, and then a small wooden desk in the far corner of the room under a closed window covered by a curtain of some pale color. The walls had no paintings or photographs, and their dusty white color completed the iciness of the place. The ceiling was so low that it almost touched his head when he went in. A man of coarse features with a scowl had accompanied him to the door of the room, then opened it and let him in, then shut the door, apparently without recognizing that he was a sheikh or well known. He showed no signs of reverence or respect. He didn't ask him what he would like to drink or tell him when Brigadier Ahmed el-Faisal would arrive. Hatem's head was full of thoughts about the possible outcomes. He knew he was in a trap. His stomach had been groaning like a millstone since he received the phone call from the brigadier while on his way home. He had been busy thinking about other things when his phone rang and Brigadier Faisal's name appeared on the screen. It was a bad sign.

"Why don't you drop in for half an hour, Mawlana, and let's have a coffee together?" the brigadier said.

Hatem found it hard to get the words out of his throat.

"It would be an honor, brigadier," he said.

"You're close by, aren't you?" Faisal said quickly.

"To tell you the truth, I'm close to home."

"We're next to your house, Mawlana. Don't you go past the State Security building every day on your way to the highway?"

Hatem tried to relax.

"To tell you the truth, I recite the first chapter of the Quran every time I go past the place," he said with a laugh.

"Why? We're not dead yet, I hope," replied the brigadier with a tense laugh.

Hatem shuddered at his bad joke.

"I recite it for the policemen who've been killed in the line of duty, brigadier," he said.

Ahmed el-Faisal gave a loud guffaw.

"Okay, come and see us now so we can say a funeral prayer for them together," he added.

"Will it take long?"

The brigadier raised his voice, giving the impression he was running out of patience. "What's wrong, Sheikh Hatem? Sounds like you're up to something. We'll be expecting you," he said.

"I'm on my way, brigadier."

"I'll leave word at the gate."

He hung up and Hatem stared into the car window. Sirhan brought him around with a question: "Shall we carry on or turn back?"

He didn't wait for an answer, or else he took Hatem's silence for an answer, and turned the car around.

Alone in the cold room Hatem thought back to the strange events of the afternoon with Nashwa at his father's house. She had completely disarmed him, overwhelmed him with her beauty and her sexuality. She made him feel alive again and reached parts of him that had gone numb with time. He could hardly believe that he was the man whose body had pressed against Nashwa's as she kissed his face and brought him to climax. Then Nashwa lay on her back beside him, with signs of regret and guilt on her face. She gathered her hair behind her back, and stared at her toes, subdued and silent. Then she ran to pick up her clothes and went back to being the committed puritan, as if their encounter had had no effect on her and he hadn't made her feel anything comparable to what she had stirred in him.

He was disappointed with himself but didn't think badly of her for it. He was dizzy with remorseful questions and, although he felt guilty, he didn't know where the feeling came from. With the mental agility of a trained sheikh, he very soon decided that what he had done didn't count as a cardinal sin. He said there was no need for him to be harsh on himself because he hadn't technically committed fornication. That would require that he ejaculate inside her. It didn't trouble him that what he had done was haram. It's true that he couldn't think of a legal ruse that would legitimize what he had done but he knew that, if he thought hard enough, he would find one. But he didn't need to because it had all happened in secret and only God knew about it, and Hatem el-Shenawi's arguments wouldn't wash with God. This act was one of many acts, and in the end they would all be added up and if the balance was good, then fine, and if the balance was evil, then that would be bad. But he was interested in how Nashwa saw him and, strangely, not so much with the way he saw her. Her innocence didn't bother him, although he had a feeling deep down that she had planned this. It made him feel worthless to think about what her opinion of him would be now, when he had yielded to her seduction, when he was supposedly the virtuous sheikh. Was she disappointed in him? Had she expected him to act like Joseph, resisting the advances of Potiphar's wife? He couldn't explain why she had locked the door when Hatem's father seemed trusting or out of the picture, or maybe his father's indifference was part of a test God had set for Hatem.

The encounter didn't last long. What annoyed him most as a man was that he had reached orgasm too soon, even if he had a good reason. The months of abstinence had been more than a man could stand, and the unexpected physical contact and the sudden surge of desire was an excuse that satisfied his male pride, but it would tarnish his image in the eyes of a female, however much she might have desired him. The fact that she wanted him might have left her more disappointed, even if he had felt that she did reach orgasm with him. She slipped away to the chair facing the bed, moved her bag aside, and sat down. She had put her hijab back on and had buttoned up her blouse over her cleavage. Without a word she put her socks back on with strange precision. She put on her shoes and headed for the door. She turned the key in the lock and then bizarrely put the key back in the keyhole on the outside as if she wanted to eliminate every trace of the encounter.

"Goodbye," she said in a hushed whisper.

Hatem thought the word 'goodbye' wasn't exactly in keeping with what had happened a few minutes earlier, but maybe she meant to convey that nothing had happened. And had anything really happened? A young woman had seduced a sheikh that she liked, compromising her religious convictions—extremist, puritanical convictions that were highly restrictive spiritually and intellectually. In the sheikh she had found someone to hold her tight, someone who would meet her physical desires instantly without disapproval or lectures on morality.

He was more surprised at himself. She had ceased to surprise him some time ago. How could it be that, after this shocking incident, which might spell ruin for him, he was worried he might have disappointed her by failing to live up to his religious commitments, or maybe by not being virile enough? Although the encounter had taken place in secret, he was fearful of a scandal and anxious that news of it might reach Omayma's ears. He was terrified that Nashwa might say something that destroyed his reputation.

In the midst of all this, Hatem received the call from Brigadier Ahmed el-Faisal. The call took him back to the case of Sheikh Mukhtar el-Husseini, the center of attention in a massive song and dance on television stations determined to defame the man and destroy his career, his name, and his family in an evil, vulgar way. His stolen pleasure with Nashwa had distracted Hatem from thinking about Sheikh Mukhtar, despite the excerpts he had seen on television programs and the pictures of Sheikh Mukhtar published on the websites, which had launched a barrage of venom against him, and despite what he had picked up from telephone calls and text messages. One of the calls was from Khaled Abu Hadid, imploring Hatem to dissociate himself from Sheikh Mukhtar and denying that he had even invited him to any of his banquets. There was also a mysterious message from Nader Nour saying, "We have to do something." Hatem didn't know what—something to save the man, or something to attack the man and wash our hands of him?

Nashwa had made him forget the serious consequences he should expect if they found out that Sheikh Mukhtar had visited him and left those things in his care, or if they heard that Mukhtar had confided his grievances in Hatem, and apparently in him alone, apart from God, or if they found out about the phone calls with Mukhtar's mother, who was distraught at her son's disappearance. The phone call from the State Security man put him back at the epicenter of the earthquake. He reached the gate and was let through after they checked his identity. Sirhan was told to drop Hatem off at the entrance to the building, then drive out and park outside. The procedure showed the mean side of the place, which Hatem had visited before as an honored guest, received by several officers who seemed to be protocol people. This time, very late in the evening, he was escorted upstairs by some lowly creature who took his cell phones from him and handed him over to a thuggish-looking man. He then found himself in the bare room, unaware that he would be staring at the ceiling till the morning of the next day.

After a humiliating one-hour wait, Hatem had tried to do something. He went to the door and tried to open it but found it was locked.

He called quietly, "Hey brother, hey sir . . ."

No one answered and he heard no reaction of any kind, so he did the only thing he could do: He went back and sat on the sofa, mulling the damage to his pride. As time passed he realized they were sending him a message: You're nothing, ignored, thrown in a room where no one asks after you. Should he take the message on board and submit passively to any demand they made or any order they gave, or should he hold his ground and refuse to surrender to their injustice and bad manners, or should he ignore it and forget all about it?

It was a test of his strength and he faced the test alone. When all the razzmatazz comes to an end and you lose their respect and your prestige and your value in their eyes, then you lose your own sense of importance and your self-esteem. You derive your value from them and not from yourself, from outside yourself and not from inside. Apparently we are not respected because of the way we are, but because certain parties, be it family, the audience, or the state, see us that way. This was a good opportunity for him to find out what he really thought of himself—thrown here, neglected, his dignity crushed in a room that was designed to humiliate. The room could do its work without words or confrontations or interrogations to extract his full confession. It would show whether he was a man who could stand his ground against cruelty and intimidation, or whether he was worthless, too meek to resist.

He stood up once again and banged on the door, but all that came back was the echo of his impatient banging. He walked around the room in a futile attempt to vent his frustration. He took off his gown and put it on the sofa and stretched out his legs in an attempt to relax that rapidly failed. He got up and went to the little desk in the corner of the room and started to look through the drawers but they were completely empty and he was angry. He moved the desk a few feet and found that it was light and of such poor quality that it almost fell over with one firm push. He felt cold so he looked up at the single small window, set as high as possible in the wall facing the door. He couldn't work out if it was open or closed. Was the cold coming through the window or was it seeping through the walls, he wondered.

The day they detained him with the young Christian converts in the security headquarters it was a ruse that he went along with. But this time the trap was well and truly set for him. It was obviously meant to humiliate him and the only reason to hold him all these hours was the Mukhtar el-Husseini case. He was convinced it was about Mukhtar. What else could it be?

Deep down inside he whispered to himself that maybe Mukhtar had come across something secret about Hatem that Hatem wasn't even aware of. The fact that Mukhtar had singled out Hatem to air his grievances to, had left those things with him, and had asked him to take care of his mother could only mean that Hatem was strong and worthy of Mukhtar's trust. Or maybe it meant that Hatem was naive and blindfolded, if not blind, Hatem thought. "And whatever happened to Mukhtar's wife? Did he manage to get her out of the country? Had she disappeared, was she in hiding or in detention, or had she withdrawn from the scene?" he wondered out loud.

He sat cross-legged on the sofa and nodded his head back and forth muttering traditional prayers that he had often recited off the top of his head. Now they were helping him calm down, reminding him of the supreme power, Almighty God, as he asked for His help. He didn't think himself worthy of His grace, but if God is entitled to give His grace to

349

anyone he pleases, then He won't deny it even to those who don't deserve it. Hatem wasn't asking for justice because he didn't think that justice would be in his interest: he was asking for mercy. He began to speak louder as he recited, saying aloud hadiths about the special powers of certain chapters of the Quran, although he knew they were falsely attributed to the Prophet. In the time of the Prophet the chapters themselves were not yet complete, so any given chapter could not have special powers that had been tested and endorsed by the Prophet. These were hadiths designed to encourage people to read the Quran and to resort to God in times of distress or crisis. The intention was good but the words they put in the Prophet's mouth were false. But he didn't stop repeating these hadiths because he had noticed over the years that they gave people peace of mind, so it wasn't a priority for him to tell the truth about such things if a little untruth did no harm.

He began reciting the Quran in the room, starting with the first verses of the Cow chapter, then jumping forward impatiently to the Cave chapter, which he muttered in a whisper. When he reached the verse that goes: *"We shall now narrate to you their story, in truth. They were young men who believed in their Lord, and we gave them additional guidance,"* he began to recite it aloud in the traditional style of formal Quran recitals, bringing back old memories of when he used to recite in funeral tents in front of hundreds of people, who trembled at his voice. Then he addressed those around him and those detaining him in a resonant voice from deep in his chest through the verse: *"And we strengthened their hearts when they stood up and said, 'Our Lord, Lord of the Heavens and the Earth, we will not call on any god but Him, for if we did, we would have transgressed.'"* Then, as if it were an act of defiance and his response to all the questions he hadn't yet been asked, he recited the next verse: *"These our people have adopted gods other than Him, though they don't show any clear evidence for them. Who is more wicked than those who speak falsehood about God?"* He recited it according to the best-known of the seven possible readings of the verse, the reading that Hafs learned from Assem, who learned it from Warsh, who learned it from Nafie. He got to the verse *"And confine yourself to those who call upon their Lord, morning and evening, seeking His face. Let not your eyes wander beyond them, seeking the luxuries of the present life. And do not obey him whose heart We have caused to forget Us and who has followed his whims. He has gone too far."* He imitated the performance of Sheikh Mohamed Rifaat, then repeated it in the style of Mustafa Ismail, then in the style of Minshawi, then repeated the last sentence of the verse: *"And do not obey him whose heart We have caused to forget Us and who has followed his whims. He has gone too far."* He echoed, in all their various styles, Mahmoud el-Husari, Abul-Enein Shuaysha, Taha el-Feshni, and Abdel-Samad, and then he recited: *"The Book shall be laid out, and you will see sinners afraid of what is in it. They shall say, 'Alas for us! What is it with this Book? It doesn't miss anything, big or small. It records it all.' They shall find their deeds listed and your Lord will wrong no one."* When he got to this verse he felt he was detached from where he was and hovering in the air far from the room. He had broken free from his detention cell and was dreaming of the streets around the Citadel, the alleys of Gamaliya, the Sufi processions, the declarations of divine love for the family of the Prophet, the sound of the sunset call to prayer at home in Ramadan, the pilgrims running between al-Safa and al-Marwa as if chasing Hagar, who was carrying Ismail and looking for a drop of water to quench their thirst. *"Your Lord will wrong no one."* He recited in the voices of all the sheikhs he had heard and all the styles he had learned and hadn't learned. *"Your Lord will wrong no one."* He repeated it until he felt that it filled every inch of the room and until he suddenly noticed movement outside the door. He froze to listen, got down off the sofa, and moved toward the door. He put his ear to the door, then knocked, in the hope it might provoke a reaction from whoever was moving behind the door, but he heard nothing.

*

He put his gown back on, though after reciting the Quran he was no longer aware of the bitter cold. He felt he had broken his shackles and armed himself with self-knowledge. Now he felt he was stronger than them, even when they were trying to humiliate him, and he realized that if he could live the rest of his life at home reciting the Quran to himself and thinking about it, and poring over books of Quranic exegesis, confident that his son Omar was in good health, then he would not need anyone and would not want anything further.

He walked briskly around the room, liberated and indifferent to what was happening, then he went to the door to bang on it with the strength of someone with nothing to lose. Then he started going around the sofa; he turned it over, and wiped the soles of his shoes on the walls. Nihilist, capricious ideas were now swimming in his blood. If they were intimidating him because he knew about Hassan, alias Boutros, and held a secret about the son of their president that would cause havoc if it came to light, and if Mukhtar was their victim and he—Hatem—their hostage, then he could take them hostage too. If they harmed him, he would harm them too. Then he felt that his bladder was about to burst, and because the door was locked and because there wasn't a stir outside, and because hours had gone by since he relieved himself, he decided to go ahead and urinate. He lifted up his galabiya, took the hem in his teeth, undid his pants, took out his penis, and started to urinate on the walls. He walked around, urinating on the desk, on the curtains, on the worn carpet, and on the back of the door. It was an expression of anger and of freedom. Now, when they opened the door, he was ready for any interrogation. He was certain they could see him through cameras planted in the room, and he was urinating on them too.

Day came but the sun didn't come. The only light in the room was the cold light from the light bulbs and they didn't show what time it was outside. Although the single tiny window was tightly closed, Hatem knew from a glance at his watch that time was passing and that it was almost morning. He was standing, unable to sit down because everywhere he looked there were puddles of urine. A sense of relief came over him and gave him the strength of someone who is no longer afraid of failure and is ready for any trial of endurance. The door suddenly opened, startling him, and someone, who looked like a blockhead, appeared wearing a suit with a smile stuck on his face—like a smiley face icon in a text message.

The blockhead bowed. He seemed to be unusually flexible for a blockhead. "Come this way please, Mawlana," he said.

So Hatem had recovered some of his prestige. Perhaps they had learned a lesson from when he urinated in all their faces. He walked behind the blockhead till they came to a corridor that led to an inner staircase, which they then went down. Hatem found himself facing a hallway that ended in a grand door guarded by two more blockheads, who were less flexible than their colleague. They knocked on the door, opened it, and waved Hatem in. He entered a large, spacious, elegant room and a welcoming, cheerful face with an exaggerated smile rushed toward him.

"Welcome, Mawlana. You bring great baraka. Your virtue does us honor," said the man.

The reception was so vulgar and disgusting that Hatem almost forgot what had happened in the previous hours. Hatem quickly recognized the man's face despite his foul mood and his physical exhaustion. It was the same man who had visited him in the Giza security headquarters. He turned and found Ahmed el-Faisal in all his impudence coming toward him with three others who were no less obnoxious than Ahmed. They welcomed him, shook hands warmly with him, then went back to their seats in a sitting area in a corner of the room while the other man sat behind a desk in the center of the room and asked Hatem to sit down too.

"Sit down, relax, Mawlana," he said.

He looked toward the blockhead who hadn't moved and was standing there awaiting an order.

"One medium coffee for Mawlana and a bottle of water," he said. "And make sure you use the Hassan Pasha coffee," he added.

He waved the flunky away and looked back.

"You realize, Mawlana, that I'm here as a guest of the gang."

He looked toward the three officers sitting there, then sprang up from his seat as if stung by a bee.

"Let's go and say the dawn prayers together, led by the sheikh, before the sun comes up," he said, pointing to a half-open door. Beyond it Hatem's sleepy eyes made out a small en suite bathroom.

"Are you going to do your ablutions, Mawlana?" the officer said.

"No, I've abluted without water," Hatem said coldly.

They all laughed. Brigadier Faisal came up to him, took his hand, and led him to the bathroom.

"We all know it's not just a basin you need," he muttered.

No doubt he was referring to Hatem urinating all over the room, which made Hatem proud of himself and what he had done.

When he had washed, he came back into the room.

"And so I guess you're all washed and ready," he said, "or do you pray without washing, since clean living doesn't count for much with you?"

They burst out laughing with strange abandon, and Faisal added, "You are being very bold with us, Mawlana."

"Or else he's very upset with us," added one of the others.

"Honestly, you people are merciless," said the most important of them, the one who called himself their guest. "No one would ever trust you. You don't know who you're dealing with and you don't respect people and their learning. Isn't that right, Mawlana?"

Hatem felt they were treating him as a toy and decided to ignore it. "Which direction is Mecca?" he asked.

Faisal pointed in one direction but Hatem turned and stood facing the opposite direction. "No, the other direction, Mawlana," Faisal corrected him.

"Are you sure you pray facing the same direction as the rest of us?" Hatem asked calmly.

"Enough, Sheikh Hatem, we know you're upset. Come on, put your trust in God and earn some merit through us by being our imam in prayer," said Faisal.

Hatem was surprised by their shallow faith and the light-hearted way they did things. They thought that praying would purge them of their misdeeds.

"Okay, are there any chapters of the Quran that are banned during these prayers, or can I choose freely?" he asked them.

The man couldn't help roaring with laughter until he started coughing and spluttering. "Generally speaking, I'd concentrate on the verses about Heaven. There's no need for the ones about Hell," he finally replied.

"Heaven? Do you think Heaven's a police club on the Nile that you can enter with a membership card?" asked Hatem.

He then said, "Allahu akbar," and started the prayers. The way they had received him distracted him from concentrating fully on the prayers. Was it a truce, a trick, or was it a final blow against him, Hatem wondered. Anxious and yet scornful of them, he recited the "Afternoon" and "True Devotion" chapters in the prayers. Then he felt free to meet his fate at their hands. When he rose from the prayer mat he found they had gotten up quickly, put their shoes on, and gone back to their places as if they were re-assuming their authority.

"May we pray together in Mecca one day, Mawlana. So tell me, what news of Hassan?" said the senior officer.

"Hassan who?"

"Please, Mawlana, we're being serious now."

"Ah, you mean Boutros."

"You're responsible for Hassan, and we need to reassure the big man that he has come to his senses and he's back to normal and the good Lord has shown him the light thanks to your piety and learning and your powers of persuasion. You're the young people's preacher, Mawlana. But tell me, can I tell the big man that everything's okay and reassure Hassan's father while we're at it? That man is patriotic and he's been serving the country since he was a young man. I tell you, Sheikh Hatem, and the guys here know it, that man is one of Egypt's most important sources of economic support. He alone is responsible for billions of pounds a year coming into the coffers from the export of gas, despite what the riffraff and the hirelings say about him. His shoes are worth more than any of those people who call themselves the opposition. As far as the gang here is concerned, the files on those guys are all much the same. We've got plenty against them, but when we pick any of them up the agents of America and their American masters make a fuss and attack Egypt, but they won't touch a single hair in this country as long as it is protected by the president and his vigilance and his wisdom."

The officer stopped for breath and then continued: "By the way, you should sit down with the president. You'll find him very simple and kind, with the decency of a real Egyptian and the patriotism of a hero of the October war. Just for your information, he understands everyone in the country and cares for them, and for us, and he's saved Egypt from some real disasters."

Hatem expected the brutish trio to sing the chorus part in this patriotic anthem but their only contribution was some mumblings and mutterings.

The coffee had arrived while they were praying. The man gestured to Hatem to drink and he took a sip. Then he put it aside because a nauseous feeling had turned his stomach. Neither the man nor his aides had yet come around to the purpose of this humiliating summons. Perhaps they had decided to wait till he asked or to let him leave in complete confusion. He decided to stay silent too, especially as his exhaustion had started to affect his limbs and his throat was dry. Then Brigadier Faisal came and sat down in the chair opposite him.

"Sir," he said, addressing the senior officer, "we have full confidence in the loyalty of Sheikh Hatem el-Shenawi. All our reports confirm that, and when His Excellency"—he now turned to Hatem, looking deep into his eyes and emphasizing each word—"invites you to meet the president, it's not just an honor to you, Mawlana, but also a sign of complete confidence in you."

The most senior official took over. "I've apologized for the evil deeds of my colleagues here in State Security. They're inexperienced, ruthless, heartless people and they don't know who's who, as I told you. I've given them a piece of my mind." At this he turned to Brigadier Faisal. "Isn't that right, Faisal? Tell Mawlana what I've done."

"His Excellency did indeed think that what we did was a terrible mistake and we're going to put it right," said the brigadier. "The man will be released soon. We just have to sort the case out and tone down the media campaign so that we can let him out quickly."

It was too complicated for Hatem, who no longer understood who the police had apologized to nor exactly why. And what he said about the case and campaign and the man, what did he mean by it?

Then suddenly it all made sense. Before he even needed to ask, the man in charge started speaking. "We know how much you like Sheikh Mukhtar el-Husseini. And before you defend him, yes, everything you're going to say is right. He was set up by us here in State Security. The man isn't a Shi'ite and he never went to Iran. He's not a spy and there's no organization, and there's no truth in any of that nonsense that's all over Egypt at the moment, and that will continue for two or three weeks. They've stigmatized the man for the rest of his life and pretty much ruined his future in this country. None of the thousands upon thousands of people who used to surround him will go anywhere near him now. No followers, no donations, no pledges, no moulid or any of that. But Husseini can thank God that he's going free without a trial or a prison sentence."

The boss turned to Brigadier Faisal and started to reprimand him, although his act was unconvincing.

"You've treated him monstrously and I'm not at all happy with what I saw of Husseini. He looks like he's suddenly aged twenty years. The marks from the beatings and the bruises on his face and his chest are very obvious," he said.

Hatem thought that maybe this was all a show designed to intimidate Hatem because they thought he was still too defiant. "And he can't go free any time soon when he's in that state," the man continued. "What will people say? Did you really have to give him that many electric shocks on his balls, you brutes? When I was alone with him in the cell and he was crying like a baby, I wanted to have you shot."

It seemed quite clear that he was threatening Hatem with a similar fate. The boss turned back to Hatem and could see that Hatem was wincing. His face was troubled and sad, as if he were about to give in and cry.

"I know you're very upset, but rest assured, everything will get back to normal," the man went on. "I promise you he will be back with his mother soon, and by the way, we very much appreciate the fact that you didn't contact her or his wife, although I heard from her father that she was going to ask to be divorced from Sheikh Mukhtar, I'm sorry to say. Oh, and I'd also like to reassure you about something else. Don't worry in the least about the things he left in your house."

Hatem was taken by surprise, and then he was surprised that he had been surprised in the first place. Of course they had done their searches and monitored him and found out all his secrets, invaded his privacy, and bugged his telephones.

"Firstly, don't bother looking for them in the house because we have them and we've seen everything that's there and we've confronted Sheikh Mukhtar with the details of what's in the notebook and the recordings and the man didn't deny anything. And by the way, when I met him, I denied you had handed them over to us. In fact I made it absolutely clear to him that we got hold of them by our own means, so he has no reason to think ill of you, Sheikh Hatem.

"Secondly, don't get the idea that we wanted to harm Sheikh Mukhtar, but he really was used by people who don't want good things for this country and they misunderstood him. He's a good man but he's naïve. He's truly religious, but he doesn't understand politics and the brutes in security had to prove to him that he couldn't perform miracles, and if he could, it wouldn't be at our expense or at the expense of the president's son."

When the man in charge said goodbye to him at the door, he reminded him of Hassan and how important it was that he didn't fail to win him over. When Ahmed el-Faisal said goodbye to him at the door to the building, the sun was up and the brigadier put on dark glasses that confirmed how creepy he was. He handed Hatem the cell phones they had confiscated when he arrived, and told him they had called Sirhan to bring the car. They had sent Sirhan off the day before and told him that Hatem would be going away on a trip with just the boss.

"Try to speak to Nader Nour," the brigadier said, "because he called your cell twenty times yesterday and left you a message saying he wanted to meet you urgently. Goodbye, Mawlana."

Hatem was in some middle zone between being confused and being tense. He didn't know if he was confused and therefore tense, or whether he was tense and therefore confused. He couldn't pin down what he felt.

Sirhan found him when he came through the door of the State Security building. They had left him to walk through the yard that lay between the inner gate and the outer gate. It was daytime but the sun was hiding behind clouds that threatened rain, and a biting wind stung his face and whipped at his turban. He walked slowly and deliberately, dragging his pain and frustration behind him. The sense of humiliation began to course through his veins again, as if he had found himself thrown abandoned on the pavement. Although he had regained his self-respect when he was alone in the waiting room (he had even had no qualms about pissing on their furniture), his one-hour meeting with the police officers had been a complete waste of time. It had shown that under their pressed trousers they had the legs of devils, like the wicked magicians in books on black magic and in spells cast by spirit mediums, but in the end he was as trapped as he had been in the first place. None of the policemen standing guard outside showed any interest in him, as if they had orders to ignore him, and when he came out through the gate, he stood there lost until Sirhan came up behind him, gave him a friendly tap on his shoulder, and showed him the way to the car.

"This way, Mawlana."

"Thank God you're safe," he added in a mutter, strangely.

Sirhan might have used that expression if Hatem had returned from a journey, if he recovered from an illness, or if he had been released from prison, but it wasn't clear what Sirhan imagined in this case.

They hadn't touched him and they hadn't beaten him. They hadn't attacked him or tortured him, so why did he feel it would have better if they had done so? The humiliating isolation he had experienced through the night hours had given him a taste of a degradation that was worse than being tortured, because being tortured means you're an enemy and important, a rival that has to be broken by this bestial cruelty. But being ignored and isolated in a room, as if that was enough to make him learn his lesson to behave properly and be compliant, sent him a message that he didn't want to hear: that he was already their man and there was no need to resort to crueler methods, or that he was so weak and cowardly that just a few hours in a room without windows would break him.

When he sank into the back seat of the car, a question hit him with full force: was it Sirhan who had stolen the things that Mukhtar el-Husseini had left with him, and given them to State Security? He had left them in his office at home, either in the cupboard or in a drawer or on top of his desk, all places within easy reach for Sirhan, but maybe it was the guard or the cleaning women who came and whose names he didn't know because Omayma changed them so often. Or was it Hassan himself? The kid was rebellious and stubborn. Or had the State Security people broken in, without anyone in the house noticing and even though the house was never left unattended? But who's to say that people like them would be seen when they broke in?

When he reached home, he just wanted to recover from the long ordeal. But Hassan and Omayma rushed toward him anxiously. Hassan almost carried him in his arms to a seat, while Omayma looked on sympathetically and tenderly in a way he hadn't seen almost since they got married. So they must know what had happened and was happening, and who was behind it.

Hassan didn't leave any space in his mind for doubt. On the contrary he swept all doubts aside. His face looked older and more mature in his anger and the indignation that he made no attempt to conceal.

"I told you they were bastards," he said.

Leaving aside the fact that Hassan hadn't in fact ever told him they were bastards, and although he wasn't sure if Hassan meant the State Security people, Hatem agreed with him by staying silent.

Omayma hurried to the kitchen meanwhile and came back with a glass of hot milk and a bottle of water and asked the maid to run a hot bath for Hatem.

"Umm Omar," said Hassan.

Hatem smiled at the name he used for Omayma. The sound of Omar's name eased his pain.

"Umm Omar heard from Sirhan that you were at State Security and that they told Sirhan to go away and they said they would give you a lift back. She didn't understand what was happening, but I did. Luckily for me, and for you, I woke up after that shit you gave me. After I took that pill and slept I woke up feeling dizzy and with a headache but relaxed, so I decided to have two more pills and I slept so much I lost track of time, and that was kind of amazing. But when I went downstairs during the night to have a drink from the fridge I heard Umm Omar talking to Sirhan on the phone, and I gathered that you were with them, and I realized at once that they had evil intentions. Imagine, the bastards were going to drag you into the Mukhtar el-Husseini case. They were going to frame you as the intermediary between him and Iran and accuse you of collecting money for the secret organization."

Hatem didn't believe him. That was perfectly clear from the indifference on his face, and this provoked Hassan.

"You don't believe me," he said. "For your information I called my father and he answered me because I hadn't spoken to him on the phone for three years. He answered quickly and he was stunned, because I let rip at him and told him that if he or his son-in-law did anything dirty to Sheikh Hatem in their usual way then by the living Christ I'd go on television and YouTube and expose them and say I've converted to Christianity and I'd drag his son-in-law's reputation through the mud throughout the world."

Hassan was speaking without inhibitions, proud of himself and strong for the first time. He had abandoned his defeatism and his depressed appearance.

"The man didn't believe what he was hearing, so I said even more and told him Hatem was in State Security as we were talking and if they touched a hair on his head I would reveal everything. I was saying, 'You're trying to get rid of him so that he doesn't talk about me, or you'll frame him on some charge so you can break him, because he knows your secret and all about your son who's secretly abandoned your religion. Do you in fact have any religion, you brutes?' He started answering back and he was so angry he didn't know what he was saying. 'Come to your senses, Hassan!' he said. 'Enough of this nonsense. I'll have you thrown in the mad-house, you worm. I'll ask about that sheikh of yours, and who told you anyway what they're going to do with him? Now mind your manners and shut up. Give me a quarter of an hour and come back to me and I'll give you an answer when you've calmed down.'"

Omayma was nodding in agreement at his story and confirming it, because she had heard him herself. She interrupted Hassan's story with a smile.

"Sheikh Hatem," she said, "you know that Incredible Hulk film when he gets annoyed or has an argument and his shape changes and he inflates and gets very tall and his clothes tear and he turns green? That's exactly how Hassan was when he was speaking to his father. I was making signs at him to calm down, because I didn't understand how he had been transformed into this creature. But I can tell you, he was very happy as he was doing it."

Hassan roared with laughter, showing a childishness that Hassan the adolescent had been trying to hide. Hatem and Omayma joined in the laughing.

"I couldn't wait a quarter of an hour," Hassan continued. "So I spoke to Abul-Makarem el-Sebai."

Hatem looked at him quizzically. He had finished his glass of milk and the maid had taken his shoes and socks away and put a cushion under his feet to raise them for comfort.

"Who's this Abul-Makarem el-Sebai?" he asked.

Hassan smiled as he stood up. He went up to Hatem, gently took off his turban, and handed it to the maid. Hatem and Omayma were surprised, especially when Hassan helped Hatem take off his gown, folded it, and put it next to him.

"Sheikh Hatem, on that day when we went to Father Mikhail's church, you were speaking as if you were the chief detective of the universe and yet you didn't know the man who came to see you at dawn today in the State Security headquarters. Of course they treated him as if he was senior to them and more important than all their leaders because he's a director in presidential security and he's the person in charge of my brother-in-law's security and something close to his private secretary. That's Abul-Makarem el-Sebai. Of course I know him from home and socially and I know he works with my brother-in-law in Zamalek, but to get to the point, he's more important than any minister in Egypt. Even the interior minister doesn't mess with him and the president's men grovel at his feet and do what he says in case he turns the president's son against them and they end up in deep shit. "

So that was the man Hatem had met in the security headquarters and then in State Security. The man had behaved as if he ran the whole country by remote control.

"Abul-Makarem answered my call and I laid into him. He puts up with me, reluctantly of course because no one's allowed to shout at him, but even if I converted to Christianity or went mad or lost my mind, he's ready to take my shit so that the president's son doesn't get angry with him. I gave him hell and told him State Security was definitely trying to frame you and I wouldn't keep quiet and I made up a couple of things, such as my brother-in-law definitely didn't know about this nonsense. He said 'You mean he's innocent?' I decided to tell a white lie. I didn't see why not if it would make him act. So I said the president's son would never forgive them and I'd spoken to Father and he'd promised me he'd stop this nonsense."

"Strangely he too asked me to wait a quarter of an hour and before he called back I found Father on the line and I ignored him because Abul-Makarem is more important. He said, 'I'm going in person to get him out, sir, so don't you worry about it, and tell his wife she'll have breakfast with him tomorrow morning.' After that I called Father and found my sister Farida answering the phone and she told me Father was angry with me and didn't want to speak to me, but he assured me that Sheikh Hatem was now drinking coffee with them and would be coming out right away, but Farida's nice and she knew of course from Father what they were planning to do. The bastards were just about to put you in detention and torture you, and they'd recorded a confession from Sheikh Mukhtar that you were in with him. Of course, God damn it, they tortured him and he said what they wanted, but with one call from Abul-Makarem they fell into line. And probably my brother-in-law knows all the details and agreed because they wouldn't torture a mouse, let alone a man, without asking him for permission, but when I threatened to make a scandal they backed off, though I'm worried about their next step, because we're never safe from those evil bastards."

This deluge of information overwhelmed Hatem, and Omayma realized he was confused. She knew her husband wasn't strong. She went over to him and whispered, "Go and have a bath so you can sleep and have a rest." He nodded submissively, but when he tried to stand up the effort was too much and Hassan hurried over to help him.

"But Hassan," he asked, "what made you feel I'd be in danger in the meeting with State Security?"

"Because you hadn't seen what they did to Sheikh Mukhtar el-Husseini on the satellite channels. They ripped him to pieces. They slaughtered him, and some of them seemed to have such strict orders that they flayed him alive. I knew he had visited you here and was dear to you."

"How did you know that?" Hatem asked, intrigued.

"What do you mean, Sheikh Hatem? I've been living in your house. And, by the way, I want you to explain to me about the Shi'a and how they differ from the Sunnis and on what exactly."

Hatem laughed. "Are you planning to give up converting to Christianity and turn Shi'ite instead?" he asked.

"Well? Would it be better or worse?"

"Ask your brother-in-law."

They had reached the bathroom and Hassan insisted on coming in with him. He asked Omayma to go out, then helped Hatem take off his clothes. Hatem lowered himself into the bath and, oddly, as he was laughing at Hassan's comment he found red blotches on his chest and arms and the lower part of his stomach like an allergic rash or insect bites. He was puzzled but his body relaxed as it slipped into the soapy water. Hassan sat opposite him on the toilet seat.

"You promised me that when I'd swallowed the sleeping pills and woken up again you'd give me advice on what I should do about my conversion," Hassan said.

Hatem looked at the signs of the cross cut on the inside of Hassan's wrists.

"Look, Hassan, you don't know enough to abandon Islam for Christianity or even to revert to Islam from Christianity, because you don't know anything about Islam, as I've told you a hundred times, and you don't understand anything about Christianity. Your problem was solved last night when you saved my reputation and my health and my life by getting your father and your brother-in-law to intervene. You hate your family and you're angry with them. You have a low opinion of what your father does and it's clear you know all the family's dirty secrets in politics and business. So you're rebelling against them and this conversion business was a good opportunity for you to punish them and give them a fright, so you decided to abandon your religion. But as soon as you give up your family and depend on yourself and people know and treat you as Hassan and not as the son of this man or the brother-in-law of that man, you won't feel the need to convert to Christianity or Shi'ism or shamanism or whatever. Look for something you love to do and fulfill yourself that way. Find a girl you love and marry her. Travel, study abroad, even go to the Vatican and study Christianity, and if you understand anything come and see me, or do proper Islamic studies at a university in London. The main thing is to throw away your identity card that carries the mark of your relationship with this family that you hate, and all the problems will be solved."

Hassan bowed his head and stayed silent for a while. Then, drained of all enthusiasm, he said, "It's hard to think after all this that I've converted to Christianity just to annoy my family. No, Sheikh Hatem, I believe that the light of the Virgin Mary has come to me and that Jesus loves me."

Hatem restrained himself. He didn't want to make fun of Hassan's confusion.

"So what? Muslims believe in the light of the Virgin as well as Christians, and as for Christ loving you, that's something we all look forward to, because Christ spoke in God's name and is the Prophet of God and we believe in him as Muslims, and we think he's living too. To be loved by him there's no requirement that you be Christian. So are you just being stubborn? As I told you, you're an idiot when it comes to religion and you don't know anything. The truth is, you're a disgrace to Islam and a disgrace to Christianity."

Hassan stood up in anger, or was possibly just pretending to be angry.

"After all I've done for you, is this what it comes to, Mawlana?"

He headed toward the bathroom door to leave but Hatem called him back. As he moved in the bath, the water spilled onto the floor with a splash.

"Come back, boy," said Hatem. "Or else I'll stand up naked and we'll have a public morals and homosexuality scandal on our hands, and converting to Christianity or Shi'ism would be a million times less serious."

Hassan came back laughing.

"Of course you know they won't give up at this round," he said. "And anyway you're damaged goods, compromised, and they won't forget that you know more than you should."

"So how do we get out of this mess?" asked Hatem sadly, sunk in gloom.

"You're asking me, Sheikh Hatem, when I'm a disgrace to Islam and a disgrace to Christianity! You answer that one please, you great scholar of Islam and philosopher of Christianity."

Hatem threw soapy water in his face and wet his clothes.

"Right then, you ignoramus, pass me the robe."

Hatem had to go to see Mukhtar el-Husseini's mother. She looked tired and frail in her large white dress, sitting like a woman in her seventies on whom the world has thrown a sudden burden, leaving her broken and sad in a spacious, empty house that once bustled with people who came to see Mukhtar. She was harsh with people and fearful. Perhaps her fear explained her harshness, because people had abandoned the house, and its master and mistress, as soon as the smear campaign began against everyone and everything to do with them. They had turned their backs on Mukhtar's house and denounced it. Then people came shouting insults and abuse from under the windows and through the keyholes. People who hated Mukhtar el-Husseini or were envious of him started banging on the doors in the middle of the night, cursing and calling him names. For three days in succession after dawn prayers, people gathered in the Ansar al-Sunna al-Muhammadiya Mosque on the edges of the town, marched to Husseini's house, and made speeches in the courtyard and at the door. They woke people up and caused unrest, describing Husseini as a Shi'ite heretic and an infidel. They accused Shi'a of heinous crimes, and slandered the people in the house and those who came to visit them, and those who liked the Husseinis, those who sought their blessings, and those who believed in them. Mukhtar's mother had put up with this day after day; she had decided to stay, unlike Mukhtar's wife and the rest of the household, who had left for Cairo because they were frightened by what had happened and by what might yet happen. The mother, exhausted and offended, had tried one day to go out onto the first-floor balcony and speak back at them.

"We're not Shi'a and we have nothing to do with the Shi'a. We're the descendants of the family of your Prophet," she said in a hoarse voice.

But they just threw stones at her.

The stone-throwers shouted insults denying she was related to the Prophet's family and offended her with accusations of heresy. The woman screamed and stumbled and fell as she was closing the balcony door. Someone was about to run and help her but people told him to stop and he was pulled back, then there was silence for some minutes and some concern that the woman might have died.

As the people walked off, one of them shouted, "You have a week to get out of town, mother of the heretic!"

So she was a broken woman when she received Hatem. It was like a breath of fresh air when she saw him and felt there was a glimmer of hope in the darkness. Hatem tried to reassure her.

"A week at the most and Sheikh Mukhtar will be out, and back in your arms," he said.

"And back in people's arms, Hatem my son," she said tearfully.

"Never mind about the people," he replied. "What matters is that he's back in your arms. The good Lord knows all about it."

He said how sorry he was and offered excuses, but he was worried the details might be too much for her. She forgave him and thanked him and prayed for him and assured him of something he already knew—that Mukhtar loved him and had always been his brother.

Before he left, she said, "Did you know that the name Husseini wasn't originally part of the family name but Mukhtar's ancestor five generations back acquired it from spending five years in the Hussein Mosque as a servant to the mosque and the people who prayed there?"

She said that Mukhtar's father, like her, was a descendant of the Prophet's family and they had all memorized the family tree of the Prophet and were buried with it when they died. She said that Mukhtar's name was Mahmoud Mukhtar ibn Zein el-Abdin ibn Jubeir ibn Taqi el-Din ibn Ibrahim ibn Oqeil ibn Ahmed ibn Youssef ibn Oday, and the line went back to Muhammad, may God bless him and grant him peace.

"And then this happens to us?" she said.

"It's a trial with which we are afflicted and from which we will recover with the will of God the Just, the One, and the Victorious, my noble lady," Hatem replied.

Hatem was keen to prove to himself that he could stand up like a man to being humiliated by State Security. He was well aware they would be following him and monitoring his visit as it happened. They may have put cameras and bugging devices in the house but he was determined to be there on the day after his miraculous escape safe and sound from the State Security building, thanks to God and the role of Hassan Abdel-Laah, as Hatem had called him when they said goodbye at home before he went to see Mukhtar's mother. Hassan had packed up his stuff and embraced Omayma in front of him as tenderly as a child saying goodbye to his mother. Omayma was surprised, but Hatem wasn't annoyed at Hassan's show of emotion toward her. Hassan told him he wouldn't see him again but he swore that he loved him and that he wouldn't forget spending time with him and staying in his house, and said he didn't want Hatem ever to be angry with him, whatever he did or whatever he found out he had done. Hatem reprimanded him for saying goodbye, saying there was no need for him to leave. He pulled his packed suitcase away from him and called Khodeiri, who had been summoned urgently to the house, and told him to take the suitcase back upstairs to his room.

"This is your house, Hassan," said Hatem reproachfully. "Go out and do what you want and come back at the end of the evening. Whether you come back Muslim or Christian, this is your house, and in order to divide the country into two halves, I'm going to call you Hassan Abdel-Laah until you land on one side or the other. Whatever god appears to you and however you decide to worship Him, take your time."

Visiting Mukhtar's mother was his first task and he did it early in the morning, then he came back a little before noon and went to the bank where he had his accounts. He was greeted with the usual welcomes and dozens of questions about religion, about his programs and fatwas. He asked the branch manager, who had long been a friend, to fill him in on the latest developments in his accounts. The man looked at the screen in front of him while Hatem looked at the closed-circuit screens around the room showing the public areas, the corridors, the entrances, and the pavement outside and people standing at the ATM in the street.

"There's a deposit of three million pounds, and there's an account with a little less than a million in it," the manager said.

Hatem sighed and said, "Praise be to God. We ask Him to bless us in worldly matters. Look, I'd like that deposit to be transferred to an account in the name of Omar el-Shenawi, who's my beautiful son and a minor, and the other money to be transferred in full and to the last penny to my good wife Omayma."

371

The branch manager smiled.

"All's well, I hope?" he asked.

"Yes," said Hatem. "I'm going to have my tonsils removed and I'm worried I might be declared redundant, so I thought I'd better protect my son and his mother instead of them having to go through the probate business and all that hassle."

"May God grant you good health, Mawlana. Sorry to hear about your tonsils."

"Thank God it's tonsils. Better than it being my testicles."

The manager laughed but the laughing didn't completely ease his concerns. Hatem signed the papers happily, with loving thoughts of Omar.

Hatem expected disaster to strike and he had decided to sort out his affairs before it struck. He expected Ali el-Kaaki to get in touch with him at any minute to cancel the programs and wheedle his way out of the contracts. He expected his glorious television career to collapse when el-Kaaki blew the final whistle. He knew how close Kaaki was to the security agencies and how he was just a puppet on strings that tied him to the State Security building. In fact he had once overheard that a former director of State Security was in partnership with the owner of the Dunya channel and the son of the current director was a partner of el-Kaaki's. He waited in silence for the inevitable phone call from el-Kaaki or his office or the program producer. He expected to hear news that Khalil had withdrawn his sponsorship of the Ramadan series. It would be quick and easy for him to abrogate the contract. A nod from the Interior Ministry to Khalil or even a malicious hint from one of his Salafist sheikhs about Hatem and his relationship with Mukhtar el-Husseini would persuade Khalil, both for reasons of faith and as a political precaution, to stop financing his program. Hatem would have to go back to being a mosque preacher, if the Ministry of Religious Endowments would agree to take him back, which probably wouldn't happen. In fact he may already have been dismissed from his old position and State

Security would make sure he never again stood in the pulpit of any mosque in Egypt. His link with Husseini would mean he could never preach in the Gulf countries, which might have been a refuge in times of hardship. Hatem was convinced he was acting out the last episode of the stage of his life to which his learning, his popularity, and his position as a television celebrity had brought him. Could he play the role of the opposition sheikh, when the only sheikhs he could see that opposed this regime were the extremist sheikhs who declared both the ruler and his subjects to be infidels? Did he have it in him to be the sheikh who spoke truth to despotic power?

Why hadn't he spoken out all these years about the tyranny of the sultan? While the sultan reigned Hatem had lived in comfort, spent his time relaxing in swimming pools, and frittered away millions of pounds made from preaching and learning. The learning might be useful, yet he was the one who benefited most. Why had he ignored the corruption that was said to be rife in the country? He had never shown any interest in it.

He imagined the voice of the producer in his ear, telling him that time was passing and the end of the program was rapidly approaching. That's why he had hurriedly transferred the money to Omar and Omayma, so that they would be safe from harm and could live the lives they were used to, and so that Omar could pay for the medical treatment that might cure his illness and then for an education if he managed to get that far, and could have money for himself and for a future that would be brighter than his past. He was grateful to Omayma despite the rift that had developed years ago. However cool their relationship was now, the experience of living together was enough to make him feel grateful. Maybe she had changed from wife to sister after all these years. He thought back to the first years of his marriage, when he and Omayma were having trouble having a child. Each of them projected onto the other feelings of guilt and suspicion that the other was responsible for Omayma's failure to get pregnant, although all the X-rays and other tests suggested that both were perfectly capable of having children, though maybe not together. At dawn they would perform the usual prayer together and then he would say a special prayer for a child. Often they would both end up in tears. She blamed him for the fact that his prayers were not answered, while he wondered why God was punishing him and then felt guilty about even asking the question. He never thought of marrying another woman. Such an idea never came into his head, but Omayma wouldn't believe he wasn't thinking along those lines and she made him pay for her suspicions, punishing him for the fact that she could never confirm them. Then one day she came back home from the doctor's and collapsed into his arms, crying and sobbing aloud, writhing in pain and trembling, mumbling broken words as she wiped the snot from her nose with her hand. "I'm pregnant, Hatem," she finally said.

It was because of that day, that moment, that he would never abandon her as long as they lived. And this knowledge, that he couldn't leave Omayma, meant that the desire that now drew him to Nashwa didn't disturb him. In fact he was happy with it, because it was like a light in the darkness at a time when he felt anxious and tense. He tried to speak to Nashwa when he woke up after his detention. He called her after leaving the house but her phone was unavailable. He called her again after reaching Mukhtar's mother's house but she didn't reply, though there was a recorded message. He loved her voice and called her four times just to hear the message again and again. He called her again when he had finished at the bank and this time the busy signal meant he didn't even hear the recorded message, and he felt an emptiness and desolation in his heart. Was she ignoring him because of the incident at his father's house? Was she apprehensive about him and his reaction? Was she wary of continuing the relationship? Did she now hate Hatem because he had disappointed her and ruined the good impression she had had of him?

The only answers were that he wanted her. He wanted her copper-brown face and her large eyes, sometimes brown, sometimes black, sometimes amber, sometimes all these colors together, and her silky brown hair when it fell loose from under her hijab, when it brushed his face and he kissed it with reverent lips and reveled in its sweet, feminine smell and plunged his face in it, rolling his head in the soft hairs that made him tingle. He remembered her bronze neck, flecked magically with tiny beads of sweat as she kissed him feverishly. He remembered her slender body, tall and self-confident, with a waist that was living proof that the Creator was a master when His hand shaped a human likeness of one of the houris in paradise. He was puzzled that he still felt the same way about her after what had happened. There was no trace of remorse, as if he felt no need to apologize for that sensual encounter. Driven by deep desire, he didn't hesitate for a moment as he tried to meet her again, though he knew that he might be monitored more strictly and that exposure might ruin him.

Stuck at the traffic lights, he tried to call her again. He pressed her name on the screen but was surprised to see Nader Nour's name pop up instead, demanding to be answered. He had ignored Brigadier Faisal's suggestion that he call Nader when he came out of the State Security building, then he had ignored two calls from Nader and even his urgent text messages. He didn't want to be bothered by chitchat with Nader, who was the reason why he was stuck in this putrid swamp in the first place, and while he missed having a friend he could confide in and tell his story to and whose advice he could seek, he could do without Nader interrogating him about things he had no doubt heard from his security contacts and from the household of the ruling family. Nader's name disappeared from the screen and Hatem tried again to get in touch with

Nashwa. Then Khodeiri, sitting in the front seat next to Sirhan, turned round to speak.

"By the way, Miss Nashwa is waiting for you at the office," he said.

When he reached the office door, Khodeiri had caught up with him and then overtaken him to turn the key in the door. Ramadan, the errand boy, opened from the inside and greeted Sheikh Hatem. He asked him what he'd like to drink and said, "I spoke to Mister Khodeiri earlier and told him the lady says her name's Nashwa."

The errand boy clearly wanted to give himself a role but Khodeiri cut him short reproachfully.

"Enough, Ramadan, go and make Mawlana a cup of tea, quickly."

Hatem made his way toward the office door and opened it impatiently, looking for Nashwa. He was shocked to find the room empty, without even a whiff of her. He looked back angrily and, unable to stop himself shouting, he asked, "You silly idiot, where the hell is the woman who was here?"

Khodeiri preferred to think he wasn't the silly idiot that Hatem was referring to. He quickly pulled Ramadan by the collar as he was about to open the door again, since Sirhan had rung the bell and was muttering from outside, asking Ramadan to open up.

Hatem was standing there waiting for an answer from the two of them. The doorbell made him more agitated and he asked the question again: "Where's the woman who was in my office?"

"She said her name was Nashwa and she wanted to see you," Ramadan replied confidently. "I told her I didn't know your schedule so she told me to speak to Mr. Khodeiri and tell him she was waiting for Sheikh Hatem, so I told Mr. Khodeiri."

Hatem thought she had probably left. He was disappointed and even more depressed than he had been. Ramadan went to open the door for Sirhan and Hatem heard him saying, "I didn't want to let her sit in the sheikh's office, so I put her in the other room, and she was praying when you arrived just now."

Hatem cheered up instantly and went slowly into his office, recovering his dignity on the way.

"Very well, show her into my office," he said.

At first he thought it was a trick, and a silly trick at that, one that deserved an even sillier response. There were a few light knocks on the door, he said 'come in,' and the door opened. He thought the idiots sitting in his office must have made a mistake: it was a fully veiled woman draped in black from head to foot. The only part with any obvious shape was a head that was completely covered, with a pair of large black glasses attached.

"Who is this thing?" Hatem stuttered. "Could this be Nashwa?" he asked, recovering from the surprise.

The niqab made her look taller, or maybe it was because he was sitting on a low sofa that he thought it wasn't her. She just stood there and he didn't know what to do. He still suspected, and hoped, that it wasn't her.

"Nashwa?" he said.

"Yes, Mawlana," she replied sharply.

"Congratulations on your new clothes," he said. "What's the big idea?"

His desire had subsided.

"God's law," she replied, in the same sharp, defiant tone.

He waved his hand toward her.

"And the expensive French designer glasses, are they part of God's law too?" he asked.

She took hold of the glasses with her black gloves but didn't take them off, though it looked like she was about to.

"Did meeting me really require this Bar Lev line you've built around yourself?" Hatem added.

She didn't answer and, since she was completely covered, he couldn't detect any reaction.

"Why are you standing there like that?" he said. "Have a seat."

She didn't respond.

"Choose the seat furthest from me and sit there."

His heart began to soften when her head began to look around the place. Then she chose a corner and went over to sit down. He felt she was uncertain and confused and that his affection for her was coming back to life.

"When did you decide to wear the niqab?" he asked. "Was it after what happened between us?"

She completely ignored the second part of his question.

"The niqab is something that God Almighty has decreed for Muslim women," she said with a forcefulness that she wanted to be clear and final.

"Really!" he replied sarcastically.

The sarcasm offended her and it took even him by surprise. He had long been uncomfortable with the latest innovations in religion and this time he hadn't been able to hold back a spontaneous reaction that was colored by his anger with her and by a sense that she was trying to escape him by repeating the endless platitudes of the neo-Salafists.

"I don't believe you any longer and I've begun to realize that everything I've heard about you is true," she said.

She knew her remark would be hurtful.

"And what have you heard in the last seventy-two hours that you didn't know before, Nashwa?"

"That you campaign against the niqab!" she said, possibly as an evasion.

He realized she was leading him on, so he followed her lead.

"I've never campaigned against the niqab," he said. "Whenever I'm asked about it on television or in seminars I always reply that it's a custom and not a religious requirement, but there's nothing wrong with women wearing the niqab, since they're free to interpret Islam as they wish. The problem is that it's the advocates of the niqab who want to claim it's the one and only obligation."

"Of course it's obligatory. It's the real hijab. In fact God Almighty told women to stay at home and not to go out in the first place," said Nashwa.

"And when exactly did He tell them that? The day before yesterday?"

"Don't make fun of it!" Nashwa shouted.

"God forbid! In fact I'm making fun of you, you idiot. That's not what you said or the way you were two days ago."

"God showed me the way."

"The way to what?"

"*'O wives of the Prophet, you are not like other women if you are pious. So do not speak indulgently to men lest those who have sickness in their hearts start to have designs on you. So speak with decorum. Remain in your homes and do not display your finery as in the first Age of Ignorance.'*"

Hatem realized he was dealing with a parrot with black feathers.

"That's right, well done," he replied. "You've memorized the Quran well, but I can't see the point of reciting these verses to me right now."

"I'm doing what God told us to do."

"Yes, my dear, me too, and all of us. But you're putting into practice what sheikhs and preachers told you to do, not what God told you to do. God said this verse, but your understanding of it comes through preachers, and notice I don't say through people who have written works of Quranic exegesis. You've never ever read any of those works, and neither have any of those other people who decide to give me lessons about Islam whenever they hear me say something they've never heard before. They just heard it from someone who heard it from someone who heard it from some preacher."

Startled by what he had said or maybe primed to confront him, she stood up.

"I heard you yourself say that this verse showed how important it is for women to stay at home, honored and respected," she shouted.

She was so upset and agitated that her glasses almost fell off.

"I can't have said that, even under duress. I know as well as anyone else that I often say things to please the customer and to go along with what the people sitting in front of the television think. I give them the benefit of the doubt and don't bother them by making them think, because all they want is a couple of words that will make them happy and that won't confuse them with other ideas, so I give them what they want of course, and may God protect the faithful from the evil of fighting, but I've never been so obliging that I'd say anything like that—that women should stay at home. And what do you mean, stay at home, Nashwa? Would I really say that to people in a country where thirty-two per-cent of the families are supported by working women, not counting the fifty percent of households where the wives help their husbands with the expenses? Perhaps I said some people cite this verse to argue that women should stay at home, as their interpretation of the phrase '*Remain in your homes*,' but I don't usually volunteer the rest of my opinion, which is that the whole verse applies only to the Prophet's wives. It's specific, not general."

"Oh yes? All the other ulema have said it applies to all Muslim women."

"Don't say ulema, sister Nashwa. Say preachers and evangelists. No ulema could ever say that. The verse itself is absolutely clear and inconvenient for those preachers. Because God is addressing the Prophet's wives. '*You are not like other women*,' He says, so how for the love of God could '*You are not like other women*' change its meaning and refer to all women? And have you read what any work of interpretation has to say about the meaning of the word 'qarna' here? Do they say it just means stay at home and don't go out, when in fact the Prophet's wives did go out of their houses hundreds of times after the verse was revealed? The most common interpretation of the word 'qarna' is that it means they should be dignified, and it's addressed to the wives of the Prophet, remember, and that's an interpretation that fits in with the rest of the verse when He tells them, '*So do not speak indulgently to men lest those who have sickness in their hearts start to have designs on you.*' It means that God wants to protect the Prophet's wives, so He asks them to stick to formal conversation with others and not to speak indulgently, not to be too friendly and familiar. And maybe the Prophet's wives really did do that, just intending to be nice and friendly, and this led to some men trying to catch their eye or get a word or a smile out of them, which shows that society in the days of the Prophet and even around his house was not some angelic ideal. No, there were men who tried to chat up the Prophet's wives with bad intentions."

Nashwa shuddered. "What do you mean?" she said.

"I mean that at the height of the Prophet's mission there were people who spoke about his honor and dignity. They talked for a month about the conduct and reputation of his wife Aisha. Do you think it was a perfect society, with wonderful people whose hearts were as pure as the driven snow? Not at all."

The moisture in her breath had steamed up the lenses of her glasses, so she took them off and wiped them with her gloved fingers.

"Next you'll tell me the hijab's only for the Prophet's wives too!" she said, in the same sharp tone she had maintained since she came in.

Hatem laughed, completely dismissive of the conversation and of Nashwa, and angry and frustrated with the ignorance that followed him like his shadow.

"In this verse, yes, the hijab is only for the Prophet's wives, and notice that you said the hijab and not the niqab. And by

the way, for the verse on the hijab, there are thirty-nine different interpretations of the form the hijab should take, including
one that says it's the same as the niqab, and just to remind
you, the niqab had just one eyehole rather than two, perhaps
because glasses hadn't been invented when those writers were
alive. And as for the phrase '*Do not display your finery as in the first
Age of Ignorance,*' before you ask me whether there was a second
Age of Ignorance, I'll tell you, yes, there was.

"Roughly speaking, the first Age of Ignorance, according
to the people who wrote Quranic exegesis, was between the
time of Noah and the time of Abraham and lasted maybe nine
hundred years. Abul-Abbas says of those times, 'In the Age of
Absolute Ignorance women didn't cover up in the way they
should. A woman would even sit with her husband and a male
friend, and her friend would have his way with the top half of
her while her husband had his way with everything below her
waist, and one of the men might ask the other if he'd like to
switch.' What do you think of that kind of Age of Ignorance
and finery like that? Do you believe it? There are people who
say that women used to wear dresses made of pearls, open at
the sides and at the breasts. That was what 'finery' meant in
the Age of Ignorance—a woman showing her body to people
as she came and went. I'm not objecting to this rather bizarre
concept, which gives the impression they were living in nudist
colonies, but were there really pearls in the Age of Ignorance
that we read about in biographies of the Prophet? They would
have been rather a luxury, completely out of place in the aus-
terity of the desert. And they wouldn't go down well with men
who were jealous and protective. The people of the Age of
Ignorance were not such dolts or pimps, Nashwa, that their
women would dress up like that. That's all a figment of the
imagination of writers who came from nomadic tribes in the
desert and it has nothing to do with Islam."

"You tell people one thing on television, and then in
private and to me you say something different. Would you

dare tell people what you really think about these verses?" asked Nashwa.

"Okay, so you're here to have an argument. Is that because you regret what happened and you feel we committed a sin?"

Nashwa stood up nervously and then sat down again.

"Did you hear what you just said?" she said. "You feel we committed a sin. Is it just a feeling or did we really commit a sin? What do you call it when there's a naked woman in the arms of a man who's making love to her as if she's his wife?"

"For a start, calm down. We don't want to create a scandal," he said calmly. "You may have noticed that I'm not short of scandals. Secondly, there was no naked woman. She didn't take her clothes off and I didn't have time to undress her, unfortunately for me or luckily for her. Thirdly, I didn't make love to her like a man to his wife, but more like a boy with the neighbor's daughter in the stairwell. And by the way, so that you've covered all the bases with your religious fatwas on what we did together, then it definitely wasn't fornication and it wasn't a cardinal sin. It was what the Prophet was referring to when he said to one man, 'Perhaps what you did was thighing or kissing.' It might count as a temporary lapse for which one can make amends by giving alms, or we might treat it as a sin for which we can repent by asking God for forgiveness and by praying and giving alms. We could also treat it as a failure on the part of a man to resist a very pretty and reckless girl who enticed him with seductive words, and the man then let her down with his dismal performance and she regretted what had happened and stayed away from him for three days, which were the most difficult days of his life, not just because she wasn't there but because he was abducted, intimidated, and taken hostage by wild dogs."

She suddenly made a dash for the door. Humiliated, he rose to catch up with her and when he tried to hold her arm to stop her rushing out she pushed his arm away roughly. He stepped back in shock. She paused and turned to him. Wet patches of tears showed on the veil over her face and tears started to drip from the frames of her black glasses.

"I can't. It's impossible. I can't go on. This far and no further," she said, her voice softening.

He realized that an intense struggle was raging inside her. As she dashed out of the room, she shouted back, "It's my fault. Why did I agree in the first place?"

He couldn't work out what she meant.

"Agree to what? What do you mean?" he said.

There are moments when one turns to God and wishes that life would return to normal, that the sick hadn't fallen ill, that those who are missing were not gone, that feelings had not changed, that links had not been broken and places had remained as they were. The life we are used to, however unpleasant it might be, can sometimes be better than a new life, and definitely better than a new life that is unfamiliar. Hatem was used to sitting in the studio set, on the sofa that was put in place whenever it was time to film. It was fetched from a storeroom at the back and the workers aligned it with the marks drawn on the floor, which they sprayed with some liquid to make it shine. The technicians finished setting up the lighting in the right positions. The lighting director who was standing on the ground gave his orders to the workers climbing on the metal gantries near the studio ceiling (Hatem often worried they might slip and fall and hurt themselves), and one of the workers held a very long pole with a metal hook on the end with which he moved some of the spotlights in the ceiling nearby to adjust the light onto his face. He looked at the screen set up in the studio to see whether the light was properly aligned on Sheikh Hatem's face. The cameramen knocked the ash off their cigarettes quickly before taking up their positions. The assistant producer asked them to stand behind the cameras since they were going on air in just five minutes. The soundman stuffed wires down the back of Hatem's neck, attached the radio transmitter to his side, and clipped the tiny microphone to the hem of his gown, apologizing all the time. Georgette the make-up woman dabbed powder on gently. She knew that the sharp smell of the powder might irritate his nose and upset him. She apologized profusely but insisted on going as far as his eyelids, and he usually ended the program rubbing his eyes. The crowd around him suddenly thinned out just as the order came down to them on the set: "Five, four, three, two, one . . . Over to you, Anwar."

Amazingly Hatem was delighted to hear the sound of Anwar Othman's voice when his phone rang on the afternoon of the day when Nashwa turned up in the niqab.

"Mawlana," he said. "I'm back from holiday and I'll be expecting you on air tonight. The audience has probably had enough of reruns."

What a relief! He couldn't deny he was really delighted. He felt that his life could go back to normal, without a trace of anything new—the same routine again and again, the same traditional approach, the cloned sermons, the recycled lessons, and the fatwa sessions about women, giving alms, and trivial questions. He had been prepared for an upheaval in his life, from the dangers that threatened him from every quarter. He was also still irked by Nashwa's mysterious remark about 'agreeing in the first place,' so much so that he stayed alone in his office, eating the food that Khodeiri forced on him, and speaking only to shout "no" in Sirhan's face when the driver told him that Nader Nour had called and would he like to answer. When Anwar spoke to him in his deep voice, he forgot his fear of being ostracized by the television channels, their owners, and the advertising agencies, and he felt that State Security must have pardoned him. He put his anger behind him for some moments as a result of this surprise reprieve, and he imagined that the president's son had intervened as a favor to Hassan. Hatem called Omayma and told her he would be back home within an hour, in order to get ready to go to Media Production City and appear with Anwar Othman. Omayma was surprised, and he replied that he was optimistic because there hadn't been any orders to stop him and cut off his livelihood.

"Hatem," she replied reassuringly, "God has been generous to us so don't worry. We could live on what we have for years, even without work."

Hatem responded to her sudden kindness. It was one of those moments when he felt he had wronged her by what he had done with Omar and what had happened with Nashwa, however trivial that had been.

"God bless you, Omayma, that's a very nice thing to say," he said.

Later, as he was about to leave home for the studio, Omayma asked Hatem what the program would be about. For some mysterious reason her question brought his optimism to the surface, showing his attachment to his old placid life of routine.

"It'll just be Anwar Othman's usual themes, exciting in their cheapness," he mumbled with a contempt for which he would pay a high price.

When he arrived, Anwar came up and welcomed him warmly.

"What's the theme for the program tonight, Anwar?" Hatem asked him.

Anwar was ecstatic about having lost ten kilos in one month and was raving on about his diet and how his female admirers were impressed by his new weight, about his old suits, which he planned to give away to poor people with pot bellies, and about the segment on dieting that he would introduce into his daily program.

This outburst by Anwar made Hatem tense and apprehensive.

"But you haven't told me what the theme is for the program," he said.

Anwar spread his arms in surprise and surrendered to the technician who was attaching the microphone and the earpiece.

"Since when have you had to ask what the theme is, Mawlana? You're like a train that doesn't care what stations it passes through," he said.

He paused to rearrange his clothing after they had attached the wires to the inside of his shirt.

"Anyway, what else could we talk about other than the subject everyone's talking about these days, Mawlana? The Shi'a of course."

Anwar went on about how, after the Mukhtar el-Husseini scandal, people were interested in the Shi'a and their secrets, but Hatem wasn't listening. Anwar brought up all the elements that would make for a lively program—the accusations that they defamed the Companions of the Prophet and slandered the Prophet's wife Aisha, and that they thought the Prophet Muhammad received the revelation by mistake, because it should have come to Ali.

So this was the ordeal they had decided to put him through, on the most popular program of its kind against a host who was a servant of State Security. Anwar's friendships with State Security officers went as far as shared summer holidays with their families, close friendships between his wife and their wives, and children at the same schools. How would he stand up to Anwar Othman's interrogation skills? The guy was a master at scheming how to undo a rival or another television station.

Hatem remembered how one night they left the studio and went to sit and socialize in the coffee shop Anwar had opened two years earlier near the beginning of the desert road to Alexandria, where there was a large garden with tables here and there, and heaters on poles in the walkways in winter and vast fans bolted onto metal stands in summer. Inside there was a fancy air-conditioned hall where they played endless traditional instrumental music and the staff provided efficient and enthusiastic service, from the maître d', who seemed to be an old friend of Anwar's, to the shisha boys, who had been trained to bring everything he or Sheikh Hatem might need after a program, when it was less crowded and the customers were less intrusive. Everyone knew it belonged to Anwar and two partners of his from State Security, so it was no surprise that it was immune from any harassment from the health inspectors, the tax people, the local council, or any other government bodies. Anwar was keen to maintain cleanliness and smartness, although he was obviously lying when he said he was losing money in the restaurant and that keeping high standards was more important to him than making a profit.

That night Brigadier Mohamedi Suleiman came to join them from another table and he coughed a dozen times from a dodgy shisha. Anwar had it changed and gave the shisha boys a sharp rebuke, while Mohamedi swore it was because of his chest problems and because he insisted on smoking shisha in defiance of his doctor's orders.

Mohamedi said boastfully, "Tomorrow you'll see your friend on television like a chicken with its head cut off."

At first Hatem didn't know who he meant but he soon found out: there was someone in the opposition who was in the news, and they had threatened to expose his lawyer brother who had been implicated in some cases of fraud.

"He'd do best to act the hero," Anwar commented at the time. "He should say he's only responsible for his own behavior and that his brother should get the punishment he deserves because we're all equal before the law. He should say he'll hand him over to the public prosecutor himself and nonsense like that. That way he would be able to turn the tables on you."

"I'm shocked, Anwar. What, do you think I went to the Police Academy?"

Anwar laughed. Apparently it was an old joke between the two of them.

"Of course not. You're a graduate of the university of life," said Anwar.

"Exactly. Where do you learn to be cunning and devious, Sheikh Hatem? From cradle to grave, after a long life."

He paused to let Hatem take in the idea, and then continued.

"I told his brother the lawyer to write a confession saying that his brother, the big opposition guy, was his partner in all the transactions because that would protect him whatever happened," he said.

"And did the bastard write one?" asked Anwar.

"Sure he did. He thanked me and kissed me and damn near danced for me too."

Hatem wondered whether Anwar had sat with Ahmed el-Faisal in the same place in the same restaurant and whether they had made a deal at his expense. He imagined the brigadier saying, "Get him onto the subject of the Shi'a, and either he'll say what we want and attack his friend Mukhtar el-Husseini and kneel down and reaffirm that he's the loyal servant of State Security, forgetting that he has secret information about the country's rulers, or else he'll be finished as far as people are concerned, and as far as we are concerned."

That would be their big plan and he could almost read it in big letters on the teleprompter. He would be crushed and he would have to cut to a break, maybe the last one in his life. But what were the Shi'a to him? He might as well say what everyone wanted to hear. He was a television sheikh, after all, not a sheikh with real learning. Isn't that what he had trained himself to be—to hold what he'd read and what he knew in reserve and only to say things that met the wishes of the red light that gave him permission to speak? He was a red-light sheikh, a television preacher who should know that he belonged to this box, this game. In this game you weren't allowed to step outside the boundary lines that marked the field. What mattered was that the audience, the advertisers, and the owners were happy with you, and you put on a show that could be interrupted for advertisements selling soap, potato chips, and tins of cooking oil that they claimed was traditional. When his old teachers at al-Azhar were giving their lessons in the mosque courtyard, seated at the base of a column, did they have to put up with someone asking them to stop so he could advertise the shops of the chief merchant or public baths that ease back pain? Why did he think it was important that he say something that mattered? Since when had he had a mission? Was he afraid he might be punished, lose his livelihood, and be humiliated, or was he afraid of losing face in front of Hassan, and Omar, when he started to understand? And where was God in all this? Why didn't he think of where he stood with respect to God when he said something he didn't approve of just to win the approval of others?

He honestly believed he pleased the audience by flying under the radar. He told himself it was sometimes better to chip away at ignorance gradually than to confront it head-on. But now he faced a choice between, on the one hand, going along with widespread deceit for fear a hammer might hit him on the head and crush him if he did not or, on the other hand, confronting the deceit however bad the consequences might be, including the possibility that his audience would turn against him and society would hate him. First a few grumbles, then you lose your livelihood and they attack your record and your faith, then you are cast out.

Anwar began, just as he had expected, with a hostile introduction that incited the audience to kill the Shi'a and endorsed the execution of Sheikh Mukhtar, by the first person who laid eyes on him, to win God's favor and mercy. "Would you like to comment on this introduction, Sheikh Hatem?" he concluded.

The question was an initial challenge in a contest in which Anwar wanted his viewers to see blood flow. It was one of those moments that television presenters relish most: emotions running high, the guests insulting each other, tears, an actor sobbing, a hot fatwa on sex from some sheikh, a politician's threats, or an exotic dancer's confessions. No learning or information would interest this television monster, which demanded something vulgar or lewd, anything raw and impulsive.

"The essence of Muslim evangelism, my dear brother and eminent friend," Hatem began, "is to bring people together rather than drive them apart, to unite rather than divide, to mend rather than break, to set right rather than to cast judgment, to advise rather than criticize, and to guide rather than threaten."

Then he paused, as if he had thrown ice onto Anwar's bald pate. But Anwar was a professional; Hatem still thought he must have been a circus presenter before he moved to television. In response to Hatem's opening punch, he came back with a counterpunch.

"Of course, Sheikh Hatem," he said. "That's all very worthy and laudable. Evangelists should keep to that approach when they preach, but provided they make clear what is halal and what is haram, provided they deter religious innovations and deviations, confront aberrations from true Islam and distortions of the Quran and the Sunna."

He stopped to give Hatem time to take in his deliberate nastiness, and then continued, "So now we ask you, Mawlana, to what extent can we consider the Shi'a to be Muslims?"

The question was crude, tendentious, and aggressive. It showed where the program was headed and that it would end in a lynching. Now Anwar wanted him to dismiss the Shi'a as heretics to save himself from the suggestion that he was taking their side and the side of Mukhtar el-Husseini. He wanted him to throw down his glove in surrender to satisfy State Security before the commercial break.

"Look, Anwar," said Hatem, deliberately using the man's name alone, without any titles or honorifics, "do you remember the hadith about the pillars of Islam? Of course you remember it, unless you flunked elementary school."

The mockery was a warning, as Hatem pulled Anwar into the ring.

"Well, so say the hadith then. You look a little flustered," he continued.

Anwar smiled and decided not to let Hatem get away with it.

"Islam is based on five . . ." he began.

"Yes, that's the right hadith. Well done. Come on, let's say them together: testifying that there is no god but God, performing prayers, giving alms, fasting during Ramadan, and, for those who can afford it, making the pilgrimage to Mecca. Of course you can afford to go every year with the Interior Ministry delegation!"

Then Hatem decided to strike. "Now we come to our Shi'ite brothers. They testify that there's no god but God, they say the same five prayers and give the same alms, and they fast during Ramadan and make the pilgrimage to Mecca. How then can you ask me if they're Muslims or not? Is the question even valid as a question? The imam Ibn Taymiya says that dismissing people as heretics or infidels was the first unwelcome innovation introduced into Islam."

Anwar attacked stupidly: "You're defending the Shi'a!"

"Are you attacking them? You asked me a question and when I answered you I defended the truth, not the Shi'a. Anyway, are you asking me because you want to know? Or is this 'Who Wants To Be A Millionaire?' and you know the answer but you're just testing me?"

The heat rose on the set and the sparks started to fly. Anwar went back to alternating between smiling and stroking his jaw.

"Don't you think that defaming the Companions of the Prophet—Abu Bakr and Omar, for example—puts one outside the Muslim community?" he asked.

"Firstly, I'm not going to tell you what I think, but the consensus of religious scholars is that this is a serious offense—besides of course being impolite, impudent, and ignorant—but not heresy or unbelief. But I'd like to say here that Omar ibn Abdel-Aziz, the fifth of the rightly guided caliphs as the early Muslims called him, when you read the great biography of him, you'll find that among the great things that he did during his reign was that he banned the defamation of Ali in mosques, and Ali here means Ali the imam of the pious, may God be pleased with him. Note that he was the eighth Umayyad caliph and the Umayyad caliphate had been around for about sixty years at the time, and Ali was being insulted in mosques. You may know that the Shi'a at that time were just opposition groups that didn't have recognized mosques or specific countries where they were in power, because the first Shi'ite state came hundreds of years after the beginning of Islam. Anyway, insulting the Companions of the Prophet was common among the Shi'a at the time, just as insulting the imam Ali was the official practice of the Umayyad state until Omar bin Abdel-Aziz stopped it for two and a half years, and then it was resumed after his death, or rather his assassination. So what I mean is that this was a mistake that everyone made and it goes far back in history. But if anyone continues to do it, they should be condemned as extremist and depraved."

"But they continue to insult Abu Bakr and Omar and Aisha even now, don't they?"

"I swear I've never heard them do that," Hatem replied. "If anyone did say something like that, then as I said, that would be an outrage. But that doesn't prove anything about either Shi'a or Sunnis."

"Would you like to listen to part of a recent sermon one of them gave in which he insulted the Companions of the Prophet?"

"Of course not. Let's not pick extremists and lunatics from here and there, and drive people apart rather than bring them together, especially since there are also people giving sermons in which they accuse the Shi'a of heresy. Look, Anwar, when you get to know Islam properly, there's no such thing as Sunnis or Shi'a. There aren't any sects or denominations. The Prophet Muhammad wasn't a Sunni. He was the Muslim Prophet of God, who brought the good news, called people to Islam, and guided them. The whole story was a political struggle for power over who should succeed the Prophet. Tens of thousands of people were killed in the struggle, which was between Ali the Commander of the Faithful and Muawiya, who rebelled against Ali's leadership and, as we would say these days, staged a coup to secede from the Islamic state. To justify this political struggle, they had to find non-political justifications, which all appeared after the war was over. The question arose as to whether it was legitimate for two groups of Muslims to fight. One group appeared that took the side of Ali and the family of the Prophet, especially after the massacre and tragedy at Karbala, which is a mark of shame on the forehead of humanity and not just of the Islamic state at that time, and then there was the group that prevailed in the war and acquired official status, which was bound to create a legitimacy with which to stand up to the family of the Prophet and justify shedding the blood of Muslims. The concept of the People of the Sunna and the Community appeared and the struggle lasted centuries between rulers and oppositions, and between a majority and a minority, and everyone was busy formulating ideas to protect either the majority and the government and its control over Muslims or, on the other hand, the persecuted minority opposition that operated underground or in prisons or was closely controlled and monitored. So it's hardly surprising, Anwar, if you haven't fallen asleep listening to me and if you understand what I'm saying, it's hardly surprising that a number of imams and interpreters of the Quran and historians were persecuted or imprisoned under the Islamic state, solely because they were accused of being Shi'a or of sympathizing with the Shi'a. The same thing is being repeated these days with the political conflict between Iran on one side and Saudi

Arabia and the Gulf states on the other. They all try to come up with justifications in Islamic law, explaining how they are defending the true Islam. But it's just a political quarrel for which the price is paid by ordinary, normal Muslims who imagine that worshiping God means they have to hate the way other people worship the same God."

Hatem might have bored Anwar but he was relieved and he hoped it was time for the break, which it was.

"The producer says we have to cut for a break now, but I want to ask you, as it's clear you're minimizing the danger of Shi'ism—"

"What! You're trying to pin an accusation on me, but you haven't even asked me about Shi'ism in the first place, for me to minimize or exaggerate the danger!" Hatem cut in angrily.

"But you said there are no denominations in Islam."

"Okay, but how does that mean one should be Shi'ite? Shi'ism is a denomination and I told you Islam doesn't have denominations in the first place."

"But you said the Prophet wasn't Sunni."

"Of course, because you can't say that Jesus Christ was a Catholic, can you? Besides, my friend, the Shi'a claim as much as anyone else that they love and follow the example of the Prophet and there are descendants of the Prophet who are Shi'ite. So the Shi'a are Sunnis from their point of view, and we are Shi'a from our point of view because of our love for the family of the Prophet, Ali, Hassan, and Hussein."

Anwar felt that the audience was losing touch with what Hatem was saying, either because it was obscure or because of his overtly defensive tone. He was more satisfied than Hatem with Hatem's performance, so he decided to finish him off before the break, as he had promised his friends in the police.

"Do you deny that the Shi'a have a Quran called the Quran of Fatima?" he asked.

Hatem knew that Anwar had left this zinger till the end so that he could leave triumphant before the wretched break.

"I tell you," he replied, "any Muslim who hears us in Iraq or Lebanon or Syria or Saudi Arabia can go into any Shi'ite mosque and pick up the first Quran they find there and tell us whether there's a single letter or word that makes it different from our Quran."

Anwar jumped in quickly. "But it's a secret Quran!" he said.

"And what's the use of a secret Quran, Anwar? You seem to suggest it's a Quran that's used for worship, so in what sense would it be secret if people used it in their prayers for fifteen centuries? Look, Anwar, as soon as you say the word 'mushaf,' people assume you're talking about the Quran, but that isn't right at all. You may know, but you probably don't, that the word 'mushaf' never occurs in the Holy Quran to describe the Book of God. 'Mushaf' is an Arabic word that was applied to the Quran after it was compiled during the reign of the Caliph Abu Bakr, but it could apply to any set of pages bound between covers. That would be a mushaf. But what is known as Fatima's mushaf doesn't contain anything that could called Quranic as far as we understand from all the stories and research. What they say is that Fatima was sad and in grief at the death of her father the Prophet and she remained in grief until she herself died just seventy-five days later. During that period the Angel Gabriel consoled her by appearing in various guises and speaking to her about the Prophet's virtues and by telling her stories written by Ali bin Abi Talib, who was her husband of course. All these accounts might be explained away, they might be accepted or dismissed, but there's nothing in them about Fatima receiving any divine revelation or about this mushaf containing a single word of the Quran. And the book doesn't exist anyway and even the Shi'a say it belongs to the twelve imams and that it's with the missing imam and no one knows when he'll return. But let me go back and say that this is all about political conflicts and anyone who has a chance to smear his rival does so undeterred and with impunity."

In a parting gesture meant to declare his interim victory, Hatem declared dramatically, "And now for our break."

The banners of victory were fluttering in the eyes of Anwar Othman during the break, as he gave his muscles a rest during the time-out. Everything he had wanted to happen had happened. It didn't matter whether what Hatem said was valid, true, accurate, or honest. It didn't matter whether what Anwar said was sound or silly. What mattered to the police officers who planned it was that it would smear and pillory Hatem. This had been achieved, because they were working on minds that were not interested in thinking or finding the truth. They were working on the instincts of an audience that had a fascination with the scandalous and that was disposed to accept personal attacks and believe anything that was slanderous. Hatem had become a television sheikh who, for the past many years, had paid no attention to the growing interest in superficial aspects of religiosity and apathy about its essence, its treasures. The most watched of his programs had been the one in which he described the moving scene when the Prophet died in the arms of Aisha, his wife. The advertisers asked for it to be repeated several times. Yet when he spoke about public finance in Islam, in a program that was unusually daring, the audience walked out and the advertisers warned the channel not to repeat it. When Ali el-Kaaki gave him the list of themes that he, as an advertising agency, wanted in his new program, they were all the obvious ones: the hijab, chastity, men and women alone together, the death of the Prophet, prayers for special occasions, almsgiving, what Islam says about envy, and the special qualities of Quranic verses. When Hatem told him that the only sources for the special powers of Quranic verses were spurious hadiths that were invented to encourage Muslims to read the Quran but didn't contain anything that made sense, Kaaki replied, "But Mawlana, why don't you want people to read the Quran?"

And when Hatem read the title "The Torments and Comforts of the Grave" he threw the piece of paper on Kaaki's desk and said, "I can't do that, Kaaki."

"Why not, Mawlana?"

"I can't say that people are tormented in their graves."

"Why not?"

"Why not! Because they're not tormented in their graves."

"But Mawlana, we've been hearing about the torments of the grave since we were in our mothers' wombs, and then you come along and say it doesn't exist!"

Hatem laughed. "For a start, it's just one hadith with a single chain of transmission, and hadiths like that can't be used as the basis for law or doctrine," he said. "It would be okay if you wanted us to include the special powers of Quranic verses, but not the torments of the grave. And besides, people would kill me and hate me if I told them people aren't tormented in their graves, because I'd be arguing based on reason and not on the texts. It's true there's nothing in the Quran about the torments of the grave but everyone hangs on to the same hadith without exposing it to the ultraviolet rays of reason that God asked us to use."

"Mawlana, don't complicate things for people."

"What am I complicating, Kaaki? After a long life, you die, and that's it," Hatem said with a laugh, even though he was being sincere. "Then they'll put you into a grave, unless you were burned to death and they couldn't find any flesh or bones, and you're just ashes. If the torments and comforts of the grave really exist, there would have to be two things. Firstly, there must be another life apart from life on earth and the afterlife—the life of dead people in graves so that they can feel the torments or the comforts, because how could they feel anything unless they're alive? The other thing is there would have to be two Days of Judgment and two Days of Resurrection instead of one of each because, if you believe in this business of the torments of the grave, then you'll be judged twice, once to decide whether you deserve to be tortured or to have an easy time in your grave and then again to decide on your fate in the afterlife, whether you go to Heaven or Hell. But this is incompatible with either Islamic doctrine or reason. There's only one Day of Judgment and we'll all rise from the dead on one day, the day the trumpet is blown, but there's no partial judgment or judgment in two stages, no 'take a little torment now and we'll settle up later on the Day of Resurrection.' Those who talk about the torments of the grave are implying that God Almighty is unfair, God forbid, because how can He punish us before He judges us? How can He torture us in our graves for our deeds before we're forced across the bridge over Hell and we've seen our good deeds and bad deeds on the scales? Should there be punishment before judgment? A verdict before a trial? Of course not. And besides, the Quran says the Day of Judgment will be so frightening that everyone will want to *'run away from his brother, his mother and father, his spouse and his children.'* But how could that be if everyone knew what the result would be from whether they'd been tortured or had a pleasant time in their graves?"

Despite what Hatem said, Kaaki was determined to have a program on the torments of the grave but without Hatem's point of view. Hatem give in and obeyed. He still remembered that famous program, in which he didn't say a single word about what he thought. He just went over the explanations and stories in the old books, with some phone interviews and a dramatic re-enactment that was followed by adverts for soap and shampoo, as if the soap was to wash the corpses.

Hatem let Anwar jump around like a piece of popcorn in the popper, delighted he had successfully carried out the orders he had received from State Security. Hatem got down from his seat slowly, aware that none of the staff had come near him. They hadn't whispered in his ear, congratulated him, or asked any questions. The smell of treachery hung in the air. Suddenly he found Nader Nour right in front of him in the studio.

The film star was standing behind the camera surrounded by the cameramen, who welcomed him, shook hands with him, and gave him a warm reception. He came up to Hatem with a group of people and took his hand to lead him off.

"Mawlana, Sheikh Hatem my dear," he said. "Come with me. I've been looking for you for days, but you just ignore me."

Anwar was standing in a corner, busy with a phone call and smoking a cigarette.

"Seven minutes of adverts left, Mawlana," he shouted across the room.

Nader pulled Hatem toward the door of the studio and took him by the hand down a short, narrow corridor, then turned into another, longer narrow corridor and opened the door into a room that was full of computer equipment and screens, but no people. It looked like it was out of use. Nader took him in and shut the door behind them. Nader sat down on a seat that he seemed to have occupied quite recently: there was a computer bag next to it, some cigarette butts, and his keyring. He asked Hatem to sit down on a chair facing a large screen. Hatem thought these detailed preparations were strange, but he went along with them out of curiosity because he wanted to know what Nader meant by being so suspiciously enthusiastic about meeting.

"We're friends, aren't we, Sheikh Hatem?" Nader said.

"No, we're not friends," Hatem replied forcefully.

"You know, if you'd said anything else I'd have been angry with you. We're not friends of course. You're my sheikh and teacher and I'm your student."

"That's not what I meant by my answer. And I don't teach in the drama academy, so I can't be your teacher."

"No, you're teacher to Nader Nour the human being, not the actor."

"Five minutes to go!"

"Till what?"

"Till the end of the break. I'm doing a live program."

"Are you sure you want to go on with the program, Sheikh Hatem?"

"Why wouldn't I?"

Nader flicked his lighter and a jet of flame shot out with a hiss.

"After the break that bastard Anwar's going to ask you about Mukhtar el-Husseini," he said, lighting his cigarette, "and any answer you give will harm you, and the answers you gave before the break have already done you enough harm. You're pretty much finished as a television preacher."

"Is that a warning, a threat, or a piece of advice?"

Nader sighed. "Okay, I want you to watch a two-minute video clip and then decide," he said, with the confidence of a dog that knows an earthquake is about to strike.

Without asking Hatem's permission, he put a disk into the computer and the biggest screen in the room went blue, then pictures started to appear and move. It was a scene from a film that Hatem didn't know, apparently a bad one, without any well-known faces. Then suddenly Nader appeared on the screen in what looked like a red bedroom, wearing an open shirt that showed his bare chest and smoking a cigarette.

Nader froze the scene by pressing a key on the keyboard.

"This is one of my silly movies," he said. "It was a low-budget quickie, and in it I'm playing a young frivolous bachelor. I want you to watch the rest of the scene carefully and see who opens the bedroom door now."

He took his finger off the keyboard and the movie resumed on the screen. In the film Nader stood up and opened the door when someone knocked. The screen showed Nader's face alone in the picture, smiling, and pretending to be overjoyed. "Welcome, signora," he says. Then there was a shot from behind Nader's back, showing the woman standing in a red dress with bare shoulders, coming in with a stupid laugh. He took her in his arms as he closed the door. For a while Hatem couldn't work out what Nader's various gestures meant, but he was stunned and his heart sank when the face of the woman in Nader's arms started to become clearer. When she looked up, her face filled the frame. She was laughing shamelessly, like a woman of the night in any other Egyptian movie. Nader froze the frame from the keyboard and looked deep into Hatem's eyes. Hatem was transfixed but couldn't fully understand what he was seeing. His eyes glazed over, his head pounded, and his skin itched. It was Nashwa. She was an actress, and she had been acting all along.

Hatem was shocked and humiliated. Out of the corner of his eye, he thought he saw Nader watching him with a mixture of sympathy and pleasure at his discomfiture, or maybe it was just the jolt of emotion Hatem felt when exposed as an older man that a young woman could toy with. Had he been the plaything of this girl, who now appeared in another shot on the screen when Nader fast-forwarded the movie? A famous young singer who liked to show off his bare chest appeared, holding the microphone stand as he sang. The words of his song were confident in their banality, and a young woman appeared, dancing in a group of other girls, though she was clearly the star, and the camera concentrated on her as she followed the singer. It was indeed Nashwa's face and body, though she looked slimmer. Her short skirt was tight on her buttocks, deliberately designed to look sexy. Her blouse was open at the top of her cleavage and showed off the shape of her pert round breasts, which were supported from beneath to make them seem fuller. Hatem was offended by Nashwa's shameless, exhibitionist strutting. She was like a slave girl advertising her charms in a slave market. It humiliated him as someone who had loved her and what remained of his love humiliated him as a sheikh. How could Nashwa be the same as this woman? A brazen whore, a vampish slave girl with a pretty face with dark red lips, black lines on her eyebrows, and green eyeshadow, long pointed eyelashes as bold as the looks she received were lascivious, and an inviting smile that served only to arouse. How could this pretty and flirtatious girl have changed into that fanatical, puritanical young woman who clung to the formalities of religion and had the illusion that her own piety was Islam? Which was the real Nashwa: the woman in the niqab or the woman who threw herself at him to kiss him passionately, unable to control her desires?

She was never this way or that way. She was just a smooth operator that had been set on him. He had to understand that she was a trap and he had walked straight into it. What had she done to him now? Had she revealed his secret? Surely the only reason she had come to see him, or had been placed in his path, had been to make sure that he had a secret that she could reveal.

Hatem sat down, exhausted and confused. He didn't bother to demean himself by asking about her or about the details of what was behind this revelation that Nader had just sprung on him, but he was shaking inside and he felt as if thousands of ants were crawling inside him. Anwar Othman opened the door and Nader quickly froze the movie at a picture of the sheikh's beloved dancer.

"Mawlana, two minutes to the end of the break," Anwar said.

"We still need time. Please extend the break, Anwar, and I promise you I'll do you a program in which I confess that I used to kill cats when I was young," Nader said.

Anwar looked at Hatem, who looked up at him and could see immediately, from the glint in his eyes, the raised eyebrow and the tilt of his head, that Anwar knew what Nader was showing him, but he didn't say anything.

Anwar went back out of the door, muttering, "We can extend the break. Whatever you say, you big shot, but are you sure your confession about cats will interest the audience?"

Nader shut the door behind him.

"Definitely, especially when I go on to say I used to gather the cats together for orgies in my bedroom and take pornographic pictures of them," he said.

Then he rolled his chair over until it was almost touching Hatem's.

"Why am I here?" he said, looking toward Hatem. "You must be wondering, Mawlana. And why did I show you that film of Nashwa dancing? Why right now, in the middle of a program in which that police informer fraud Anwar Othman is going to ask you about Sheikh Mukhtar and the Shi'a and all that shit?"

Hatem didn't answer. He just swallowed Nader's words.

"They invited you to this program to get rid of you or finish you off if you decide to go on defending Mukhtar el-Husseini and the Shi'a," Nader continued. "And please don't tell me you're not defending them but just stating the facts. These days if you don't denounce them, then you're with them. The whole country treats religion like the movies, Mawlana. It's very clear and simple. There are good guys in the movies and there are bad guys, and of course we have to be the good guys if the movie's going to be a success. Don't speak to me about drama, or the dramatic context, or the logic of events, because that ruins the movie. If you go out now and tell us there are some bad things about the good guys and there are some good things about the bad guys, that will get you in deep trouble, as you know."

Nader stood up and took hold of Hatem's chair.

"It's not just a matter of your work and having your programs banned," he said. "I'll bet no one would dare produce a program with you, or invite you on as a guest, or even shake your hand in the street. It's gone way beyond that. What you say will pave the way for them to include you in the Mukhtar el-Husseini case. At first it was just a matter of playing around and framing the poor guy, but now it's gotten bigger and they want to spite Iran and take a shot at Hezbollah, so they decided to make a big deal of the case. I know they promised you that the man would soon be able to go home, and I'm sure he will, but first they'll drag him through the mud and destroy his reputation and the reputation of other prominent people such as you. You know why, Mawlana? Because they thought you were one of them and under their control. When they realized they couldn't wind you up with a key, they were stunned and decided to punish you. But there's still a last chance, in just a few minutes. You can go back on air and abandon the courageous stance that took them by surprise, abandon Mukhtar el-Husseini and go back to being the sheikh they knew before, the one they trained, I'm sorry to say. That's the down payment on a truce between you and them. To make things worse Nashwa will reappear, God alone knows under what circumstances and what your involvement with her was, but anyway, you did get involved, though I don't know to what extent. But definitely you know and they know, because they're the ones who sent her."

Hatem finally spoke. "Why are you doing this to me?" he asked.

His voice sounded as if it came from deep under the sea, from a man who was drowning or from a diver. Nader smiled, ignoring the fact that Hatem has said 'you' rather than 'they.'

"You're the most famous sheikh in the country, Mawlana. And the most popular, the highest paid, the most influential, and the most widely viewed. They were the people who allowed all that. The mosques would close their doors to your lessons and the television stations would ban you from appearing, and the producers would stop making your CDs, if they wanted. If you want to be a sheikh, Mawlana, you have to be their sheikh."

*

In the past, he had always said what the red light wanted him to say.

When the light went on he set off, as if in a race that he always won. The learning was carefully measured, the dose precisely controlled. He had walked on safe paths and chosen areas that were interesting and important without disturbing people's expectations. He was a merchant of religious knowledge, not a doctor who treated people and ordered them to take their medicine, even if it was bitter. He was a singer who sang what pleased his audience and what his listeners requested, not what he wanted them to hear. He received applause in the form of sighs of admiration and cries of 'Allahu akbar' in the mosque or from the studio audience, and in the form of the adverts that poured into his programs. His fees rose and there were pictures of him on billboards in the street and on the covers of magazines. He was the modern sheikh, but nothing of what he said was modern. It was just the same old ideas drawn from the same old books, following in the footsteps of the old sheikhs, without any innovation, without shocking the audience, without any original thinking. Yet they still saw him as 'the modern sheikh,' because he spoke in an easygoing style, simplified things for them, told amusing anecdotes, cut back on the traditional complicated talk, and gave plenty of examples. He made jokes that made people laugh, talked about things that happened in soccer matches, included the world of soap operas in his explanations of religious matters, slipped in technical terms, and set up a Facebook page and his own websites on the Internet. He brought together a group of young people to film his program and had young singers of the same generation sing the intro, but he was very conservative about never straying from the mainstream.

There were two kinds of learning in his life. There was the learning he had studied and loved and treasured. Like a camel roaming free in the desert, he found himself in it, silently and in seclusion. He used it, warily and stingily, only to provoke rival sheikhs and show off to conformist preachers who always gave textbook answers. What he liked most about Hassan was that he brought him back to that kind of learning: debate, reasoned disputation, history, and reason. One of the things he liked most about being with Nashwa was that she challenged him to dig up that learning, rub off the rust, and give it a shine. The other kind of learning was the learning he dealt with on television and when he spoke in public—the learning associated with the red light. When the light went on, he spouted it out, earning hundreds of thousands of pounds, millions in fact. His contract as exclusive main guest three times a week on Anwar Othman's program was worth a million and a half pounds a year, and the days he appeared were the days the station made the most in advertising.

On that particular day, after Nader asked Anwar Othman to extend the break in Hatem's program, they ended up running adverts for twenty minutes.

"Hey guys," shouted the producer from the studio door, "no one ever has commercial breaks this long. It's very unprofessional and we're the only ones who do it."

"Go to hell and let's make some money," Anwar replied.

Nader followed Hatem back to the studio to go back on air. He watched as Hatem met Anwar at the door to the set. He was surprised to see the sheikh take Anwar by the arm and say, "I'd like a quick word with you in your room, Anwar."

Hatem had tiny beads of sweat all over his forehead and his body was bent with fatigue and dejection. His face looked tired and earnest. His roaming eyes were slightly bloodshot, with a trace of tears in the corners. When he and Anwar went in, Hatem noticeably clenched his jaw and ground his teeth.

He had often been in Anwar's room, which deliberately and foolishly tried to show visitors how stylish it was. It was small, like all the rooms in the studios, but it was the least cramped and it had an en suite bathroom, a bed with soft, expensive sheets, and a large mirror to satisfy Anwar's vanity, with a gilt frame indicative of his old-fashioned taste. He also had famous and expensive brands of perfume, an extraordinary selection of ashtrays and lighters, a wardrobe that covered the wall, left open to reveal Anwar's suits and shirts, a sample of what he owned and what he spent on clothes. In front of a picture of his boorish face, Anwar invited Sheikh Hatem to sit down on a black leather massage chair that filled half the room, with big armrests and a high, adjustable back. But Hatem maneuvered Anwar into turning a half-circle and Anwar ended up sitting on the leather chair. Hatem pushed him onto it and said, "Relax a minute. I have a surprise for you."

Anwar was surprised, but he raised his eyebrows in defiance of the sheikh because he knew he was in the stronger position.

"I might have asked you," Hatem said, "to tone down your questions and the way you ask them, and not to carry out the plan to destroy me as faithfully as you usually obey your orders, but I couldn't be sure you would agree if I asked you to make sure the evening went off well. It's also impossible for me to back out of continuing with the program because they would immediately see it as a sign that I was running away, as a sign of weakness and fear, and that would damage my image in the eyes of the audience and State Security."

"So let's go and finish off the program," Anwar replied gloatingly as he rose from his chair. "I'll ask you questions and you can save yourself by answering as the situation dictates."

Hatem reached out and put his hand gently on Anwar's chest as he stood up.

"No, there's another solution you haven't considered," he said. Hatem pushed him back violently, throwing him down on the massage chair, which was opened all the way and lying flat. Then Hatem stepped forward and put his knees on Anwar's supine body. He managed to immobilize him by pressing his arms down on Anwar's chest and shoulders.

Anwar had no idea what was happening. All he could feel was Hatem's clenched fist punching his nose and chin with a strength that amazed him. Then the pain began and he screamed. He caught a glimpse of Hatem's fist, colored red with the blood pouring out of his nose and jaw. When the fist hit his eye like the head of a hammer, Anwar passed out.

"The other solution is you back out of the program and I continue by myself," Hatem panted.

He stood up, left Anwar's prostrate body, and opened the wardrobe door. He lifted Anwar's back from behind till it was upright, then gave the body a big push, over the edge of the chair and toward the wardrobe door. Anwar's head smashed into the door and his body slumped onto the floor.

"Help, guys!" Hatem shouted. "Mr. Anwar tripped and slammed into the wardrobe door and passed out."

The red light went on after a twenty-six minute break for commercials. Sheikh Hatem was alone on screen.

"Assalam aleikum, we're back again after a rather long break, for which we thank God," he said. "That means our program is a great success and the advertisers are showing great interest, a sign of high viewer ratings, and we hope and pray to God that they will always think well of us. Unfortunately my dear friend the great star Anwar Othman became indisposed during the break. It seems he had too much fatta for lunch, so he says he's sorry he can't come back for the rest of the show and he promises you he'll stay away from fatta. So I'm here with you on air, with the help of God. I'm going to ask you questions and you answer, or you ask me questions and I'll answer. And in line with the theme of the show, which was set by our friend Anwar, let me speak to you about the etiquette of disagreement in Islam, as we learned it from the Companions of the Prophet and the generation that followed, may God be pleased with them all. Unless it's a friendly disagreement or a disagreement simply for the sake of disagreement, then it's the kind of discord that God and His Prophet would not approve of."

Hatem took the first call: "Hello? No, I can't hear your voice, madam. What? You're busy changing the ringtone on your cell? Is that really necessary? Hello? Hello?"

But what Hatem was really wondering about was if and when someone would call in and ask him about Mukhtar el-Husseini.

Hatem wanted to ask Omayma if she remembered the girl who had come to visit a while back.

Of course she would remember Nashwa. Omayma had sat with her and spoken to her and had breakfast with her. The way she looked that day suggested that Omayma hadn't digested either her breakfast or the presence of that girl in her house so early in the morning. Omayma's face suggested she was suspicious. But somehow Nashwa's visit and Hatem's recent ordeal had shaken things up and restored some warmth to the relationship between Hatem and Omayma. The passion Hatem had felt for Nashwa had made him more passionate about Omayma, maybe because he felt guilty or remorseful.

When he got home, he felt wrecked, shattered, wounded, and threatened. He hadn't received any phone calls asking about Mukhtar el-Husseini. In fact, after he went back on air alone, without Anwar Othman, he received only two phone calls, and they had both been set up by the production team. They were dull questions from fake viewers and he felt that orders had arrived to wrap up the show quickly, especially since they were puzzled about the mystery of Anwar Othman getting injured in his room. After the show he found out that Anwar hadn't told anyone that Hatem had attacked him. It may have been pride, or fear of a scandal. Nader also vanished after the show, as if he had accomplished his mission, the purpose of which Hatem hadn't quite fathomed. Had he really wanted to save Hatem from a trap? The idea that he would be motivated by affection must be suspect, given that Nader loved only himself. Or maybe the fact that he had come was a sign that the people who set the trap were unsure what they wanted the outcome to be. Some of them wanted to destroy Hatem completely, while others wanted him to survive with just an arm missing or a foot ripped off.

He wanted to say to Omayma, "I betrayed you with that girl that tricked me." But no, he wouldn't say "I betrayed you," because he hadn't betrayed her. For a start they were living almost separate lives, albeit under the same roof. The last time they had had sex was so long ago that he could hardly remember when it was. Second, he hadn't slept with Nashwa. It was just a quick hug and some fondling. Under sharia law that wasn't adultery, sexually it wasn't intercourse, and it hadn't amounted to anything. Third, he was in love with Nashwa. If Omayma was sensible she could forgive him for a hundred reasons, because a man of his age couldn't live as a virgin, even if he had forgotten what sex with love was like. He hadn't asked Omayma how she put up with celibacy, or why she no longer saw him as a means for sexual gratification. In fact she had never rejected him, any time he felt like sleeping with her, but she accepted so grudgingly, and her body was so cold and she made the minutes he spent on top of her seem so tedious that he lost interest and desire. She didn't criticize him or complain. She just asked, with casual disrespect, "Have you finished?" He would ignore her and get up, numbed psychologically and physically.

He hadn't betrayed her, so he wanted to tell her about the person who had betrayed him, about Nashwa, who had dragged him to the edge of love and then turned out to be an actress, playing with this sheikh, while someone had fun at his expense by recording his conversations with her or taking pictures of him with her. They were definitely spying on him and eavesdropping and maybe taking pictures too. It's true it might have been her that made the recordings and took the pictures, and he was sure she was the one who stole the things that Sheikh Mukhtar el-Husseini had left with Hatem. He had looked for the flash drive and the files and the papers and he couldn't find them. He had accused everyone in the house of taking them, and then accused himself of negligence, but now he knew how State Security had obtained them. That morning when Nashwa had visited him and slept in his office while she was waiting for him, she had stolen Mukhtar's things. He had opened the door that day and found her asleep on the sofa. She was pretending to be asleep, but she had accomplished her mission. Would he find the pictures of him with her in his arms on the Internet the next day? A one- or two-minute show of the famous, upright sheikh in the arms of a young woman lying on him in his bed. Not only that but he came quickly too. What virility! Of course the woman might be his wife, so why would people think he was doing anything wrong? But even if there was nothing wrong about it, it was an affront to his prestige and an insult to his worth, and there would be endless comments about it, and they would fill out the scandal with the girl's story and her allegations. Hatem wondered what she would allege he had done. Would she even need to make up allegations? Surely she wouldn't need to, since everything had really happened.

He wanted to tell Omayma, but he was afraid he would cry out of weakness, not for fear that the world would collapse on his head, but weakness toward Nashwa. He hated the fact that he couldn't bring himself to hate her even now. He had a horrible stabbing headache, not from the flood of disasters that had almost overwhelmed him but from the deceit of a pretty woman he had thought was his angel, sent to bring him mercy. Where was God in all this?

Why didn't he find himself impatient to pray, on his knees, prostrate, imploring God to save him from the thunderbolt that was coming?

He was ashamed in God's presence. He hadn't even said one of the hundreds of prayers he taught people. He didn't address God as you might expect from someone who's been struck by disaster and who asks God to ward it off or to give him some relief. He was shy and embarrassed, because what could he tell God when God already knew? He just stayed at home with the door closed, staring up at the ceiling all the time as if he could see through it to the sky, silent because there was nothing to be said.

So immobilized that he couldn't even pray, he found himself drawn toward an abyss, feverish with a fear that made his body tremble.

He wanted to tell Omayma that he wanted to see his son and to ask her where Omar was. He no longer thought about anything but Omar.

OMAYMA PREPARED EVERYTHING. SHE SAID it would be a bad idea for them to go to visit Omar in the clinic. They might assume he was trying to escape or realize how dangerous it would be if he was free and far away; they might take stringent measures to stop him coming back, or drive him into exile. Hatem was grateful to Omayma for her conspiratorial way of thinking, which stemmed directly from her female cunning. He took the opportunity to tell her, half in conjugal teasing and half in philosophical speculation, that all the conspiracies in the world originated in the feminine side of men and that Islamic civilization was indebted to palace slave girls, who taught men the art of refined living and were not just pretty concubines.

"Your high opinion of women gets you into trouble, Sheikh Hatem," Omayma threw back.

Omayma couldn't be unaware. Her intuition was better than her information. Hatem took the right hook with the desperation of an old boxer who knows that taking a punch is in itself a form of heroism when you can't punch back.

Omayma thought the best solution was for them to take a holiday soon, and not necessarily a short one. She had agreed with him ever since the day after his last show that he was in the last stage of his life as a famous sheikh and a preacher with a mass audience, and that winning now meant cutting one's losses. Neither of them could take it if they cooked up a charge against him and threw him in jail. The disgrace would threaten everything. All he could do then was bide his time for a chance to get out of the country, because all the evidence suggested he had broken the law of loyalty and he didn't think he could easily win back the trust of the security people and, behind them, the presidential palace and the approval of the president's son.

He clearly wanted to win back that approval. He hadn't yet become the obstinate hero.

Omayma made reservations at a resort in Hurghada on the Red Sea. In the winter there was hardly anyone there. Rain pelted down on the balconies and roofs of the wooden beach houses, adding to the sense of desolation and gloom, especially with the long silences between them, interrupted only by remarks about food or about Omar. Their cell phones didn't ring because she had turned them off and used them only when necessary or behind his back. He had no computer, no iPad. They had left technology alone at home. As soon as she went into the hotel room, Omayma pulled out all the wires to the television. At the last moment Hatem had brought with him the complete set of Sayed Qutb's *In the Shade of the Quran*, and lived off it. To make him inconspicuous during the daytime when he was sitting by the pool or by the sea, Omayma forced him to dress like a tourist—in Bermuda shorts and a colored African-style shirt and the kind of hat that the English wear on safari. It may have been the first time in the history of beaches and swimming pools that anyone sat reading Sayed Qutb's work of Quranic exegesis while a blonde European woman walked past him in skimpy beachwear. The contrast between what he was reading and the scantily clad women around him made him laugh at times. Omayma understood how he felt and although she sympathized with him, all she did was look at the water and eat. There was nothing she could say that would help him. On the third day the boredom was killing her and then he felt guilty for imprisoning her with him, and told her he was willing to go back to Cairo with her, to whatever awaited him there, in return for escaping the boredom.

"Don't be silly, Hatem, it doesn't suit you," she said. "If they wanted to do you harm, do you think they would wait till you came back to Cairo? They'd come right to the door of the beach house. We're not hiding from them here, because they knew we were coming before we even arrived. The hotel reservations office, the tourist police, and the State Security office in Hurghada all know. We're hiding from your viewers—the ones who love you and the ones who hate you."

Hatem had to admit she was right. "It is hard to hide. I mean, anyone who reads Sayed Qutb on the beach would have to be a sheikh disguised in a funny hat," he said.

But at the time he felt safe, as if he had escaped. It seemed the president's son hadn't yet decided he was a threat to his reputation because he knew the story of Hassan, his brother-in-law, in every detail. Perhaps he realized that the intimidation had had the right effect, and Hatem had been frightened into silence. What they had done to Sheikh Mukhtar el-Husseini had also helped to deter Hatem, especially now that they had stripped Hatem of the strength that his popularity gave him. And God alone knew what incriminating documents Nashwa had got hold of and handed over to the security people, or maybe they would accuse him of sexually assaulting or raping her if they wanted. The last he had heard before coming to the Red Sea was that all the programs and shows he was doing had been suspended, which confirmed what he was already sure of: that all the television stations would boycott him. In short, as far as they were concerned, he was under control. He didn't pose a risk and they didn't need him.

Hatem and Omayma sat drinking tea on the terrace of the beach house, next to the puddles of water on the gravel surface. It was still raining and there was a chilling wind, while the sun lurked behind a thick cloud that promised more rain.

"Where do you think Hassan is now?" asked Hatem. "Do you think he's left Egypt? Would they let him go abroad and do what he wants there? His sister was terrified they might do something to him, especially when it was clear I'd failed to bring him back to his senses."

"Do you really feel you failed to bring him back to Islam?" Omayma replied.

"He never abandoned Islam, so he didn't need to come back, Omayma. He didn't know anything about Islam and he never found out much about Christianity. I told him his problem was with his father, not with his religion. Sometimes I felt he was just a stupid kid, and sometimes I was sure he was a stupid kid, but it was like he was my kid and sometimes I was frightened how much anger and rebellion he had inside him. When it came to knowledge about religion, he was like everyone in his generation, or rather like everyone in the country. It doesn't go beyond hearing a couple of Friday sermons, in which they dozed off toward the end, or a couple of church services where they don't understand half of what the priest says. But even so, I have to respect his intelligence and worry about how mysterious he is."

Omayma poured more hot water into her cup and the tea bag gradually turned it brown.

"And Nashwa? Did you find out who was behind her?" she asked. His discomfort at the question turned into surprise that his wife was behaving like a sister.

"She's an actress. The Interior Ministry put her up to it, and she probably stole the documents and other things that Sheikh Mukhtar left with me."

"Didn't you ever suspect her?"

"Did you have any suspicions about her?" Hatem replied.

"I didn't have any suspicions because I knew who she was."

Hatem was shocked. "You knew she was an actress and she was playing me for a fool?" he asked.

"As for being an actress, she used to be one but then she gave it up. As for her playing you, well, you like to play, and

418

I didn't think you'd lose that game with her. But it looks like you did."

Omayma stood up with a smile. He took her hand and pulled her back down to her seat. She was surprised but gave in.

"You haven't slept with me for ages, Omayma," he said.

"Have you asked yourself why?"

"Often. But I haven't found an answer."

"Maybe the answer's clear. For four nights now you haven't even thought of giving me a hug, even though we've been together twenty-four hours a day and we've been sleeping a few inches apart."

The confrontation made him feel embarrassed.

"Don't you desire your wife any longer, Mawlana?" she asked.

"But it's you who became cold toward me. The last time we were together I was hurt, but I tried to be a gentleman. I didn't force myself on you and I didn't touch you, out of respect for your decision to reject me. What would you expect me to do if you throw up after sleeping with me? That happened the last two times, and before that you pushed me away so hard I almost fell off the bed. I felt like a disgusting rapist and I didn't put any pressure on you and I didn't have any suspicions about anything."

When he said the word 'suspicions' and saw her reaction, his suspicion became a terrible certainty that was like a slap in the face. When Omayma saw that he had understood, she ran into the beach house in tears as if she couldn't bear the weight of her secret and wanted to throw it off. Hatem stood transfixed, paralyzed by the surprise and unable to think clearly. He followed her in and found her lying on her stomach on the bed sobbing. So Omayma had thrown up because she was disgusted with herself, not with him, because she hated what she had done and not because of what he had done to her. She wasn't cold; she was remorseful that she had betrayed him.

Omayma tired of sobbing and her sobs changed into a suppressed whistling because her face was buried in a pillow and she had put another pillow on her head. Hatem was sitting in the corner of the room and, for the first time since he had arrived, the room seemed cramped and oppressive. He stared at the floor in silence, his senses overwhelmed. He went through a gamut of emotions—shock, anger, crushing sadness, denial, a raging sense of humiliation, contempt for his own carelessness, a desire to hurt her, an inability to imagine anything he could do, pity for himself and then for her, growing hatred of her, and, strangely, a desire to have violent sex with her. The questions that tormented him seemed to pull him deep into a dark sea. Who had she betrayed me with? Had she make love to a man in my bed? Is she still doing it? Had she seen his penis, and had he squeezed her breasts? Was it just one man or had Omayma, the wife of a man of religion and good morals, been whoring around?

Omayma was shocked and terrified. Her arms and legs moved under the bedding but she didn't turn and look at him. She just listened and the bed creaked as her body trembled.

"O God," Hatem stammered in a whisper. "I wonder how Hilal bin Umayya felt when he went to see the Prophet about his wife's infidelity. He told the Prophet he had come home for dinner and found his wife with a man. 'I saw it with my own eyes and heard it with my own ears,' he said."

That was how Hatem felt now—devastated, because he had brought this on himself. The Prophet hadn't wanted to hear what Hilal bin Umayya said about his wife. In fact he almost had him flogged. He told Hilal he needed to produce clear proof of his wife's infidelity, to which Hilal replied that seeing a man on top of his wife was surely enough.

"Do you know what happened then, Omayma?" asked Hatem. "From beyond the seven heavens God took pity on

Hilal and revealed the Li'an verses to the Prophet. The solution was that if a man makes accusations against his wife but has no other witnesses, his evidence will stand if he swears to God four times that he is telling the truth and then swears a fifth oath that God should curse him if he tells a lie. But the wife can avoid punishment if she swears by God four times that her husband is telling a lie and then swears a fifth oath that God should curse her if she is lying. But we don't need to waste time taking oaths because you've confessed. In Hilal's case, his wife was told to think carefully before she swore the fifth oath because she would be punished in the afterlife if she lied. The woman hummed and hawed, beat around the bush and mumbled, then she made up her mind and swore the fifth oath. The Prophet decreed that they should separate and ruled that if Hilal's wife had a child, the child should not take a father's name but no one should call the child a bastard. The Prophet had said earlier that he would be able to tell the paternity of any child by its appearance, depending on whether it looked like Hilal or like the man she was accused of sleeping with, whose name was Sharik bin Sahma. In fact that child grew up to become a military commander in Egypt. See how lucky Egypt is!"

Hatem stood up. Omayma was startled and sat up in bed in fear he might approach her, but he moved away to a corner of the room, then turned around, then leaned against the wall, then walked, then stood stock still and said nothing, then stared at her, then looked away from her toward the ceiling with his head up and his neck stretched out frozen for some moments, then turned to her with a rigid face that frightened her.

"In my capacity as Hilal bin Umayya, I would have had such self-control when I saw my wife with another man that I would have gone to the Prophet to ask him what to do. So I'd like to know if you're still seeing your lover!" Hatem shouted.

Omayma bristled as soon as she heard the question and then lashed out like an enraged lioness, her face wet with tears and snot and the sweat from burying her head for hours between the pillows. She picked up and threw everything she could get her hands on—flower pots, lampshades, pillows, the plates on the table, cups, a key ring. She even grabbed the pictures in wooden frames on the walls and threw them at him, covering the floor with pieces of glass. She threw things at him as if demented, while he tried to dodge them. Although he took some hits on his arms and shoulder he stood still, watching her as she screamed hoarsely at him in wounded pride.

"Shut up!" she said. "How low can you stoop? You think I'm a whore, Hatem el-Shenawi? That's the limit, Mawlana! Did you pick me up off the pavement, or was I a dancer in a video clip that tricked you? I'm more honorable than you or any woman in this country."

With that she collapsed into such a stupor that he thought she might be dead.

In the distance the muezzin gave the dawn call to prayer, possibly through the radio of one of the security men at the beach houses. Omayma was waking up and Hatem was sitting on the balcony watching the sun rise from the sea on the morning of a day that would be a strong contender for the title of most miserable day of his life. The hotel staff had heard Omayma screaming and smashing the contents of the room, although it was some distance from the main offices and the hotel building did not overlook the beach houses. But because there were few guests around in the winter lull, apparently people were all ears for the scandal raging in the sheikh's beach house. They knocked on the door and Hatem opened it quickly. He was unsure what to do with Omayma because she was lying rigid and her skin had turned sallow. He was worried something bad might have happened to her. He brought in two of the hotel staff quickly and they helped him lift her up and lay her on the bed. One of them called the hotel doctor while

Hatem got a bottle of perfume from the bathroom and almost poured the whole thing onto her face. He patted her cheeks in an attempt to revive her. One of the hotel staff advised him to check her pulse at her wrists. He established that she was breathing, albeit rather slowly and with a rasp. When the doctor arrived, he turned out to be a young man from somewhere deep in the countryside who was taken aback when he recognized Hatem. Hatem told him Omayma had lost her temper when she heard some bad news and had started crying and screaming and smashing things in the room. The doctor diagnosed it as a nervous breakdown. He used his stethoscope on her and took her blood pressure, and then assured Hatem that all was well, especially after he opened her eyelids and shone his little flashlight into her eyes.

Omayma stirred and mumbled, "What's going on?"

The doctor gave her an injection and said it would send her to sleep but it didn't seem to work, because after a while she got up from the bed, wrapped herself in a blanket, and walked slowly and weakly out to the balcony, taking Hatem by surprise. She sat next to him, breathing heavily from exhaustion.

"And what did the boy turn out to be?" she asked.

The question took Hatem by surprise and he didn't know what she meant.

"Which boy?" he asked.

"The son of the woman whose husband accused her of betraying him, or the one who became governor of Egypt. What did he look like? Was he blond and thin like Hilal her husband, or dark and fat like the man she was accused of sleeping with?"

"He turned out to be a bastard, dark and fat," Hatem replied, with a bad-tempered laugh despite himself.

"And what did the Prophet do with her? Did he punish her for lying? Did he have her stoned?"

"He didn't do anything to her. He only separated her from her husband."

She started to sob again, but not as violently or loudly as before. She gave Hatem a deep, sad look.

"I'm sorry, Hatem. I couldn't keep it a secret from you any longer," she said. Is she sorry for betraying me or for confessing, Hatem wondered.

"Do you know why?" she continued. "Because I love you. I love you as my husband and as the father of my son. And because I really appreciate what you've been going through recently and because once again I've seen the Hatem who taught me about religion. I'm ready for any punishment, because I'm guilty. When my friend who works in the bank called me and told me you'd transferred all the deposits to Omar's account and my account, I was very worried about you. Even when I knew you were in love with that girl Nashwa, and although I was jealous, I was more worried about what she might do to you. Ask, so you feel better, Hatem."

"Who was it?"

"I imagine you remember what happened to you after Omar had his accident. Suddenly I found myself alone with my child, who had almost drowned in the swimming pool and had gone into a coma. He had oxygen tubes in his nose and inside him and he was lying in front of me in the intensive care unit. I felt like someone had cut my heart out with a knife and thrown it down on Omar's bed. Remember after that how I asked you about God several times and how He described the mother of Moses as having *a void in her heart*. Well, my heart had a void in it and was lonely. You had abandoned me and Omar at that time in a strange, painful, wounding madness, and I tried to forget about you. What did it mean when our son was in the hospital unconscious and on the verge of death and you left me alone and disappeared? And then I found out you had gone to the mosques and tombs of the holy men to work as a servant, cleaning the washroom for prayers, mopping up in the bathrooms, sweeping the carpets and floors, and sleeping in the street. You were like one of those Sufi dervishes in the mosques of el-Hussein or Sayeda Zeinab. So my husband had abandoned me. The great sheikh, the most famous preacher in the country, had become a crazy dervish. You were the man I went to for protection but you almost went mad and you ran away from facing up to your terrible weakness toward your son and your crazy love for him and your morbid fear of losing him.

"You threw yourself into the mosques so that God would cure your son or relieve your pain. Okay, but where did I come in? I was stuck with my son and I was hurt. I was weak and fragile and I missed my husband. Dr. Adel, the neurologist who was treating Omar, was very kind to me and made friends with me. He was a married man in his fifties but he made me feel that someone was interested in me. One day in his clinic he took me in his arms and I submitted. After that I hated myself and I broke down and I felt that God would punish me and take my son from me, but even so I couldn't resist Adel. He was attentive and said he loved me and was going to divorce his wife and that you were no longer in full control of your mental faculties and I should get a separation. I lived in this whirlwind for a while. Omar was in a coma for seven weeks and you almost drove me mad, Hatem, when you told people about Omar's illness and said he was in a coma for twenty-two days. I don't know where you got that number from. As soon as Omar moved his hand and his body functions started to get back to normal, I realized how confused I had been, with the pain and the sadness and betraying you, and I was unhappy with my relationship with Adel and I asked him to stop looking after Omar and assign another doctor to the case. Omar's condition improved and I began to realize he would need time to recover his health and there were areas in his brain that had been affected by the coma. But I did have him back and he gave me new life and hope, and of course you remember when you came to your senses after Sheikh Mukhtar el-Husseini intervened, may God honor him and set him free, and we went home with Omar and started the physiotherapy and the rehab and everything we went through together."

"And did your relationship with the doctor continue?"

"Of course he tried to resume the relationship," Omayma said. "He put pressure on me and called me. But just as I tried to forget you earlier because you were weak and ran away and abandoned me, I then tried to forget about him because he had exploited the weakness of a miserable woman who was frightened for her son and had been hurt by her husband. He wasn't at all a gentleman, and basically I don't have memories of any of the time I spent with him because I was like a patient who was drugged. I forgot about the sex right away but when you wanted me as a wife I felt that I had betrayed you for nothing and I was so disgusted with myself. And you just gave up and I couldn't believe it."

"And has the doctor tried to get in touch with you recently?"

Omayma sighed.

"The doctor died," she said.

"What do you mean, he died?" Hatem asked in surprise.

"There's no 'what do you mean' about it. He died, about two months after you and I went back home. He had a heart attack while he was operating on a patient and he fell down dead."

Hatem couldn't help joking about it.

"You finished him off, Omayma," he said.

"Not really," she said with a laugh.

The balcony was flooded with daylight and Hatem felt that his head was heavy and his body lethargic from all the events of the night.

"Come on, Omayma, go and rest. Go to sleep because you're tired," he said as he rose and took her hand.

She started crying again and leaned on him as she went into the room.

"Have you forgiven me?" she asked.

"But you haven't forgiven me my weakness and the fact that I fell ill over my son and ran away from you," Hatem replied, helping her lie down on the bed.

"No, I haven't," she replied, with painful honesty. "Something cracked in the way I felt about you, and it tormented me, along with the agony I felt for my son, who's bound to continue to suffer."

"So remind me to show you the program I did about happy marriages in Islam," Hatem said with an uneasy laugh.

"God is forgiving and merciful," said Omayma, her face taut and pained.

He nodded. Tired and overcome, he stretched his legs out over the side of the bed.

"He is indeed," he said. "You know, there's one saying of the Prophet I really like. If all the sayings of the Prophet turned out to be untrue, and just one true one was left, it would be the one where he says, 'If you did nothing wrong, God would find others who had done wrong, so that when they asked for forgiveness, He could forgive them.'"

"Our Sweet Prophet," whispered Omayma in tears.

As they returned to Cairo, he knew there was no going back. The silence between them had been too heavy for either of them to lift since they had woken up, their faces bloated and exhausted, defenseless against the wrinkles of the years.

Hatem was moving painfully slowly, while Omayma dealt with the hotel, the bill, the car reservation, and the flight times, like one of those automated female voices that ask you to press "1" if you want customer service or "2" if you want technical assistance.

In a small plane several rich passengers looked at Hatem in recognition. It was the kind of greeting you give to a celebrity, not to a man of religion; Hatem could tell the two types of greeting apart. The newspapers the passengers were holding were the first thing that brought him back into a world that was closing in on him like a metal ring around his neck, and Omayma added lock upon lock to it. Was it possible, he wondered, that Omayma's betrayal of him had been noted in a file in State Security? It's true it had been some years back, but who was to say that for years State Security hadn't kept files on him and his wife, along with all the other people and their wives? He was afraid to ask her to confess if she had had any other affairs after the doctor who had died. She would think he had classified her as a whore. It wouldn't be good for him if he asked a question that she wouldn't answer properly, if she even answered at all. Hatem couldn't go back to being what she wanted him to be and who knew what she wanted him to be anyway? Why had she confessed to him? She would have done better to keep quiet, keep her secret, not just to protect herself but to protect Hatem from himself and from her guilt.

He would never go back to being her husband in her bed or in her heart, because that's not what he was, and it was absolutely clear that she too hadn't been like that for years. But he couldn't divorce her. He would never deprive his son of his mother, living in his father's house, and anyway he still cared what people thought of him.

They finally got out of the car outside their house. He sat on his favorite seat in the corner of the bedroom while she quickly started to unpack the bags.

"Do you have any suggestions as to how I might react?" he asked her, breaking their silence for the first time that day.

She arched her back and bristled.

"Do as you please," she said.

"So you'd clearly like me to spring to the defense of my dignity and honor, and divorce you," he said. "Or kill you or have you stoned perhaps," he continued when he saw she was troubled. "Especially as you've confessed, so there's no need for me to find four witnesses who saw the act of penetration, and by the way there are some jurists who require that one or all of the witnesses confirm that they tried to slip a thread between the genitals of the man and the genitals of the woman to be sure there was no space between them and that intercourse really did take place."

"You know, you're not only insulting me by what you say. You're also insulting yourself," Omayma whispered.

"Everyone else has already insulted me, so there's only me left, Omayma," Hatem replied calmly. "And while we're on the subject, it would be no use me trying to kill you, because I'm not the killing type and I don't feel angry enough to kill you. Maybe even the opposite. I sympathize with you. I care about you, and myself and Omar, and for all the time we've spent together and everything we've struggled to achieve. Besides, for you to be stoned for confessing to adultery, you'd have to make your confession in person to the appropriate authorities. If I reported you, you could be summoned to testify, and if you denied it, we wouldn't have achieved anything. It would also require the authorities to announce that they were going to start implementing sharia law. Then there would have to be a fatwa from a sheikh and they might come to yours truly and ask me to give a ruling. 'Should we stone her to death, Mawlana? She's a married woman who committed adultery with a married man.' And I would reply, 'Does she have any children?' And they would answer, 'She has a fourteen-year-old son who almost drowned in a swimming pool and went into a coma after they took him out of the water, and he stayed in a coma for twenty-two days—sorry, seven weeks—and then he miraculously regained consciousness, but he was no longer in full physical or mental health. He continued to receive treatment and had to go abroad for more treatment and for education in a specialist clinic that's a combination of a hospital and a school for those with special needs. The woman in question looks after him, Mawlana.' And I would rule that she shouldn't be stoned to death but she should be available to look after her son, so until her son recovers, she's free.'"

Omayma was sobbing, but Hatem continued. "Then they would ask, 'Should she be separated from her husband, Mawlana?' And I'd reply, 'Her husband can forgive her, or he can separate. She has no say in the decision.' 'But Mawlana, what if he forgives her and then some time later the wife thinks her husband is like a pimp and approves of her adultery?' And I would reply, 'That depends on her character. If she's generous, she'll think her husband is either kind-hearted or easily fooled. If she's not generous, there's no harm in a pimp marrying a whore.'"

Then came the long days of disengagement: Hatem had no one to see and nothing to do. He treated his new-found freedom as if it were a gift from God, because the only possible outcomes in the long term seemed to be imprisonment or banishment. Things had calmed down suddenly and the tears dried up. He came back from their holiday and found that the furor on websites had subsided and they had lost interest in him and his circle and in Mukhtar el-Husseini. Apparently the massive remote control that was in the hands of the country's security services had put an end to all discussion of the subject overnight. It was an extraordinary show of submission to the security services and their ability to emasculate all those television stations and programs—the presenters, the sheikhs, the broadcasters, the whoremongers—as well as the newspaper columnists and reporters, all in one fell swoop. Hatem tried to call Mukhtar's mother but he couldn't get through. Her phone was out of order or out of service. He hadn't heard anything about Mukhtar's case being sent to court or about him being released. He expected they had already fulfilled the promise they gave him that the case would be wrapped up, so what was happening to Sheikh Mukhtar now, Hatem wondered, and where was he?

Khodeiri and Sirhan undertook to stay in the house with him. They reminisced about the past, with smiles and sighs of sorrow. No phones rang because the contracts had been revoked, the programs canceled, and the lessons banned. No friends called either, because he didn't have any friendships. His father came to visit, accompanied by his wife, who took a shot at figuring out what was going on in his relationship with Omayma.

"Are you upset with each other?" she asked. "God protect us from evil."

The three of them—Hatem, Omayma, and Hatem's father—ignored her. His father did refer sadly to the fact that Hatem was under siege and out of work and suggested he try to find out why the authorities were angry with him (which Hatem already knew, of course), and try to placate the people who were hostile toward him. Hatem knew his enemies had been kind to him and the only way to placate them was to submit and hide away at home until they summoned him. No group or movement saw Hatem as a hero, and neither did he. He couldn't find anyone who felt sorry for him. Since the smear campaign against him, even his old followers on Facebook had been regularly dropping him, Omayma told him. Not many stuck with him or pinned great hopes on him. He had lived a two-faced life—the scholar and the merchant of learning, the original thinker and the conformist—and he had never let either side win total victory, out of fear for his livelihood. He really was 'Mawlana' in both senses of the word: it could mean 'our master or leader,' but it can also mean 'our servant or follower.'

Khodeiri surprised him one day as he put a cup of coffee on the table in the garden for him.

"Mona Ramzi called, Mawlana," he said, "and asked you to call her as soon as you find time."

"I'm certainly not short of time. Why didn't you tell me when she called?"

"You were asleep upstairs at the time, Mawlana."

Hatem phoned her. Her voice sounded as soft as ever, although she had given up acting and had started wearing the hijab, a pioneer in the long list of actresses who became known as 'the penitents.' In fact she had tried hard to defend acting and she hadn't renounced it in principle. She had only renounced her own acting. Acting was one thing and Mona Ramzi's acting was something else entirely. If acting was a woman in a bikini walking in front of the camera then Mona Ramzi was a great actress because her breasts were renowned well before the invention of silicone. Hatem once met her in the lobby of a religious television channel in which she was apparently a partner and she had joked about not being able "to find a solution for her breasts," as she put it. She couldn't find a gown or a shawl that would disguise them. She was more than seventy years old and for twenty of those years she had been wearing the hijab and living in seclusion, but she still remembered that sheikhs don't get embarrassed. Hatem told her that a woman's breasts were the most important part of her body and that they were mentioned in the Quran.

"The phrase in question, Madam Mona, means '*draw their head coverings over their bosoms.*'" She laughed and said, "And the breasts they have these days, is it halal to show them off?" as she walked off laughing, leaning on the arm of an assistant.

His face lit up when he spoke to her. "To what do I owe this honor? To have Mona Ramzi herself ask after me," he asked.

She laughed like a lewd old woman.

"The honor is ours, Mawlana," she said.

She waited while Hatem mumbled something complimentary and thanked her.

"Of course I know our phone calls are all on air and monitored," she continued, "but you know me, Mawlana. I'm a woman who doesn't get frightened and who doesn't care, because I never do anything that would make the Lord angry, and the Lord knows that, and Brigadier Salama knows too."

He laughed at her self-confidence, and she laughed back even louder.

"You know what?" she continued. "I'd like to see Salama on the Day of Judgment and beat him with my shoes, and you know what? That would weigh heavily in the balance as one of the good deeds I'd done."

"Okay, but he might be listening to our conversation and he might cause you problems," said Hatem.

"I couldn't have said that to you while he was still in the police force, but thank God, he's gone to hell."

"He's retired?"

"No, he's six feet under. I cursed him every day at every prayer, on the prayer mat. 'O Lord,' I said, 'let me one day see Salama Abdel-Muhsin Fathel-Bab al-Gizi meet his comeuppance.' And in the end he died a fitting death."

"Oh my God!"

"You know what happened? He fell into a sewer. He really gave me hell, Mawlana, and I even complained about him to the interior minister. Would you believe it, three interior ministers came and went and none of them treated me fairly. So now, whenever someone calls me from the ministry, I say, 'Look, Mister, if you're going to do wrong by me, you'd better pick your sewer pretty quick.'"

Mona continued with the sewer story, until Hatem interrupted.

"Was that Salama guy from State Security?" he asked.

"No, Mawlana, he was from the waterways police."

"What on earth did you have to do with the waterways? I know you had your ways, but waterways, that's ridiculous!"

Mona cackled with laughter, then dropped the punchline.

"The bastard was my husband!" she said.

Hatem played back the whole conversation from the start in his head and let out a long laugh.

"Great to chat with you, Mawlana," she said, "but look, I called you up and I swear if it wasn't for my health I'd come and see you at home."

"It would be an honor."

"The honor would be ours. But look, I have a small company that my grandson's running. He's a young lad but very smart. It's a ringtone company."

"A what company?"

"Cell phone ringtones and things like that. And we wanted to make an ad for the new Islamic ringtones. The call to prayer and a few prayers. We'd like you to do us the honor of doing the ad in your voice. It's a one-minute job."

Hatem felt insulted, but he decided to let it pass. "Of course. Send your grandson over and we can arrange a time."

"Thank you, Mawlana," she said, "and by the way I'm sure we won't disagree on the money. I know I'm just a very humble old woman and not at the same level as you, but the advertisement will have your baraka."

"What money, Madam Mona? I'll do it as a gift and if you want, I'll do you a ringtone as well. In fact I'd be very good at that."

"That's sweet, Mawlana, really. Listen, I don't want you to get upset about that girl Nashwa. She's a poor girl, I swear."

The shock made him reel in his seat and his face twitched. He felt dizzy as if her words were twisting around him, circling his neck.

"She's had a really hard life," said Mona. "She failed at acting and she took up the hijab here in my house. Then she went to the Institute of Missionaries and studied for a master's as well. She's enlightened and the Lord blessed her with a love for learning, but she got into trouble and what she did to you she did unwillingly, I swear. If you knew how she felt you'd feel sorry for her."

"Which film is that from, Madam Mona? Is it *A Very Naughty Girl* or *Love on the Desert Road*?" Hatem asked coldly.

"God bless you, Sheikh Hatem. Do you think I'm pulling your leg?"

"No, sorry, I think you've already pulled it."

"You really do have it in for her, don't you?"

"I feel very bitter."

"But you still remember my films, *A Very Naughty Girl* and *Love on the Desert Road*. You're the naughty one, Mawlana. And by the way, when my grandson sees my films he says 'You were totally hot, grandma.' Niazi Mustafa, may he rest in peace, before he was killed, used to say to me, 'Fatin Hamama is the lady of Arab cinema and you, Mona, are the breasts of Arab cinema!'"

Hatem tried hard to keep Mona from going through the rest of the body parts of Arab cinema. When the conversation ended, he couldn't help praying to God to forgive Salama Abdel-Muhsin al-Gizi.

Omayma woke Hatem up in a panic and he came to with a jolt. It was still dark and the muezzin hadn't yet called the dawn prayers. Hatem had been sleeping for about two hours. Omayma was pale and was shaking him by the shoulder.

"Has anything happened to Omar?" he shouted.

His question unexpectedly helped to calm her down by reminding her that there were things more frightening than whatever it was that had frightened her. She fell silent and thoughtful, as if she was recovering her strength.

"They've blown up a church," she said.

Hovering between restless sleep and being awake and tense, Hatem didn't understand. "What do you mean exactly?" he said.

"A church has been blown up and it looks like a lot of Copts have been killed."

Hatem woke up properly and jumped out of bed.

"And Hassan?" he said.

Omayma nodded. "That's what I said too. I was worried about Hassan. My heart tells me that Hassan's in danger. I immediately connected the explosion with Hassan," she said.

She reached out for the remote control and switched the television to a news channel that was reporting the explosion.

"I was watching a movie," she explained, "but a friend of mine called me and told me about the explosion at the church. I went online and found the news and then I went through all the channels till they started reporting on the event."

The details started to pour in. Hatem and Omayma moved into the living room and turned both televisions on to different channels covering the same event, and turned on their iPad to pick up any extra details. Omayma showed him a Coptic website that had pictures of the dead, with bodies blown up and mangled limbs. They looked through the faces of all the young men who appeared—whether dead, or injured, or rescuing the injured, or shouting angrily about the killing.

At midnight, hundreds of Copts had been gathered in a church hall for a performance of a play put on by young people from a church in Zeitoun when they heard a car alarm. The alarm didn't seem to be working properly because it went on and on without stopping. Two young men went out to find out what was going on and were standing on the pavement looking for the vehicle that was making the noise when another alarm started up from another vehicle and the noise became unbearable. The young men asked the guards at the church to intervene, but the guards were pathetic and indifferent. One of them said, "The car probably belongs to someone in the church." One of the men from the church went up to the guard and shouted, "Why don't we figure out which car it is first?"

One of the church ushers appeared at the door to find out what was going on and called the two young men over. One of them went over to the usher to explain while the other kept shouting angrily at the guards. Suddenly the alarms stopped and the only sounds to be heard were the passing cars and the footsteps of people on the pavement opposite, where there was a bank with a big glass window, closed at that time of night. Then there was the boom of an explosion from inside the church hall and pieces of concrete from the walls of the hall flew into the air like a fireball, blasting everything that stood in the way. A gap in the shredded concrete and the twisted reinforcement bars revealed a hall choked with smoke. There was the deafening sound of wooden beams crashing to the floor, flames cracking and popping, and window panes shattering. Through the gap a man emerged from the grey smoke, reeling and staggering. He had lost an arm and his chest was spattered with blood. He fell to the ground unconscious. Dozens of Copts followed, screaming and looking around in confusion as they came running out of the hall in terror, as if on the Day of Judgment, fleeing the flames and the smoke and the bleeding bodies that covered the floor and the stairways. People were pushing and shoving to escape and to save the injured. Some shouted for people to call ambulances and others were angry that the fire brigade had not yet shown up. Then the tone shifted to expressions of defiance, and outrage at the injustice, and prayers to God and Christ and the Virgin Mary for help. Two priests soon began to organize people to save the injured and instructed people what to do. Young people still wearing their costumes for the play gathered around them and obeyed their instructions. Suddenly the alarm on one of the vehicles started up again giving everyone a start and, seconds later, the vehicle itself exploded in a ball of fire that melted the asphalt and sent a wave of death and destruction down the street, picking up and then dropping everything in its path. The blast ripped up paving stones and sent them flying in all directions, along with shards of glass and pieces of metal from the parked cars, impaling, smashing, and tearing into the flesh of the people standing nearby.

Then there was just the groaning, the sighs, the rattling sounds, the rasping, the sobbing, and the bleeding.

Hatem called Hassan's phone but was told it was 'out of service.' He didn't stop trying to call him for the next twenty-four hours.

Omayma called Farida from Hatem's phone but she didn't answer. There was just a short recorded message.

Hatem woke up Sirhan and did his best, with explanations and insults, to remind him of the priest they had once visited in a church outside Cairo to get him to dig out the priest's telephone number. Sirhan started stammering drowsily, telling some story about his cell phone, the gist of which was that the phone was broken and the memory lost.

Hatem spent the rest of the day counting the dead and looking for their names. Omayma looked on websites, especially the Coptic websites, while Hatem checked the television stations. Omayma shouted out twice when she came across the name Boutros among the thirty dead whose names had been announced. Hatem stopped at the same name among the seventeen in the second batch of victims. It was a total of forty-seven killed, men, women, and children. The media were careful to give prominent coverage to an Interior Ministry statement that said there were three Muslims among the victims, ignoring of course the fact that two of them were the guards at the church, and they later found out that there was no third Muslim.

Hatem tried to get in touch with the hospitals that took in the victims through the hot line that the Ministry of Health had announced but he discovered that the line was completely dead. Omayma spoke to every doctor she had met since childhood and the ones in her new social clique in an attempt to obtain any scrap of information from the hospitals. The Coptic websites started to publish photographs of the victims, and there was only one person called Boutros left and they were worried it might be Hassan.

That afternoon, when they were both exhausted, Hatem asked Omayma, "Why are we so worried about Hassan? By what kind of crazy coincidence could he have been in that particular church at that time?"

Omayma agreed and they realized they had upset themselves more than necessary.

"Either Hassan was there or he wasn't there, let's hope," she said.

Despite his exhaustion, Hatem rushed back to his iPad and, with trembling fingers, looked for something that was troubling him. Puzzled, Omayma asked him what he was looking for. He didn't hear her, so she sat behind him as he browsed.

"Why are you looking at that website?" she asked.

It was a website that specialized in attacking Christian missionary activity in Egypt and the bombing was on its home page.

As Hatem read the lines to himself, he muttered, "I want to know what the play was about, the one they were performing when the bomb went off."

He stopped anxiously on two lines at the end of the story. Omayma read from over his shoulder in a loud, breathless voice.

"This play, which has previously been performed in several other churches, is about a confrontation with a terrorist who breaks into the home of a Christian family. When he sees how strong the faith of the family members is, although some of them have been killed, the light of the Saviour shines in him and he converts to Christianity," it said.

"I doubt that information is correct," said Hatem, after Omayma had finished reading. "But for sure it's been planned. The explanation is meant to counteract the sympathy people feel for the victims and suggest excuses for the killers."

So far no one had claimed responsibility for the explosion.

Mona Ramzi's grandson sat on the other side of Hatem's desk. He had brought along a computer that was way too advanced for Hatem to understand. Hatem broke into a big smile at the contrast between the amazing modern device and the way her grandson was dressed. In a loose gallabiya that stopped short of his ankles and an Afghan-style turban, and with a long shaggy beard, he looked like he had just arrived from the Abbasid era. He had dispensed entirely with a mustache and he was holding a traditional tooth stick with which he cleaned obsessively between his teeth. He had a big brown mark on his forehead from bending forward and touching the ground when he prayed. Hatem learned that the man's name was Hadhifa and that he was twenty-three years old.

He decided to ask him a question he had asked himself dozens of times: "Why do you think it is, brother Hadhifa, that of all the Muslims in the world it's only those in Egypt who have prayer marks on their foreheads? Is it some genetic feature unique to Egypt and nowhere else?"

He had the impression that Hadhifa was taken aback by the unexpected question.

"What do you mean, Mawlana?" he said. "All Muslims who pray develop a mark on their foreheads from prostrating themselves."

"Who told you that?" Hatem replied. "Come, let's turn the television on and watch any Arabic religious channel and take a look at the sheikhs and the audience and the speakers, or let's go to Mecca on pilgrimage and you'll find that only the Egyptians, in the million circling around you, have prayer marks. Or go and get a picture of Osama bin Laden and Ayman al-Zawahiri together. They're brothers in arms, they've slept in the same camp for years and prayed together in the same mosques for days on end, but even so it's Ayman al-Zawahiri who has an obvious prayer mark on his forehead, whereas there isn't a trace of one on Osama bin Laden."

"But it says in the Quran, *their marks are on their faces, from the trace of prostration*!" Hadhifa said in surprise.

"And who told you, Hadhifa, that 'their marks' refers to prayer marks? Prayer marks have nothing to do with the marks mentioned in the Quran. There are different opinions on these marks. There are several accounts attributed to Ibn Abbas in which it refers to a radiance or a whiteness on their faces on the Day of Resurrection, in other words, nothing to do with this world to start with. There's also an interpretation that says it means their faces are yellow from not sleeping, and in that version it says that if you saw them you'd think they were sick, but they're not."

Hatem stopped when he saw that Hadhifa wasn't concentrating.

"But Hadhifa, who gave you the name Hadhifa?" he asked, getting back to basics.

"My grandmother Mona. Because in a dream she saw Hadhifa the Companion of the Prophet and he told her he wanted her as a wife but only after you wear the hijab, Mona, he said. She woke up from the dream, gave up acting, and started wearing the hijab," Hadhifa replied.

Hatem liked the story.

"That's very strange!" he said, hiding his sarcasm. "I mean, Companions of the Prophet who are better known than Hadhifa might have visited her in her dream, but it's very strange that it should have been Hadhifa in particular. Did your grandmother tell you how she'd even heard about Hadhifa?"

"Didn't you know she acted in the film *al-Qadisiya*?"

Hatem was surprised. "Really? But what's *al-Qadisiya* got to do with Hadhifa ibn al-Yaman?"

"He was in the film."

"No, come on!"

"Yes, and that's why she remembered him."

"But I think Hadhifa took part in the battle of Nahavand and not the battle of Qadisiya," said Hatem, "but it's not important because it sounds like the actor who played him was amazing."

Hadhifa gave him the text of the advertisement and a small microphone attached to the computer and asked him to read it several times. Hatem sighed, then began to read.

"The Muslim ringtone," he said.

Hadhifa interrupted him, finally took the tooth stick out of his mouth, and said, "No, Mawlana, we want it to be moving and solemn."

Hatem laughed heartily. "Okay, Hadhifa, I'll be solemn right away," he replied.

Hadhifa finished the recording and started to pack up his stuff. He put his hand in his pocket and took out a wrinkled envelope with crumpled corners, and offered it to Hatem, who assumed it was his fee for the recording. The amount in the envelope clearly wasn't very much, in fact so little that Hatem felt as insulted as he had been when he found himself doing voiceovers for adverts, like an amateur or a fading celebrity. Hatem declined to take the envelope and told Hadhifa that his work was a gift to his grandmother, but Hadhifa left the envelope on the desk anyway. Hatem felt his telephone vibrating. He glanced at the number and was curious, because the call was from a landline at the Media Production City, where the studios and television stations were based.

"Assalam aleikum," he said.

"Wa aleikum assalam. Is that the evangelist Hatem el-Shenawi?"

"Yes."

"This is Medhat el-Shahhat, producer for the *This Evening* program on the Dunya channel. We'd like you to take part in a phone conversation on the program and give us your comments on the explosion at the church," said the caller.

Hatem was surprised. He assumed this was some young man who hadn't heard he'd been banned from the airwaves.

"I can't, Medhat," he said. "Forgive me but I'm busy right now."

Hadhifa took advantage of the fact that Hatem was busy on the phone. He shook Hatem's hand and walked toward the door. Hatem took advantage of the call to accept the envelope.

"But Mawlana, what you say at this time and about this incident is very important and we all need to hear it," said Medhat.

Hatem was shaking Hadhifa's hand and escorting him to the front door. Sirhan then went out with him while Hatem tried to end the conversation without being rude to the enthusiastic producer.

"I'm not playing hard to get, I just can't do it."

The producer insisted. "We only need you for two minutes," he said.

"Who's the editor-in-chief of the program, Medhat?" Hatem asked impatiently.

"It's Mr. Mushir el-Shenwani."

"Is he with you in the control room?"

"Yes, he's here."

"Okay, ask him. Tell him you've got Hatem el-Shenawi on the line and you want me to speak on the program. Tell him and let me hear what he says."

"But he asked me to call you. Anyway, here's Mr. Shenwani for you."

The new voice was different, rougher. "Mawlana," he said, "I miss the great scholar. We haven't seen your face on screen for a while." The tone was welcoming but a little harsh.

"God preserve you, Mushir," Hatem said sharply. "But it looks like young Medhat isn't fully informed of the change in circumstances, so please accept my apologies for not being able to speak on the program."

Mushir reacted with a whole dramatic performance. "No, not at all, Mawlana, we'd be honored to have you speak. Don't worry about us. I have with me a list of names sent by the Ministry of Information, on headed notepaper with a seal and from the ministry's fax machine, and it lists the ten sheikhs and eminent scholars that the television channels should ask to comment on the church incident, and your name is number three on the list."

Was it a mistake? Would the person who made the mistake pay a price? Was it a gesture of approval to bring him back under their patronage? Hatem had no ready answer but before long he was doing a fifteen-minute call-in interview with the program, condemning and denouncing the attack on the church. He trod cautiously for fear he might lose the chance to go back on air that loomed on the horizon.

When they punished him they gave him his freedom. When they pardoned him they put him back in their cage.

Hatem was free when he was banned from television and from making any other public appearance: no one asked him to say anything he didn't want to say or even to say anything at all. But now just by offering him, whether deliberately or by mistake, an opportunity to make a comeback, he found himself unable to resist the temptation. He began calculating what he could say and what would make them angry and what would make them happy and win their approval.

He hated his own vulnerability, which followed him like his shadow. He started going over in his mind what had happened to Mukhtar el-Husseini and to him and Hassan, as a way to maintain his self-respect and keep his distance from the temptations of the limelight. But the lights certainly caught his attention.

THE INSTRUCTIONS FOR THE EVENT were clear: "Brigadier Ahmed el-Faisal will come and take you himself because you won't be able to reach the cathedral in your own car and because you'll go with him first of all to the headquarters of the Sheikh of al-Azhar. Don't worry, we'll take you back home when it's over."

Everything had happened in such a rush and in such confusion that he had abandoned any residual objection to the idea of reverting to his old role as sheikh of the red light. For a time he had harbored hopes that he no longer needed to operate in their world. He thought that the fact that those in power were angry with him had put an end to the uncertainty and made his decision for him, but in just a few hours his powers of resistance had collapsed and the lure of resuming his role in the theater had taken charge. Once you start acting in the theater, you run the risk of becoming the person whose role you play and your life becomes a drama in itself.

The invitation to the event in the cathedral strongly suggested they had put him back on the stage and that he was still a star that the director needed. His telephone had rung and the screen had shown a private number. He sighed and took a deep breath, then answered. The man on the other end was Abul-Makarem el-Sebai, the office manager of the president's son.

"Mawlana," he said, "you were interesting and informative in your comments on television yesterday."

445

"May God honor you and keep you, Abul-Makarem Pasha. It was an honor," replied Hatem, trying to disguise his jubilation.

"It was a horrible and tragic incident," Abul-Makarem replied, combining a somber, dignified manner with the tone of voice of a fridge thermostat. "It confirms that Egypt is being targeted and that foreign forces are lying in wait to attack this country, which is peaceful and stable. They're trying to strike at us by creating strife and chaos."

He didn't wait to hear what Hatem thought of his geostrategic analysis, but went on to explain Hatem's assignment.

"We're all at the service of this country at a time when it needs us and expects us to save it from the crisis. Thanks to God's will and the wisdom of our great president, who is a symbol and guarantor of stability for all Egyptians, the crisis will not give rise to any strife between the two elements of the nation. Mawlana, we've welcomed a great initiative on the part of our men of religion, who are going to get together as a delegation to visit the Pope in the cathedral to offer their condolences and preach in the heart of the church about Islam's tolerance. They're going to say long live the crescent and the cross and there's no difference between Muslims and Christians, we're all Egyptians. You're one of Egypt's greatest and most famous evangelists and people love you and trust you so you have to be there with us in the delegation, so that we, and the Copts and the whole world, can hear from you and from the other eminent sheikhs about how Islam condemns this cowardly terrorism. In fact, as soon as the interior minister and the minister of information put the idea to the president's son he presented it enthusiastically to the president. Between you and me, they drew up the list of names themselves and you were high on the list, Mawlana."

The assignment declaration was over. Hatem thanked the man for his exhaustive and fascinating presentation. He obeyed the call with mumbled thanks for having confidence in him and with remarks on the great responsibility. Then Abul-Makarem told him that Faisal was coming to pick him up for the mission.

It was still early and he didn't know exactly when Faisal would come, so he decided to sit in his office browsing through books and do the kind of reading he had abandoned when he started making public appearances, because the material he used in his public appearances was all material he had memorized in the past and he didn't need to review any of it. He asked for a cup of coffee to be brought to his office. He had opened the curtains and the rays of the sun flooded the room. He opened one half of the window to let the cool winter breeze refresh him. His heart skipped a beat when he saw the envelope that Hadhifa had left the day before. It seemed to be calling him.

He sat on his chair and picked up the envelope, which was printed with the production company logo. "Hadhifa Islamic Media," it said, and then "Private—to Mawlana Hatem el-Shenawi" in handwriting. Hatem tried to open the envelope where it was sealed, but the edges tore and a flash drive fell out. It took him by surprise. His trembling fingers continued to open the envelope and eventually he managed to pull out the pieces of paper without tearing them, irritated at how well sealed it was. He opened two folded pages. The first was in small, delicate handwriting. His heart beating and his veins throbbing, he realized immediately that it was written by Nashwa. She had signed her name at the end. Impatiently and with troubled thoughts he started to read it.

"In the Name of God the Merciful, the Compassionate," it began. "My sheikh, my teacher, and my love . . ."

The words 'my love' hit him in the spot that hurt him most. The fact that the word came next to expressions of respect brought tears to his eyes.

I know you're angry with me and that hurts and pains me. While I respect your position and recognize your right to it, I am unable to ask you for forgiveness, because my sin is too great and unbearable. God alone knows how wretched I am and I don't know what will happen to me if they find out that I've sent you a copy of the flash drive that Sheikh Mukhtar el-Husseini left in your charge. I stole it from your office on their instructions and I swear by God Almighty that I copied it for you that same day and didn't look at the contents and never thought of trying to find out what was on it. I hid it somewhere that no one could ever come across it and I'm sending it to you through Mona Ramzi and I don't have another copy, because it was left in your care. I no longer fear anything but God, whereas I used to be afraid of devils too. I ask God alone for protection and pray that you don't come to any harm because of me.

Hatem's feelings and thoughts were confused and conflicted. He fluctuated between desire and pain, then he laughed with abandon in spite of himself as he read the last line.

By the way, I've applied to do a doctorate on the thought of the Mutazila and my supervisor told me he was a colleague of yours at college and he's sure you're a Mutazilite. So I didn't say anything, Mawlana.

Had he forgiven her? All he knew was he now had visual and auditory hallucinations of Nashwa: Nashwa smiling and laughing, Nashwa frowning, Nashwa playful, stern, and wearing the niqab, with long loose hair, tense and dry when she announced her strange, fanatical opinions, her taunting dance in the film, the way she had stood up in his program and asked him an aggressive question, the way she lay in his arms with beads of sweat on her neck, the time when she stood in front of him draped in loose black cloth that made her look mysterious and gloomy, they way she flirted with him for days and moved closer until she touched him, while she spoke to her masters at night, telling them his secrets and violating his privacy.

After sipping the coffee for a while he noticed the other folded piece of paper. With a nervous wave he again asked Sirhan to keep away for the moment. He made sure the door was firmly closed. He ignored the breeze that had picked up and was blowing the papers on the desk and rustling the pages of a book that was open on the shelf of the bookcase, making a noise like leaves on a windy night. The sun had withdrawn so Hatem put the electric lights on, and read the piece of paper. It was a letter of thanks from the production company for reading the adverts for the ringtones for free. He couldn't help laughing out loud at Mona Ramzi and her grandson with the tooth stick, but he was grateful to Mona for intervening and arranging Nashwa's letter. He thought back to what Mona had told him in the telephone conversation about how Nashwa had been unfairly treated.

He put the flash drive into the laptop and opened the folder. There was a file that looked like a copy of a letter, an audio file that looked like a download of some recording, and a third file that looked like a long text file. Hatem opened the letter file and it turned out to be a scan of a handwritten piece of paper. Hatem thought it must be Sheikh Mukhtar's handwriting, especially as the letter had a stamp that included his signature and his title as the head of the Sufi order. He tried to shift from his feelings toward Nashwa to his responsibility toward Mukhtar and to the onerous and oppressive question of what there was in this file that was so serious that they had to hunt it down when they were persecuting Mukhtar. He suddenly worried that Ahmed el-Faisal might have arrived or called, so he checked his cell and there was a message from Faisal warning him that he was on the way, so he hurried to find out what had made Mukhtar el-Husseini their enemy.

The writer of these lines is Sheikh Mukhtar el-Husseini and this is my testimony to Almighty God, to meet my obligations to the truth and to set the record straight for all Muslims.

Things have come to a head and it is no longer possible to remain silent. We have endured and we have stood firm. We have tried to resolve the disagreement and suppress the anger and pain that we feel. We have reached out to cooperate with good will, but all we have received in return is obstinacy, persecution, deliberate humiliation, the harassment of our families, and the violation of our dignity. We have only God to whom we can appeal for protection and we ask Him to remedy the injustice and ease our distress. We appeal to our ally on the Day of Judgment, our chosen ancestor, may God bless him and grant him peace, who was sent by God out of compassion and to show us the way, and whose family was cleansed by God of any impurity. How strange it is that some people lie in ambush for the noble, righteous, and saintly descendants of the Prophet and think God does not notice those who do wrong. God Almighty will eventually show you His signs and you will see what fate they meet, because we have been the victims of daily harassment and persecution—financially, spiritually, psychologically, and in our family lives—by unjust and corrupt policemen and Interior Ministry officials and by officials and civil servants in the provincial headquarters, who take orders from their masters.

All this came about because of a sequence of events that began one day last year, when a former general in State Security came to us, apparently as a Sufi disciple. He came with a friend of ours, a judge who has regularly served the order since he was a young man and law student. Because we liked and trusted this man, we welcomed the general, especially as we do not turn away those who knock on our doors and we do not deny those who come to us with requests. The man cultivated our friendship and found time to help us for months, and one day, when there were only a few members in the place, he told me that Mr. Abul-Makarem el-Sebai had heard how highly people thought of us because of our relationship with God Almighty and wanted to arrange a discreet meeting with us at a quiet time. This was the first time I had heard the man's name and I found out he was the secretary or office manager of the president's son. We willingly agreed. We knew that people said good things about us and believed us to have special powers, although some of this is baseless nonsense. We also knew that in private people gossiped about us having something to do with magic. This idea was propagated by those who found fault with us and it was accepted and believed by those in whose hearts Satan had planted hatred for us and for descendants of the Prophet, because in fact the relationship between us and the Lord is like a lover's attachment to his beloved. We worship Him in love, not in fear. We may not be perfect but we dissociate ourselves from anything associated with Satan or Iblis. When Abul-Makarem el-Sebai came to see us we found out that he wanted to arrange a meeting between us and the president's son, who was seeking baraka from us, and we were delighted because, although we like to keep our distance from power and from rulers, we told ourselves that God had sent him to us to bring him close to God, to divert him from things that make God angry, to persuade him to do things that please God, and to put him in a position where he could help someone who had been mistreated.

We later found out that it was Abul-Makarem in person who ran the campaign of intimidation against us: he supervised it daily and sent his boss reports morning and evening on what was happening to us.

Saying that he wanted to put his mind at ease, he asked us to come to a meeting at the mansion that the president's son has in a beach resort, because it was the height of summer, may God protect all of us from the heat of Hell. I went willingly and enthusiastically without any companions other than a driver and a member of the order, but they wouldn't let them into the mansion, an arrogant gesture that upset us, though we let it pass because we didn't want to make too much of something minor. Until the president's son came in, we thought he would respect the status of the person who was coming to see him in his house, but his coldness and his hostile disdain prevented him from seeing the truth about himself or his visitor. He dashed all our hopes in him and we soon lost all sympathy for him. It quickly became clear that the man we were sitting with was destined to be useless. Despite his arrogance, he seemed troubled when he opened the subject, after some introductory remarks that made us even less sympathetic toward him because they showed that he was ignorant about us and about others. Attached to this file you will find an audio file with a complete recording of our conversation with him and what he said to us. The president's son said, "I've heard things about you that made me ask to meet you to consult with you on a private matter. It should be clear of course that we will be sharing a secret that no one else should be privy to. You appreciate how serious it would be if any of these private matters leaked out and what a bad effect it would have if what I tell you in confidence was disclosed to anyone else." Even a deaf ear could not have mistaken the threatening tone. "In fact," he continued, "the subject is not grave but it is troubling, and I'd like to find a solution through a man of religion such as you, since you are said to resolve such matters."

It was then that I realized that the man's intelligence staff had got their information from ordinary uninformed people, without checking it, so they had set him up to seek help from someone who wasn't going to help him and were implicating me in the failure of something I had never said I could succeed at.

The president's son continued: "A while back I started to have a recurring dream. In fact it's a nightmare. At first I took it lightly and tried to ignore it, but it started to occur again and again and put severe strain on my nerves. I started taking tranquilizers but they didn't help in dealing with the nightmare. Because of the headaches, the tension, the loss of concentration, and the lack of sleep, I went abroad and consulted a doctor in London who prescribed some medicines for me, but they were all designed to deal with the side effects of the nightmare. They were anti-depressants or drugs that stop disturbing thoughts, but they didn't stop me thinking about the same subject."

I waited for him to explain, without asking him directly what the dream or the recurrent nightmare was because I gathered that he didn't want to tell me.

"Here's the problem, Mister Sheikh," the president's son continued. "How can I get rid of something that dominates my thoughts and forces me to behave in a way I don't want? I won't lie to you. This conflict is unnerving me and worrying me. I'm worried it will affect my work, and you know how sensitive and important that is, and that it will affect my family life too. In view of my responsibilities I have to keep my stress under control so that I look composed in public, and that makes me even more stressed, and I don't know how to break out of this cycle, especially, and I'm going to be frank with you, given that my situation is so critical I've resorted to doctors in America as well, but they told me that the cultural and social differences mean I have to resort to a doctor from my own country and my own culture, language, and religion. As soon as we got to the word 'religion,' I said 'That's that.' I did research until I decided to resort to you and ask you, in confidence."

He had used the word 'resort' several times, but his arrogant tone was incompatible with the idea that he thought he was seeking refuge. I couldn't avoid asking the president's son the inevitable question about the nature of the dream. When he replied, he was not only hesitant but also aggressive.

"I dream that someone naked is taking my clothes off, then throwing me down on my stomach. I'm submissive and I can't resist him, and then, you can guess the rest of course," he said.

I found his dream as puzzling as he did. But I noticed that his face relaxed once he had gotten the dream off his chest.

"Does the dream recur in the same form every time?" I asked.

"Well, it can vary," he said.

"Does the same person always appear in it?"

"At first it was the same person, but later that changed."

"Are they people whose faces you recognize?"

"Some of them."

"Did the dream occur in your childhood, your adolescence?"

"I can't say I had the same dream when I was young, but it's possible. You forget things easily as a child, you know. Anyway, this began not so long ago and started to recur."

"May I know how long ago that would be? Do you mean a year ago? Or more? Or less?"

"Some time ago."

"Is it connected to a situation you were in recently, and then the dream started after that?"

"It is."

"Might it be possible for you to tell me about the situation?"

"I don't think it's important," he said.

At that point I made the biggest mistake of my life. I looked at his fingers drumming on the arm of the chair, at his blank stare, the pallor of his face, his chin held high, his head turned toward the void, and his dry smile. Suddenly black rings seemed to spread under his eyes.

"This isn't a dream, is it?" I said. "It's real, and we want to find a solution, if I've understood correctly."

His veins bulged, his eyes glazed over, and his face twitched. He jumped to his feet and I had a feeling they were going to come across me drowned somewhere that very night. I was too frightened to move but he went back to his seat and sat down after a tense moment of hesitation. The strange thing was that he resumed his air of superiority, though now it seemed to be just a defense mechanism.

"So, do you have a solution, Sheikh Mukhtar? And please, don't tell me to read the Quran and seek God because I've already read the Quran several times to try to overcome this weakness. I've gone on pilgrimage, I've prayed, I've fasted, and given alms to try to get rid of this weakness, which has started to take control of me."

Then, as if he had finally thrown off his protective shell, he said, "I hate my weakness. I don't want it to break me. I can't stand my secret."

In fact I was very understanding and sympathetic but I didn't have any solution to offer. I don't know that there even is a solution in such cases.

"Really, sir," I said, "I'll try my utmost. I'll pray for you until you find peace of mind."

I wanted the meeting to end, because each of us had just discovered that the other was powerless. He had confessed his own secret weakness and I had admitted my own inability to help. Thank God he said a quick and abrupt goodbye and told me to get in touch with Abul-Makarem if there was anything I wanted to tell him, and off he went. A few minutes later Abul-Makarem came in, apparently quite unaware of what had happened. He kept up his cheerful, welcoming tone as he escorted me to my car.

A few weeks later a relentless campaign of harassment began. One of the members of the order took me by surprise by taking my hand one day and slipping into it what I later discovered was a recording of everything that had taken place in my meeting with the president's son. I still don't know who was eavesdropping on the man who holds the keys to the country and has access to reserves of influence and money. Who decided to give me the thing that I believe has so far given me immunity from the most serious consequences?

Sirhan came in to tell Hatem that Brigadier Faisal had called him from the car a few minutes earlier but he hadn't replied, and now the brigadier was waiting for him at the gate.

Hatem hurried to pull himself together. He shut the office door and then went back, opened it, went to the open window, locked it shut, then went out again. He put the key in his pocket for the first time, and went off to where he was awaited, dispirited and confused.

Ahmed el-Faisal got out of the car as soon as he saw Hatem coming. He rushed toward him, embraced him, patted him on the back, kissed him on the shoulders. Hatem had the distinct impression that the man was deranged. Such a transformation in someone who has been tormenting you, humiliating you, trying to deprive you of your livelihood, spying on you, strangling you with his own hands and who then puts on a show of warmth and affection, as if you were old friends meeting after a long absence, must be, if not a sign of an illness that needs treatment, then at least of the kind of disease that would persuade you to steer clear of a person who behaves in such a manner. Hatem sat down next to him in the back seat of the car. He was wearing his religious vestments—the kakoula, the gown, and the turban on his head. Someone else, apparently of lower rank, was sitting next to the driver. Hatem greeted them. Hatem was in an emotional state after what Nashwa had done and what Mukhtar had confided to him. He had completely overcome his anxiety about returning to the life of a celebrity. As he was going out to meet Faisal, he had caught sight of Omayma. She was looking at him sympathetically, with none of her old distaste for him. He realized he had forgiven her because she had not forgiven herself.

"Look after yourself," Omayma said.

"As soon as I get back we have to go and see Omar or you can call up and have him come back," he replied with a smile.

*

Faisal noticed that Hatem's mind was elsewhere, so he decided to make conversation.

"Was all well in Hurghada?" he asked.

"What about Hurghada?"

"Your holiday, Mawlana."

Hatem smiled and his spirits started to lift.

"I bet you know all about it, you people. So what do you think? Was it pleasant?" he said.

Faisal sighed. The car had reached the ring road, which was unusually empty.

"Mawlana, all of us in this world have a machine that we stand at and it's our job to operate the machine, whether that makes people angry or happy," he said.

"Okay," said Hatem, "I'd like to oil your machine and ask you what news you have of Sheikh Mukhtar el-Husseini."

Faisal's lips quivered a little, then broke into a sly smile that he made no attempt to hide. "I told you, Sheikh Hatem, that he'd be released and the case would never go to court," he said.

"Because there was no case in the first place," Hatem said defiantly.

"No, because we didn't want there to be a case," Faisal replied sharply.

"Please, Ahmed Bey, I'd like to be sure the man's safe."

Faisal's face relaxed. "Rest assured, Mawlana," he said, patting Hatem on the shoulder.

"We released him a few days ago and he went to Sudan and he's living in a house in Khartoum. I can give you his address, but we've asked him not to appear in public until things calm down and not to speak to any television stations or newspapers. You know how the Salafists there have been denouncing him as an infidel and saying he should be killed. We were worried the Iranians might try to meet him in Sudan, so we warned him before he left."

Hatem tried hard to digest the news. "And why Sudan in particular?" he asked.

"You may well be surprised. The truth is he had to leave the country quickly and Saudi Arabia refused to give him a visa. We tried to have him go to Kuwait but apparently they were worried that a sheikh accused of converting to Shi'ism would provoke a crisis there. You know about the suppressed tension between the Sunnis and the Shi'a in Kuwait. It was the same story in Bahrain and the other Gulf states, and quite honestly we refused to send him to Lebanon or Libya, so all we had left was Yemen or Sudan, and he chose Sudan, saying he had lived there for two years when he was young."

Faisal changed key. "We want to make a fresh start with you, Mawlana," he continued. "There's a very good chance you'll become the number one sheikh in Egypt, and we know you, and you know us, so we can coordinate with complete confidence and trust. With everything the country's going through—the enemies in waiting, the traitors, the foreign agents, the terrorism that's trying to drive a wedge between the country's Muslims and Christians—everyone in the government has to pull together to win this war. A sheikh like you who's popular, and everyone knows you're independent and you've had your ordeals, even from the government itself, but you're patriotic, and an agency like ours and decent people in the media and politics and even in the opposition parties, we all have to coordinate and plan with each other, just like our enemies and the foreign agents are coordinating with each other to destroy Egypt."

Hatem nodded in agreement. He felt that the face of the man sitting next to the driver was not unfamiliar. He searched through the files of his memory but he couldn't pin down his face or where he had seen him before, but he knew that he had.

The car had driven into the courtyard at the offices of the Sheikh of al-Azhar. Hatem and Faisal got out and walked to some stairs. At the bottom of the stairs some men were standing in black uniforms and with walkie-talkies.

They saluted Faisal as a senior officer, greeted Hatem, and took them off to a hall. As soon as he went in Hatem felt the power of the machine that Faisal had spoken about, the machine where he stood all day doing his dirty work. All the evangelists and preachers from the satellite channels, and the Salafist sheikhs who filled the programs of the religious channels, had gathered together as if it were the day to pay homage to Yazid ibn Muawiya.[5] There were about twelve of the most famous, influential, and popular evangelists of the elegant variety that wore Italian suits and whose programs were interspersed with adverts for soft drinks, bathroom tiles, potato chips, steel factories, and banks. Then there were the ones in short galabiyas and Saudi-style shawls with hennaed beards and whose programs carried adverts for blankets, pots and pans, mountain honey, nigella seeds, and Kardasa cloaks at a hundred pounds each plus delivery charges. The minister of the interior might give a bonus at the end of the day to the religious activities department in State Security, and the president's son and the secretariat of the ruling party might reconfirm their confidence in the interior minister and the information minister for their extraordinary ability to muster all these sheikhs in one funeral tent. Some of them exchanged cursory greetings with Hatem, tinged with shock at his presence since his name had almost been struck off the lists they kept of their rivals and competitors. The sheikhs kissed each other mawkishly on the shoulder or on the head.

Hatem kept to himself in a corner, took out his cell phone, and called Sirhan, who answered after a minute that felt like an age. He whispered into the phone, his mouth shielded by his cupped hand.

"Take the car and go at once to Sheikh Mukhtar's mother. . . . Yes, in their village, Sirhan. And tell her that Sheikh Hatem wants to know if they've really released Sheikh Mukhtar and if he's gone to Sudan. If she tells you this is true then get his address and telephone number from her. . . . Yes, you idiot, in Sudan."

Before hanging up, when he felt the people around him wouldn't notice because they thought that maybe the Sheikh of al-Azhar was coming, or the interior minister himself, he said to Sirhan, "Did you find Father Mikhail's number?" Sirhan's answer took him by surprise.

"Really?" Hatem replied in response. "He called on your phone? It's strange he thought it was my phone. My God, and I've been looking everywhere for him. Okay, I won't be able to call him now. Tell him I'll be in the delegation of sheikhs in the cathedral in Abbasiya with the Pope, and I'll call him later."

When Hatem hung up, he was still wondering why Father Mikhail had called him. Did he want to check on Hassan through Hatem, just as Hatem had wanted to check on Hassan through Mikhail? It would be a disaster if the massacre at the church drove Hassan to do something crazy that would be the ruin of us all. It looked like Father Mikhail had the same worry.

The Sheikh of al-Azhar came in through a side door and walked to the seat of honor at the large round table. Oddly, he was holding the hand of the information minister, who looked happy that the Grand Imam was treating him with such honor, and in the presence of other imams who were grand themselves.

On the wall behind the Grand Imam, Hatem noticed a large picture of the president kissing a copy of the Quran. He couldn't tell whether the reason for the picture was the president or the Quran. The room had arabesque stained-glass windows, high-backed dark brown wooden seats with padded arms, bookcases with glass doors on all four walls, full of books with leather bindings and gilt lettering, a massive chandelier that looked like a replica of the ones in the

Fatimid mosques nearby in al-Muizz Street, and bottles of water around the table and small teacups with filigree holders. Some of the sheikhs had put their prayer beads in front of them on the table, next to their cell phones. They sat there, proud to be present and happy to listen to whatever was said. The Sheikh of al-Azhar spoke gently in a low voice. He talked about going to pay his condolences to the Pope the previous evening and how the wicked and criminal attack on the church could only have been committed by someone who hated Islam and knew nothing about it, and that on the Day of Judgment God would punish anyone who did harm to Egypt. He asked the Egyptian evangelists, sheikhs, and religious scholars present to come with him to visit the Pope and offer their sincere condolences and to enlighten the nation by explaining that Islam was not responsible for murders by the faithless or the sins committed by terrorists and attributed to Islam, a religion that, through its tolerance and compassion, will win over anyone who takes issue with it.

The minister of information listened to the sermon with his head bowed like someone who was hearing such talk for the first time and had just now discovered that Islam was tolerant. His drooping eyelids and his regular nodding in agreement almost made Hatem feel seasick, and when the sheikh stopped talking, apparently satisfied that there was no need to explain what had already been explained or to repeat what he had already said several times, the minister leaned over to him and whispered something. The sheikh then said that now they would listen to the eminent scholar and esteemed professor, Dr. Rifaat Hashem, who might be able, by what he said, to set the outlines for what they should all make clear to Egyptians, Muslims and Christians alike, when they addressed the whole world in the cathedral. Rifaat Hashem, whose mission was apparently to pass on orders from the chairman of the religious affairs committee in parliament, who was the chairman of the same committee in the ruling party, started his speech by thanking the sheikh and praising him so profusely that Hatem thought they must be going to the Pope to thank the Sheikh of al-Azhar.

Then Hashem recited from the Mumtahana chapter of the Quran: "*As for those who do not fight against you for religion's sake, and do not drive you out of your homes, God does not forbid you from showing them kindness and treating them fairly. God loves those who act fairly.*"

They all bowed their heads reverently, endorsing the compliment to Islam and flattering the Sheikh of al-Azhar.

Hatem realized that the more anyone tried to make this farce succeed the more it would fail, but Dr. Hashem didn't give anyone a chance to form their own judgment. Instead he added lots of words about the tolerance of Islam, as though he were trying to persuade his audience of it. Then he struck the blow that hit Hatem the hardest, with the subject most likely to make him angry: how Islam treats the People of the Book, such as Christian and Jews. He said the Prophet forbade their mistreatment or murderous attacks on them, as in the hadith recounted by Safwan ibn Salim, quoting several Companions of the Prophet as saying, "If anyone mistreats someone with whom he has contracted an agreement, or impugns their character, or makes excessive demands on them, or takes something from them with ill will, then I will argue against him on the Day of Judgment." Abu Daoud and al-Bayhaqi related the hadith, and even toughened up the threat against those who violated the sanctity of their blood and attacked them without good cause. Bukhari, citing Abdullah ibn Amr, quotes the Prophet as saying, "Anyone who killed a person having a treaty with the Muslims shall not smell the smell of Paradise though its smell is perceived from a distance of forty years."

Hatem felt he would die if he couldn't speak. Clearly these people hadn't seen the bodies that had been burned or torn apart by the explosions in the church. They hadn't heard the groans and the screams of the injured and the victims' relatives. They hadn't read what the Coptic websites were saying. They hadn't seen or heard or understood the outbursts of Coptic anger and pain.

"With all respect, Your Grace and Dr. Hashem," Hatem broke in impulsively, to the annoyance of all. Hashem's face turned pale and then flushed red, "if this is what we're going to say in the church to console the Copts on their losses, then it would be best if we don't go at all."

There were huffings and puffings and mutterings. Some of the people objected to him interrupting Dr. Hashem.

"Be polite in the presence of your betters," said someone Hatem couldn't identify because he wasn't looking in Hatem's direction.

Hatem tried to continue despite the disruption and despite the irritation evident in the silent reactions of the Sheikh of al-Azhar and the minister. "When you have people who are grieving and feeling persecuted and wanting revenge, it doesn't make sense for us to go and tell them they're dhimmis, which is a label they can't stand in the first place. The country keeps saying "citizenship, citizenship" and then our sheikhs talk to us about dhimmis. Okay, so if the Copts are dhimmis, we should ask them to pay the jizya, stop recruiting them into the army and have done with it."

Sheikh Younis sprang up right in front of him, just like he did with members of his audience on the Rawda channel. "Do you want us to change our religion to please the Copts, Sheikh Hatem?" he said. "I swear, this is our religion and we'll hang on to it and defend it and if people want to live among us by its laws they're welcome and safe, but those who don't like it can go and find themselves another country."

Hatem stood up and addressed the Sheikh of al-Azhar. "Oh, and by the way, Your Grace, I think we should tell the Pope his best bet would be to emigrate," he said.

There were shouts and cries and Sheikh Younis was so excited that some of the other people stood up and tried to calm him down. The minister of information whispered something in the ear of the Sheikh of al-Azhar, who then called for calm in a voice that was anything but. The uproar soon died down and the sheikh took the floor, maintaining the same soft tone.

"In fact, this has been a useful debate and we have benefited from it, though it has been a little heated," he said. "I have a suggestion from the minister of information, a responsible man who carries on his shoulders a burden that would crush a lesser man and who has our esteem for honoring the halls of al-Azhar, which always welcomes those who serve this country, which we hope will remain safe until God inherits the earth and everyone living on it. He suggests that it be a visit by a delegation of ulema to pay condolences in full view of the world and that the eminent sheikhs may then make individual statements to the media one by one but without a formal speech to the Pope and his priests by the delegation as a whole."

When everyone nodded in agreement, Rifaat Hashem looked defeated and peeved. Younis and the group that had rallied behind him were about to lynch Hatem, who suddenly found the minister coming up to him and shaking his hand warmly.

"I thank you for your wise observation," the minister said. "By the way, you ought to work with us in the Ministry of Information."

The minister was joking and Hatem answered back flippantly. "I could work as one of your many antennas," he said.

The joke shocked the minister and he glowered, but Hatem embraced him as if they were school friends. "Don't be angry with me, sir. I couldn't resist. And the dreary sheikhs you brought along rubbed me up the wrong way."

"I understand why the guys at the interior ministry recommended you. They told us you should be with us on the *It's Our Country* program," the minister said with a laugh.

They were walking toward the place where the delegation was being herded onto a bus.

"As for *It's Your Country*, it really is your country," Hatem said.

When he got on the bus he looked at his watch and then at his phone. He was wondering whether Sirhan had reached Sheikh Mukhtar's mother yet or if he was still on his way.

The road was clear and they had an escort of motorcycles of a size that matched the volume of their sirens, ridden by policemen in helmets that covered their faces and boots that came almost up to their knees. They controlled the route taken by the bus, which was accompanied by some black cars in front and some others behind. As the bus approached the cathedral, the sheikhs looked through the windows at the hundreds of policemen lined up in front of the building with weapons, shields, helmets, and batons. From the direction of the cathedral in the distance they could hear the roar of people shouting or chanting, but the words were not clear. The bus drove down the narrow lane that led from the big gate decorated with crosses to the open space outside the cathedral. The sheikhs saw the tension in the police officers who were walking around in the company of church officials. Dressed in black, they were moving quickly and nervously and calling out to each other curtly and at cross purposes because they were so on edge.

As soon as the bus drove into the open space in front of the building with the domes and the round arches, they were surprised to find thousands of Copts taking part in a demonstration at the cathedral, sheltered by its walls. They held up wooden crosses smeared in blood, carried statues of Christ coated red, and waved cloth and paper banners saying Christians were being persecuted, demanding vengeance for the massacre, and accusing the state and the security services and terrorists of committing the crime. Their eyes were red with tears and anger. The sheikhs muttered anxiously and some of them cringed in fear, murmuring fragments of questions as the bus inched forward. The protesters were mixed up with security people, and church officials who had come to welcome the delegation. Young people started jumping up and down to find out who was on the bus. One of them noticed a sheikh's turban and let out a cry, then other people started jumping and peering and climbing up to discover that the visitors were Muslim religious leaders. Suddenly there was no restraint to their anger. The crowd started shouting curses and beating their fists against the sides of the bus, as they chanted in rage. The crowd began to hit the windows of the bus with their wooden crosses, sporadically at first. Then the pace picked up and the windows were smashed to pieces. The sheikhs were aghast and terrified. They huddled together for protection. Then people in the crowd started throwing stones through the broken windows and the sheikhs had to crouch on the floor of the bus to avoid them. They went down on their knees under the seats. The thousands of people shouting terrified the sheikhs, who started screaming and swearing and crying for mercy. Despite the mayhem, Hatem couldn't help gloating over his companions in the delegation, who had imagined they were going to some kind of celebration or a condolence session on television. The Copts were so angry that the lives of this busload of sheikhs were now under serious threat in the chaos for which the authorities were completely unprepared. Some of the priests, the police, and some young Copts tried to calm things down but they were overwhelmed.

Some of the demonstrators were shouting, "Murderers! Extremists! You kill the victim and then walk in the funeral procession! We don't want condolences from you hypocrites. May the Lord exact revenge on you."

On the bus Hatem turned to Dr. Rifaat Hashem. "How about you going out, Dr. Rifaat, and giving them a lecture on the role of dhimmis in Islam?" he asked with cruel sarcasm.

The sheikhs were now so frightened that they were pale and silent. They didn't even notice when the crowd suddenly fell still and thousands of people moved aside to let the bus come through safely. It seemed that intervention by the priests and the cathedral security people had succeeded. But the sheikhs were still stumbling around in the broken glass, their turbans out of place, and their clothes soiled and trampled underfoot in the confusion. They didn't get themselves together again until the bus door opened at the foot of a grand marble staircase that led up to a large platform with double wooden doors carved with Coptic symbols in bright colors. A few clergymen were standing there in their immaculate clothes, their awesome black headgear and cast-iron crosses hanging on their chests. One of them got on to the bus to welcome the visitors, apologize to them, and ask for their indulgence. The people in charge of the bus and some of the sheikhs recognized him as someone important in the church, so they stood up straight and smiled and some of the color returned to their ashen faces, especially when the camera lights came on and two cameras started to film the august arrival of the most famous and most important sheikhs and preachers in the field of Muslim evangelism, come to offer their condolences to the Pope and the church. A quick-witted clergyman quickly put up his hand and stopped them filming. He scolded the cameramen and pushed them out of the way.

Dr. Rifaat Hashem, who was at the front of the delegation as the senior member, turned to Hatem and said, "Sheikh Hatem, why did that priest make the cameramen move away?"

Hatem smiled, knowing how important it was for Hashem to be filmed.

"For a start, he's a bishop and not a priest. Secondly, it was so they wouldn't take pictures of the damage to the bus and the broken glass, which would have ruined the whole story," he said.

Hashem embraced Bishop Mousa, who was standing to greet them with a dignified smile, a kindly face, and open arms.

"Good thinking, Hatem," the minister whispered to Hatem, who was being pushed forward by the crush behind him. "Stick by my side to give me cover," he added.

"Shall I tell them about the dhimmis?" Hatem whispered back.

When they had finished hugging and kissing and were waiting for the rest of the delegation to do the same, Hashem turned to Hatem again.

"What makes you think I'd distort my religion to spare the feelings of the Copts or anyone else?" he said. "Of course they're dhimmis."

"You really think they're dhimmis, doctor? Surely the conditions and requirements for people to be dhimmis came to an end hundreds of years ago," Hatem replied.

Hashem had walked on behind Bishop Mousa, who was going up the stairs. Both of them were muttering polite greetings such as "Pleased to see you" and "My condolences" and "Thank you for your efforts," while Hatem was giving Hashem a piece of his mind.

"If you think they're dhimmis," Hatem said, "we'd have to revive the slave trade and apply the rule that alms money can be spent on converting people to Islam. We'd have to give alms money to the treasury and people could atone for breaking the Ramadan fast or for failing to fulfill their oaths by freeing a slave. We'd have to exempt them from military service and we couldn't get angry if the Byzantine Emperor Nicephorus treated the Muslims in his country as dhimmis too."

Hashem gasped in awe at the splendor of the place and leaned over to Hatem. "Okay, things are Byzantine enough without bringing in the emperor," he said. "Let's just make sure the next hour passes safely."

"If you go on longer than half an hour you'll have to let the sheikhs make speeches, and if one of them drones on about the tolerance of Islam, we'll pay the price and the several thousand Coptic demonstrators in the cathedral may well dissect us like frogs."

They crossed the carpet in the hallway, passing under a vast dome. In an opening in the center of the dome there was a stained-glass window showing the Virgin Mary carrying the baby Jesus. On the walls hung brightly colored pictures telling stories or illustrating parables or conferring benevolent power. Bishop Mousa slowed down and they all slowed down behind him. He looked at Hatem with a smile.

"I'm a real admirer of yours, Sheikh Hatem," he said warmly.

The other sheikhs were surprised and the ones who preached on Salafist stations were annoyed. Hatem realized he had gone straight onto their lists of infidels, no doubt about it. He glimpsed something coded in the way the bishop was looking at him.

"That's an honor, Your Grace," he said.

People were crowding around them now and the cameramen rushed toward them. They realized they had reached the Pope's office, and the Pope had indeed appeared, in his black cassock decorated with crosses, his shiny black headgear, and his white beard flecked with black. He had the complexion of someone from southern Egypt and eyes that looked tired and old. He welcomed them with a smile and opened his arms for Dr. Hashem, while the others tried only to shake hands, keeping their distance or embarrassed by the hospitality or hesitant to be equally effusive in return. When Hatem shook hands with him, the Pope held his hand for a moment and looked deep into Hatem's eyes, to Hatem's surprise. Bishop Mousa went up to the Pope, who tilted his head to hear what the bishop was whispering into his ear. He nodded and squeezed Hatem's hand hard.

"Listen to Bishop Mousa, Mawlana," he said.

Before Hatem could take in the request the Pope had let go of his hand, turned to another sheikh, who shook his hand

and muttered feebly, "I hope that next time we visit it won't be such a sad occasion."

It was clear that the priests in the church were anxious not to say anything to the delegation of sheikhs about the noisy protest that was taking place a few yards away in the heart of the cathedral. Maybe they intended to send two separate messages: that ordinary Copts were angry and vengeful, and at the same time that their leaders were wise, moderate, prudent, patient, and willing to wait for the state to take the next step, but their calm was so exaggerated that it seemed artificial and temporary, or maybe it reflected a deep faith that transcended any desire for human intervention. They sat in the seats allocated to them in the hall while Dr. Rifaat Hashem sat in the chair next to the Pope. Just as he was about to speak, the minister sneaked a glance toward Hatem, who had taken a seat as far from him as possible.

"In the name of God, the Merciful, the Compassionate," Dr. Hashem said. "And may God bless and grant peace to His beloved, the chosen and faithful one. There is no power or strength other than in God Almighty the Indulgent. We are all grievously afflicted and we all feel the same pain. Your losses are our losses, your injured are our injured. How else could it be when we are all Egyptians, born of the same nation under the same skies, living on the same land, drinking the waters of the same Nile, and worshiping the same Lord?"

Sheikh Younis was fidgeting. Hatem, who was sitting right next to him, caught him tapping his feet on the ground like someone trying to hold back a scream. A few months earlier Sheikh Younis had devoted several programs to proving that Christians were infidels. The title he chose was "The trinity is threefold disbelief" and it brought in more advertising revenue for ringtones than any other program in the history of satellite broadcasting. So it was no surprise that Sheikh Younis found it hard to put up with what Dr. Hashem was saying about worshiping one god. Hatem leaned over toward him.

"Rifaat Hashem is about to turn infidel, Sheikh Younis!"

Younis looked at him reproachfully and with distaste.

Hashem was finishing up. "We come to you with patient hearts, willing to wait for recompense in the afterlife. As God Almighty said, '*The patient shall be given their due without us counting the cost.*' Remember that if God takes something from you, then it is His and if He gives you something it is His, so how can you be angry if He takes away what is His? 'What God takes is His and what He gives is His,' as the Prophet said. So if God takes away something you love you should say, 'It belonged to God, He can take what he likes and He can give what he likes,' because if God makes you suffer it is always in order to make you happy later. If He deprives you of something, it is always to do you a favor in some other way. If He takes something from you, it is always in order to give you something else. God will never harm you, because in fact He loves you. As it says in the hadith, 'When God loves a group of people, He sends afflictions to test them. Those who are content win His approval and those who are discontent face His anger.' Al-Tirmidhi cited the hadith and said it was sound."

Hatem felt that Dr. Rifaat Hashem was behaving as if he had come to give the Pope his condolences on the death of a grandson, assuming, that is, that the minister didn't realize that popes don't get married or have children. It didn't sound as if his words were for a massacre that had been committed against Copts in a church and that had caused massive anger and deep sadness among members of the Coptic Church. For a moment Hatem was worried that Rifaat Hashem might slip up and talk about the role of the dhimmis in Islam, so he got up and crept quietly past the cameras, disappeared behind them, and walked on toward a far corner that seemed quiet and remote from the noisy meeting. The eyes of the priests and church security people tracked him as he went. He held up his cell phone as a pretext for moving away, and bowed his head into a corner between a column and a wall and called Sirhan, who had put his favorite song, sung by a young singer who preached abstinence, as his caller tune. He hadn't wanted to deflate Sirhan's enthusiasm by telling him how much the singer earned for a single performance. The song cut off when Sirhan answered.

"Wa aleikum assalam," Sirhan said.

The driver clearly thought of the caller tune as the equivalent of saying 'Assalam aleikum,' so when he answered the phone he went straight to the conventional response.

"Did you make the journey?" Hatem asked him.

"You won't get a word out of her," said Sirhan. "She's not talking."

Hatem didn't understand what Sirhan meant, so Sirhan repeated it, but Hatem still didn't understand.

"Because she's almost paralyzed," Sirhan finally explained, "and she can't speak, but she wrote some words for Khodeiri on a piece of paper. She's very old and sick, it's true, but she's clearly well educated and smart."

Hatem hung up on Sirhan and walked slowly and sadly back to the hall, confident that his suspicions were well-founded.

He suddenly felt sick and stopped, his head spinning. The black gowns on the men by the door suddenly looked white. In his mind's eye he saw swirling colors and a succession of ghostly figures. He heard himself playing music with a blind musician, mixed with the sound of himself reciting the Quran in an empty funeral tent, with adverts streaming across his chest. He imagined strange creatures running between his legs, so many of them that he almost tripped and fell on the floor, but someone pressed on his shoulder and that seemed to stop the drum of the washing machine that was turning in his head. He found his footing and got his breath back and there was a young man smiling at him and patting him on the back as if to strengthen his resolve.

"Don't you remember me, Mawlana?" the young man said. It sounded like he was speaking from behind a fog in a dream.

Hatem looked him over carefully and recognized him. It was the young officer who had been with Ahmed el-Faisal and had been sitting next to the driver. It was then that he realized he had seen him before.

"Have I seen you before?" Hatem asked.

"At Sheikh Mukhtar's, a few years ago," the man said. "My grandfather was a follower of the Sufi order, and I was with him that day."

"So why do I remember you so clearly? I must have seen hundreds of people who look like you, even thousands."

"Because that day you told me I looked very much like you."

"Of course," Hatem said in surprise, like someone who'd been looking for his glasses and then realizes he's already wearing them. "You look the way I looked twenty-five years ago, the way I looked in the black-and-white photo in the first passport I ever had."

"Do you know what they've done to Sheikh Mukhtar?" Hatem asked.

The man squirmed in pain at the question, mumbled something incomprehensible, and vanished into thin air.

Hatem was puzzled. He looked for the man to ask him to explain what he had said because it worried him. But he couldn't find him so he went back to the hall in the hope of finding him there. He turned and saw his reflection in the mirrors in the corners of the room. He really did look as if he had changed into a black-and-white photo, either pale or ghostly.

The audience was growing actively bored and no one knew how the meeting would end. Rifaat Hashem and the delegation of preachers couldn't decide. They seemed to be waiting for someone else to give the order, worried that they might appear remiss if they cut it short or if there was something else required of them that they hadn't accomplished.

The Pope didn't want to say anything that anyone would understand to mean that the time was up and thank you all very much, and those around him were worried the Pope might make a mistake out of exhaustion or illness and the others would think he was disrespectful or inattentive. Hatem wanted it to finish so he looked for any of the security men who had escorted the delegation but couldn't find any of them in the hall, which was crammed with people. He waved to a cameraman who was a familiar face from many years of working in the satellite channels. He went up to him, whispered in his ear, and seconds later the cameraman jumped up and, with the intensity of someone pretending to be important, said, "Dr. Rifaat, do you think you could come to the press conference? The journalists and the television stations are all waiting outside."

It had the effect of a final-boarding announcement at an airport. Everyone stood up before the minister could respond and hurried to exchange kisses and farewells. They raced each other outside while Dr. Hashem was still asking where the press conference would be. The cameraman avoided the minister and looked instead to Sheikh Hatem for help.

"It's downstairs, Your Excellency, down in the lobby," Hatem replied.

Hatem went downstairs exhausted, thanking God that his son Omar had lost his memory, because what was worth remembering when reality produced nothing better than plausible lies. He was walking with the other sheikhs, who were asking each other anxious questions about the way back and whether they would again be stoned and cursed and attacked by angry Copts. Back at the bus, more and more church fathers had gathered around the sheikhs to say good-bye, as if to protect them from the unpredictable protesters.

"Sheikh Hatem, Your Grace," said a young priest, speaking politely and firmly. "Please come this way. Bishop Mousa is expecting you."

Hatem looked at the bus and then at the priest.

"Don't worry, Mawlana," said the priest, reading his mind. "We'll call your driver and he'll wait for you here at the cathedral, or if you want we can give you a lift anywhere you want to go. But please tell the other sheikhs you won't be going back with them."

"I don't think any of them will miss me," Hatem replied.

He followed the priest up the same stairs they had just come down, and then down some corridors that led to another building. The priest told him they were now in the church of Saint Reweis inside the patriarchate. There were paintings, statues, and icons everywhere—on the ceilings, the walls, the columns, the windows, the seats—and candles burning in bowls of oil and molten wax. The candle flames danced in yellows and reds in the lusters of the giant chandeliers hanging from the ceilings. The air was full of the scent of incense and perfumes. For a moment Hatem froze to the spot and a phrase rang in his ears: the words spoken by the young officer who looked like him and then vanished. The officer had spoken the words moments after Hatem asked him about Sheikh Mukhtar. Now Hatem could hear the whole sentence clearly: "God have mercy on his soul," but had he really said that? Had Hatem really heard it?

Bishop Mousa stood waiting for him at an arched wooden door. The bishop smiled and Hatem, exhausted by questions, reciprocated with an inquisitive smile, puzzled at what the secret might be that lurked behind this meeting. Bishop Mousa opened the door and waved Hatem in. Suddenly he was inside a room that had nothing in common with the rest of the church. It was small, the walls were bare of any decoration, and it appeared to be soundproofed. On all four walls there were massive computer screens connected to keyboards on a long wide wooden counter rather like the desks that draftsmen use. Bishop Mousa took Hatem to a small sofa and Hatem sat down. The bishop then took a chair facing him.

"By the way," Hatem said, trying to decipher the atmosphere of mystery and slightly irritated that he didn't know what he was being dragged into, "I've begun to see computer screens as a very bad omen."

The bishop laughed. "They deserve to be seen as bad omens," he said.

At that point a man with sharp features, a sullen look, and a noticeable stoop came in carrying two cups of green tea. He put them between the two men and moved off without a word. Hatem was reminded of the mute servant in horror films.

Bishop Mousa sighed. "In fact we've been trying to get in touch with you since yesterday. I asked Father Mikhail to tell you we'd be honored to meet you," he said.

Now Hatem understood what was behind Father Mikhail's unexpected call. He bowed his head, confirming what the bishop had said. "That's right," he said. "He left me a message to call but I didn't get it, though I did want to ask him if he knew whether Hassan was okay, or Boutros, if you like. Isn't that why he called?"

Bishop Mousa nodded. "Of course, it's not unconnected with Hassan. In fact that's exactly what it's about," he said.

Now Hatem was really worried. "Has something bad happened to him?" he asked. "I've been worried about him ever since the explosion at the church. I'm sure you know all about him, Your Grace, and I imagine his conversion to Christianity isn't of great importance to the Church, despite his enthusiasm."

Mousa bowed his head, weighed down by sadness. "Unfortunately his conversion is now something of great importance, Mawlana, but for reasons that are quite the opposite of what you might think."

Hatem had no idea what he meant. Mousa then turned one of the screens on with a remote control that he picked up from the table. Hatem was reminded of Sheikh Mukhtar's testimony and Nashwa's dance on Nader Nour's favorite CD.

"That's why I was pessimistic," he said. "I've certainly been subjected to quite a few of these private viewings recently."

The screen showed video footage of the church that had been attacked a few days earlier. It showed the façade, the gate, and a few cars parked along the curb outside. Some cars stopped and people got out and went into the church— men, women, and families with children. Hatem noticed that the footage had a date and time stamp in the bottom left-hand corner.

"Is the date in the picture right?" Hatem asked. "The evening of the explosion and about an hour before it happened, right?"

Bishop Mousa froze the picture by pressing a button on the remote control and turned to Hatem.

"It's right," he said. "Now I'm going to show you some shots from some other cameras. The first camera, the one you're watching now, was at the bank opposite the church. We had a cooperation agreement with the bank to share the camera with the bank to save costs. We had a camera that covers the street in front of the bank and they do the same for us with another camera, and the two cameras send images to both the church and the bank. Then there was another camera we'd put inside the church, behind the priest who's reciting the prayers, and that one films the congregation and anyone who comes through the main door. Let's go back to the first camera and watch what happens about forty minutes before the explosion."

The bishop pressed the fast-forward button until he reached the time he wanted, then put it on play. In the video a car stopped and the driver waved to a group of young church workers who were standing at the gate. They greeted the driver, removed some traffic cones, and helped him to park outside the church door. The driver got out and shook hands with them, then turned to the car and locked it with the remote key. At that point Hatem's heart skipped a beat. He jumped up to check. Mousa helped him by stopping the picture to show the young man locking the car. It could only be Hassan.

He sat down in shock. He realized that his anxiety and his misgivings, and Omayma's too, were completely justified. Hassan had no doubt died in the explosion but they were keeping it a secret. He was devastated and heartbroken. Bishop Mousa ignored Hatam's anguish.

"Mawlana, note that Hassan has a backpack on his back," the bishop said, pointing at the screen.

Despite his grief, Hatem took a close look at the backpack, which looked like the ones that schoolchildren use and seemed to have a drawing on it.

Bishop Mousa played the rest of the scene, showing Hassan go in with the church staff, the young men who had been waiting for him outside.

The picture now switched to shots taken inside the church ten minutes before the explosion. Bishop Mousa pointed to the fourth row of seats and someone slipping out toward the door. He stopped the picture and it was clearly Hassan. Hatem's heart raced and he felt a wrenching in his guts. Mousa then switched to a shot from the camera at the bank: Hassan appeared, hurrying out of the church and hitting the parked car with his hand, then walking past it and hitting another car with his hand. He was strolling along toward the pavement opposite the church. Mousa went back and played the footage taken from the other camera: Hassan was holding a cell phone in his hand and looking at the church. Then he dialed a number on the keypad and pressed the call button. At just that moment his face was lit up by the flash of the explosion. The shock wave hit him and panic broke out all around him. While others fled the destruction, Hassan stood his ground undaunted.

Hatem's nerves were in pieces. He felt crushed, as if an elephant had stepped on his chest. Everything certain he had known was shattered, along with everything he had trusted, every truth, all his peace of mind. Hatem no longer had anything to say. He was in fragments, paralyzed. He sat there stunned in front of the frozen picture.

"Impossible! Hassan a terrorist?" he said. "Hassan?"

Bishop Mousa sat down to get his breath back. The pictures had shaken him too, though he had apparently seen them several times.

"He was cleverer than everyone else. It looks like they didn't tell you the security people had monitored him looking at al-Qaeda websites and other extremist sites on the Internet and that he tried to get in touch with them several times. Apparently he did get in touch with someone. The security people warned his family and you know what his family's like. They confronted him and he denied it. Then he said he was just curious and they thought it was a whim or just an adventure, a young man with spare time and nothing to think about, especially as he had completely stopped looking at those websites. A few months later this conversion business started and you know what happened then. Some young Christians adopted him. They were delighted and treated it as a victory for Christianity. We warned them several times when we found out about it, given how sensitive it was both in public and in private, because of whose son he was and whose brother-in-law. But he managed to build relationships with some members of the church, and we know you tried to stop him converting. When I heard you were involved, I said at the time that they'd made a good choice asking you to help, but it's clear that the kid was going ahead with his plan anyway. And then he carried out this operation."

Hatem froze. His arms and legs had turned to ice. Beads of sweat formed on his forehead and began to trickle down his cheeks, mixed with tears. His lips trembled and he ground his teeth audibly as he tried to keep a grip on himself. But the stream of images, the feelings, the voices, the conversations, and moments he remembered completely overwhelmed him.

Bishop Mousa, distracted by the enormity of what he was about to say, didn't notice what Hatem was going through.

"I have a terrible problem, Mawlana," he said, "a problem that's way beyond our means to handle in the patriarchate, and way beyond us. It threatens the whole country and we don't know what to do about it."

He finally noticed that Hatem wasn't with him.

"Are you all right, Mawlana?" he said, patting him on the shoulder.

The only response was the ghost of a smile that flitted across Hatem's lips and a slight nod that made Hatem wince, though it was hardly visible.

Bishop Mousa continued: "We have to move quickly. There are young Christians who are furious, as you've seen for yourself. And it's not just the Copts in Egypt, but all over the world. With this attack they've reached the stage where they can't take any more. Some of them have got hold of these pictures and other evidence, and for them it's a clear-cut case and they're making threats, even to us in the church, that if Hassan doesn't hand himself in within seventy-two hours they'll show these pictures all over the world and publicize the fact that people related to the president are personally involved in killing Copts and blowing up churches. Unfortunately, Mawlana, they've collected all the information there is about Hassan, including your role and the fact that you've spent time with him. Some people claim there's a suspicion that you are in complicity with Hassan, though we in the church fully believe you're the last person to be an extremist and that you've been fighting against bigotry toward Copts in particular."

Bishop Mousa pressed a button and the picture moved again. Dozens of people were running around in panic outside the church. Some of them had lost arms or legs, some had mangled flesh, missing eyes, burns, or faces covered in blood. Hassan stood watching them from the pavement opposite. He pressed a button on his remote key. His car alarm began to wail and then the car itself exploded. The body of the car rose off the ground and flew over some of the neighboring cars, which themselves caught fire and exploded from the heat and the flames. Balls of fire, shards of glass, sharp pieces of metal flew through the air and more bodies fell to the ground. In the distance, through the smoke, Hassan could be seen, still standing, still watching the scene of devastation.

Bishop Mousa leaned over and whispered in Hatem's ear. "You have to find him, Mawlana," he said, "and persuade him to hand himself in."